JIG NEVER WANTED TO BE A HERO—

He would have been perfectly happy just not to be pummeled on a daily basis. But after being kidnapped and dragged off on a quest adventure, he had inadvertently become a legend. And while he no longer got pummeled, he did get the jobs no one else wanted—the dangerous jobs.

So it was inevitable that when there was a threat to the whole mountain down in the part once claimed by the Necromancer and the Dragon—both now dead thanks to Jig—he was the one they'd expect to clean up the mess.

Burdened with some truly pitiful companions, and led by an ogre who'd made it all too clear what the price of failure would be, Jig went off to face certain death.

Actually, he was almost looking forward to dying. After all, that seemed to be the only way he'd ever convince anyone that he really wasn't any kind of hero at all . . . .

JIM C. HINES

Jig the Goblin Series:

GOBLIN QUEST (Book One)
GOBLIN HERO (Book Two)
GOBLIN WAR (Book Three)

GOBLIN HERO

JIM C. HINES

DAW BOOKS, INC.
DONALD A. WOLLHEIM, FOUNDER
375 Hudson Street, New York, NY 10014
ELIZABETH R. WOLLHEIM
SHEILA E. GILBERT
PUBLISHERS
www.dawbooks.com

Cover art by Mel Grant.

DAW Book Collectors No. 1400.

DAW Books are distributed by Penguin Group (USA) Inc.

First Printing, May 2007
3 4 5 6 7 8 9

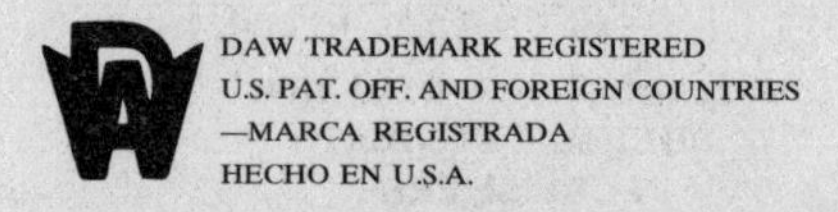
DAW TRADEMARK REGISTERED
U.S. PAT. OFF. AND FOREIGN COUNTRIES
—MARCA REGISTRADA
HECHO EN U.S.A.

PRINTED IN THE U.S.A.

ACKNOWLEDGMENTS

I am absolutely delighted to share *Goblin Hero* with you all. Poor Jig wasn't thrilled at the idea of another adventure, but that's his problem. As with the first book, this one wouldn't have happened without the help and support of a great many people.

First and foremost, my thanks to Sheila Gilbert, my editor. Not only does she demonstrate tremendous insight and great judgment in buying my books, but her suggestions on *Goblin Hero* have made it a far better story. Thanks also to Debra Euler and the other wonderful people at DAW Books.

Mel Grant has done it again, creating another amazing cover.

My agent, Steve Mancino, deserves a huge round of applause (not to mention pizza) for all his hard work. Not only did he help sell the goblin books to DAW, but thanks to Steve, you can also find Jig the goblin in Russia, Germany, and the Czech Republic. Just in case you wanted your own copy of Приклн очеия Гоблина.

Then there are the terrific people who read and critiqued my early drafts, particularly Catherine Shaffer, Heather Poppink, Mike Jasper, and Teddi Baer. Not to mention all my virtual pals who read the occasional snippet and offered support and encouragement.

To my wife, Amy, and to my own little goblins, Skylar and Jamie, your love and support mean more to me than I could ever say.

Finally, my humble thanks to all my readers. I'm both honored and thrilled to be able to share the second goblin book with you. I hope you enjoy it.

The Song of Jig
(to the tune of the wizard drinking song
"Sweet Tome of Ally Ba'ma")

Heroes entered the darkness,
A dwarf, an elf, and two men,
Seeking fame, seeking glory,
Slaying goblins as they went.

But one lone goblin dodged their blades and their bow.
That lone goblin, he survived.
They tied him up, to be their guide down below,
But Jig's the only one who came out alive.

Hail, Jig Dragonslayer.
His sword is strong, his aim is true.
Hail, Jig Dragonslayer.
Treat him well, or he might slay you too.

Jig led them down through the darkness,
To the realm of the dead,
Where corpses leaped from the shadows
And the heroes nearly lost their heads.

Jig the goblin did not cower.
His sword is strong, his aim is true.
No, Jig the goblin did not cower.
He drew his sword and ran the Necromancer through.

So Jig, he led those heroes deeper,
To the darkness where the dragon dwelled.
Steam was rising from his night black scales,
And his eyes were pits from hell.

Hail, Jig Dragonslayer.
His sword is strong, his aim is true.
Hail, Jig Dragonslayer.
While others fled, Jig grabbed a spear, and he threw.

Hail, Jig Dragonslayer.
His sword is strong, his aim is true.
Jig finished off that beast of hell.
Then he finished off those heroes too.
So treat him well, or else he might slay you.

CHAPTER 1

"How come goblins never live happily ever after?"

—Jig Dragonslayer

Jig the goblin was no warrior. His limbs were like blue sticks, his torn ear tended to flop to the side, and his fangs barely stretched up past his upper lips. As a child he had been relegated to muck duty, hauling caustic sludge through the goblin lair to fill the fire bowls that illuminated the cavern. The putrid, rotting-plant smell of muck would seep into his clothes, his hair, even his skin. And muck duty was far from the worst he had survived. He tried not to think about his time cleaning privies.

His grand quest a year ago hadn't changed him. Well, except for the nightmares about the dragon Straum coming back to eat him, or the Necromancer casting a spell to wither Jig's body until it crumbled to dust, or giant carrion-worms crawling into his bed-roll and—

Jig shook his head, trying to banish those images. Suffice it to say, he was still the same nearsighted runt he had been before. But he had emerged from the dragon's lair with one potent gift: the ability to heal various injuries.

Given the nature of goblin life, this made Jig one of the busiest goblins in the lair.

His current patient, a muscular goblin named Braf, was everything a goblin warrior should be. Strong, tall, and dumb . . . even for a goblin. Somehow Braf had managed to wedge his own right fang deep inside his left nostril.

Jig shook his head. Braf raised stupidity to new heights, then threw it down to shatter on the earth below.

A dirty rag looped around Braf's jaw held the fang still. Blood and other fluids turned the rag dark blue. Braf gingerly wiped his nose on his wrist, momentarily halting the seepage. He stared at the goo on his hand, then wiped it on his too-tight leather vest.

"Can you fix it?" Braf said, his voice muffled and nasal.

"Don't talk," Jig said. He closed his eyes. *How much longer?*

Tymalous Shadowstar, forgotten god of the Autumn Star, stifled a giggle only Jig could hear. *I'm sorry, I'm doing the best—* The god's voice dissolved into jingling laughter.

Jig had discovered Tymalous Shadowstar during that adventure a year before. Or maybe Shadowstar had discovered Jig. Shadowstar was the one who gave Jig the power to heal the other goblins. What Shadowstar got out of the deal, Jig still wasn't sure. There were days he thought Shadowstar did it purely for his own amusement.

How did he do this to himself anyway? Shadowstar asked between giggles.

Braf's not exactly the sharpest blade in the armory, Jig said. *But I'm guessing he had help.* Someone had tied those bandages on to Braf's head. Had Braf tried to do it, he probably would have hanged himself.

Goblins. Why did it have to be goblins?

It was a complaint Jig had listened to ever since he discovered the forgotten god. Now was when Jig would traditionally try to defend his people, to point out the things they had accomplished in the past year. Things like achieving a shaky truce with the hobgoblins deeper in the mountain, and sealing off the outer tunnel to protect them from adventurers.

Yet when he looked at Braf, Jig couldn't find it in himself to speak up on behalf of the goblins.

I think I'm ready now, said Shadowstar.

"Good." Jig crossed the small temple, trying to ignore the mosaic on the ceiling. Bits of colored glass formed an image of the forgotten god, a tall, pale man dressed in black, with silver bells striping his arms and legs. Sour smoke from the muck lanterns floated around the image, never quite reaching the pale face. The face had a definite smirk, one that hadn't been there earlier in the day.

Jig placed his hand over Braf's nose and tried not to grimace. Goblins had never been known for their attractiveness, and Braf was a spectacular example of why. Old disease scars dotted his skin, and his misshapen nose looked a great deal like a pregnant frog that had settled in the center of his face.

Shadowstar started to snicker again. *Now it looks like a frog with a huge yellow fang up its—*

"Hold still," said Jig. He tilted Braf's head back and slipped one finger beneath the bandage as he waited for the magic to start. The flow of Shadowstar's power through Jig's body always made him feel bloated, and he shifted uncomfortably as the magic warmed his hands.

Before he could do anything more, a glowing orange insect landed on his arm and began to creep forward. Jig yanked his hand back. The last thing he needed was for a bug to crawl up Braf's nose. He swatted it, splattering glowing bug goo over his arm, even as two more of the pests buzzed around his head.

"What are they?" Braf asked.

"I don't know. They started showing up a few weeks ago." Jig waved his hands, trying to bat them toward the spiderweb in the corner of the temple. "And stop talking!"

The bugs drew back. Jig slapped his free hand over Braf's swollen nose.

Slowly, Shadowstar warned.

A hair's breadth at a time, Jig slid the offending fang out of the nostril. He tried very hard to ignore the fluids that followed, coating Jig's hands with blue slime. He also ignored the feel of the fang moving beneath the nostril, the way the tooth scraped against the bone.

Braf's eyes crossed. The warmth in Jig's hands increased. His fingers felt like swollen tubers, and the orange bugs were circling Braf's head. Jig's arms tingled.

Got it, Shadowstar said.

Jig slid the tip of the fang free, and there was a loud popping sound as the jawbone slipped back into the socket. Jig swung one hand at the bugs. He missed, and the motion splattered blood across Shadowstar's mosaic.

Braf sneezed. He touched his nose, and a broad grin split his blood-crusted face. "Thanks, Jig!"

Blood, spit, and snot had misted Jig's spectacles. He slipped them off and wiped the lenses on his pants. "So how did you do this to yourself?"

"I was on guard duty," Braf said. "My partner bet me I couldn't touch my nose with my fang. When I won the bet, he punched me in the jaw."

A shining example of the goblin race, Shadowstar commented.

"I guess you showed him," Jig said.

Braf laughed. "Yeah." He scratched his chin and turned to go. As he stooped through the low doorway, he hesitated. "Hey, don't tell anyone I came to you. Some of the other goblins don't like you that much, and I don't want them to—"

"To think you've been coming to the runt for help?" Jig asked, his voice tight. Nearly every goblin had needed Jig's help at one time or another over the past year, but not one wanted to admit it.

"Yeah!" Braf beamed. "That's right. Thanks!" He disappeared down the tunnel before Jig could find anything to throw at him. Some things never changed. No matter how many goblins he healed, no matter how many quests he survived, he was still Jig the scrawny, half-blind runt.

Jig sat down on the altar. A dark, red-spotted fire-spider the size of Jig's hand crept up the side and scurried toward him. Jig straightened his arm so the spider could climb onto the singed leather pad Jig wore strapped to his right shoulder. Fire-spiders grew hot when threatened, and Jig had the burns to prove it. Despite the scars, Smudge still made a better companion than most goblins.

"It's not that bad," Jig said to Smudge. "They can't afford to kill me. Who would fix their wounds?"

He glanced at the blood on his trousers and sighed. Another improvement from a year ago was the quality of Jig's clothes. Jig had spent most of his adult life in a ratty old loincloth so stiff he could have used it for a shield. Now he wore soft gray trousers and a loose black shirt. His old sword hung at his side, and he had his favorite boots on. The leather was bright blue, with red flames painted down the side and white, furry fringe on top.

Most importantly, he had his spectacles. Large, amethyst lenses covered his eyes, letting him see the world as clearly as any goblin, except for his peripheral vision where the lenses didn't quite cover. Steel frames kept them hooked over his pointed ears. They weren't perfect, and the frames irritated his bad ear, which had been torn and scarred in a fight with another goblin. But being able to see the world around him was worth a little pain.

Recently Shadowstar had suggested another addition to his wardrobe: socks. It had taken a long time to persuade one of the children to weave a pair of cloth tubes, then sew them shut at one end, but the result was literally a gift from the gods. No more blisters, no more dark blue marks on his legs where the dye from his boots rubbed off, and best of all, his boots didn't smell quite so horrid when he took them off.

"Jig?"

The voice came from the darkness of the tunnels, but Jig recognized it. "What do you want, Veka?"

Veka stepped into the temple, drawing her long black cloak tight around her considerable bulk. Broad-shouldered and thick-limbed, she had sent more than one goblin to Jig with missing teeth or a broken nose.

Veka worked in the distillery, turning rotted fungus, smashed glowworms, and pungent mushrooms into muck. As a result, she always smelled like decomposing plants. Her hands were covered in greenish stains, and the fumes of the muck room had left her eyes bloodshot.

"You didn't cast a binding spell when you healed Braf's nose. How did you do that?" She rapped the end of her staff on the floor for emphasis. Glass beads, bits of metal, and what looked like a mummified finger all clattered against the staff, tied there with scraps of leather and braided hair.

The staff, like her cloak, was part of Veka's obsession with all things magical. An obsession that unfortunately included Jig.

"I don't even know what a binding spell is," Jig said, hopping down from the altar. He walked toward the tunnel and hoped she would move out of his way.

Veka didn't budge. She raised a tight fist and slowly spread her fingers. Faint threads of light formed a dim, fragile web between her fingers. "The binding is the way the wizard taps into the magical powers that surround her. It is the first step of the journey toward—"

At that point, one of the orange bugs landed on Veka's hand. The binding spell flickered out of existence. "Stupid bug!" She smooshed it flat.

"Veka, I can't—"

She didn't let him finish. Scowling, she set her staff against the wall and fished through her clothes. From a pocket within her cloak, she produced a stained brown book. The cover had been torn off and resewn, and many of the pages were coming loose from the binding. "Josca says in chapter two that the Hero will find a guide, a mentor to lead them to the path." She waved the book at Jig like a sword. "You're the only goblin who knows anything about magic, and you won't even—"

"Who is Josca?" Jig asked, stepping back.

Veka tapped the cover. Oversize silver letters read *The Path of the Hero (Wizard's ed.) by Josca.* "Josca says every Hero follows the same path. Only the details change. I need a mentor. By refusing to teach me magic, you're blocking my way."

Her teeth were bared, and the long lower fangs looked freshly sharpened. Jig took another step back. "Josca should write an edition for goblins. In the first chapter the hero sets out for adventure. In the second he dies a horrible, painful death."

"You survived." Her scowl turned the words into an accusation.

Heavy footsteps running up the tunnel saved Jig from having to answer. Braf shouldered his way past Veka and said, "I forgot. The chief said she wants to see you. It's about the ogre."

"What ogre?" Jig asked.

"The one who showed up right after my . . . problem," Braf said, with a quick glance at Veka. "He smashed up a few other guards. He said he was looking for the Dragonslayer. The chief said to go right away."

Jig covered one of the muck lanterns and scooped up the other by the handle. Green light reflected from the dark red obsidian of the walls as he followed Braf into the tunnels. The clomp of Veka's staff followed close behind.

"What do you think the ogre wants?" Braf asked.

"I'm more worried about what the chief will do to me for taking so long to answer her." Ever since Kralk took control of the goblins, she had been looking for a way to get rid of Jig. He frowned, thinking about the rest of Braf's story. "Why didn't the other guards come to me for healing?"

"What guards?"

"The ones the ogre injured."

Braf laughed. "When I left, the older goblins were scrubbing what was left of them off the walls."

Jig swallowed and began to run.

Two guards stood outside the entrance to the goblin cavern. Fire bowls provided a cheerful yellow-green light. Jig ignored the blue bloodstains on the wall and floor. He flattened his ears as he walked inside. He had been away most of the day, and even the subdued, nervous conversation of five hundred goblins was louder than he was used to.

Smudge shifted restlessly on Jig's shoulder. The heat from the fire-spider's body caused drops of sweat to trickle down Jig's neck. Not that Jig needed the warning.

The ogre was easy to spot. He sat near the back of the cavern, surrounded by armed goblins. Steel blades and long wooden spears trembled as the goblins fought to control their fear. For his part, the ogre didn't seem to notice.

Why should he? His leathery green skin was strong enough to turn away most attacks, and his hands were as big as Jig's head. He sat on the floor . . . probably because if he stood, his head would scrape the ceiling. His teeth were smaller than goblin fangs, but still sharp enough to sever a limb. He could cut a swath through the cavern bare-handed. Shadowstar only knew what he could do with the huge, brass-studded club resting across his knees.

"Jig! It's about time you got your scrawny arse

down here," shouted Kralk. The lanky goblin chief was smiling, which made Jig nervous. She wore a necklace of jagged malachite spikes and an ill-fitting dwarvish breastplate. Metal spikes adorned the shoulders and . . . chest area . . . of her armor. Kralk collected weapons, rarely carrying the same one two days in a row. Today a nasty-looking morningstar hung from her belt, clanking as she walked toward Jig.

Jig hadn't been around when the last chief died. At the time, he had been around the fifth or sixth stanza of "The Song of Jig," somewhere between fighting the Necromancer and cowering before the dragon. When Jig came back, many of the goblins had encouraged him to take over as chief, a prospect he found as appealing as dancing naked in front of tunnel cats.

Ultimately, three goblins had emerged as potential candidates, ready to fight for control of the lair. The morning of the fight, only one of those three showed up for breakfast. The other two were found curled up near the garbage pit with most of their blood on the outside of their bodies.

Kralk had been trying to get rid of Jig ever since. She never challenged him openly. No, it was always "Jig, could you slay that rock serpent that snuck into the distillery?" or "We need someone to lead a raiding party to steal food from the ogres," or "Golaka is experimenting with a new soup, and she wants someone to taste it."

Naturally, Jig always said no. Each refusal chipped away at his reputation, reinforcing Kralk's power over the goblins and making his life miserable. Why couldn't she see that he wasn't a threat?

The ogre's voice thundered through the cavern, making Jig jump. "This is the Dragonslayer?"

A path opened between Jig and the ogre. Goblins

moved away like blood flowing from a wound. Jig reached up to stroke Smudge's head. The fire-spider was warm, but not hot enough to burn. They weren't in any immediate danger.

For an instant Jig considered lying. If he said Braf was Jig Dragonslayer, the ogre wouldn't know any better. One look at the grin on Kralk's face shattered that plan.

"I'm Jig," he said. His voice sounded like a child's squeak compared to the ogre's.

"You're the one who killed the dragon Straum?" The ogre picked up his club and made his way toward Jig, keeping his head and shoulders hunched.

Jig glanced at Kralk, then nodded.

"You put a spear through that monster's eye?"

He nodded again.

"You? You're the one they sing that song about, the one—"

"Yes, that's me!" Jig snapped. His momentary anger ebbed as quickly as it had begun, leaving his legs so weak he thought he was going to collapse. *Brilliant*, he thought. *Shout at the ogre. Why not kick him in the groin next?*

The ogre knelt, peering down at Jig, then back at Kralk. "He's like a little goblin doll!"

Jig's claws dug into his palms. Better a toy than a threat. "Braf said you wanted to talk to me."

"That's right." The ogre took another step, putting him almost within arm's reach. Almost within Jig's reach, at least. The ogre could have grabbed Jig by the head and bounced him off the nearest wall without stretching. His green scalp wrinkled into a frown. "We need . . ." His voice grew quiet, muffling the last word.

"What was that?" Jig asked.

The ogre's face turned a deeper green, almost exactly the same shade as the mold that grew on the privy walls. "Help. We need help."

Jig stared, trying to put the pieces together. He understood the words, but his mind struggled with the idea that ogres would come to goblins for help. What next? The Necromancer returning from the dead to start a flower garden?

"What kind of help?" Jig asked.

"A few months ago something showed up in Straum's cave and started hunting us. At first we thought it was those hobgoblin types, or maybe you goblins, so we came up and slaughtered a few of you." He gave a sheepish half shrug. "Sorry about that."

Kralk stepped closer. "You killed far more hobgoblins than goblins. We considered it a favor."

"Right. So you won't mind doing us a favor in return." The ogre stared at Jig. "Whatever they are, they've got magic on their side. Many of us have already died. Others have been enslaved. They're hunting down those who remain, the families who fled into the deeper tunnels."

Jig had met two wizards in his time. One had been a companion on his quest. The other was the dreaded Necromancer. Both had tried to kill him. To be fair, a number of nonwizards had also tried to kill him, but wizards tended to be much nastier about it.

"We've heard of you," the ogre said. "You've got magic of your own, right?"

Jig knew where this was going, and his mouth was too dry to answer. He managed a weak nod.

Kralk's smile grew. Smudge responded to that smile with enough heat to sear the leather shoulder pad. Tiny threads of smoke rose from beneath his feet. Interesting that the goblin chief frightened him more than the ogre. Jig had always known Smudge was smart.

"What do you say, Jig?" asked Kralk.

Jig took a step back. There had to be a way out of this. He whirled and pointed at Veka. "What about her? She can cast a binding spell, and she *wants* to be a Hero."

The closest goblins started to laugh, either at Jig's cowardice or at the idea of smelly, overweight Veka as a hero. As for Veka herself, she flashed a grin nearly as wicked as Kralk's own. "Sorry, Jig. If you had taught me magic, I might be powerful enough to help. But I guess you'll have to do this on your own."

"But—"

"This is your path, Jig Dragonslayer, not mine." Veka tapped her staff on the floor, rattling the beads and bones. "A Hero must make her own path. To quote the valiant Duke Hoffman, who transformed himself to rescue the mermaid Liriara, 'I have chosen my way, and it is the way of the squid.' "

The ogre stared. "What's she talking about? What's a squid?"

Say yes. Shadowstar's voice was calm and firm.

Jig's was not. "What?" He closed his eyes, trying to shut out the rest of the cavern so he could concentrate on Tymalous Shadowstar. *You want me to say yes?*

I can't see everything that's happening, but I can tell you this much. Something about your ogre friend feels wrong. There's a residue of some sort, almost a magical shadow. Whatever's happening down there, it's dangerous. You have a choice, Jig Dragonslayer. You can go with the ogre and discover what's happening, or you can wait for the problem to come to you.

Waiting sounds good. Shadowstar didn't answer. Jig sighed. The god always meant business when he used Jig's full name. *What do you expect me to do? They're ogres! If they can't fight this thing, how am I—*

You've fought dragons and wizards and adventurers, and you survived. Veka is peculiar, even for a goblin, but she's also correct. A Hero is one who finds a way.

Kralk is trying to get me killed! She—

Or you can refuse. Tell the ogre no, and see how he reacts.

Right. Jig looked at the ogre. "I'll go," he muttered.

"Excellent!" The ogre slapped him on the shoulder, knocking him to the ground. "Whoops. Sorry about that. I forget how fragile you bugs are. Nothing broken, I hope?" He grabbed Jig's arm and hauled him upright.

Jig stepped back, testing his arm. Fortunately, the ogre hadn't struck the shoulder where Smudge was perched. The fire-spider was crouched into a hot ball, staring at the ogre. Smudge extended his legs. With a burst of speed, Smudge raced down Jig's chest and burrowed into a pouch on his belt, leaving a trail of smoking dots down Jig's shirt.

"Take Braf along for protection," said Kralk, sneering. "Whoever's hunting the ogres might not have heard 'The Song of Jig.' They might mistake you for a stunted coward and rip you apart before you have the chance to tell them of your great deeds."

Jig glanced at Braf, who was busy picking the scabs on his nose. He couldn't decide if bringing Braf would improve his chances of survival or make them worse. Braf grimaced and stretched his jaw, using the tip of his fang to scratch inside his freshly healed nostril. Definitely worse.

"Someone else volunteered to accompany you," Kralk added.

"I'm coming, I'm coming," said a goblin from the back of the cave, in a voice so old it creaked.

Kralk grinned again. "Jig will certainly need a nursemaid to look after him."

Goblins snickered as Grell made her way through the group to join Jig. If there was any goblin who would be of less use than Braf, it was Grell.

The canes she used to support her weight were smooth sticks, dyed dark yellow with hobgoblin blood. Grell was older than any goblin Jig knew, with the possible exception of Golaka the chef. But where Golaka had gotten bigger and meaner with age, Grell had shrunk until she was almost as small as Jig himself. Her face reminded Jig of wrinkled rotten fruit. Grell had worked in the nursery for as long as Jig could remember, and generations of teething goblin babies had covered her hands and forearms in scars. Dark stains covered her sleeveless shirt. Jig tried not to think about the origins of those stains.

"Are you sure?" Jig asked. "It will be dangerous. The ogres—"

"Ogres, ha!" Grell said. One whiff of her breath made the rotten fruit comparison much more apt. One of her yellowed fangs was broken near the gums, and the smell of decay made Jig want to gag. "Spend a week with twenty-three goblin babies and another nine toddlers, then we'll talk about danger."

"But—"

Grell jabbed the end of one cane into Jig's chest. "Listen, boy. If I spend one more day with those monsters, either I'm going to kill them or, more likely, they're going to kill me. I refuse to die buried in sniveling, crying brats. Kralk agreed to give me a break from nursery duty if I went with you and this green-skinned clod, so I'm going. Understand?"

"What about the nursery?" Jig asked desperately. "Who's going to take over?"

"Riva's still in there, but you're right. Without help, they'll probably overpower her pretty quickly." Grell turned toward the kitchens. "Hey, Golaka. Send one of your drudges over to help watch the brats!" To Jig, she added, "That should work. They can always threaten to barbecue the older ones if they get out of line."

Golaka peered out of the doorway. Sweat made her round face shine. She waved her stirring spoon in the air, spraying droplets of gravy over the nearest goblins. "My helpers are all busy mashing worms for dinner."

"I only want one. And your worm pudding tastes like week-old vomit anyway," Grell shouted back.

Jig cringed. He could see other goblins creeping out of the way, as far from Golaka as they could get. On the bright side, maybe he wouldn't have to take Grell along after all.

Golaka shook her spoon at Grell. "Last one who complained about my cooking got his tongue ripped out. The taste didn't bother him at all after that."

"Pah," said Grell. "Just send over whatever idiot overspiced the snake meat the other night. One day dealing with teething goblin babies, and they'll work twice as hard once they're back safe in your kitchen."

Golaka's spoon stopped in midshake. The rage on her face slowly melted away, and she began to chuckle. "I like that." She spun and headed back to the kitchen. "Hey, Pallik. Stop licking the hammer and get over here. I've got a new job for you!"

Jig turned to the ogre, who had watched the entire exchange with an increasingly skeptical expression.

"Come on," said Jig. *Before anyone else volunteers to "help."*

The laughter of the other goblins followed them out of the lair, stopping abruptly when the ogre spun around and snarled. The silence drew a faint smile from Jig. His goblin companions might be worse than useless, but he could get used to having an ogre along.

Jig studied the two goblins. "What is that supposed to be?" he asked, staring at the object in Braf's hand.

"A weapon, I think," said Braf. "I traded a hobgoblin for it a few days ago."

The so-called weapon was the length of Jig's leg. A thick wooden shaft ended in a brass hook, wide enough to catch someone's neck. The other end was barbed and pointed.

"Do you know how to use it?" Jig asked.

"I wanted to name it first. I was going to call it a hooker."

Jig cringed.

"But that didn't sound right," Braf went on, rotating the weapon and testing the point on his other hand. "I thought about calling it a goblin-stick, because I'm a goblin. But I think I'm going to name it a hook-tooth, because it's sharp like a tooth, only the other end is hooked, see?"

Standing behind Jig, the ogre snickered. He could probably snap Braf's hook-tooth with one hand.

"I wish I could remember where I put my shield though," Braf continued. "I had it at dinner last night because I used it as a plate, and I remember Mellok kept stealing my fried bat wings."

Grell's wrinkled face tightened with disgust. Shifting her balance, she raised her cane and slammed it into Braf's back, making a loud *thunk*.

Braf hardly budged, but his face lit up. He craned his neck and patted the edge of the shield, still strapped to his back. "Thanks, Grell!"

Jig turned to the ogre. "What's your name?"

"Walland Wallandson the Fourth."

"The fourth what?" asked Braf.

"The fourth Walland Wallandson."

Braf stared. "Couldn't the other ogres come up with enough names?" He seemed oblivious to the glare Grell shot him, so she slapped the back of his head.

"It's my father's name," said Walland. He flexed his fingers, and his knuckles popped with the sound of cracking bones. "He was Walland Wallandson the Third. His father was the Second, and my great-grandfather was Walland Wallandson the First. Your name is your legacy. Your family is everything. Anyone who mocks the Wallandson name had best prepare for a long, painful death." That last was said with a glare at Braf.

"Seems awfully inefficient," said Grell. "All those ogres taking care of their own offspring. How do you find time for anything else?"

Walland shrugged. "They don't stay young forever." He turned to Jig. "Well?"

"Well what?"

"Are we going?"

Jig had forgotten he was supposed to be in charge of the other goblins. "Right. Sorry." He raised his lantern, then hesitated. Going first meant leaving two goblins and an ogre at his back. Walland probably wouldn't do anything, not if he really wanted Jig's help. But the other two, well, they were goblins. Worse, Kralk must have talked to both of them before Jig even arrived.

"What's wrong?" Braf asked.

It wasn't that Jig didn't trust them. He trusted them to behave like goblins. "I'm wondering which one of you has orders to kill me."

He hoped his bluntness would startle the guilty one into confessing. Instead, Braf and Grell glanced at one another, then at the floor. Neither one would meet Jig's eyes.

Jig was in trouble. "Braf?"

Braf scratched his nose. "Kralk said she'd chop me up and toss me in Golaka's stewpot if you came back alive. She thinks you want to kill her and take her place."

"Why, so the entire lair can plot my death instead of just you two?" Jig asked, his voice pitched higher than normal. Borderline hysteria had that effect on him. "What about you?" he asked, turning to Grell. "What did she promise you?"

"She said if I killed you, she'd make sure I never have to work in that miserable, foul-smelling nursery again."

"You can't do that," Braf protested, raising his hook-tooth. "Kralk told *me* to kill him."

Jig's hand brushed the handle of his sword. From this angle, he could probably stab Grell in the back, but Braf was out of reach. Besides, Tymalous Shadowstar frowned on stabbing people in the back. Jig had never understood that, but he knew better than to argue the point.

Walland snorted and stepped past Jig, giving Braf a light shove that sent him bouncing off the wall. Braf landed on his backside, nearly impaling himself on his own weapon. "Trustworthy lot, you goblins," said Walland.

Jig didn't answer. Despite common belief, the goblin language did include a word for trust. It was derived from the word for trustworthy, which in the goblin tongue, was the same as the word for dead.

Jig stared at the ogre's leathery face, hoping he wasn't about to make a mistake. "Walland came to us for help," he said. "He asked for me. For Jig Dragonslayer." He narrowed his eyes and tried to look menacing as he turned to the other goblins. "I imagine he'd be very unhappy if something happened to me before we could help him."

Braf stood up, rubbing his behind. "I'm not afraid of some ogre," he said, lowering Jig's estimate of his intelligence even further. But he tucked his hooktooth through the shield on his back and made no move to attack.

"Grell?" Jig asked.

Grell shrugged. "The way I figure it, there's a good chance you'll get yourself killed down there and save me the trouble."

"Fine." Knowing she was probably right gave Jig a sick feeling in his gut, as though he had eaten something that wasn't quite dead yet. His only consolation, as he raised the lantern and set off down the tunnel, was that whatever killed him would no doubt kill the other goblins as well.

CHAPTER 2

"The path to glory begins with a single step. Of course, so does the path to the headsman's block."

—Jasper the Godhunter
From *The Path of the Hero (Wizard's ed.)*

Veka's books bounced against her sides as she hurried out of the goblin lair. She pulled her cloak tighter to minimize the jostling. She should have sewn more padding into the pockets.

She mumbled to herself, practicing the grand speech she had worked up to explain her departure to the guards. She would start by saying she had heard the call of destiny and had decided to set out on her own to fight the invasion of their mountain home. The path promised great danger and mighty trials which only the greatest of Heroes might survive.

She stopped when she reached the guards, who were in the middle of a game of Roaches. Both guards stomped their feet, each trying to scare the three roaches toward the other side of the tunnel. The goal was to get them to flee past your opponent without touching either the roaches or the other goblin. The game usually ended with crushed bugs and broken toes.

Veka tapped her staff on the ground. Nothing happened. "Aren't you going to challenge me?"

They kept stomping. "Move, you stupid bug!" shouted one.

Veka cleared her throat. "I said—"

"I heard," said the guard. "Who do you think I was talking to?"

His partner laughed, and the first guard took the opportunity to jump in front of the closest roach, sending it racing back.

Veka hunched her shoulders and hurried past. She tried to comfort herself with the fact that many Heroes endured the mockery of their peers. Look at how the warriors used to treat Jig Dragonslayer, back before he had the luck to get himself captured by adventurers and dragged along to fight wizards and dragons and such.

Well, it was her turn now. She imagined returning with the power to cast a spell that would transpose the guards and the roaches, letting the goblins scurry about until they were crushed beneath giant roach feet. She had set out on the Hero's Path, and when she returned, she would have the power to punish all the goblins who had laughed and jeered over the years.

The first chapter of *The Path of the Hero* talked about The Refusal, when the Hero first sees the Path and turns away. Veka wasn't sure why the Hero did this, especially since they all ended up on the Path anyway, but Josca was adamant. All true Heroes began by turning their backs on the Path, just as Jig had done when he tried to get Veka to go with the ogre instead of him.

Fortunately, Jig had given her the perfect opportunity to announce her own refusal, and she got to make Jig look like a fool at the same time. Served him right for hoarding all that magic for himself. Veka had worked so hard to set Braf up, all so she could watch Jig perform his healing magic. Yet for all of her planning and spying, she had seen nothing new. Jig never used a spellbook. He never cast a binding charm. He didn't use a wand or a staff or any of the traditional wizarding tools. He grabbed the wounded goblins, and magic simply *happened*. "How am I supposed to learn anything from that?" Veka muttered.

The last trace of light disappeared behind her as the tunnel curved to the left. Veka moved to one side, brushing her fingers along the grime-covered wall as she walked. She had brought a small muck lantern from the distillery, but any light would make her far too visible.

The smell of the air changed as she walked, taking on the musty scent of animal droppings and hobgoblin cooking, both of which smelled equally foul to Veka's nose. She had come this way only twice in her life, both times sneaking through with other goblins to raid Straum's lair below. That was where she had found her spellbook, along with her copy of *The Path of the Hero*.

The harsh sound of hobgoblin laughter interrupted her thoughts. She hurried through the tunnel until she caught a glimpse of Jig arguing with the hobgoblin guards. Jig had left his companions behind, facing the guards alone, as a true Hero should. The twisting of the tunnel meant she couldn't see the hobgoblins, but she heard at least two different voices aside from Jig's own.

The other goblins and the ogre all waited before the bend as Jig said, "We need to get to the lower tunnels."

"Is that so? What did you bring for the nice tunnel guards?" said one of the hobgoblins.

"Fresh-cooked meat?" asked the other. "Maybe some of that spicy lizard tail your chef makes with fire-spider eggs."

"If you haven't got that, we could always settle for a few strips of your flesh." Both hobgoblins laughed.

Veka leaned forward, straining to hear how Jig would respond. Would he draw his sword and slay both guards, or would he use magic? She hoped for the latter.

Jig did neither. "We haven't got any food to spare, so you're going to have to settle for strips of flesh." Veka crept closer, hoping the other goblins wouldn't look back. Jig waved his hand at the ogre, who lumbered into the light. "Why don't you start with his?"

A disappointed sigh hissed through Veka's teeth. That was so typical of Jig, always finding ways to sneak out of anything heroic. It made her wonder again about "The Song of Jig." Had Jig really slain the Necromancer and the dragon? More likely he had skulked in the shadows while the adventurers did the real fighting, then stabbed them all from behind when they weren't expecting it. Though that was still pretty heroic for a goblin.

By now the hobgoblins were stammering and cutting each other off in their eagerness to let Jig pass. Veka waited for them to leave, moving only when she could no longer hear the tapping of Grell's cane.

Now it was her turn to face the hobgoblins. She had

no ogre to protect her if the hobgoblins decided to punish her for their humiliation, which they almost certainly would. Veka had endured enough humiliation in her life to know what it was like.

So be it. This would be the First Obstacle. Just as the dwarven Hero Yilenti Beardburner had to overpower the nine-armed guardian of the black river, so would she, Veka the goblin, face these two hobgoblin guards.

Yilenti's First Obstacle sounded much more impressive.

She braced herself for the encounter. Aside from her books and staff, she had brought very little. Her muck lantern, currently hanging from her rope belt. Her wizard's staff. A skewer from last night's dinner, which she had swiped to use as a weapon. Bits of blackened rat meat still stuck to its length. At first she had tried to carry it up her sleeve, but after twice stabbing herself in the armpit, she settled for tucking it through her belt and hoping it didn't fall out.

Veka straightened, throwing her shoulders back and attempting to walk with the proper confidence and poise of a Hero. The hobgoblins watched from the junction of the tunnel. Both stood at least a head taller than Veka herself. One leaned his weight on a thick spear. A curved sword hung from the belt of the other, who was sipping what smelled like beer from a bloated skin.

A statue of a hobgoblin warrior stood beside the guards. Made of black glass, the statue marked the border of hobgoblin territory. A similar statue used to stand by the goblin lair, until one of the guards tried to climb it a few months back. Jig hadn't been able to save that one.

The statue towered over the guards, the spikes on

its helmet nearly touching the ceiling. One ear had broken off, and the double-headed ax in its hands was heavily chipped. A burning lantern hung from the left fang, gleaming off the statue's angry scowl.

Structurally, hobgoblins resembled larger, uglier goblins. Their skin was yellower and their muscles stronger, but they had the same sharp fangs protruding from their lower jaws, and large, goblinesque ears topped the broad heads.

Between the guards and the statue, Veka felt like a child. For Veka, used to being the largest one in any group, it was an unpleasant feeling.

The one with the spear scratched a long scar cutting down the side of his face. He wore a hardened leather breastplate, and his pants were white tunnel cat fur. A small animal skull served as a belt buckle. His black hair was greased back in the style of a hobgoblin warrior. After a cautious glance down the tunnel, probably to make sure Jig and the ogre were really gone, he sneered and said, "Another rat-eater."

His companion punched him on the arm and said, "Forget rats. This one looks like she's eaten a whole tunnel cat."

Veka's nervousness disappeared. Bad enough her fellow goblins called her "Vast Veka" behind her back, and worse things to her face. She didn't have to take that kind of disdain from a couple of hobgoblins.

She slammed the end of her staff against the ground hard enough to make both hobgoblins jump. "I am Veka," she said. "I go to join the others in their quest."

She liked that, especially the quest part. It sounded very haughty and heroic.

"Is that so?" asked the one with the scar. Veka mentally dubbed him Slash. The scar nicked the outer edge of his eye, and that eye tended to look off in random directions. He glanced at the other guard. "Well if that's the case, go right ahead. If you hurry, you should be able to catch them before they reach the lake."

"Thank you," Veka said graciously as she passed. She saw a nasty grin spread across Slash's face, but before she could react, he yanked back with his free hand. In the dim light, she could barely see the line looped around his wrist, running to a small hook on the wall, then to the ceiling.

A wooden panel fastened to the roof gave way, showering her with sharp rocks. She stumbled forward, cursing and clutching her head.

"I told you," said the other hobgoblin. "Rocks don't do enough damage. We need to mount crossbows to the ceiling."

"You can't leave a cocked crossbow on the ceiling," Slash snapped. "They'll lose tension, and the strings will rot, especially with all the moisture from the lake."

"Look at the rat-eater. All your little rock shower did was make her cry."

"We need bigger rocks, that's all," said Slash.

Veka sniffed. One of the rocks had caught her on the nose. She reached for the skewer tucked through her belt.

Instantly both hobgoblins raised their own weapons. "Don't be foolish, little goblin."

Slash snickered. "Not so little, really."

Veka's hand shook, she was so angry. But there were two of them, both better armed than her. And no matter how badly they had humiliated her, they *had* allowed her to pass.

She straightened her robes, brushing away the dirt and pebbles. A true Hero shouldn't just scurry off into the darkness. A true Hero would make a disdainful remark about their personal hygiene, slay them both, and stuff their broken bodies into their own trap. She couldn't even think up a suitably scathing comment.

This was only the first step on the path, she reminded herself. Every Hero suffered setbacks and failures in the beginning. That's why the first part of Josca's book was subtitled "Stumbling Along the Path."

She rubbed a lump on her forehead as she hurried down the tunnel. Why did the stumbling have to sting so badly?

Veka moved fast enough to catch a glimpse of Jig and his companions as they reached the underground lake, the passage to the lower tunnels. A stone archway stood at the edge of the lake, a long tunnel stretching down beneath the water. A long swath of black sand covered the open stretch before the lake. No matter how quietly one moved, the scrape of that sand was more than enough to summon the guardians of the lake, the poisonous lizard-fish.

Jig and the other goblins used their weapons to knock swarming lizard-fish back into the water as they crossed the sand. The ogre didn't bother. His bare feet stomped lizard-fish into pale pink goo.

The lizard-fish kept coming. The white-skinned creatures were as long as Veka's arm, with clawed front feet to drag their bodies through the sand. Their bulging eyes swiveled independently, giving them addled expressions. Long white antennae flattened against their necks as they attacked. As she watched, another lizard-fish scurried up to the ogre and whipped its tail about, jabbing the needle-sharp spines of its tail into the ogre's leg.

The ogre kicked it across the cavern to slam against the wall.

Veka stared. Lizard-fish spines had enough poison to kill a full-grown goblin in the time it took to scream. The ogre had barely noticed.

And they needed help from Jig Dragonslayer?

"Come on, Walland," Jig shouted.

With one last stomp, the ogre followed them into the tunnel. From the look of it, he had been enjoying himself.

Veka untied her robe and grabbed an old grooved fire stone from the pocket of her apron. Setting her muck lantern on the ground, she felt the end of her staff until she found the metal striker dangling by its cord. She drew the striker through the groove in the rock, shooting sparks into the lantern. The muck whooshed to life, spreading green light through the cave.

Black sand covered the ground in front of her. The water was still, smooth as black glass, save for the occasional ripple or bubble where lizard-fish and other creatures surfaced in search of insects. Toward the back, water dripped from the rock overhead, too far away to see.

Bits of broken green malachite studded the roof of the cavern, sparkling in the light of her lantern. The truly impressive formations were farther out, beyond the reach of greedy hobgoblin hands.

Veka could still hear the faint tapping of Grell's cane as they moved through the tunnel. Years ago the only way down had been through an enchanted whirlpool at the center of the lake, but generations of adventurers had left their marks throughout the mountain, blowing up bridges, smashing doors, triggering rockslides that blocked various tunnels, and generally making a mess of the place. At least the tunnel through the lake was a useful alteration. Veka grabbed her lantern and stepped onto the sand.

Instantly the lizard-fish returned, swarming from the water and spraying sand as they dragged their bodies toward her. Veka leaped back into the tunnel, and the lizard-fish slowed. Their claws couldn't find enough traction on the bare obsidian, so lizard-fish rarely left the sand of the beach. Unfortunately, the sand covered every bit of stone between Veka and the lake tunnel.

This wasn't fair. Jig hadn't done anything heroic to get past the lizard-fish. His ogre had done most of the work. All the goblins had to do was knock away the few lizard-fish the ogre didn't smush.

"I want an ogre of my own," Veka muttered. She tried again, moving as softly as she could, but it was no good. The instant the sand scraped beneath her feet, the lizard-fish returned. Veka's throat began to tighten.

"There has to be a way past," she said. There was always a way. She couldn't fail now, only a few steps into her journey. She sat down in the mouth of the tunnel and drew her spellbook from her cloak. The spellbook was in even worse shape than her copy of *The Path of the Hero*. At one time it must have been magnificent. Charred red leather covered engraved copper plates that formed the cover. The metal itself had survived the flames, but the pages within hadn't been so fortunate. Those few that weren't burned beyond legibility were incomplete and blackened around the edges. That was to be expected when you grabbed your spellbook from a dragon's lair, she supposed.

How many weeks had it taken her to decipher even the basic binding charm she had tried to show to Jig?

The next page was a levitation charm, but no matter how many times she tried, she had yet to levitate even the hairs she plucked from her head for practice. All her long nights of concentrating had gotten her nothing more than aching eyes and a sore scalp.

The mocking laughter of the hobgoblins echoed in her memory. She started thinking about Jig, and how he had cowed the hobgoblins into submission. By the time she managed to follow him into the tunnel, Jig probably would have found whatever was hunting the ogres and destroyed it.

"This should be my quest. My path!" She brought the lantern over the spellbook and squinted. Her other hand clenched into a fist for the binding spell. Josca wrote that the true Hero would find new strength and power when her need was great. This time, the spell had to work. It had to!

Slowly she spread her fingers, imagining lines of power spreading from each fingertip to a point in the center of her palm. She moved her hand over her staff, forcing the magical star outward until it intersected the wood. According to her spellbook, her staff would help her control the magic. A wave of the staff would send her soaring gracefully into the air, and she would be able to slip past the lizard-fish unnoticed. She didn't need much power, only enough that her boots didn't touch the sand. Surely she could summon that much magic. She concentrated on the binding spell, staring so hard she almost believed she could see the silver lines wrapped around the end of the staff. Her hands trembled from her effort. If she could only—

A bit of muck spilled from the lantern, landing on the open spellbook. Veka yelped and flung the lantern away, slamming the book closed to smother the flames. Smoke continued to rise from the pages. She scrambled forward, scooping sand from the beach and dumping it over the book. She could see the tiny green flame burning through several more pages. She dumped more and more sand onto the book, covering the whole thing until at last the fire died.

Only then did she think to look up. Lizard-fish formed a half ring around her. Slowly she backed away, into the mouth of the tunnel. Several of the lizard-fish tried to follow, only to hiss and retreat when they got too close to the muck that had spilled from her lantern. Whether it was the light, the heat, or the smell, they refused to pass the lantern to get to Veka.

Moving as slowly as she could, she picked up her spellbook and slipped it into her cloak pocket. She used her staff to right the lantern, then hooked the end of the staff through the handle. Keeping the lantern between her and the lizard-fish, she backed hastily into the tunnel. The spilled muck continued to burn on the sand.

Once she was safe on bare obsidian, she set the lantern down, grabbed her spellbook, and flipped to the levitation spell.

The muck had burned through most of the spell, searing the next ten or so pages for good measure. One of the few intact spells in the book, gone in an instant. She touched the browned edges of the hole, and flakes of burned paper stuck to her fingertip. She stared at the now-empty beach, wishing hatred alone was enough to destroy those hideous lizard-fish. "How am I supposed to become a Hero without a spellbook?"

She couldn't. Without magic, she was nothing but a fat, useless goblin who would probably spend the rest of her life working in the distillery until the fumes finally drove her mad.

She pulled out *The Path of the Hero* and set it down next to the spellbook. For a moment, she was tempted to throw both books onto the muck still burning in the sand. What kind of Hero lost her spellbook before she had even begun her journey?

She flipped to the beginning of the spellbook, cringing as more charred paper flaked loose and floated to the ground. The binding spell was still there, mostly legible, but that was only the first step in spellcasting. The binding was like her fire striker, providing the sparks to fuel true magic. Without those spells, her sparks simply fizzled and died.

Josca wrote that the Hero was supposed to overcome all obstacles, but he didn't explain how. Veka didn't have an ogre along to stomp lizard-fish. She didn't have anyone.

She blinked and wiped her eyes. Picking up *The Path of the Hero*, she flipped through the pages and began reading chapter nine, "The Sidekick."

"While not a prerequisite for true heroism, many legendary wizards have been known to take a companion. Whether it is the half-giant apprentice of the dwarven sorcerer Mog or the three-legged frog familiar that accompanied his master Skythe through the Bogs of Madness, the sidekick provides much-needed aide and support for the Hero's journey."

Veka's jaw tightened. She gathered her books and stood, brushing sand and ash from her robes. She might not have a three-legged frog, but a hobgoblin was the next best thing.

The hobgoblins were standing in the middle of the tunnel arguing. The wooden panel on the roof hung down, though the rocks had been swept to one side. Slash waved his hands and shouted, "There's not enough height for iron spikes to do any serious damage, not unless we add a lot of weight, and then the hinges won't hold it."

"So what's your idea?" snapped the other. "Nail rock serpents to the platform by their tails again?"

Slash's face darkened. "That would have worked if they hadn't turned on each other," he muttered. He started to say more, but stopped when he spotted Veka. He elbowed the other guard and pointed. "Speaking of more weight—"

They took in Veka's damp dirty robes and disheveled appearance in one glance and smirked.

Until now, Veka hadn't been sure how she would persuade of the hobgoblins to accompany her. Studying the creaking platform, she knew. The beads and trinkets on her staff made a nice dramatic rattling sound as she pointed it at Slash. "You. Come with me."

Slash stepped to one side and retrieved his spear, which had been leaning against the wall. "Much as I'd love to follow a rat-eating goblin around, I'm on duty."

Veka scowled, hoping it appeared menacing. Setting her staff and lantern on the floor, she loosened her belt and began fishing through the pockets of her apron until she found a small package folded inside several layers of smoky yellow cloth.

"What's that?" asked Slash.

"The last piece of your trap." She unfolded the cloth, revealing what looked like a pile of black dirt. Being careful not to touch the granules, she held it up for the hobgoblins to see. "This should solve your problems."

When they leaned closer, she blew the contents into their faces.

She leaped back, dodging a swipe of Slash's spear. The other hobgoblin was fumbling for his sword. "I'm going to cut you into strips and feed you to the tunnel cats!" he roared.

By now, the powder was already having an effect. Slash had dropped his spear and was scratching furiously at the tiny spots breaking out on his face. His friend had been hit with even more. His arms, neck, and face were all coated, and his eyes were watering so badly he couldn't see to stab her.

"Do you have any of that beer left?" Veka asked. They didn't answer, not that she expected them to. "Alcohol will neutralize the worst of the itching."

Both hobgoblins scrambled for the skin. Slash reached it first, pouring most of the contents over his face before handing it to his partner. He grabbed his spear.

"What do you think would happen if you coated the top of your platform with that powder?" Veka asked.

Slash hesitated. He glanced at the other hobgoblin, who was cursing and hopping about as he tried to shake the last few drops from the skin. "What is that stuff?"

"It's magic," Veka lied. "It's called turgog powder." She had been saving that packet to slip into the waterskin of a goblin warrior who had insulted her a few days back.

Slash was still pointing his spear at her. "How do you make it?"

Veka hesitated. Turgog was a by-product of corrupted muck. Rats would occasionally sneak into the distillery, and they had an insatiable appetite for the dried, treated mushrooms used halfway through the muck-making process. Their digestive systems processed the mushrooms into the highly irritating substance she had blown on Slash's skin. But she doubted Slash would want to know she had covered his face in powdered rat droppings. So she waved her hand and said, "It's a complicated magical formula."

Slash's eyes narrowed. "Magical?" He glanced at her staff. "What are you supposed to be, some kind of witch?"

"Wizard," Veka said. She pointed her staff at him. His companion had already fled into the hobgoblin lair, screaming for beer. "Come with me, and I'll provide you with enough turgog powder to douse a whole party of adventurers."

A smiling hobgoblin was an ugly sight, especially when that hobgoblin's face was still covered in an orange rash. "Let's go," he said.

"Grab one of those lanterns," Veka said. Hobgoblins used a different mixture of muck, one that burned with a bluish flame, but the basic formula was the same. "We'll need it." She stifled a grin as she turned and set off toward the lake. She had sent one hobgoblin fleeing, and convinced another to join her quest.

She was going to be a Hero after all!

The splashed muck on the beach still burned, giving them a clear view of the black sand. Veka stepped onto the beach and watched the lizard-fish crawl from the water, antennae waving.

"Why don't you use your magic on them?" Slash asked.

He wasn't as dumb as he appeared. "All power comes with a price," she said, quoting Josca's book. Unless you were Jig Dragonslayer. Then power was simply dropped in your lap through sheer stupid luck. "I see no reason to waste my magic on such low creatures as these lizard-fish, not when there is a simple alternative."

Before he could respond, she said, "We'll go together. They're afraid of the lanterns. Hook the handle over your spear and wave it behind us. I'll do the same with my staff to clear a path as we go. Once we reach the tunnel, they won't follow us."

At least she hoped they wouldn't. They hadn't followed Jig and the others into the tunnel.

Holding the lantern in front of her, she began walking. Slash didn't move. "This is your plan?" he snapped.

Veka scowled and hurried back onto the rock. She fished *The Path of the Hero* out of her cloak.

"What's that?" Slash asked.

"My spellbook," she said. She would have used the real spellbook, but *The Path of the Hero* looked much more impressive, plus it had better pictures. She thrust the book at him, keeping one finger on the illustration of an elf fighting what looked like a cross between a dragon and a dungheap. "And this is what I'm going to transform you into if you don't help me."

She slapped the book shut, nearly catching the tip of his nose. Without giving him time to think about her threat, she strode to the edge of the beach. "Well?"

To her amazement, Slash hurried to join her. "I'm coming, I'm coming."

"Good." Her heart thudded with excitement. He believed her. She had stood her ground, confident and in control. She should have been terrified. Slash was a hobgoblin, and everything about him screamed *danger!* Yet she wasn't afraid, and Slash didn't know how to handle it.

This time Slash followed close behind as she set out

across the beach. As before, the lizard-fish hurried out of the water but stopped a short distance beyond the lanterns. Several tried to scurry around to attack from behind, but Slash swung his lantern back and forth, splashing drops of burning muck. One splashed a lizard-fish's tail.

With a high-pitched squeal, it raced back into the water. The still-burning flame was a blue glow disappearing into the depths of the lake.

"I didn't know they could make noise," Slash said. He shook his spear, trying to splash more lizard-fish. "Ha! Look at that. They run like scared goblins."

Veka glared but said nothing.

Slash shook his lantern again. The butt of his spear jabbed Veka in the side, not hard enough to draw blood, but enough to make her stumble. Her lantern dropped into the sand.

"Oops," said Slash.

Veka tried to get her staff through the handle, but the lantern had fallen on its side. Already the remaining muck oozed out through the broken panels of glass. By the time she got it upright, only a tiny bit of muck remained, emitting a feeble green flame.

The lizard-fish closed in around her. She smashed the lantern onto the nearest, then glanced back at the tunnel. The lizard-fish had closed in behind them, cutting her off. The edge of the lake was only a few paces away.

"Run," she said.

"What's that?" asked Slash.

Veka used her staff to fling the broken lantern forward, causing several lizard-fish to dodge out of the way. Slash sprayed a few more as he spun and ran after her.

Sand sank and shifted beneath Veka's feet as she

fled. Shadows leaped crazily ahead of her as Slash swung his spear around, nearly setting Veka's hair and robes on fire. She couldn't tell if it was deliberate or not.

She was concentrating so hard on running, she nearly missed the tunnel. Only when her feet slapped solid rock did she realize they had made it. She turned around.

Outside, the lizard-fish waited, climbing atop one another in their eagerness, but never leaving the security of the sand.

Behind her, Slash was removing his lantern from the spear. He raised it high, examining the inside of the tunnel.

The rock was smooth and polished, far brighter than the grimy obsidian of the goblin tunnels. Puddles splashed beneath their feet with each step. She could see tiny snails in several of the puddles.

Slash's foot crunched three of them as he looked around. The sound echoed strangely.

The tunnel was too cramped, so she had to hold her staff parallel to the wall to keep from banging it. "Come on," she whispered.

She found herself hunching as she walked, and forced herself to lift her chin and straighten her spine. Heroes didn't slouch. They stood proud and tall.

But how often did Heroes travel through a lakebed tunnel, with all that water held back by nothing but a thin layer of rock? The silence was nearly as palpable as the moisture in the air.

Sweat dripped down her back. Cold water dripped onto her neck. She flattened her ears and kept walking. The tunnel sloped downward, following the bottom of the lakebed deeper and deeper.

The end of the tunnel was a black hole in the dark,

glistening stone of the floor. A ladder made of the same magically shaped obsidian led down from the far edge.

"Give me the lantern." Moving the blue flame over the hole, she dropped her staff into the room below. The clatter sounded terribly loud after passing through the tunnel, but nothing happened. With the lantern heating her left arm, Veka climbed down into the throne room of the legendary Necromancer.

The walls and floor were black marble, thick with dust. She could see footprints where Jig and the others had come down. A glass mosaic covered the ceiling, reminding her a bit of the one in Jig's temple, though the images here were abstract and meaningless. The smell of preservatives and old bat guano made her sneeze.

Behind her, Slash was humming as he climbed down the ladder. Veka's jaw tightened as she recognized "The Song of Jig." She picked up her staff, horribly tempted to break it over Slash's head, but it was too late. The melody had already wormed its way into her mind. She thrust the lantern back into his hand, hoping the muck would splash his wrist, but no such luck.

How did that verse go? Something about corpses leaping from the shadows, until the noble, valiant, wonderful Jig managed to slay the Necromancer. She turned, searching the darkness for any hint of movement. There was none, of course. Goblins and hobgoblins alike had passed through here many times since Jig's little adventure, and not one had been torn apart by the animated dead.

Another pit on the opposite side of the room led down to the dragon's realm. Like the lake tunnel, this was a magical shortcut left by that same band of adventurers. They had used magic to carve their own path through the mountain, including the stone ladder on the far side of the pit. Veka's envy was so strong she could taste it, like the backwash of good slug tea. She stared, wondering what it would be like to have the power to reshape the stone itself.

She squinted and moved closer to the edge. "Cover the lantern."

The blue light diminished, and gradually Veka's vision adapted enough to see the faint silver light shimmering below. The ladder should have extended all the way to the ground below, but the rungs rippled and shimmered, and the bottom half didn't seem to exist at all.

"What is that?" asked Slash.

"I don't know. Whatever the ogres were afraid of, it's—"

"The ogres were *afraid*?" Slash asked. He stared at the pit, then at Veka.

"The ogres have been hunted down and wiped out," she said. "There are only a handful left. That's why this one came to us for help."

Slash was still staring, his spear hanging loosely in his hand. "And you want to go down there?"

"We should move quickly," Veka said. "I don't know what's happening to the ladder, but I don't trust—"

That was as far as she got before Slash's foot slammed into her backside, launching her headfirst into the pit.

CHAPTER 3

"No night is so dark, no situation so dire, that the intervention of the gods cannot make it worse."
—Brother Darnak Stonesplitter, Dwarven Priest

As Jig climbed down into the cavern where the ogres made their home, the first thing he noticed was the cold. The wind made him shiver, especially where it slipped up his sleeves and down his back.

The second thing he noticed was that the last few rungs of the ladder were too insubstantial to support his weight. Unfortunately, he noticed this only when his feet slipped through the rungs, dropping him onto his backside.

He looked up to warn the others, then groaned. Braf had never been an attractive goblin, but from this angle . . .

"Something's wrong with the ladder," Jig said, turning away to retrieve his lantern. He scooped sand from a pouch on his belt to extinguish the flames. "The last three rungs aren't completely there."

"Like Braf," Grell said.

Jig ignored her. He was too busy trying to absorb the changes to this place. When the dragon Straum lived here, he had used his magic to recreate the outside world. Straum had been trapped, doomed to remain as a guardian for various treasures, so he had done everything in his power to make himself at home. Jig remembered blue skies overhead, the unnaturally bright light of a false sun, the rustling sound the trees made in the wind, like the slithering of a thousand snakes.

Some elements of Straum's world had been illusory, such as the sun that crossed the sky each day. Others were real, like the trees and plants Straum had spread throughout the cavern, feeding them with his own magic until his woods were a match for anything in the outside world.

Those trees were bare and skeletal now, encased in a thin layer of ice. The ice was everywhere. The whole place had a faint smoky smell, reminding him of the crude forge back at the goblin lair.

Jig knelt, and the grass crunched beneath his knees. He broke off a single blade and studied it. Was he only imagining the silver swirl of light trapped within the ice? Frigid water trickled down his palm as the ice melted. The grass inside was brown and brittle.

He blinked and squinted, flicking the grass aside to study his own hand. His skin appeared faded, having taken on a faint bronze pallor. Looking around, he saw the same metallic tinge everywhere. The ice sparkled silver, and the trees had the dull tarnish of old lead. The illusory sky had a dull gray glow, and there was no sign of Straum's false sun, which Jig appreciated. Even knowing it was an illusion, he had always half expected the sun to fall on him.

"Hideous, isn't it?" Walland said, dropping down beside Jig. "The change was slow at first. Cold winds coming from Straum's cave. Frost spreading over the grass each morning. The leaves withered and disappeared. And then there's the snow." He spread his arms to indicate the silver flakes floating down around them. Already they had begun to stick to the lenses of Jig's spectacles, blurring his vision.

Grunting and swearing marked the arrival of Braf, who either hadn't heard or had forgotten Jig's warning about the ladder. He got to his feet, brushing ice and snow from his clothes as he moved around behind Jig.

"Someone get me off this stupid thing," Grell shouted. Her canes were hooked over her belt, and she clung to the ladder with both hands. One foot gingerly poked the rung below. Black specks shot away from the rung as her sandal passed through it.

Wordlessly, Walland reached over and plucked her from the ladder.

"Where do we go?" asked Braf, making Jig jump. One of the first rules of survival was never to let another goblin get behind you, yet here he was, gaping at the trees and giving Braf a clear shot at his back.

They promised they wouldn't kill me until we dealt with the ogres. Not that a goblin promise was worth much, but fear of Walland's retribution might carry a bit more weight. And since whatever problems the ogres were having would probably kill them all, he really shouldn't have to worry about Braf.

A rustling at his waist made him glance down. Smudge was using his forelegs to push his way out of the small pouch on Jig's belt. Smudge's head appeared, took in the world around him, and promptly disappeared again. Jig wished he could do the same.

He started to tie the lantern to his belt, trying to

find a place where the hot metal wouldn't burn his legs. Finally he hooked the handle over the hilt of the sword, so the metal rested against the scabbard. He ended up shifting several pouches to the other side of his belt to balance its weight.

Walland tilted his head and sniffed the air. He turned slowly, his eyes scouring the trees around the clearing. He took a step, paused, and turned again. Jig had no idea what he was looking for, but if possible, the ogre's behavior was making Jig even more anxious.

"You do know where you're going, don't you?" asked Grell.

Walland cupped one hand over his eyes and searched the sky, nearly bumping his head on the ladder as he circled.

Grell snorted. "He reminds me of a deranged rat the kids used to keep as a pet, until one of the older girls ate him."

"Just making sure we weren't seen," Walland said.

"Maybe we should go find the other ogres," Jig said. The longer they stayed in this clearing, the faster they would be caught and killed, and Jig preferred to postpone that as long as possible. "You told us there were some who had escaped whatever's been hunting you?"

To Jig's left, a small creature waddled out of the woods to stare. It resembled a cluster of icicles with a wrinkled pink face and a long snout. The icy spines glistened with color that changed from blue to green to purple with every movement. It seemed to be sneaking up on a pair of glowing orange bugs, the same kind that had been bothering Jig back in his temple. The bugs flew lower, circling the creature again and again. A bright spark leaped from one of the spines near its head, and the insect dropped dead.

The creature pounced, shoving the bug into its mouth with both paws.

"What is that thing?" Jig asked.

"We've had all sorts of strange creatures creeping into our woods," Walland said. He scooped Grell up, holding her so she sat on his forearm with her canes dangling down and her heels kicking Walland's thighs. "Quickly. We don't have much time."

Soon Jig and Braf were running as fast as they could to keep up. Ice and grass crunched beneath their feet as they followed Walland into the woods. The ogre carried his club in his free hand. He didn't bother to stop for trees or low-hanging branches. Instead, that huge club smashed them out of his way, leaving Jig to wipe chunks of wood and ice from his face. Even if the falling snow hid their footprints, all an enemy would have to do was follow the path of destruction. But Jig was breathing too hard to say anything.

He could hear Grell swearing over the noise. Her voice shook with each step, giving her curses a choppy rhythm, almost a marching chant. An extremely vulgar and angry chant, but so were a good number of goblin songs.

As he ran, Jig occasionally saw movement to either side: a flash of white light that disappeared among the branches, a bit of snow shifting and crumbling, a shadow leaping away, brushing through bare shrubs as it fled. Nothing attacked them though. Not yet, at least.

Finally Walland slowed to a jog, momentarily stopping Grell's complaints until she could adjust to the slower rhythm. "Where are we going?" Jig asked, wiping sweat from his face.

Walland pointed. "That fallen tree over there." The tree appeared freshly toppled. The base of the trunk was wider than Braf's neck. Only a thin shell of ice coated the upper part of the tree. Given how hard the ice and snow were falling, Jig guessed the tree had been chopped down no more than a day before.

A closer look suggested "chopped" was the wrong word. Some of the trunk showed the toothy bite of an ax, but the rest was splintered, as if someone had grown impatient and simply shoved the tree down with his bare hands.

The branches shivered, sending bits of ice into the snow. Jig stopped in midstep. Behind the tree, partially concealed by broken branches, lay another ogre.

"You're being attacked by trees?" Braf asked.

Walland set Grell on the ground. She immediately walked over to slap Braf's head. To Jig, it wasn't a completely stupid question. This whole place had been created by magic. Who knew what was or wasn't possible? Though he doubted a sentient tree would have taken the time to tie the ogre's arms and legs to its trunk. Nor would it make much sense for the tree to lie there while the ogre struggled.

"My sister Sashi," said Walland, resting one hand on the broken tree. A rough hood was tied over the ogre's head. The muffled sounds coming from within suggested she was gagged. She appeared almost as large and muscular as Walland himself.

Grell limped closer, studying the knots. "That's good technique, tying her joints to the tree so she doesn't have the leverage to break free. There are a few kids I would have liked to use that with." She glared at Braf as she said this, but he didn't appear to notice.

"I told you we were being enslaved," Walland said. He held his club in both hands, twitching nervously every time the trees creaked in the wind or a bit of ice fell to the ground. "I led my family away from the others, hoping we could hide in safety. Sashi here disagreed. She wanted to go to Straum's cave and face this enemy head-on. She's always been the impulsive one in our family."

"What happened?" Jig asked.

Walland shrugged. "She found the cave. She returned a day later and nearly killed me."

"So you hit her with a tree?" Braf asked.

"Not right away. I pretended to lose consciousness. She didn't seem to want me dead. She started to tie me up, and I managed to get an arm around her throat." He rubbed his forearm, and Jig noticed dark scabs near the elbow. "Sashi always did fight mean," he muttered. "I tied her up and brought her here. That's when I went looking for Jig Dragonslayer."

"I thought you wanted us to help your people fight, to battle alongside ogre warriors . . ." Braf's voice trailed off as Walland gave him an incredulous look.

Jig looked at the bound ogre, then at Walland. He had an unpleasant feeling in his stomach that he knew where this was going.

Walland shook his head. "First you save my sister. Whatever spell they've put on her, I need you to break it."

"Whatever spell *who* put on her?" Grell asked.

"I don't know. Anyone who's gone to face them has either died or turned against us. We see lights in the sky sometimes, but never close enough to make out the shape of our tormentors. Ogres aren't what you'd call sneaky."

Sashi's muffled shouts had grown louder at the sound of Walland's voice. The tree shivered and creaked as she struggled to break free. She actually managed to lift the entire tree off the ground before collapsing again.

"Don't worry," said Walland. "I kept her blindfolded when I brought her here. Even if her masters are watching through her eyes, they won't know where we are."

This was why Shadowstar had sent him with Walland? Jig didn't have the slightest idea how to start. This wasn't a matter of broken bones or a pierced nostril. Jig took a tentative step toward Sashi, who had stopped moving. The roughspun bag over her head tilted to one side, as though she were listening to his approach.

What do I do?

Tymalous Shadowstar didn't answer.

Hello? A little help would be nice. Still nothing. It figured. There was never a god around when you needed one. Jig circled the tree, studying the ogre and stalling for time. She wore the same rough deerskins as her brother, though hers were damp and filthy. Her nails were broken, and several of her fingers bled where she had struggled to claw through the ropes. From the gouges in the wood, she had also tried to scrape the tree itself apart.

"Go on," said Grell. "Fix her up and let's get out of here. This place is cold enough to freeze snot."

Shadowstar? I don't think Walland is going to be happy if I can't help him, and I really don't want to be trapped down here with an unhappy ogre and his crazy sister.

"You can help her, right?" Walland said, giving his club an ominous twirl.

Jig nodded and stepped closer to the tree. "Um . . . I can't really get to her with all those branches in the way. Can you turn the tree over?" No doubt she had taken some scrapes and bruises in her fight with Walland. Maybe Jig could start with those while he tried to figure out what to do next. Though if Shadowstar had truly abandoned him, he wouldn't be able to heal so much as a hangnail.

Walland stomped over to the base of the tree, setting his club on the ground and gripping the trunk with both hands. Jig glanced around, trying to gauge his chances of escape if he started running now. He guessed he'd make it four, maybe five paces before Walland crushed his skull. Six if the ogre stopped to kill Grell and Braf first.

Walland grunted as he hoisted the end of the tree onto his shoulders, suspending his sister with her head toward the ground. More branches snapped as he gripped it with both hands and twisted, turning Sashi faceup on the tree, still secured by the ropes around her hands and legs.

That was the moment Sashi arched her body and slammed her back into the tree. At first Jig wasn't sure whether the horrible cracking sound had come from the tree or Sashi's spine. Then she was flexing again, using her legs to swing the lower half of the tree upward. This time the crack came from Walland's jaw as the broken tree smashed his face. He staggered back, blood dripping down his face. Sashi squirmed, twisting and flailing to free herself. She rolled away, dragging her wrists down past her ankles, then bringing them to her mouth. She tore the sack from her head, yanked the gag from her mouth, and bit through the rope. She glanced at the goblins. With an amused snort, she turned to her brother.

Walland had his club out and was circling around Sashi. She scooped up the lower half of the tree and flung it at him. He dove back, but it gave her time to loosen the ropes around her ankles.

"What now?" Braf asked. He had his hook-tooth out, and appeared perfectly willing to leap into the fight. How had he survived this long?

"We run," Jig said.

Grell was already hurrying through the trees as fast as she could. Jig passed her in the time it took Braf to say, "Does that mean you're not going to help Sashi?"

Glancing back, two thoughts crossed Jig's mind. The first was that there would be no way Grell could move fast enough to escape. No matter which ogre won, they would overtake her with ease. The second thought was that the time it would take the ogre to kill Grell was more time for Jig to get away.

He waited for the inevitable chastising from Tymalous Shadowstar, but the inside of his skull was silent. Shadowstar had such peculiar ideas about leaving one's companions to die. Even when those companions had orders to kill you.

Jig looked back again, trying to decide what to do, and ran straight into a tree. Ice and snow sprinkled down on him as he landed on his back, staring up at the dull gray sky. Hot blood trickled from his right nostril. He saw Braf and Grell running toward him. With her canes, Grell looked like a withered, four-legged bug. Jig scooped a handful of ice and snow and pressed it against his nose as he climbed to his feet. He could still see Walland and Sashi fighting in the distance. Walland was the larger and stronger of the two, but Sashi appeared to be winning. Maybe it was because Walland was still using his club, while Sashi was swinging half a tree.

Sashi's attacks were slow, but Walland didn't seem willing to kill her. Several times Jig saw openings where Walland could have smashed Sashi's skull while she recovered her balance, but he kept going after her hands and arms, trying to knock the tree away.

Walland tried again, and Sashi kicked him in the knee. Walland howled in pain. By the time the sound stopped, Jig and the others were fleeing again.

"We should fight," said Braf. "There are three of us."

Jig glanced at Grell. Sashi had snapped a tree in half. She would do the same to the old goblin without breaking stride. As for himself, he couldn't even run away without being knocked down by a tree. Braf was the closest thing they had to a warrior, and he was waving a weapon he had never used before.

"You killed the dragon," Braf said. "Why are you so afraid of a stupid ogre?"

The reasons would take far too long to list, so Jig didn't answer. Grell was watching him, waiting for his decision. They both were. What did they expect him to do, pull a dragon out of his pouch and turn it loose on the ogre?

Not that running away was doing much good. Already Sashi was closing the distance between them.

"Spread out," Jig said. His breath puffed from his mouth in silver clouds. He removed his spectacles and wiped the worst of the snow from the lenses.

Braf had his hook-tooth ready, though he kept changing his grip, first aiming the hook at the oncoming ogre, then the point. Grell leaned her canes against a tree and pulled a short curved knife from somewhere inside the blankets bundled around her.

Jig reached into one of his belt pouches and scooped Smudge free. The spotted fire-spider was already hot to the touch, and Jig swiftly set him on the ground. The ice began to melt, sending up clouds of steam as Smudge crawled toward the closest tree. As he climbed, he stopped several times to shake drops of water from his legs.

"Sorry about that," Jig said. "Trust me, you're better off there than with me." With that, he set his lantern on the ground, drew his sword, and turned to face the ogre.

A scream of rage startled him so badly he nearly dropped his sword. Weapon raised, Braf charged the ogre. As Jig stared in dumbfounded amazement, Braf thrust the sharp end of his hook-tooth toward Sashi's chest.

She dropped her tree as she twisted out of the way, then backhanded Braf to the ground. She glanced at Grell, raising one eyebrow as if daring her to attack. Grell shrugged, put her knife away, and stepped aside.

That left Jig. He raised his sword, holding the blade across his body in the guard position he had seen adventurers use. Sashi hadn't even bothered to retrieve her tree. She strode toward Jig, giving him his first good look at Walland's sister.

Her time tied to the tree had left her hair wet and tangled, like limp seaweed stuck to her skull. Dirt and bits of bark clung to her clothes. An enormous green bruise covered the upper part of her right arm. Apparently Walland had landed at least one good blow. She held that arm close to her body, but Jig had little doubt she could finish off a few goblins one-handed.

"So you're Jig Dragonslayer," she said.

Jig wiped more blood from his nose. If he ever learned who had come up with "The Song of Jig," he was going to push them into a fire-spider nest.

"Is it true what my brother said?" Sashi asked. "Can you use the magic of this world?"

Jig studied Sashi's face, trying to guess which answer

would keep him alive the longest. If she thought magic was a threat, the truth would give her more incentive to kill him. On the other hand, what were the odds of an ogre seeing a goblin as a threat?

"Yes?" It was the wrong answer. Sashi lunged, her good arm outstretched to grab him by the face. Jig ducked, jabbing the point of his sword into her wrist. She howled and staggered away as blood the color of pine needles dripped onto the ice and snow. Braf tried to stab her with the tip of his hook-tooth, but it skidded off of her thick skin. Braf stared at his weapon, probably double-checking to make sure he had used the right end.

Sashi reached up and twisted a thick branch from the closest tree. Smaller branches rained ice as she swung at Braf. She attacked again, then yelped. Grell's little knife protruded from the side of her thigh.

They had gotten a few lucky shots, but it wouldn't be enough to kill an ogre. Jig knelt beside the cold lantern, jabbing the end of his sword through the panes and scooping as much muck onto the blade as he could. The muck was cold, and he had nothing to produce a spark. Well, almost nothing. He steadied the blade with his other hand as he brought it to the tree where Smudge was cowering.

One of the greatest challenges of Jig's life had been training Smudge to ignore muck. To fire-spiders, the caustic goo was like candy. When Jig was younger, a fire-spider had managed to sneak into the distillery, with disastrous results. Goblins passing by had never fully recovered their hearing, and Jig had been one of the unfortunate few assigned to clean what remained of the muckworkers inside.

He tried not to think about that as he brought the sword to Smudge. The fire-spider watched Jig closely as he took one step, then another. Jig had used Smudge's hatred of water to train him away from the muck. The only time fire-spiders went near water was to breed. He could tell Smudge fully expected to be spat upon the instant he went after the muck.

"Come on, you stupid spider," Jig said. Sashi was chasing Braf around a tree. Grell had produced another knife and held it ready to throw, but she didn't seem able to get a clear shot.

Smudge's training held. He turned around and began crawling away. Jig gritted his teeth, grabbed the spider, and dropped him onto the sword. Smudge was already terrified, as the burns on Jig's fingers proved. The muck burst into flames. Finally realizing Jig wasn't going to punish him, Smudge began scooping muck to his mouth with his forelegs.

It figured. Now that Jig needed his sword back, Smudge refused to leave. Jig stuck the tip of the sword back into the lantern and shook it until Smudge tumbled free. Leaving Smudge to gorge himself in the green flames, Jig turned back to Sashi. She had ended the ridiculous pursuit around the tree by ripping the tree from the ground. Now she stepped toward Braf, arms wide.

Jig rested his blade on his shoulder, grabbing the handle with both hands. Before his spectacles, he wouldn't have been able to aim well enough to do this. He swung the sword forward. Muck flew through the air like tiny green fireballs, splattering Sashi's back.

"Good spider," Jig whispered. Smudge didn't look up from his feast.

Grell threw her second knife. This one barely nicked Sashi's shoulder, but it was enough to distract her from Braf. She didn't even seem to notice the flames making their way up her back, into her hair. What was wrong with her? Smudge had given Jig a number of unintentional burns over the years, and he knew for a fact that fire *hurt.*

Jig charged, swinging his sword at Sashi's thigh. If they could take out her legs, they could run away. Also Jig was too short to aim much higher.

Sashi kicked him. The world flashed white, and Jig found himself on his backside, with snow down his shirt and pants, staring at the sky. He raised his head, and the pounding in his skull almost overpowered Braf's shouts. Braf grabbed his hook-tooth and attacked again. This time he hooked Sashi's ankle from behind.

She barely noticed, dragging Braf from his feet and ripping the weapon from his hands as she walked toward Jig.

"Don't you know you're on fire?" Jig asked. She acted like she'd happily let the meat cook from her bones as long as she got to slaughter a few goblins first.

Jig pushed himself to his knees. Where had his sword landed?

Sashi screamed. Oh, there was his sword, protruding from the flames that now engulfed her back and shoulders. Behind her, Grell hobbled back to retrieve her canes.

Sashi reached around, trying to grasp the sword, but her arms didn't bend enough to reach. She spun around in circles, like a tunnel cat chasing her tail. Finally she appeared to give up. She took several shaky steps toward Jig, then collapsed face-first on the ground.

"Is she dead?" Braf asked.

Jig crawled toward the still-burning body. He would have walked, but he wasn't sure his trembling limbs could hold him yet. "I think so."

Braf used his hook-tooth to catch the handle of Jig's sword and tug it free. Snow and steam hissed where it landed. Jig decided he could wait a few minutes to retrieve his weapon.

A loud whoop startled him so badly he fell back into the snow. Braf was shaking his hook-tooth at the sky and laughing. "Three goblins against an ogre. Did you see when I hit her with my hook-tooth? And, Jig, the way you flung that muck was brilliant! That ought to teach her not to attack goblin warriors."

Grell rolled her eyes. With a pained groan, she hobbled closer and spread her hands, warming them over the still-burning ogre. "So does this mean we're finished?" she asked.

"No!" Jig said quickly. Once their quest was over, Grell and Braf were free to kill him. "I mean, we don't know Walland's dead, and he did ask us to help his people. We should at least find out what's been enchanting them. Whatever it is, they're not doing a great job." He stared at Sashi's body. "We should be dead."

"What?" Braf stopped dancing. "But you're Jig Dragonslayer."

Jig ignored him. Hot footsteps dotted his leg as Smudge returned. There was a distinct bulge in the fire-spider's fuzzy belly. Smudge headed straight for Jig's belt pouch, no doubt for a long nap.

"Jig's right," Grell said. "The only way so few goblins have ever overpowered an ogre is by sneaking up and killing him in his sleep."

Braf chuckled. "Yeah, I know that song." He raised his voice and began to sing.

"Their weapons drawn, the goblin party snuck through darkest night,
lusting for revenge after the morning's failed attack.
But tonight the goblins meant to wage a goblin's kind of fight.
With numbers great they stabbed the ogre squarely in the back."

"Do you remember the last verse?" Jig asked.

"The ogre yelled in red-hot rage, the goblins yelled in fright,
and as he died the ogre seized a goblin's neck and . . . crack!"

Jig clenched his hands together like an ogre killing his attacker. "Ogre Attack" was a children's song, with gestures to accompany each line.

"We shouldn't have survived," Jig said. Whatever was controlling the ogres, it slowed their reflexes, made them clumsier. That might also explain why Sashi hadn't seemed bothered by the flames. The enchanted ogres would be less effective fighters, but they wouldn't stop fighting until they were dead.

Jig stared through the trees at the gray sky beyond. He doubted very much that Shadowstar had sent him here to kill the ogre he was supposed to be saving, but so far, the god hadn't chastised him. Come to think of it, Jig had heard nothing at all since they descended into Straum's realm.

Shadowstar?

Silence. What a wonderful time for the god to abandon him.

Grell had retrieved one of her knives, and was helping herself to a bit of well-done ogre meat from the shoulder, where the flames had died down. "So tell me, Jig. With all that running around, do you have any idea how we get back to the ladder?"

Jig stared. Already the snow had begun to cover their tracks. The trees all looked alike to him. It was one of the things he hated about this place. No tunnels, no walls, nothing but open land spreading in all directions. How was anyone supposed to find their way around?

"I—"

Grell snorted. "That's what I figured."

And people wondered why Jig hated adventures.

CHAPTER 4

"The difference between a Hero and an ordinary man is that when the ordinary man comes upon a flaming death swamp full of venomous dragon snakes, he turns around and goes home. The Hero strips down and goes for a swim."

—Saint Catherine the Patient, mother of Glen the Daring
From *The Path of the Hero (Wizard's ed.)*

Snow and ice cushioned Veka's fall, but the impact still knocked the wind out of her. She groaned and rolled over, spotting her staff a short distance away. She crawled over and used it to prop herself up.

From atop the ladder, Slash grinned down at her. "Where's all your fancy magic now, wizard? I'll bet you can't cast your spells on a target you can't see." He disappeared, no doubt heading back up to the lake tunnel.

He was laughing at her, just like the other goblins had always done. Between one tight breath and the next, Veka forgot all about Jig and ogres and heroic quests. She shook her staff and shouted, "And how exactly are you planning to get past the lizard-fish alone, you ugly mound of dragon droppings?"

Slash reappeared soon after, looking far less cocky than before. "About that—"

That was as far as he got. Veka drew back her arm and threw her staff like a spear. It caught Slash right in the stomach.

Slash grunted and doubled over, clutching his gut. Time seemed to slow as Veka watched him recognize his mistake. His spear fell, and his eyes widened. He reached out, flailing for the edge of the pit. His fingers scraped the stone as he tumbled forward. In a slow, graceful dive, Slash somersaulted down and landed flat on his back, almost in the exact same spot Veka had fallen.

She picked up her staff and Slash's spear while he gasped for breath. Large as she was, Slash was even bigger, and he had landed far harder than Veka. She nudged him with her toe. "Get up. Quickly, before we're discovered."

Slash touched his head, as though he were testing to see if the skull was intact. A fall from that height could easily result in broken bones, but hobgoblin skulls were notoriously thick. "Discovered by what?"

Veka pressed her toe to Slash's head, turning it to one side. "Those things, for a start."

Twin streaks of fire raced over the trees in the distance. Given the subdued coloration of everything from the sky to the rash on Slash's face, which looked like old rust, the brilliance of the two flames was even more startling. The nearer of the two was bright green. The other was a deep red. They swooped back and forth, their paths crossing again and again.

"They look like they're searching for something," Slash said as he got to his feet.

Jig and the others. She wondered if they were in trouble. The two flames appeared to be coming from the direction of Straum's cave. "What are they?" That they were magical in nature was beyond obvious, but they were too far away to make out any details.

"They're dangerous." Slash reached for his spear.

Veka yanked it back, out of reach. "You're lucky I don't kill you for pushing me through that pit. If I weren't in the midst of a quest, I—"

Slash leaped forward, seized the spear just behind the head, and yanked. Veka stumbled, but she didn't let go. She tugged back, putting all of her considerable weight into it.

With a wicked grin, the hobgoblin released the spear.

For the second time, Veka landed in the snow. Slash pounced, grabbing the spear with both hands and twisting. He nearly snapped Veka's wrist as he wrenched it from her grasp. Before she could recover, he smashed the butt into her forehead. "Some wizard."

Right then Veka would have given everything for just one spell that would take away that smug, arrogant smirk. Maybe something that transformed his teeth into worms. That would be fun to watch.

Slash looked at the ladder. The closest rungs were little more than shadows. Even with his spear stretching as high as he could reach, the tip barely scraped against the lowest solid rung. "We should get out of this clearing," he said.

Blood heated her face. She had read Josca's book so many times she knew most of it by heart. Nowhere did it say anything about the Hero being shoved into pits or taking orders from her own sidekick. A true

Hero would have wrestled the spear away from Slash and beaten him senseless.

"We need to find Jig Dragonslayer," Slash said.

Veka rubbed her head. "Why?"

"Unlike a certain oversize goblin braggart, Jig won't have been stupid enough to come down here without a plan for getting out. If nothing else, that ogre he had might be big enough to hoist us up to the ladder. Unless you want to try your magic?"

Slash didn't wait for an answer. Veka bit back a squawk as he grabbed her by the ear and yanked her toward the trees. He released her after a few steps, apparently trusting her to keep up.

Veka's mind filled with all the things she would do to him once she was a real wizard. Her books thumped against her stomach as she ran, painful reminders of how far she had to go to truly follow the Hero's Path.

They found Walland's body sprawled upside down against half a broken tree. Another of the flaming lights, a yellow one this time, had already discovered it. Veka and Slash crouched behind a cluster of pine trees. The brown needles were encased in so much ice and snow it was nearly impossible to see beyond them.

"So much for your idea," Veka whispered.

"Maybe if we dragged him back and used him like a stool?" Slash said.

Shadows twitched back and forth as the yellow light behind the body moved, almost as though it were pacing. Veka flattened herself to the ground. There were fewer branches down here, but now the snow began to chill her whole body. She gritted her teeth and remained, her ears wide as she listened to the high-pitched mumbling coming from the light.

"No life left in this one," the voice said. "Is it really so difficult to subdue an enemy without smashing them to a pulp?"

The light brightened abruptly, shooting sparks in all directions as it leaped up to land on Walland's shoulder. This was it: Veka's first real view of her enemy, her nemesis, the foe she would battle as she traveled the Path of the Hero.

"The ogres were beaten by a bunch of pixies?" Slash whispered. He sounded as if he was fighting not to laugh.

Standing atop the ogre was a small winged man. If he stood on the ground, the top of his head wouldn't even reach her knees. He had two sets of wings, like an insect, and the yellow sparks seemed to come mostly from the lower set. The wings had an oily shimmer around the edges. Otherwise they were clear as glass, save for faint yellow lines that spread through them like veins on a leaf.

Black cloth crossed around his chest, cinched into a knot at his waist. His black trousers were decorated with red beads that took on an orange shine when they caught the light from his wings.

The pixie gave Walland one swift kick, then flew into the air. "Where have your friends run off to, ogre?"

A low growl made Veka jump, but it wasn't Walland. The sound came from an enormous dog that sniffed the air as it approached the dead ogre. It walked with a limp, and one of its rear legs was matted, probably with old blood. Gaps in its fur showed older scars, mostly near the throat. Strings of drool swung from its flat, wrinkled face as it bared its teeth and snarled at the pixie.

The pixie barely hesitated, glancing back only long enough to swing one hand in a lazy gesture.

The dog took a few more steps, snapping at the sparks falling from the pixie's wings, before giving a sharp, pained yelp. As the pixie flew through the branches and disappeared, the dog sat and began to gnaw at its rear paws.

"What happened?" Veka whispered. Slash's jaw tightened, but he said nothing.

The dog snarled, attacking its own legs with even greater ferocity. The pixie didn't appear to be coming back, so Veka crawled out from behind the tree.

"That dog will rip you apart," Slash warned.

Veka was more curious than afraid. What had the pixie done?

She was almost at Walland's body when she saw. The roots of the nearby trees had coiled around the dog's paws, anchoring it to the ground. Smooth black bark crept up its legs. Blood and splinters sprayed from its panicked jaws, but the pixie's magic was too strong. No matter how the dog struggled, the bark continued to spread. It had reached its hips by the time Slash joined her. The dog's yelps grew higher in pitch, and foam dripped from its mouth as it panicked. Slash reached for the dog and nearly lost his fingers.

"That's no way to die," Slash said. "Can you stop this?"

Veka shook her head, too fascinated to lie.

He grabbed the end of his weapon and swung it like an oversize club against the dog's neck. There was a loud crack, and the dog dropped.

"Stupid pixies." Slash nudged Walland's body with his toe. "The dog was just looking for a meal."

"How did it get down here?" Veka asked. "I've never seen a dog like that before."

"Probably came with a group of adventurers." He pointed to a worn scrap of leather buckled around the dog's neck. A few rusted spikes protruded from the collar, though most had torn away over time. "They bring their animals along on their little quests, get themselves killed, and their pets either wind up in some other creature's belly, or they go feral like this poor thing. I remember one fellow who carried around a pair of trained ferrets who could disarm traps, chew through knots, all sorts of tricks."

"What happened to them?" Veka asked.

"We caught one of his companions and tied her up for the tunnel cats. Sure enough, he sent his ferrets to free her while he fought the cats." He grinned. "He should have taught them to be sure nobody had spread poison on the ropes they chewed."

Veka turned her attention back to the dog. By now the tree had nearly consumed the body. Only the wrinkled face and one ear still showed, and soon those too disappeared. Tiny branches began to sprout from the dog-shaped stump.

The pixie had done this with nothing more than a wave of his hand. No wonder the ogres were so desperate for help.

Slash gave the wooden head a sympathetic pat. "What now?"

Veka didn't hesitate. "Walland said they had taken over Straum's lair. We'll sneak into the lair and discover their secrets. That should give us the key to destroying them."

For a long time Slash simply stared at her. When he finally spoke, he sounded almost resigned. "There's something very wrong with you, even for a goblin."

Veka didn't answer. If she tried to explain, he'd only laugh at her. That, or he would go ahead and kill her.

But deep down, she knew. These pixies were her nemesis. Nemeses? It didn't matter. The magic she had seen proved they were the archenemy she must defeat to finish her journey along the Hero's Path. If she could overthrow these pixies, it would be a triumph unmatched in goblin history. Nobody would even remember Jig and his stupid song. When she returned, she would be Veka the Great. Veka the Mighty. Veka the Bold. She would have so many adjectives, the other goblins would take all morning just to greet her!

Better yet, Jig and the others might be in trouble. They had lost their ogre companion, after all. What a thrill it would be to rescue the great Jig Dragonslayer.

"Come on," she said, tugging Slash by the arm. He wrenched free, staring at her as if she had suggested raw carrion-worms for dinner. He didn't understand. The longer they stayed here, the more time Jig would have to save himself, and that would ruin everything.

She started to walk in the general direction of Straum's cave. She wondered if the pixies would have spellbooks she could steal. She would have given anything for the kind of power she had just witnessed. Well, maybe not that spell in particular. The ability to make trees swallow your enemies wouldn't be much use back in the stone tunnels and caves of the goblin lair. But if the pixies could do that, they certainly had other spells she could use.

Crunching footsteps told her Slash had decided to follow. The scowl on his face made it plain he would have preferred to leave her broken body here with the dog, but given what they faced, it was smarter to stick together.

That was how a sidekick was supposed to behave.

Veka kept her ears twisted, tracking Slash's footsteps to make sure he didn't try to stab her in the back. Though he could just as easily throw his spear, if he really wanted her dead. But to do that, he would have to shift his weight, which she would also hear, thanks to the crunch of ice and snow. Hopefully that would give her enough warning to dive behind a tree.

Her enthusiasm began to wane the longer they walked. She found herself constantly stumbling over snow-covered roots or bumping into branches which dumped snow down her neck. The sky had begun to darken, making progress even more difficult. The last branch had nearly cost her an eye. "This whole place is out to get me," she muttered.

By the time they reached the edge of the woods, Veka was hungry, cold, and soaked. Her only consolation was that Slash had been equally abused.

"Straum's lair is there, the edge of the cavern," Slash said.

"You think I don't know that?" Veka tried to sound haughty and disdainful, but her stomach gurgled as she spoke, ruining the effect. She should have brought food, or at least grabbed a few bites of Walland.

A wide clearing separated them from the edge of the cavern. In Straum's time, the dragon had kept that stretch empty so nobody would be able to sneak into his lair without being seen. Over the past year, shrubs and saplings had begun to pop up, though none were tall enough to use as proper cover.

Veka leaned on her staff as she studied the entrance to Straum's lair. The horizontal crack was like a dark mouth in the cliff curving up before them. Vines hung over the entrance like unwashed hair. The ground closest to the cliff was overrun with dying wildflowers. Over the centuries, Straum had tried many things to relieve his boredom, including gardening. The sweet, rotten smell made her nose wrinkle.

A knotted rope hung down the cliff, courtesy of some early traveler. Even from here Veka could see it was frayed and useless.

She saw no sign of any guards. The pixies should be easy to spot. The one by Walland had lit up most brightly when he used his wings, but even when resting, he gave off as much light as a good lantern. If there was a pixie anywhere near that cave, Veka would see.

"Stay with me," Veka said, stepping into the clearing.

Slash's fingers snagged her cloak and yanked her back. She fell, banging her shoulder on a tree. "What are you doing?" she shouted, climbing to her feet and shaking her staff at him so hard one of the glass beads broke and fell into the snow.

"Keep your voice down, idiot! If you're so eager to get yourself killed, at least let me do it." He used his spear to knock her staff to one side. "Any hobgoblin child would know better than to go out there."

Veka stared back out at the clearing. "It's not even guarded."

"Exactly."

Veka's fingers traced the outline of *The Path of the Hero* beneath her cloak, wondering if Josca included any instances of the Hero killing her own sidekick.

Then she spotted it. The body of a small rabbit, half buried in the snow. In the dying light, she had mistaken it for a bit of wood or dirt. She couldn't see any blood, so it hadn't been killed by predators. From the amount of snow on the rabbit, it had been dead a while. Someone could have killed it with a rock, she supposed. A number of goblins were quite good with rocks. But why would they leave the corpse?

No, this had to be a trap of some sort. Judging from the angle of the body, the rabbit had been coming from her left. It had died a bit short of the cave. The trap must cover the area in front of Straum's lair. Using the rabbit as a marker to judge the distance, that meant it probably extended right up to the edge of the woods. A few steps and she would have triggered it.

That only made her angrier at Slash. A Hero shouldn't need her sidekick to save her. She knelt, determined to figure this out for herself. Slash leaned against a tree with his arms folded, amusement plain on his face.

The land looked no different. Ice encased the grass and shrubs poking up from the snow. The grass was a bit taller here, maybe. And there were holes in the snow where the ice protruded, almost as if the grass had melted the newfallen snow around it. But if that was the case, why hadn't the ice melted as well?

She pushed her staff forward, breaking bits of ice and snow. She glanced at Slash for some clue whether this was a good idea, but he only smirked. Her face burning, she jabbed the staff farther.

The ice didn't break. She tried again. A bit of snow fell away, but the ice was solid as rock. It seemed to pulse with a dim red light. Another jab confirmed it. "There's something inside the ice."

The taller shards of ice were literal spikes. She could see it now, how they came to a sharper tip than the rest of the grass. They had to be magical, probably strong enough to pierce the leather soles of her boots, as well as her feet.

She crawled forward, using her staff to test and break the ice until she reached the closest of the spikes. With one finger, she brushed the snow away.

The base was as thick as her thumb, and appeared to extend a little way into the dirt. The ice was perfectly smooth, so clear she could see something coiled at the base. She gave it a quick tap.

The ice flashed red as a thin tendril uncoiled, shooting up to the very tip of the spike.

"Looks like the rabbit managed to hit two of them," Slash said. "I'm guessing whatever's inside is poisonous. Their prey dies on top of their little trap, and they get enough food to last for weeks."

Veka's stomach rumbled again at the mention of food. "So how do we get past them?"

"If it were me, I'd toss a bunch of goblins out there. The spikes would hold them in place, and all I'd have to do is stroll along the goblin path."

What she needed was the ability to fly, like the pixies. If only she could make her levitation spell work. She pulled out her spellbook and opened it to the spell. The covers were cold on her hands where the copper was exposed through the peeling leather. The darkening sky made it almost impossible to read, even if she hadn't accidentally burned the page, but it didn't matter. She had long ago memorized every word on the page.

She knew the spell. Even though it had never worked before, it would work now. She had set foot on the Hero's path. This was the time when her powers would blossom, giving her the means to complete her journey. She glanced at Slash. Should she warn him, or simply pluck him from the ground and drag him along behind her as she flew? The latter, she decided, smiling as she imagined his frightened cries.

Her fingers twisted through the binding charm, and she closed her eyes as she finished the spell, wrapping tendrils of magic around herself and her companion and hoisting them both from the ground.

Nothing happened. She couldn't even complete the binding spell. Slash cleared his throat. "Go on, keep waving your hands like a madwoman. Maybe the little ice creatures will all get scared and run away."

Veka blinked back tears. Heroes didn't cry. Not even when their magic deserted them. She slammed the book shut.

The book . . . She stared at it for a long time. Perhaps the answer she needed was within her spellbook after all.

"You look like a fool," Slash said.

Veka didn't care. Planting the butt of her staff on the ground in front of her, she took another step. Already she was halfway across the clearing.

Strips of black cloth bound the copper covers of her spellbook to her feet. The ragged edge of her robe flapped behind her as she took another step. Red lights flashed beneath her feet. Elation at her success helped to ease the pain of ripping the covers from her spellbook. Most of the binding had torn in the process, and already the pages were separating. She had ripped an extra strip from her robe and used it to tie the pages together for now. She had hoped she would be able to repair the covers, but one look at the stiff, torn leather told her it was probably pointless.

"That doesn't matter," she whispered, taking another step. The pixies would have new books, better spells.

The ice gave way beneath her, and she clung to her staff to keep from falling. The end of the staff caught her in the chin, but she managed to keep her balance. She had reached the cliff, and the patch of ground here appeared to be natural. This was where the smell of dying flowers was strongest. Maybe the smell repelled the ice worms as well, or maybe Straum had done something to the soil to protect his garden. It didn't matter. She was safe.

She slipped the copper plates from her feet and sent them spinning through the air toward Slash, then turned back to the cliff. By stretching, she could just reach the old rope hanging down from the cave. A quick tug snapped it, and dirt sprinkled her face as the rope fell. She spat and tossed the rope aside. An ogre could probably reach the lower lip of the cave, but it was well beyond her. Or Slash, for that matter.

Slash hopped down from the field of spikes and walked over to test the vines dangling down over the cave. One tore loose in his hand, and he tossed it aside. "Kneel."

Veka raised her staff. "What?"

"Unless you have a better way to get up there?"

Oh. Veka looked up, then at Slash. "You should kneel. I'll climb up and—"

"Break my spine," Slash said flatly. He tossed the covers of her spellbook on the ground. "I'm taller, stronger, and lighter. If you're serious about getting up there, this is the only way it's going to happen."

Had he laughed, had he even smiled, Veka would have punched him in the face. For once, he didn't appear to be mocking her.

He studied the cave entrance carefully. "You really think we'll find something in there to help us?"

"Do you have a better idea?" Veka shot back. She

picked up her battered covers. The leather covering had torn completely loose on one, flapping from one corner and revealing dented, tarnished copper. The other wasn't in much better shape. She stuffed them both into her pocket with her spellbook and dropped to one knee.

Slash leaned his spear against the rock and put one foot on her outstretched thigh. Keeping his hands pressed to the rock, he placed his other foot on her shoulder and jumped. Veka fell flat into the snow and mud, but Slash had managed to grab the edge of the cave. He pulled himself up and whispered, "Pass me my spear."

Veka wiped mud from her face and grabbed his spear. "You did that on purpose," she hissed.

"Of course I did. Now give me my spear!"

Only the fact that she needed his help to get to the cave stopped her from throwing it. She handed the weapon to him, and he wrapped both hands around the end, beneath the spearhead.

Veka passed her staff up, then grabbed the other end of the spear. Her feet scraped against the rock as she searched for traction. She heard Slash grunt, and the spear slipped slightly. At least if he let go, the spearhead would probably take a good slice out of his hands.

The vines tickled her wrists as she struggled to climb, digging her boots into every crack and irregularity she could find. Dirt stung her eyes, and already her hands were beginning to cramp, but she said nothing. A Hero didn't complain about such things, even when her muscles were burning and she was hungry enough to eat hobgoblin cooking.

After what seemed like an eternity, her fingers

found the edge of the cave. Slash grabbed her other wrist, bracing her. She tried to swing one foot up to the ledge, but she couldn't stretch high enough. She tried again.

On her third attempt, Slash snorted with disgust and reached down to grab her ankle with his other hand. She half climbed, half rolled her body up into the cave and lay there gasping for breath.

"That was pitiful, even for a goblin," Slash commented.

Forget hobgoblin cooking. What Veka really wanted were some of Golaka's special spiced hobgoblin ribs, with lots of gravy.

Ignoring Slash's mocking grin, she grabbed her staff and set off down the tunnel. The dim light from outside soon faded to total blackness. Normally the dark didn't bother her. She had lived her life in the goblin tunnels and moved around comfortably by sound, smell, and touch alone. But as she listened to the breeze whistling past the cave mouth behind them, she found herself wishing they could risk lighting a lantern.

She kept to the left of the tunnel, one hand following the rough stone. Her staff she kept extended in front of her. As the sound of the wind faded, even her breathing began to sound loud.

Her heart pounded. The journey through darkness . . . could she have reached The Descent so soon? According to Josca, the Hero first endured The Trials, a series of tests through which she would prove her worth and gain the power she needed to triumph. The Descent was the fifth chapter, in which the Hero explored the darkness and prepared for the final confrontation.

Her toe hit something hard, and she fell, landing on what felt like a metal boulder. Her staff clattered to the ground next to her.

"What was that?" Slash asked. He sounded anxious.

Veka's hands explored smooth, cold metal until it gave way to dry flesh. "A body. An ogre, from the size of it." She frowned. The skin felt . . . crunchy, and was almost as cold as the armor. The ogre had been dead for some time. Long enough it wouldn't be safe to eat, she thought regretfully.

The armor had a few dents and dings, but it was still intact. She couldn't find any holes or wounds in the ogre's exposed flesh, either.

"How did it die?" Slash asked.

Veka hissed with pain as she sliced her fingers on the sword still clutched in the ogre's hand. She shoved her bleeding fingers into her mouth. "How should I know?" she said, her voice muffled. "Maybe he killed himself so he wouldn't have to listen to stupid questions."

She found a second sword in his other hand. Several knives were strapped to his belt and thigh. "He's got enough weapons to fight half the creatures in this mountain," she added.

"Probably looted them from Straum's lair."

Among the dragon's other eccentricities, Straum had been a bit of a collector, saving trophies from the various failed Heroes who tried to slay him over the years. Weapons of all conceivable design had lined his walls, along with the armor, lanterns, jewelry, even the chamber pots of the men and women he had slain.

Most of those valuables had disappeared soon after Straum's death. Centuries' worth of weapons were looted in mere days as ogres, goblins, and hobgoblins poured into the cavern. This new influx of weaponry caused a brief escalation of conflicts, decreasing the goblin population by about a quarter. Veka wasn't sure how many hobgoblins had died. Not enough, at any rate.

In many cases it was the looters themselves who died, learning too late that a sword that had done nothing but gather dust for centuries tended to break at the most inopportune times.

She could hear Slash crouching on the other side of the body. "Feels like he was burned."

Before Veka could begin to guess what might have killed the ogre, she realized she could just make out the shape of Slash moving around. In the distance, a dim green aura filled the tunnel. She tapped Slash with her staff to get his attention, then pointed to the light.

"We must be getting close," he said.

Veka watched a little longer before answering. "No. That's coming to us." Now she could hear the buzzing of wings, slightly lower in pitch than the pixie they had seen in the woods. "I only hear one. If we're fast enough, we should be able to kill it before it can use its magic." Or if not, hopefully the pixie would go after Slash first. She would have time to hit it from behind, and she might even get to see a new spell.

The light brightened as the pixie neared. The tunnel curved a bit up ahead. Soon the pixie would come into sight. "Get ready," she whispered.

"I'm . . ." Slash's voice trailed off, and he stared at her hand. Even in this dim light, she could see that his face had gone pale.

She glanced down. Blood from her cut fingers had run down her arm and begun to dry. She flexed her hand, grimacing at the sting of sliced skin.

"You're bleeding," Slash said. He swallowed and turned away. He appeared to be swaying.

"What is it?" Veka asked.

Ever so slowly, the hobgoblin fainted. His spear clattered against the rock.

Veka blinked. Hundreds of hobgoblin warriors, and she wound up with the one who was afraid of blood. She couldn't wait for him to wake up so she could taunt him.

But first . . . she raised her staff and strode toward the oncoming light. From the sound of it, the pixie had picked up speed. It had probably heard Slash drop his spear.

Time to show these oversize bugs what a Hero could do.

CHAPTER 5

"This is my *quest. I shall be the one who leads us to victory."*

—Prince Barius Wendelson, Adventurer (Deceased)

By the time Jig and the others made their way back to the clearing, the sky was dark. The land, on the other hand, still gave off enough light to keep them from walking into the trees. The light appeared to be trapped within the ice and snow, which had grown steadily deeper in the time they had been searching. The snow came to their ankles now, and beneath it the ice was thick enough to support their weight. Braf had fallen three times already.

Jig stared across the clearing, refusing to accept what he saw. "This is the right place. The ladder should be here."

He glanced at his companions, hoping they might have a suggestion. Braf yanked his finger away from his nose and tried to look nonchalant. Grell passed gas, something she had done quite regularly since their fight with Sashi.

"Ogre meat disagrees with me," she snapped. "You have a problem with that?"

Jig pulled off his spectacles and cleaned the lenses on his shirt. Given the condition of his shirt, it didn't help much.

"If the ladder's gone, how do we get back?" asked Braf.

Jig didn't have the slightest idea. They were still looking to him for answers, as if he were supposed to conjure another ladder out of thin air. Or were they simply getting ready to kill him? With Walland dead, it could be argued that their little quest was at an end. Jig squinted at the sky, pretending to search for the ladder as he stepped away from the others.

"Maybe we could ask those ogres," Braf said.

Jig tensed, one hand going for his sword before he spotted the ogres in question. They were marching through the trees on the far side of the clearing. Jig counted six, maybe seven. He had trouble distinguishing the shapes, even with the lantern the lead ogre carried.

"Don't ogres usually use torches?" Grell asked. "I thought wood burned orange, not pink."

The pink light coming from the lantern popped and sparked as the ogres made their way through the woods.

"They might be using muck," Jig said. "Hobgoblins change the recipe a bit to get those blue flames." He had always believed they did it on purpose, purely so they could have flames the color of goblin blood. But why would anyone want pink fire?

"Where are they going?" Grell asked.

Jig clenched his fists. How was he supposed to know these things?

"We should ambush them," Braf said. "We can torture them until they show us the way out. There are three of us, and we have the element of surprise."

Grell smacked the back of his head.

"Thanks," muttered Jig.

Walland had acted nervous from the moment they arrived, glancing around and jumping at the slightest sound, like . . . well, like a goblin. These ogres could not have cared less who saw them, which meant they were probably controlled the same as Sashi had been. Hopefully, that meant they shared her lack of alertness as well. "We'll follow them," he said.

"Why?" asked Grell.

"Because I don't know what else to do!"

Grell grunted. Braf looked disappointed.

"We can cut around the clearing. That light carries pretty far in the dark, so we should be able to keep them in sight."

A noise in the woods made him jump. He turned, orienting his good ear toward the darkness as he peered into the trees. The branches had been creaking in the wind since he arrived, and occasionally the weight of the snow and ice would cause one to break. The first time it happened, Jig had yelped and drawn his sword. Braf had hidden behind a tree, proving himself smarter than Jig in at least this one thing. No doubt this was just another branch collapsing beneath the snow and ice.

Another crunching sound, like a footstep.

Braf was already looking for a place to hide, while Grell hobbled after him. The tightness in Jig's stomach grew as he realized he was probably the most capable warrior in the group.

He drew his sword and pressed his back to the nearest tree. Smudge was still safe in his pouch. If he could have, Jig would have crawled in after him.

There were at least two sets of footsteps. Had it been only one, Jig might have been able to kill whoever it was without alerting the ogres. Any real battle would no doubt be loud enough to bring them running.

"Jig?"

For a moment, Jig stood frozen. Then he recognized the voice. "Veka?"

Veka crept out of the darkness, her staff rattling, and her cloak dragging through the snow. A hobgoblin trailed along behind her.

"Well met, Jig Dragonslayer!" she said.

Jig stared. "Huh?"

"A good thing I changed my mind about helping you," Veka added, a huge grin on her face. "Beating those pixies is a job for a Hero."

Pixies. Jig had encountered only one in his adventures. The Necromancer had been one of the fairy folk, a little blue-haired man with a nasty sense of humor. It was cosmically unfair that anything so small could be so frightening. The tiny dark wizard had nearly turned Jig and his companions into animated corpses. Pure luck had kept Jig alive.

"How many pixies?" he whispered. Ogres couldn't hear as well as goblins, but he wanted to be safe.

"A lot," Veka said cheerfully. "They're holed up in Straum's lair. I killed one, then we fell back to plan our next attack."

Grell limped toward them. "These things enslaved the ogres, but you and your hobgoblin pet killed one and got away?"

The hobgoblin growled, pointing his spear toward her. Grell smacked his hand with her cane, and the spear dropped into the snow.

"We were sneaking through the tunnel toward the lair," Veka said. "Slash here was—"

The hobgoblin snarled again, loud enough to make Jig cringe.

"He was distracted," Veka said. "I picked up my staff and waited as the pixie came closer . . . closer . . ." She waved her staff, clearly enjoying the tale. "Suddenly he spotted me. His eyes widened with surprise. Surprise, and a little fear. He tried to cast a spell on us, but I was too fast. I leaped out and hit him with my staff, sending him flying into the far wall. He was stunned, but not out. He tried again, and the air tingled with the power of his evil magic. Another moment, and we would have been done for."

"Did you win?" Braf asked.

Veka rolled her eyes. "Just as his hands began to burn with magic, I reached him, crushing his skull with my staff." She showed them the end of the staff, then frowned. "I guess the snow washed the pixie blood away."

"So you beat this all-powerful pixie by hitting him with a stick?" Jig asked.

"That sounds like fun," Braf said. He hurried away, presumably to look for a pixie-hitting stick.

"How did you find us?" asked Grell.

"We didn't." Veka pointed to the ogres. "We were following that pink pixie."

"That's a pixie?" Jig asked.

"A lazy one," Veka said. "She was making the ogres carry her so she wouldn't have to fly."

She walked to the edge of the clearing, ignoring the others as if she had nothing to fear and making Jig wonder what had really happened. Normally, putting a goblin and a hobgoblin together was a sure way to rid yourself of the goblin, but here was Veka, turning her back on Slash and the spear that could punch a bloody hole through the middle of her back with one thrust.

Smudge was squirming out of his belt pouch. Jig loosened the ties enough for Smudge to scurry up to his leather shoulder pad. Flakes of snow hissed as they landed on him. The fire-spider turned this way and that, trying to keep an eye on Veka and the hobgoblin both. Jig didn't blame him. He had healed enough victims of hobgoblin traps to know how dangerous they could be, and as for Veka, what could be more dangerous than a goblin who wanted to be a Hero?

"Well?" Veka asked. She had already begun walking after the ogres. "Our way lies with those ogres, and I for one will not shirk away from the call of destiny."

Jig glanced at the hobgoblin, his fear unexpectedly giving way to sympathy. "Has she been talking like that the whole time?"

"Ever since she fought that pixie." Slash's nails dug into the shaft of his spear. "When she wasn't narrating her own little adventure, she was trying to compose a song about her triumph. I nearly ripped off my own ears."

"Wouldn't it make more sense to rip out her tongue?" Braf asked.

"Come on," Jig said. He didn't like the thoughtful look Slash was giving Veka. The pink light of the lantern—no, the pixie—was already fading with distance. They would have to hurry to keep up.

As he walked, he comforted himself with the thought that at least Slash didn't have orders to kill him when this was all over. On the other hand, when had a hobgoblin ever needed orders to kill a goblin?

* * *

Light had begun to return to the sky when the ogres finally reached their destination. Jig's legs felt like dead wood, and his socks and boots were soaked through. He would have blisters the size of his fist from all this walking.

The others seemed to be doing a little better. Jig didn't know who surprised him more, Veka or Grell. Despite her weight, Veka hadn't stopped once, nor had she shown any willingness to rest so the others could catch up. As for Grell, she hobbled along at a steady pace, never quite losing sight of the group. She didn't even appear to be breathing hard.

"I work in the nursery," she explained when she caught up. She waved one of her canes at Veka. "I spend every night chasing idiots. The only difference is, I don't have to clean her arse after she squats."

Jig hurried ahead to see what the ogres were doing, as much to drive that horrible image from his mind as anything else. They had come to the edge of the huge cavern. "Are we near Straum's lair?"

As soon as he asked, he realized the stone wall ahead of him wasn't the same as the one he had seen a year before. For one thing, the trees grew right up to the edge of the rock. The only exception was a small area of freshly cut stumps. The stone itself was covered in dying brown moss, and it sloped upward at a much gentler angle than he remembered.

He also realized something else. The snow and ice were thinner here by the edge of the cavern. The few flakes that blew onto the rock were white, not gray. The ogres' skins started to lose their metallic hue as they gathered around the cliffside. Their coloration still wasn't right, but it was closer to normal than anything Jig had seen since he arrived down here. Whatever was affecting the cavern, they seemed to be reaching the edge of its range.

One of the ogres dropped to his hands and knees to crawl into a dark hole in the cliff. Rock and dirt had been piled to either side of the hole, suggesting this was a new addition. Jig had always believed the hardened obsidian walls were indestructible, but he had believed the same thing about the ladder back at the clearing.

A high-pitched scream made Jig shrink back. The ogre's feet reappeared. He backed out, both hands clutching a rope as thick as Jig's wrist. The others crowded around, blocking Jig's view.

An answering scream came from one side of the cleared area, where an enormous brown bundle flapped and struggled against a rope. Powerful wings knocked into the branches, spilling snow and sticks. Even Veka seemed a bit taken aback by the size and ferocity of the trapped bat.

Farther on, Jig realized that what he had first assumed to be a pile of rubble was actually the bodies of several more giant bats.

"Ugly things, aren't they?" Braf asked.

Jig nodded. The ogres were dragging another trapped bat from the tunnel. The rope was looped around the bat's neck, and the wings were folded and pressed tight against its body. Tiny black eyes bulged from a flat, pale face. The bats' only redeeming feature was their oversize flopping ears, which reminded Jig a little of goblin ears.

Given how roughly the ogres grabbed and pulled, Jig wasn't at all surprised by the number of bat corpses in the pile. What he couldn't figure out was why they were collecting giant bats in the first place.

With a flash of pink, the pixie launched herself into the air. She waited until the struggling bat was clear, then darted into the tunnel. The ogres looped more rope around the bat, securing its wings to its body. Several ogres began to do the same to the other bat. The smell of guano grew stronger as the bat struggled, but it was no use. Soon the ogres had both bats tightly bound. A pair of ogres hoisted each bat onto their shoulders and set off into the woods.

Several more ogres were now crawling out of the tunnel. Brushing dirt and rocks from their bodies, they hurried to join their companions.

By the time the pixie returned, the ogres were already heading back the way they had come. Jig crouched behind a tree, holding his breath and praying Braf or Veka wouldn't do something stupid like challenge the ogres to single combat.

The pixie looped through the air toward one of the ogres. She landed on what appeared to be a small hammock tied to a wooden handle. The ogre held the handle perfectly flat as the pixie settled into place. Her shimmering wings twitched slightly, folded to either side of the hammock.

All of this was accomplished without the pixie or anyone else ever speaking a word. Jig was still staring, trying to understand it all, when Veka strode past.

"Come on," she said, stepping around a tree stump. "This is our chance."

"Our chance to do what?" Jig asked. "The only thing we know about that tunnel is that wherever it goes, there are giant bats on the other side."

"The Path will present itself to the True Hero," Veka said. She was quoting that book again. She always tilted her head back the same way when she did that, with her eyes half closed and one corner of her mouth curled up. "But the Hero must have the strength and courage to follow where the Path leads."

"What about the book's last owner?" Jig asked. "His path led him straight into Straum's stomach!"

Veka sniffed and turned away. "Then clearly he was no Hero, was he?" She reached into her cloak for her book, eliciting a pained groan from Slash. Ignoring him, Veka flipped through the pages and read, "Sa'il stared at the mountain of skulls leading to the temple of the black goddess, and his friends urged him to turn back.

" 'Do you not see the bones of those who have tried to reach the goddess?' pleaded his faithful companion Tir.

" 'Without those bones, there would be no path to climb,' replied Sa'il."

Jig glanced at the others. Slash was using his finger to test the tip of his spear. Grell looked ready to fall asleep. Braf, on the other hand, was wide-eyed as he listened.

"I don't understand," said Braf. "There aren't any bones here. And wouldn't all those skulls roll away when you tried to walk on them?"

Veka slammed the book shut. "It means you can't let the failure of others block you from the Path." She walked to the hole in the cliff and peered inside. "Hurry, before they return."

They looked at Jig, who shrugged. It wasn't as though he had a better suggestion.

Veka had already stepped into the tunnel. Where the ogres had crawled on hands and knees, Veka merely had to duck her head a little. Jig started to follow, when a surge of heat seared his neck.

"Veka, wait!" Jig shouted. He leaped back, poking Smudge with his fingers to drive the fire-spider away from his neck. Smudge's heat dissipated almost as quickly as it had begun. Jig searched for a source of light, a lantern, a bit of dry wood, anything that might burn. All the lanterns had either run out of muck or been broken during the fighting.

"If you're afraid, you can wait here while I explore the tunnels," Veka said.

It would serve her right to let her go on and get eaten or stabbed or killed by whatever Smudge had sensed. Jig ran to the dead bats and ripped tufts of fur from their brown bodies. They smelled faintly of mold. He rolled the fur between his palms, spinning it into a crude bit of rope. He held one end up to Smudge as he returned to the tunnel.

A smelly orange flame appeared on the end of the rope. Jig moved quickly to catch up with Veka. Already the rest of the fur was beginning to burn. He saw Veka's shadow just ahead and tossed the fur to the ground beside her.

"What are you doing?" she snapped.

Jig pointed. "What's that?"

Pairs of tiny yellow eyes hovered in the darkness. There were too many to count. Veka untied her robe and searched through her pockets, finally producing a small cloth packet. She unfolded the cloth and dropped a long, thick tube of brown fungus onto the fire. Jig recognized it as a firestarting stick. The fungus would burn slowly and steadily, and was far safer than flint and steel for lighting fires in the distillery. The flames brightened, taking on a greenish tinge.

"That is another trial I must face," Veka said.

"No, that is a multiheaded snake thing," Jig snapped, grabbing her arm and pulling her back.

Jig counted at least fourteen heads on the tangle of snakes, all of which were watching him and Veka. This must have been what the pink pixie was doing when she flew into the tunnel. Even the ogres would have had trouble getting past it. The creature completely blocked the way. Looking at any one segment of the snake, it would appear to be a normal rock serpent. Reddish brown scales perfectly matched the obsidian tunnels. A whiplike black tongue flicked the air, sensing prey.

The pixie had apparently taken a group of rock serpents and joined them into a single creature. Their bodies merged into an irregular ball of scaly flesh at the center of the tangle. There were no tails. Every sinuous length of snake had sharp venomous fangs at the end.

Jig could see why Smudge had been afraid.

"Out of my way," Veka said, pushing Jig back. Jig hopped out of the tunnel, Veka's staff rapping the ground at his heels. She strode to Slash and said, "I need your spear."

"The pixies left a snake creature to guard the tunnel," Jig explained. Though what Veka planned to do with the hobgoblin's spear was beyond him. He doubted it would be enough to kill one of the bodies. Killing a segment of a carrion-worm only made the rest of the worm angry. She would probably have to kill every piece before the thing would really die, and while she was going after one head, the rest would go after her. "Veka, if you try to fight that thing with a spear, you're going to get killed."

Slash's expression brightened. "Here you go," he said, handing over his weapon.

Veka set her staff against a tree and marched back into the tunnel.

"What are you doing?" Jig asked, hurrying after her. Her triumph over the pixie had obviously damaged her mind. What did that say of him, though? He was the one following her back into the tunnel.

"Chapter Four: The Trials." She handed her fire-starting stick to Jig. Her hands gripped the shaft of the spear near the bottom. "All Heroes must overcome a series of harder and increasingly dangerous obstacles."

Jig stopped, momentarily puzzled. "Why do the obstacles always get harder? Why wouldn't the Hero face the most dangerous one first? The rest should be easy after that."

Veka ignored him. Raising the spear, she thrust the point at the center of the snakes.

Every head, except those few supporting the creature's weight, lashed out at Veka. Four sets of fangs sank into the wood of the spear, wrenching it from her hands. Smudge curled into a ball on his shoulder pad, and Jig smelled burning leather.

Splinters flew as the snakes ripped the spear apart. The thought of what those snakes would do to a goblin nearly made him throw up. They were clearly ravenous, some of them so desperate they were actually trying to swallow the broken bits of wood before spitting them to the ground.

Jig gathered up some of the splinters and used the firestarting stick to light a small fire on the side of the tunnel, then studied the snakes more closely. If he wasn't mistaken, the pixie had made a mistake when she created this monstrosity.

"Stupid hobgoblins can't make a decent spear to save their lives," Veka muttered. Jig grabbed her sleeve and tugged her back outside.

"So did you kill it?" Slash asked, a wide grin on his scarred face.

"I need your help," Jig said, cutting Veka off. "Help me butcher one of those dead bats."

"I'm a hobgoblin warrior," Slash said. "I don't do that kind of work. And where's my spear?"

"I'll help," said Braf. "I was getting hungry again anyway."

Jig didn't bother to explain. He and Braf worked together, cutting chunks of meat from the body while Slash stormed off to search for a replacement weapon. Veka watched, her arms crossed.

"What do you plan to do, beat them to death with raw meat?" she asked. "That's the best plan the great Jig Dragonslayer can devise?"

"Come on," Jig said, scooping some of the meat into his arms. His shirt would be ruined, and it would take ages to get the smell of dead bat out of his nose. Even before he dropped the meat, he could see the snakes quivering eagerly. The pixie's magic seemed to bind them in place, but the heads stretched and strained toward the smell of food.

Jig was happy to oblige. He tossed every bit of bat meat at the snakes, trying not to watch as the heads fought one another in their eagerness to gorge. Then Jig retreated back out of the tunnel to wait.

"What did you do?" asked Slash. He had returned empty handed, and the glare he aimed at Veka's back promised murder. "They're not dead. I can hear them from here."

"Give it time. It will die soon enough," Jig said.

"Poison?" Grell guessed.

Jig shook his head. "Most poisonous creatures have some immunity to toxins." He peered into the tunnel. The flames were dying again, but he could just make out the shape of the creature. Already several of the heads drooped to the ground. This was working even better than he had expected.

"What did you do?" Veka demanded.

"It's what the pixie did. She bound those snakes together, but she didn't think it through." They stared at him. "Look, that thing just ate most of a giant bat, right?"

Braf nodded.

"What happens next?" Jig asked.

"Dessert?" Braf guessed.

"What happens to the *food*?"

Grell snorted. "If you're me, it builds up in your gut until you need some of Golaka's special mushroom juice to get things moving, and then—" She broke off, hobbling past Jig to stare at the creature, following the lines of the snakes' smooth, unbroken bodies back to the juncture. "They can't—"

"The back part of those snakes got lost when the pixie put them all together," Jig said.

Grell pursed her lips. "Poor thing. That's a horrid way to die."

Jig was all too happy to let Veka be the first to climb over the dead snake creature. Even though Smudge was cool and calm, he still half expected one of those heads to lurch to life and sink its fangs into Veka's leg. Only when she was safely past did he stop worrying about the creature.

That simply meant he could resume worrying about other things, not the least of which was what he would say to Kralk when and if they found their way back to the goblin lair. "Let's see, our ogre escort was killed by his sister. We lost the ladder to the upper tunnels. And oh yes, the pixies have conquered the ogres and should be coming along shortly to do the same to the goblins."

Jig tried to console himself with the fact that he was unlikely to survive long enough to see that invasion.

This tunnel seemed to slope downhill, carrying them deeper into the mountain and farther from home. Even if they evaded the pixies, the odds were good he would never make it back to face Kralk.

It was scant comfort.

It's not the pixies you should be worried about.

The voice of Tymalous Shadowstar, coming after such a long silence, made Jig jump so hard his head slammed into the top of the tunnel.

"What is it?" asked Braf, his face barely visible in the dull glow of Veka's firestarting stick.

"Nothing." Jig rubbed his head and glared upward. *Where have you been? I could have used some help down here. I had to fight an ogre and a snake thing and what do you mean it's not the pixies I should worry about? Do you remember the Necromancer? He was just one pixie. Now we have—* He didn't actually know how many pixies had taken up residence in Straum's lair. *—more than one,* he finished.

That pixie was not the original Necromancer, Shadowstar said. *Don't you remember?*

I try not to. But Shadowstar's prodding had brought the experience back to the surface: the smell of decaying flesh, the screech of the Necromancer's voice as he gloated about killing the original Necromancer and stealing his magic.

He wasn't from our world, Shadowstar said. *Whether he came willingly or was exiled, he left his world behind to enter ours. The pixies below haven't done that.*

But I saw them! I saw the snake creature that pixie created. And what about the ogres? They—

Shut up and listen, Jig.

Jig blinked. Rarely had Shadowstar sounded so abrupt.

The pixies haven't left their world behind because

they're bringing it with them. That's why I couldn't reach you. Even gods have limits, and my power doesn't extend into other worlds.

The snow, the strange colors, that's—

It's an imbalanced juxtaposition of realities, said Shadowstar, escalating Jig's headache from "pained throbbing" to "Dwarven drinking party inside Jig's skull." *It's a bubble.*

That was better. Jig could understand bubbles. *So what's going to happen?*

I'm not sure. Shadowstar actually sounded embarrassed. *It may be a temporary thing, a transitional zone to help the pixies to acclimate to this world. Or it could become a permanent pocket of their world within yours. I suppose it could also pop, to further the metaphor. In that case, I imagine the magic of the pixie world would simply disperse.*

Jig's headache was getting worse. *What do you expect me to do about it?*

I don't know, snapped Shadowstar. *I was the god of the Autumn Star, remember? A god of evening, of peace and rest. Protector of the weary and the elderly. I didn't spend a lot of time repelling pixie invasions.*

Jig stopped so suddenly that Grell bumped into him. Up ahead, Veka turned back to ask, "What's the matter?"

Let me make sure I understand this, Jig said. *You, a god, can't set one metaphysical foot down there, and you have no idea how to fight them. Yet you expect me, a goblin, to take care of it? To beat an army of ogres, pixies, snake-monsters, and whatever else they fling at us, and also to push their little world-bubble back into their world?*

Bells jingled, Shadowstar's equivalent of a shrug.

Jig glanced at his companions. A hobgoblin, an old

nursemaid, a warrior who was more likely to kill himself than the enemy, and a muckworker with delusions of wizardry. *Is there anything else you want to tell me before I go back to getting myself killed?*

Veka and her hobgoblin friend. They're cocooned in the magic of the pixie world. I'm guessing they've been enchanted. The pixies are probably watching every move you make.

Jig massaged his skull, trying to ease the pounding in his head. His fingers warmed, swelling with a brief pulse of healing magic. The throbbing receded slightly. *Thanks.*

He glanced ahead to where Veka was impatiently tapping her staff on the ground. Slash was right behind her. At least Veka had destroyed the hobgoblin's weapon. Still, an unarmed hobgoblin could beat an armed goblin nine times out of ten, and the tenth time applied only when the hobgoblin was asleep.

So everyone here either had orders to kill Jig, or else they were controlled by pixies who would also kill him.

With an exaggerated sigh, Veka plopped herself down and drew out her spellbook. The spellbook was worse for wear, little more than a handful of ragged pages. She picked one and, after shooting an annoyed glare at Jig, began reading. Behind her, Grell sucked on a candied toadstool.

Is there any way we can break the enchantment? Jig asked.

Not that I know of. They may not even realize they're being controlled. Sorry.

I don't suppose there are any other gods I could talk to?

Tymalous Shadowstar didn't bother to answer.

CHAPTER 6

"True heroism requires the wisdom to find the proper path, the courage to face all obstacles, and the magic to blast those obstacles to rubble."

—Aurantifolia the Blackhearted

From *The Path of the Hero (Wizard's ed.)*

Veka walked with her firestarting stick in one hand and the pages of her spellbook clenched in the other. Her staff was clamped beneath her arm as she muttered under her breath, reading through the tattered pages. She had already rapped Braf in the head twice and knocked one of Grell's canes from her hand, but she couldn't help it. She *had* to keep reading. For the first time, as she read through the mystical incantations and charms, things began to make sense. Her body tingled with magical energy just waiting to be released.

A bit of ash dropped onto the instructions for distilling pure bile from rat corpses. She wasn't sure what she was supposed to do with the rat bile once she had it, but with so many pages damaged or burned, she was picking up a lot of random tidbits. One page gave instructions for calling fire from river stones. Another listed step-by-step instructions for planting elvish corn, which apparently required the use of a platinum-gilded spade and water collected from the morning dew of an oak leaf, all of which was way too much trouble for a silly vegetable.

She grabbed another page. Most of the spell was illegible, but as far as she could tell, it was supposed to turn the caster invisible. In the margins, the previous owner had scrawled a note in blue ink:

Fire-breathing cat guarding Lynn's chambers can apparently pierce invisibility spells.

Veka crumpled that page back into her pocket and picked another. Before she could start reading, another chunk of ash fell onto her wrist. She jumped, blowing frantically to dislodge the burning ash. Her staff clattered to the floor, stirring dust into the air.

Jig whirled, his sword halfway out of its sheath. He and Slash had squeezed past her to lead the group, which would have irritated her if she hadn't been so absorbed in her spells.

She ignored him as she squatted to retrieve her staff. Chunks of rock and dirt covered the tunnel, a far dingier place than the smooth, polished stone of home. Ogres dug ugly tunnels. In several spots, rough wooden planks were wedged against the walls and ceiling to provide extra support.

Jig still hadn't relaxed his grip on his sword. He didn't trust her. Veka saw the way he had been watching her ever since she returned. He was jealous, threatened by her victory over the pixie. That was why he had shoved her aside to fight the snake creature.

She would have defeated it eventually if he hadn't been in such a hurry to prove himself.

"Be more careful," Jig said at last. "I don't know when those ogres are going to come back, and we don't know what else might be hiding down here."

Slash laughed softly. "Don't worry, if the ogres show up, I'm sure she'll use her mighty magic to stop them."

Veka's ears grew warm. She brought the dying flame of her firestarting stick closer to the pages and kept reading, hiding in her book. The stick had burned down until it was as short as her thumb. Soon she wouldn't have enough light to read.

She sorted through the pages until she found the illumination spell. Old water damage smeared part of the middle, but most of the spell was still legible. She had tried this one before, in the privacy of the distillery. If she could find a way to create light without fire, it would make the muck work so much safer. In the past all she had managed was to burn herself.

But now her eyes devoured the page. "Nothing more than a basic transference and enhancement enchantment, really."

She blinked. She didn't even know what that meant, though the rhyme was catchy. Her mind was clearly leaping ahead, instinctively grasping more advanced concepts of magic. Her heart pounded as the arcane instructions became clear. She squinted at the damaged section. "Probably talks about providing an initial source of light, like the spark to start a fire. Pretty basic spell. Not so much generating magical light as stealing it from somewhere else."

Her fist tightened around the firestarting stick. First she needed to use the binding spell to tap into the surrounding magical energy. "That should be simple. There's enough magic trapped in this place to light up half the world."

"Hush," said Grell, poking her in the backside with one of her canes.

Veka ignored her. She spread her fingers, drawing a web of magic in the palm of her hand. The silver lines connecting her fingertips were far stronger than anything she had managed before. "That's only the first part of the binding. The magic needs to be linked to the light itself in order to manipulate it."

Veka smiled as she studied the binding. The silver lines weren't true light. Bringing her hand closer to the page didn't illuminate the words, nor did the light cast any shadows. The others didn't seem to notice it at all. Her hand felt warm . . . healthy. She began to mutter the second part of the binding, then changed her mind.

"Why bother? The words are useless, a crutch for the weak-minded." Her hands flexed of their own volition, and the silver web bowed outward. A tendril of light crept through the air until it touched the flame of the firestarting stick.

"Interesting," she muttered. "Magic is more sluggish here. Probably an ambient effect of the sterile nature of this world."

Veka stared at her hand, trying to understand the words coming from her own mouth. More sluggish than what? She tried to convince herself she was simply remembering passages from her reading. Josca liked to use big words, many of which Veka still didn't understand. What was the historical unification of mythological heroism anyway? So she blurted out a few strange phrases as she cast her spells. It was part of her growing awareness, nothing more.

Josca did say the Hero would tap into previously unknown reserves of strength and power as she traveled along the path. This crisis had simply helped her discover those reserves.

She giggled. She should have snuck away years ago instead of waiting around for Jig Dragonslayer to teach her his worthless flavor of magic.

"What's so funny?" Slash asked.

Without thinking, Veka pushed the flame with her mind. Orange light leaped from the end of the stick, splashing as it collided with Slash's nose. The firestarting stick went dark.

Slash's nose lit up like a muck lantern with an oversoaked wick. He leaped back, smacking his head against the wall, then falling as he tried to scramble away from his own nose. Dirt and dust swirled around his body. "What did you do to me?"

"Quiet," Veka said sweetly. "We wouldn't want the ogres to hear you."

Jig had turned around, his hand again going to his sword. The tunnels had widened a bit, back at the junction where the ogres' tunnel breached a larger one, but Jig still had to squeeze past Braf to reach her. "What happened?"

She tossed her firestarting stick aside. "The light was dying. I made a new one."

"Take it off, goblin," said Slash, "before I—"

Veka shook her staff, rattling the beads and trinkets at the end. Slash cringed and took a step back. A gleeful giggle tried to escape her lips at the sight of his fear, but she fought it down. Heroes didn't giggle. "Calm down, hobgoblin," she said. "Right now I've only channeled the light to you. Would you like the flames as well?"

Slash's eyes crossed as he stared at his nose. The

orange light turned his face pale, almost white. Veins traced dark lines throughout his nose, especially around the nostrils. "Could you at least dim it down a little? You're giving me a headache."

"He looks like a pixie flew up his nose," Braf said, grinning. Slash stepped toward him, and that grin vanished.

Veka thought she was going to explode from sheer joy. She had cast a spell. She had mastered the magical energies around her and harnessed them to do her bidding. And she had shown that stupid hobgoblin a thing or two in the process. That would be the last quip he made about her magical abilities. He was lucky she hadn't done anything worse.

"The light *is* pretty powerful," Jig said. They had left the ogres' tunnel behind, crossing once again into familiar obsidian, and the orange light reflected from the rock for a fair distance in both directions.

"Say no more," Veka said, waving her hand in what she hoped was a gesture of generosity. She turned to Slash, reached out her hand, and tried to pull some of that light back into herself.

Nothing happened. She frowned and tried again. The spellbook said the caster would have total mastery of any effects they produced.

"I . . . I've changed my mind," she said. "Leave the hobgoblin to his discomfort. He can tie a rag over his face if he wants. At least that would spare us the ugliness of his features."

She saw the muscles of Slash's neck and shoulders tighten, but he didn't say anything. He was too afraid of her!

"Here," said Grell, handing him an old stained cloth.

Slash's hands shook with anger as he tied the cloth around his nose. The light shone right through the cloth, but it was significantly softer. "What is this?" he asked.

"Old diaper," Grell said. "Don't worry, I rinsed it out before I packed it."

"Veka. . . ." Jig's voice trailed off. He looked nervous. Was he starting to realize she would soon replace him in the eyes of the other goblins? Already Braf stared at her with new respect, and Grell . . . well, Grell looked annoyed. But she always looked annoyed.

Veka smiled. "Shall we proceed, Jig Dragonslayer?"

Beside her, Grell shrugged. "Might as well. I've got no interest in standing here staring at the hobgoblin and his amazing glowing nostrils." She turned away and started walking. With a shrug, Braf fell in behind her.

Veka gave Slash one last smile before she followed. Fortunately, Slash had no magic of his own. Otherwise the hatred on his face would have melted her to a puddle of goo right there.

Veka found herself walking beside Slash, to the annoyance of them both. Without her firestarting stick, the only way for her to read was by the light of his nose. Several of the glowing bugs she had seen in Jig's temple circled Slash's head, evading his angry swats.

"I'm going to kill you and feed your body to the tunnel cats, you know," Slash said.

Veka ignored him. His bluster reminded her of the goblin guards boasting about what they planned to do to the hobgoblins. They were too afraid to follow through. Those few who tried tended not to return.

"What are you planning to do when the ogres and the pixies find us?" he asked. "Making pixies glow isn't going to do much good."

"There are other spells," she said, giving him a sidelong glance. Though they would be far simpler to master if her spellbook weren't in such wretched condition. Here was a spell to fling fire at one's enemies, but most of that page was blackened beyond legibility, all except the warning at the top: *Do not cast near a privy.* Another page contained the first few steps in what seemed to be a very advanced spell, but the last part of the title was smudged.

"Shadow Beam of what?" she muttered. Shadow Beam of Darkness? Shadow Beam of Death? This could be Shadow Beam of Endless Belching for all she knew. If the rest of the spell had been present, she would have tried it on Slash anyway, but without the later instructions, the page was worthless.

A draft of warm air brushed her face. She glanced up and, for the first time since leaving the woods, really noticed their surroundings.

The dust ahead was heavily scuffed. She spotted large footprints ahead of Jig and the others. Ogre footprints.

She could hear a humming sound farther down the tunnel, like a giant playing the world's largest wind instrument. The air was drier than before, and it smelled of bat guano.

Ahead, Jig had stopped moving. He looked frightened.

"What is it?" Veka asked.

"I know where we are. Where we're going, at least. I hoped I was wrong." He leaned against one wall and wiped sweat from his face. "The Necromancer transformed his tunnels into a labyrinth full of traps and spells, and every tunnel led to the same place: a bottomless pit where he could dispose of those who weren't 'worthy' of joining his dead servants."

"I know the song," Veka said. Keeping her voice low, she sang,

"Deep in the mountain, to the blackness below,
that's where the Necromancer's victims all go.
Your screams start to fade as you plummet and fall,
so bring a good snack and don't bounce off the wall
of the Necromancer's Bottomless Pit.
The Necromancer's Bottomless Pit.
You can fall for a lifetime, if you come prepared.
Bring food and klak beer, there's no need to be scared
of the Necromancer's Bottomless Pit."

Slash grunted. "We hobgoblins sing something like that. The chorus is a little different, though.

"How many squirming goblins will fit
in the Necromancer's Bottomless Pit?
Keep tossing them in as they beg and they shout,
keep tossing them in if you want to find out
just how many terrified goblins will fit
in the Necromancer's Bottomless Pit."

"Will you please both shut up?" Jig asked. "Those giant bats, there was a whole nest of them living in the pit. That must be where the ogres are going to collect them. You can already feel the wind. This tunnel leads to the pit. We'll be trapped if we go there."

"So let's go back," Veka said. The others stared. "We passed at least one other tunnel, back where the ogres had broken through. All we have to do is—"

"The ogres have been following us for a while now," Jig said. "Can't you hear them?"

Veka's ears swiveled, trying to shut out the sound from ahead as she listened. She flushed. Jig was right. The sounds were faint, but the grunting and clomping of the ogres was unmistakable. How could she have missed it?

"They don't know we're here though, right?" she asked.

"I wouldn't bet on that," Jig mumbled.

Braf was looking back and forth between them. "So what do we do?"

"We go forward," Veka said. "Follow the path."

"And hope it branches off again between here and the pit," Jig added. He mumbled something about ogres being the least of his worries, but by then Veka was once again scouring the pages of her spellbook.

The wind picked up, ripping the page Veka had been studying from her hands. She barely managed to clamp down fast enough to keep the rest from following. She watched as the instructions for transforming urine to beer fluttered down the tunnel. The wind was making it impossible for her to study.

She grabbed Slash by the arm. "Come on. I need the light."

Slash growled deep in his throat as she led him back down the tunnel, chasing the flapping paper. After several failed attempts, Slash shoved her aside and stomped on the page. He picked it up, ripping the edge, and shoved it into her hands.

"Thank you," said Veka.

Grell shook her head. "Next time you go running off like that when we're trying to avoid an ugly, ogre-inflicted death, I plan to put a knife in your belly. I thought you'd like to know."

Veka bristled. Didn't Grell understand this was the magic that would save them from the ogres and the pixies, not to mention this bottomless pit? Well, maybe not the urine-to-beer spell, but magic in general.

The wind grew stronger, tugging wisps of hair from her braid and whipping it into her face. Grudgingly she conceded the older goblin might be right. If she kept trying to read, it would probably cost her any number of spells.

Her muscles tightened as she shoved the pages into the pocket of her cloak. It was as if her body were physically rebelling against the idea of giving up her studies, even for a short time. So many things had begun to make sense, so many possibilities were becoming clear, and she was supposed to simply set it all aside?

The noise was louder here. Despite Jig's hopes, the tunnel had taken them farther and farther down, following a relatively straight line through the rock. They were trapped between the ogres and the pit.

The pit itself was visible now, a black shadow at the end of the tunnel. Jig stood to one side, staring at the darkness as if he could somehow transform it into a bridge or a ladder.

For a goblin who had fought and triumphed over adventurers, the Necromancer, and even a dragon, Jig didn't act like a Hero. He acted . . . well, more like a goblin, really. He preferred to cower and hide, to run away from danger and avoid the glory of battle.

Jig was what Josca called a Reluctant Hero. Chapter ten discussed the various kinds of heroes. For herself,

Veka had every intention of becoming a Hero of Legend, one whose triumphs would inspire her people for generations after she was gone.

But Jig was clearly a different breed. She rested one hand on the comforting weight of the book, reciting the passage to herself from memory. *The Reluctant Hero wants nothing more than to be left alone, but such is not the fate of the Hero. The Hero is destined for great things, and destiny is not easily fooled. Destiny uses a variety of prods to push the Hero into adventure, the destruction of his village being one of the most common. The murder of friends and/or family is also popular. If you feel you may be a Reluctant Hero, you are advised to go forth into the world as soon as you can. It may be your only chance to protect your loved ones from the cruel, crushing hand of destiny.*

Yes, Jig was definitely a Reluctant Hero. Given what she had seen, Jig was a Dragged-Along-Kicking-and-Fighting-the-Whole-Time Hero.

How had he survived everything that happened to him in "The Song of Jig"? He wasn't strong. He looked more like a child than a full-grown goblin. His poor vision handicapped him further, even with those ridiculous lenses. His magic seemed to be limited to fixing wounds. Faced with an impending battle against the ogres, his whole heroic plan was to run away.

Veka moved past him, keeping her head and shoulders high to project an air of confidence. Whatever luck had saved Jig in the past, it didn't appear to be helping him now. He didn't know what to do.

She beckoned to Slash. "Come with me." His silent obedience was proof of how far she had come since leaving the goblin lair.

Crumbling, sloping rock marked the end of the tunnel. The ground tilted downward, and it would have been easy for her to lose her footing and fall. Bracing the end of her staff against the opposite wall, she pressed her other hand to the stone and crept forward until she could see out into the pit.

Orange light from Slash's nose barely reached the far side of the pit. The wind rushed downward, sending a low hum through her bones as it passed the tunnel entrance. Slash had stopped a few paces back. His tiny pupils never left the emptiness beyond.

Veka leaned forward and looked up, trying to see how high the pit went. The pit itself seemed to extend as far upward as it did down. She supposed it couldn't go up forever. The mountain itself only went so high. That started her wondering if the pit were truly bottomless. Not that it mattered much. If the bottom was deep enough, a regular pit was just as effective as a bottomless one. A bottomless pit just sounded more impressive.

A good thirty or so feet up, a dark shape arched over the center of the pit. That would be the bridge at the center of the Necromancer's maze. This last tunnel had sloped deeper down than she had realized. "Bring your nose closer."

Slash took a half step, then folded his arms, refusing to take another. Veka squinted, trying to make out the details of the bridge. She could see square gaps where the blocks or tiles or whatever they were had fallen loose, but the bridge itself still appeared to be stable. All they had to do was reach it.

"The ogres will be here soon," Grell commented. "If you're through sightseeing, maybe we ought to figure out how to fight them."

Veka was tempted to wait. Once the others were dead and dying, she would stride through to stand in the center of the tunnel. The ogres would pull back, momentarily confused by her confidence. There, with the wind rushing past her face, fluttering her cloak in a dramatic fashion, she would slam her staff against the ground and say in a booming voice, "Go home, you stupid ogres!"

No . . . that wasn't dramatic enough. Slamming the staff was good, but the dialog needed work. She would have to sit down with *The Path of the Hero* and reread Appendix C: Heroic Declarations and Witty Remarks.

The end of her staff slipped, and she fell back, kicking to keep from falling. On second thought, maybe fighting wasn't such a great idea. Not when a misstep could send even a Hero tumbling into the darkness.

She could hear Jig mumbling to the others, trying to come up with some sort of battle plan. She ignored him, setting her staff to one side as she yanked the pages of her spellbook from her pocket. The pages rustled and slapped her hands in the wind, fighting to escape, but she held tight until she found the burned page with her levitation charm. Still prone on the ground, she tucked that page beneath her arm and shoved the rest back into her pocket.

She had to sit up in order to read the charm. Slash had turned away to listen to Jig's plan, but he was still bright enough for her to skim the words that hadn't been seared away. A quick binding spell to tap into the magic. A second to anchor the spell to her staff. She ignored the margin notes and a doodle of an overly endowed elf girl as she read the true heart of the charm.

"Another straightforward bit of sympathetic magic, with the magical component providing the necessary leverage." Whatever that meant. She tucked the page back into her cloak pocket, grabbed her staff, and finished the charm, carefully enunciating each tongue-twisting syllable.

Slash yelped as his head bounced against the roof of the tunnel. He kept yelling as he floated and bobbed, so the damage couldn't have been too bad.

"Veka, if we're going to fight the ogres, we'll need that hobgoblin!" Jig shouted.

She could hear the ogres running, and the far end of the tunnel had begun to take on a pinkish tinge. "Not yet," she muttered. "I'm not ready."

A twitch of her staff shot Slash out of the tunnel and into the pit. His shrieks grew higher in pitch as his arms and legs whirled, as if he were trying to swim through the air itself. Veka slowly spun her staff, rotating him until he was facing the tunnel.

"What are you doing?" Braf asked.

"Saving our lives," said Veka. She gave him a fierce grin as she cast the charm again.

Nothing happened. She tried a second time, tracing the binding with her free hand, then connecting Braf to her staff. He should have floated out to join Slash in the pit. She had done the spell correctly. Why wasn't he flying?

"You're doing that?" Jig asked, pointing to Slash.

She nodded.

Jig glanced at the approaching light, then back at Slash. Sliding his sword into its sheath, he moved to the end of the tunnel, muttering, "I hate magic." When he reached the end he braced himself and leaped. His arms clamped around Slash's waist, his legs locked around the hobgoblin's knees.

"Get off of me, you stupid goblin!"

"Don't squirm," Jig yelled. "Do you want me to bite you to keep from falling?"

Slash stopped moving. A wise choice, given where Jig's face had ended up.

"Bring him closer to the tunnel," Jig yelled. "If we all pile onto Slash, can you float us up to the bridge?"

This was *her* plan! Why was Jig giving orders? She scowled, trying to come up with a reason it wouldn't work. But she was having no trouble levitating the additional weight, and the bridge wasn't too far away. It would probably work, darn it all.

She turned away. "Grell, you go next," she said quickly, before Jig could make the decision.

Grell tucked her canes through her belt and limped to the edge of the tunnel. Veka twitched her staff, bringing Slash and Jig closer . . . closer. . . . Slash stretched out his arms, trying to reach the rock. Veka spun him around again, rapping his head against the stone for good measure. "None of that, you."

She lowered him a bit, and Grell half stepped, half skidded off the edge. Her arms circled Slash's neck, and one of her feet kicked Jig in the ear.

A high-pitched scream echoed through the pit, and for a moment, she thought Jig had fallen. She froze, trying to sort out whether she should feel guilty or relieved. Perhaps a little of both? But as the scream repeated, she realized it was too loud and too high to have come from goblin lungs.

"Veka, we have a problem," Jig shouted.

A flick of her staff moved them to one side as she peered into the pit. Far below, a giant bat flew toward them, its huge wings flapping hard against the wind.

"You there, goblin!" Two ogres had come into view. One pointed a crude wooden spear at her and Braf. "We've come for Jig Dragonslayer."

Veka felt as though the ogre had walked up and

slammed a fist into her stomach. "Jig?" she repeated. "You want *Jig*? I'm the one doing all the work!"

Beside her, Braf squeezed past to leap onto Slash. She was too stunned to even notice whether or not he made it. After everything she had done, the ogres wanted Jig. She was the Hero here, not him. She was the one wielding the magical energies. Didn't they see the floating, glowing hobgoblin?

"Veka," Jig shouted. "The bat!"

She ignored him. "Why do you want Jig?"

"That's not your concern, goblin." The two ogres began to move forward. The pixie still hadn't shown herself.

"Veka, stop playing around and do something about this bat," Grell shouted, her tone so sharp Veka started to obey without even realizing it.

The other ogre shoved past his companion. "Jig is there, in the pit. Kill the fat goblin and grab him before he escapes."

Kill the fat goblin. She was nothing but an obstacle to be tossed aside. Her fangs bit into her cheeks, and her hands shook with the grand injustice of it all. Nothing she did would ever be good enough to erase the mighty Jig Dragonslayer. Forget her victory over the pixies, forget her mastery of powers Jig couldn't even understand, none of it made one bit of difference. She was nothing. Nobody.

A squeal from the pit told her the bat was here, its wings adding to the wind as it hovered beside Slash and the others. Feet with claws as long as her hands stretched toward Braf. He dangled at the bottom of the group, clinging to his hook-tooth, which was hooked through Slash's belt.

Braf kicked uselessly, nearly dislodging himself. "Jig, help!"

Veka screamed. She tilted her staff, flinging Slash and the goblins aside. At the same time, she reached out with her other hand, her fingers curled into claws. Magic swirled through her arm as she bound the bat to herself, forcing the binding spell into the bat's body, until her power pulsed through every vein, every bone, every drop of blood. Like a magical web, her will closed around the bat, controlling its every motion.

Veka closed her eyes and leaped from the tunnel. She could still see, using the bat's own senses. To the bat, Veka was a sharply defined shadow arching into the emptiness, and it was a simple matter to fly beneath and catch her.

The bristling fur stank, and the pounding wings nearly dislodged her, but she clung with one hand to the bony edge of the wing where it joined the body. Pulling herself up, she pressed her knees into the bat's side. For one horrifying moment, she thought the bat would be unable to carry her, but this was an animal built to snatch and carry prey even larger than Veka. Wings pounded, moving them away from the tunnel and wrenching Veka's arms as she clung. She opened her eyes, seeing the others both with her own vision and with the colorless shadow-senses of the bat. Never had she seen so sharply, and the bat's hearing made goblin ears seem feeble and weak as a human's. She heard every footstep the ogres took, every curse Slash whispered, everything.

Giddy excitement swelled through her. She fought to keep from laughing, afraid she wouldn't be able to stop. Even Jig was staring at her, fear and awe etched on his scrawny face. Let Jig Dragonslayer try to take credit for this rescue. Never again would she have to suffer the mockery of goblin guards or the disdain of a hobgoblin. She was Veka the Batrider. She . . . she . . .

She had no absolutely idea how she had cast that last spell. The bat tilted to one side, fighting to break free of her control. It didn't appear to be going after Slash and the others anymore. It simply wanted to get away. And it wanted to be rid of the goblin clinging to its back.

"No, fly up to the bridge, you stupid bat." She moved her staff, floating the others higher. Why wouldn't the bat obey? "Of course. It can't understand me. I have to control its actions."

The bat was a stupid animal. When Veka first sent it flying beneath her, it had assumed the idea was its own, and taken over. All she had to do was start it moving, and the bat would keep going until something changed its mind.

Something like bait. She made the bat raise its head, fixing its attention on Slash and the others. At the same time she increased the speed of its wings, forcing it higher. "You want to eat them, you ugly, filthy, smelly creature. Eat them!"

Slowly the bat seemed to get the idea. A spear flew past, barely missing Veka's arm as the bat flew upward. The ogres stood at the edge of the tunnel, staring.

Veka moved Slash higher, twitching him back and forth to keep the bat's interest. "That's right," she said. "You're hungry. You'd rather eat a good meal than worry about me."

"Hurry up, goblin," Slash shouted. "My legs and shoulders are killing me, and if that fool Braf keeps squirming, I'm going to lose my trousers!"

In a moment of inspiration, Veka moved them toward the wall of the pit, directly above the ogres. If the ogres leaned out to try to throw their spears, they would probably fall into the pit. As long as Veka kept them close to the wall, they should be safe. "Unless the pixie comes out after us."

They were about halfway to the bridge when a flicker of motion caught her eye. She closed her eyes, allowing the bat's senses to take over. It saw much more clearly than she ever could. She spotted another crack in the wall, a tunnel immediately ahead of Slash and the goblins. Standing at the edge of the tunnel, an ogre flung a thin line into the pit. A loop of rope settled around Slash and the others, drawing them toward the tunnel.

Before she could react, a second rope flew out, cinching her to the bat. She could feel the bat fighting to breathe as the rope tightened around its throat.

She tried briefly to goad the bat into flying back, dragging the ogre into the pit, but the bat was already tired from carrying Veka, and it was too panicked to obey. The harder it struggled to breathe, the faster it used what little air remained in its lungs. Soon Veka found herself swinging toward the rock, tied to an unconscious bat. The bat hit first, cushioning the impact. She twitched her staff, trying to use her levitation charm on Slash to drag the other ogre down, but they were too strong.

So be it. Fighting was more heroic than fleeing any day. She tightened her grip on her staff and prepared for battle.

CHAPTER 7

"Keep your enemies close, but your friends closer. That way your friends are between you and your enemies."

—Goblin Proverb

Normally Jig was good at considering his options and discovering the best way out of whatever situation he had been flung into. He was finding that much more difficult now, as the ogres' rope squished his face against Slash's hard leather vest. He didn't know what the hobgoblin carried on his belt, but a number of pouches and tools kept jabbing Jig in the chest and armpit. Adding to his discomfort was the cheeselike odor of Grell's right foot, currently resting on Slash's hip, so close Jig could have licked her sandal.

The only options he could come up with all centered on how they were going to die. The male ogre carried a large ax on his belt, which seemed a likely way to go. Though ogres were known to enjoy crushing their enemies bare-handed. They could also settle for simply tugging the rope tighter until it squeezed Jig and the others to death, though that probably wouldn't be as much fun for the ogres.

He glanced at Veka. Given what she had already done, she might be even more dangerous than the ogres and pixies. At the moment though, the ogres' second rope had her face pressed against the back of the strangling bat. Jig doubted she could cast a spell with a mouth full of bat fur.

That meant Braf was their best hope. Perhaps "hope" wasn't the right word. Dangling from his hook-tooth, Braf had been low enough that the rope only caught his wrists. He had been wiggling and squirming ever since the ogres pulled them into the tunnel. With a triumphant snarl, Braf yanked himself loose and dropped to the ground. Jig and the others floated slightly upward as Braf fell.

Unfortunately, Braf had left his weapon hooked through Slash's belt. That didn't seem to bother him. He spread his hands and snarled, "Set the others free, ogres, before I—"

The closer of the ogres, the female, tugged her rope. Jig yelped as he, Slash, and Grell were yanked forward, crashing into Braf from behind. Braf stumbled forward, directly into the path of the ogre's fist. He slammed into the wall and slid to the floor. The female ogre grinned and scooped him up, tucking him under one arm. She hadn't even bothered to release the rope.

The male ogre followed them into the darkness, dragging Veka and the bat along the ground behind him. Jig did his best to protect himself as he bounced off the walls and ceiling. He couldn't use his arms, but he kept his feet out to absorb the impact when he could. He heard Veka spitting and cursing.

Jig wrinkled his nose. Wherever this tunnel led, it stank worse than any part of the mountain Jig was familiar with. The smell of rotting garbage and burned meat overpowered even the fungal scent wafting from Grell's toes. Small brown-shelled insects scurried away, avoiding the light.

These ogres don't seem to be possessed like Sashi or the ones with that pixie who were chasing you through the tunnels, said Shadowstar.

That's good.

Don't get me wrong. They're just as likely to kill you.

Jig didn't answer. He closed his eyes, trying to orient himself. Every goblin learned to navigate the darkness, but as far as Jig knew, none of them had ever tried to do so after floating about in the darkness. If he had to guess, he'd put them thirty or forty feet below home. He wondered if they were out from below the Necromancer's maze yet.

Once they had gone far enough from the pit for the wind to die down some, the ogres stopped. The female pushed Grell with one finger, rotating the group. Jig was starting to feel motion sick. The light from Slash's nose illuminated moldy rock and ground so caked with mud and dust the stone beneath was invisible.

"Do something about that nose," the ogre said. She tugged them closer, so Jig could see the pine-colored freckles on her leathery face. An emerald-studded loop of gold hung from one ear. Jig could have worn it as a bracelet.

"Unless you want to lead the pixies to us," added the male. He was larger than his companion, a hulking brute whose hair hung in dirty braids past his shoulders. Spiked gauntlets covered his fists. A single blow from one of those gloves would leave the victim perforated in four places.

The female rolled her eyes. "I don't need your help, Arnor."

"Don't be like that, cousin. I was—"

"Just because you're older doesn't mean you can—"

The male, Arnor, tossed Veka and the bat to one side and stepped toward his companion. "Look, Ramma, I'm only trying to help."

Dumping Braf on the ground, Ramma used her free hand to draw an enormous blade from a curved leather sheath on her belt. There was no handle. Oversize finger holes pierced the base of the crescent blade. She slipped it on like a glove, so the edge covered her knuckles, and shoved the blade toward Slash's face. Glancing at Arnor, she said, "Like I told you, I don't need your help."

"Threaten her, not me," Slash said, frantically tilting his head toward Veka. "She's the one who did this to me."

Ramma handed the rope to her cousin. With one hand, she hauled both Veka and the bat into the air.

"Release us," Veka said haughtily, or as haughtily as was possible considering she was still spitting bat fur from her mouth. "Then I'll consider your request."

Veka didn't seem the least bit frightened. She stared defiantly at the ogre, silently daring her to proceed. If Jig had retained any doubts about Veka's sanity, those doubts would have been dispelled.

Ramma pressed the edge of the blade against the knot of the rope. Both Veka and the bat dropped to the ground. Moments later Jig and the others had been cut free as well.

Jig didn't know whether to feel grateful or worried. The ogres wouldn't have freed them if they felt the slightest bit threatened. Given that their goblin warrior was currently snoring on the ground while the hobgoblin squirmed and swore from the ceiling, pinned by Veka's spell, Jig really couldn't argue with the ogres' assessment.

Veka stood, brushing dirt and fur from her robes.

"End the spell," said Ramma, tugging Slash down by the ankle. "Or I'll slice the nose from his face."

Veka grinned. She was actually thinking about defying two ogres.

She's a goblin, said Shadowstar. *Brains have never been your strong suit.*

"Stop fooling around, girl," snapped Grell. "I'd bet my canes there are more ogres farther down this tunnel. All it will take is one with a crossbow to put an end to your wizarding nonsense." She jabbed a cane into Veka's belly. "If you're so eager to die, run back and throw yourself in the pit. Don't take the rest of us with you."

Veka glared, her mouth still open. Jig held his breath, fully expecting to see Grell floating into the air and flung back to the pit. Eventually, Veka nodded. How did Grell do that?

Grell walked to the side of the tunnel and eased herself down, groaning as her joints cracked and popped. "Goblin trying to be a wizard. Never heard of anything so ridiculous."

Veka's face turned a darker blue, but she didn't react. Had the comment come from Jig, he had no doubt Veka would even now be turning him into a carrion-worm, but something in Grell's tone kept Veka from reacting. Jig really had to learn that trick.

"Well?" Ramma asked, waving her blade. "The longer he shines, the greater our danger."

"I'm trying," Veka snapped. She picked up her staff and pointed it at Slash. "I . . . the spell . . . I'm having a little trouble, that's all." She reached into her cloak and grabbed the ragged pages of her spellbook. "It's not . . . the binding, it's stronger than . . . I'm trying. Let me find the right page."

Ramma shrugged and stepped forward. "No skin off my nose." She raised her blade, adding, "So to speak."

"No, wait!" Slash's voice squeaked, almost unrecognizable. "Move me toward the goblin. Let me talk to her."

The ogre gave him a shove, sending him floating toward Veka. She looked up, and her words dripped disdain. "What do you intend to do? You're no wiz—"

Slash's heel caught her square in the forehead, knocking her back into the wall. Her head smashed into the stone, and she slumped to the ground.

The light vanished. Slash squawked as his body came crashing down. A pained groan marked the hobgoblin's location.

Jig rubbed his forehead. "If you'll give us a little more time, we'd be happy to finish incapacitating ourselves, and then you can do with us whatever you'd like."

He heard the ogres picking up Slash and the two unconscious goblins. "Follow," said Ramma. "Try to escape, and I'll beat you to death with your own wizard."

That was good enough for Jig. "Where are we going?" he asked.

"We're taking you to meet my mother," said Arnor.

Jig kept his good ear up, listening to the footsteps of the ogres and the tapping of Grell's canes. The stench grew worse as they walked, despite the breeze. Jig shuddered to think how much worse it would be without the wind of the pit to circulate the air through the tunnels.

Despite the darkness, the ogres navigated the tunnel without a single misstep. They had been living here for a while then. The tunnel followed no pattern, veering left and right, upward and downward, all seemingly at random. Though the aches in Jig's thighs and hamstrings suggested they were walking mostly uphill.

Several times he felt shifts and eddies in the air that marked other passages. From one came the sound of dripping water, and the heavy, sickly sweet smell of mold. Another breathed warm, dry air onto Jig's skin, carrying a smell like charred bones. Smudge stirred as they passed that one, climbing halfway down Jig's arm. Jig could feel the fire-spider quivering, as if he were ready to leap away and flee. Jig stroked the spider's fuzzy back to reassure him.

"Hold," said Ramma. She chuckled softly. "We don't want our guests to die before they meet Aunt Trockle."

Jig listened as Ramma jogged ahead, wondering what she meant. That they wanted him and the others alive was the best news he had heard in days.

The only sounds came from Ramma's bare feet on the stone and the raspy breathing of the still-unconscious Braf. From the sound of it, his nose still wasn't properly healed.

Tell him to keep his finger out of it, and maybe it will improve, said Shadowstar.

A loud hiss and the dry scrape of scales on stone interrupted the ogre's footsteps. Jig heard a muffled thump, like a fist striking a mattress.

"You little—" Ramma grunted. "Got you."

The hissing grew louder and more frantic, then stopped abruptly with the sound of cracking bone.

"Are my ears failing me," asked Grell, "or did your friend just tangle with a rock serpent?"

"They like to hunt these tunnels," said Arnor. "They give one another space, but there's always a few between here and camp."

And ogres were immune to most poisons, which made the rock serpents ideal guardians . . . assuming you didn't mind a few fang wounds. Rock serpents would eat just about anything, even carrion-worms. More than once Jig had been rushed to the garbage pit to heal some unsuspecting kitchen goblin who had dumped the spoiled remains of a meal and found himself face to face with an enraged, if somewhat greasy, rock serpent.

Now that he thought about it, the smell here was similar to the garbage pit back home. Stronger and fouler, but the same basic filth.

The ogres knocked two more rock serpents out of the way before they reached the end of the tunnel. Jig could see the orange flames of torches, and a voice called out, "Who's there?"

Both ogres spoke their names at once, then glared at once another. They reminded him of young goblins competing for the chief's favor. "Fetch my mother," Arnor added.

They had stopped at a wide, arched opening before a cavern. For an instant Jig thought they had somehow returned to the goblin lair. But the smell alone was enough to dispel that idea. He turned to his left. Straum's caverns should be in that direction, somewhere beneath them.

A few small fires brightened the cave, but the putrid smoke was enough to make him gag. Most of it pooled at the top of the cavern before flowing through a crack to Jig's left.

Thick columns of obsidian were scattered throughout the cavern. The ogres had built crude shelters at several of the larger columns, stringing rag curtains for privacy. Jig guessed there couldn't be more than a dozen ogres living here. The few he spotted appeared weary, dirty, and *hungry*. Jig comforted himself with the fact that Slash was a much meatier meal than he was, and the hobgoblin was already conveniently knocked out and ready to roast.

Braf coughed and gagged. Arnor dropped him, and he landed hard on the ground. "What is that stench?" Braf mumbled.

Ramma pointed to an open doorway at the far side of the cavern. Bits of wooden framing and rusted hinges still clung to the stone. "The pit you goblins use to dispose of your waste passes close to this cavern. Some of it is worth burning."

"Even goblin dung burns, if it's dried first." The speaker was an older, hunchbacked ogre, presumably Arnor's mother. Her knuckles were swollen and callused. A small, hooded lantern hung from a thick metal chain around her neck. With her spine so badly bent, the lantern never touched her body. The flames probably helped keep her warm. One whiff of the sweet-smelling smoke told Jig she had added something extra to the lantern fuel, something with a bit of a kick to it.

"Aunt Trockle—" said Ramma. That was as far as she got.

"We found these goblins fleeing the pixies," said Arnor. "Ramma and I spotted them coming up the pit, and—"

"I said we should kill them," Ramma piped up. "But he—"

"You told us you wanted to know of anything

strange at the pit," Arnor said, glaring at Ramma. "This—"

"Shut up, both of you." Trockle stepped forward, scowling at the goblins. Her fingertips brushed the floor as she walked.

"Sorry, Aunt Trockle," said Ramma. At the same time, Arnor said, "Sorry, Mother."

"I told you I wanted to know what was happening at the pit," Trockle went on, her voice growing more and more shrill. "I didn't say you should bring goblins into our homes."

"He's a hobgoblin," Braf said, pointing to Slash. Grell smacked his head before he could say more.

"They were coming up the pit," Arnor said. "I thought we could question them to learn what's happening back home."

"They were running away from the pixies," said Trockle, her voice stern. "So you thought you'd lead them straight to us?"

"I told you," Ramma said, elbowing Arnor in the side.

"And you went along with him," Trockle said sharply. Ramma flushed and glared at Jig.

In that instant, Jig knew exactly what was about to happen. He had been on the receiving end far too many times. Ogres were larger and stronger, and their family arrangements were bizarre, but the humiliation and anger on Ramma's and Arnor's faces was universal. Just like goblins being chewed out by the chief, they had been shamed in front of the others. Next they would need a victim, someone upon whom they could vent their rage, to help them regain their sense of power and strength.

How many times had Jig been punched, chased, tormented, and teased because a larger goblin got caught messing around on duty?

"Do you want me to—" Arnor began, stepping toward the goblins.

"No, I can—" Ramma interrupted.

Jig was already moving. He grabbed Braf by the arm and said, "Get behind me."

Braf stared. Jig pulled his sword, swiping the blade past Braf's face so he stumbled away. Jig spun around, waving his sword back and forth at the three ogres.

"Just kill them and be done with it," snapped Trockle. Her face scrunched with annoyance as she regarded Jig's sword. "Leave the bodies by the pit. Make it look like they turned on one another."

"That won't work," said Braf. "The pixies will never believe we just killed each other for no reason."

Jig answered without turning around. "Sure they will. We're goblins."

Arnor pulled out his ax. Next to the ogres and their weapons, Jig's sword looked little better than a kitchen knife.

"But they won't believe it when Braf runs screaming down the tunnel," Jig continued, praying Braf would understand. He would have preferred the hobgoblin. But Slash and Veka were unconscious, Grell was far too slow on her feet, and if Jig tried to run, he had no doubt the others would do the same. So Jig clutched his sword with both hands, tightening his jaw to keep it from trembling. "Go, Braf. Grell and I will slow down the ogres. You tell the pixies they missed some ogres. They'll probably retreat through one of those tunnels on the far side of the cavern. I'm sure the pixies will be fast enough to catch them."

He glared at Trockle, who hadn't moved. "That way we all die."

Arnor glanced at Trockle. "Mom?" Beside him Ramma had drawn her weapon and stepped sideways.

Grell limped forward, and her cane made a ringing sound against Ramma's blade. "You wait right there until your aunt tells you what to do, girl."

"The pixies will kill you anyway," said Trockle. "They plan to kill every last thing in this mountain. My boy here will make it quick. Put away that sword, and he and my niece will finish all three of you before you can feel it." She sounded completely calm and reasonable, as if letting the ogres kill them was the most sensible thing in the world.

Jig shook his head. Trockle might be right about the pixies, but the pixies weren't here yet. The ogres were.

And they were still going to kill him. For the moment they were at an impasse, but already Jig could see other ogres moving toward the tunnel. From the sound of it, Braf had taken a few steps back toward the pit, but even if he did manage to reach the pixies, it wouldn't do Jig much good. They couldn't stand here forever. Arnor was playing with his ax, and Ramma had drawn back her fist to strike.

"You take your ogres to safety," Jig said. "I'll take care of the pixies."

His heart pounded as Trockle stared at him. Slowly she began to chuckle. "You? You're going to fight the pixies?"

"You must have knocked this one on the head when you caught him, cousin," said Arnor.

"How exactly do you intend to do that?" asked Trockle. "We saw what they did to our people, and you're nothing but a goblin runt."

Jig straightened his spectacles. "No," he said, feeling like a fool. "I'm Jig Dragonslayer." Gods how he hated that name.

"Jig Dragonslayer?" repeated Ramma.

Jig's cheek twitched. "That's right."

Ramma glanced at the others. "He's the one who—"

"I know who he is," snapped Trockle. She studied Jig more closely now. "You're shorter than I imagined."

Jig couldn't think of a suitable response, so he said nothing.

"You're no ordinary goblin, that much is obvious," said Trockle. "Most of you would have either run away or charged in like idiots."

Both of which were time-honored goblin tactics, and both would have gotten them killed. Jig waited. His arm was beginning to hurt from holding his sword like this.

"Go on then," said Trockle. "Fight the pixies."

Jig lowered his sword, resting the tip on the ground. His hands were shaking, and if he tried to put it back in the sheath, he would probably cut off his own belt.

"We should wake up Veka and Slash," Braf said, stepping toward them. "Veka's magic would help against the pixies. Maybe she can fling the hobgoblin at them."

"Not with the pixies controlling them," Jig said wearily. "More likely she'd fling us all into the pit."

Absolute silence. Jig could feel Smudge growing warmer. Slowly Jig realized what he had just said.

"These two are pixie-charmed?" asked Trockle.

"Um." Jig glanced at the other goblins. Braf was still staring at him, as if he didn't quite understand.

Grell looked annoyed. Ramma and Arnor had both raised their weapons again. Jig could feel his brief respite disappearing as quickly as gold from the dead.

"Kill them all," said Trockle.

"Wait," said Jig. "We can tie them up."

"The pixies can see through their eyes," said Arnor, reaching toward Jig.

Jig twisted away from that huge hand and nearly lost his balance. "We'll blindfold them," he said. "Even if they woke up, they wouldn't know where they were or how they got here."

"They'll know we exist," said Trockle. "That's enough."

"What if—" Jig bit his lip. Once again he could see what was about to happen. His stupid comment was about to get them all killed. And this time he couldn't see a way out.

"Oh, for Straum's sake," Grell said. "You know what you have to do, Jig."

Jig stared. She was looking at his sword. Did she expect him to fight the ogres? "I can't—"

"That's your problem." With an annoyed grunt, Grell pushed Jig to one side and grabbed the sword from his hand. "Sorry about this, hobgoblin," she muttered. "At least it'll be quick." With one cane hooked over her arm, she shoved the blade into Slash's chest.

Slash jerked once, then his head dropped to the ground. Grell lost her grip on the sword and stumbled back. She would have fallen if Braf hadn't caught her shoulders.

"A shame," Grell said. "He wasn't such a bad sort, for a hobgoblin."

Slash's breath turned to tight, wheezing gasps. Jig didn't move. Neither did the ogres.

"Otherwise they kill us all, chief," said Grell, stressing the last word. "Now, are you going to take care of Veka, or do I have to do that too?"

Before Jig could respond, the voice of Tymalous Shadowstar overpowered everything else.

Jig, heal the hobgoblin.

Grell was wiping blood from her hands. "Should have stayed on brat duty," she muttered.

JIG, HEAL THE HOBGOBLIN.

The force of Shadowstar's command made Jig clutch his head. *I didn't know Grell was going to kill him, but you can't blame her for—*

He's not dead yet, and the spell dissipated the instant your blade pierced his chest.

Jig stared at Slash's body. His sword stuck up from the hobgoblin's chest like a skewer in one of Golaka's barbecued rat kebabs. *So all we have to do to break the pixies' spell is stab the victims?*

Now, Jig.

Jig moved forward until he stood in the puddle of blood seeping from Slash's body. He knelt, cutting his fingers on his own sword as he probed the wound. In the corner of his vision, he could see the ogres reaching for him.

"Let me help him," he said. He ripped the sword free, and blood spurted like a miniature fountain onto hands and arms. He put both hands over the wound, feeling hot blood cover his fingers and seep onto the ground. He would have hobgoblin blood all over his favorite boots. "Bring that torch closer."

"What are you doing?" asked Ramma.

A new kind of heat flowed through Jig's limbs, past the blood and into Slash's body.

Grell missed the heart, but she nicked one of the arteries. This is going to require a bit of precision. Put your fingers inside the wound.

"Ick." Jig closed his eyes and pressed two fingers through the skin. Something scratched the back of his finger. Was that bone? And what was that pulsing thing pressing against his knuckle? Everyone talked about how Jig Dragonslayer could cure any wound, but nobody realized how truly gross the process could be.

Got it.

The flow of blood slowed. Jig slid his fingers free and wiped them on Slash's pants. He reached down to retrieve his sword. It was warm to the touch, or maybe the intensity of Shadowstar's magic had left his body feeling cold.

"When Grell stabbed him, it broke the pixies' spell," Jig said to the confused onlookers.

He couldn't have gotten a stronger reaction if he had told them Straum himself had returned from the dead and would be dropping by later for deep-fried bat wings. Arnor and Ramma started talking again, each trying to drown out the other.

Trockle rolled her eyes and grabbed each one by the ear, her nails digging cruelly into the lobes. "Stop talking."

To Jig's great surprise, they obeyed. Arnor and Ramma were both younger and stronger than Trockle. If this scene had been played out by goblins, Trockle would have found herself beaten and tossed into the cavern. But the ogres merely glared at one another and rubbed their ears.

"After the invaders began killing us, we sent a group to Straum's cave to try to bargain with them," Trockle said. "We offered to share the cavern, or even to leave the mountain altogether. Those ogres returned the next day, enslaved. They killed dozens of us before we managed to stop them." Trockle stared at nothing. "I cracked my own cousin's skull with a club, and he remained a slave of the pixies until the last breath left his body. How can you be so certain this one is free?"

Jig hesitated. *Because my god told me so* wasn't the most convincing answer, but it was the only one he had.

"They want us dead, Jig Dragonslayer. Only when this mountain belongs entirely to the pixies will they feel safe."

"Aunt Trockle," whispered Ramma, "the hobgoblin is stirring."

"I see that," Trockle snapped. The ogres stepped closer, forming a partial circle around Slash, with Jig crouched near his feet.

Slash's tongue slipped out, moistening cracked lips. He groaned. "My chest feels like Veka sat on it. What—" His fingers touched his bloody vest. His eyes widened, and he sat upright. "Which one of you ugly, blue-skinned rat-eaters stabbed me?" He looked around, and his eyes fixed on Jig.

Jig glanced down. Hobgoblin blood covered his arms and sleeves. If that weren't incriminating enough, his sword was dripping with the stuff. Blood had dripped down the blade to form a sticky mess near the hilt. Really, Jig's entire outfit had been recolored in a kind of "slaughtered hobgoblin" theme.

"You did this!" Slash roared, pushing himself to his feet. The ogres glanced at Trockle, who shrugged, obviously waiting to see what would happen.

"Wait, I didn't—" Jig scrambled back. "Oh, dung."

Slash took two steps, and then the color faded from his cheeks. He stared at the blood on Jig's clothes. His breathing quickened, and he wobbled a bit. "I hate goblins," he muttered.

With that, he dropped to his knees and passed out.

"I think you might be right," said Trockle. "I've yet to see a pixie-charmed slave faint." She reached over to pluck the bloody sword from Jig's hand. "It doesn't seem to be an enchanted blade," she said, holding it close to her lantern. She wiped a bit of blood away from the blade by the hilt. "Magical steel wouldn't tarnish like this."

She handed the sword back to Jig, who nearly dropped it. He was still shaken by Slash's near-assault. "Do you mind if we tie him up before he wakes up and tries to kill me again?"

Trockle produced a thick coil of what appeared to be gray string and handed it to Arnor. He shoved Slash onto his stomach, then began binding his arms and legs.

"Are you sure that stuff is strong enough to hold a hobgoblin?" asked Braf.

Arnor gave it a sharp tug. "This is elven rope. Got it from Straum's lair. Thin as string but strong enough to hold four ogres. After a few of us escaped to these tunnels, we tried to use it to haul the rest of the family up after us."

"What happened?" asked Jig.

He spat. "Ever try to climb string? It's impossible to grip the stuff. It's so darned thin you slice your hand to the bone. Stupid elves."

Jig stared at his sword, wondering if he should stab Veka as well. If it worked for Slash, there was no reason it wouldn't work for Veka. Of course, there was no real reason it would work, either. Perhaps it would be better to simply tie her up until he figured out what had broken the spell.

He glanced around, and his stomach began to hurt

again. "Um . . . does anyone know where Veka went?"

There was no sign of Veka. She must have fled while they were busy stabbing and saving Slash.

"I should have stabbed 'em both," Grell muttered.

Jig had a hard time disagreeing. He was a bit surprised Veka hadn't attacked them the moment she awakened. If she could fling Slash about and seize control of giant bats, surely she could do a fair amount of damage to a few goblins and ogres. He remembered the wild glee on her face while she was riding the giant bat. The only reason Jig could think of for her to retreat was so she could return with reinforcements.

Trockle seemed to be thinking along the same lines. She scowled at her son and niece. "You've brought the pixies down upon us."

"Sorry," said Ramma and Arnor in unison.

Trockle turned to Jig, and he raised the bloody sword. She shook her head. "Killing you wouldn't help us now. Go fight the pixies, if you can. You might buy us a brief head start. Or if you prefer a quick death, we can—"

"We'll fight the pixies," Jig said.

Trockle turned and punched Arnor in the arm. "As for you and your cousin, you're going to be on dung-drying duty for the next month!" Both ogres shot hateful glares at Jig as they left.

Grell and Braf looked at Jig.

Jig knelt, wiping his sword on Slash's pants. Why did they keep expecting him to tell them what to do? Any other goblin would have killed Slash and Veka the moment they learned of the pixie spell. Because of Jig, Veka had escaped to warn the pixies.

You goblins are so quick to deal out death. What

happens when you err? Some deserve death, it's true, but can you restore life to those who don't?

Jig glanced at Slash's body. *Well, it was pretty gross, but—*

That's not what I meant, Shadowstar said, sounding cross.

I'm a goblin, remember? We don't care who deserves death and who doesn't. We care about not getting killed ourselves.

Will you just go fight the pixies? snapped Shadowstar.

Right. Jig stared at his sword. One old goblin, a runt, and an idiot against Veka and the pixies. Not to mention a fainting hobgoblin warrior.

"Braf, would you wake Slash up?" Maybe this time the hobgoblin would stay conscious long enough to help.

Not that he really expected it to make much of a difference.

CHAPTER 8

"A lot of fledgling heroes have asked me to teach them, but I tell them to take a hike. Mentor a newbie, and next thing you know you're getting slaughtered by some demon from the depths while your student escapes. Sure, the Hero eventually avenges the poor Mentor, but I'd rather be the avenger than the avengee any day."

—Nisu Graybottom, Gnomish Illusionist
From *The Path of the Hero (Wizard's ed.)*

There was nothing quite like watching someone run a sword through your traveling companion to help you shake off the last vestiges of unconsciousness.

Veka kept her free hand on the rock as she hurried through the tunnel. Blind panic had brought her this far, with no thought except to put as much distance between herself and Jig Dragonslayer as she possibly could.

She should have expected this. Jig had seen her true potential back there in the pit. He felt threatened. He preferred the old, pitiful Veka. Josca had warned of the jealousy a Hero could expect from those closest to her. She touched the comforting outline of the book through the outside of her cloak. Veka was a victim of jealousy, just like Li'ila from chapter five: The Descent.

And when Li'ila had flung her attacker to the ground and bound him with the mystical energies of the earth, she drew her sacrificial moon blade and demanded of him, "Why do you accost me here, as I enter the domain of the foul one to complete my destiny?"

And the frightened mercenary responded, "Have mercy, Li'ila. I come on behalf of your husband, who wishes only to save you from these powers that have seduced you into dark witchery."

"This is how he proposes to save me?" the astonished Li'ila demanded. "Using a hired thug to accost me in the dark and drag me back to his cottage?"

Too cowed to lie, the mercenary hung his head and said, "Not precisely. He hired me to cut out your heart and bring it to the temple of Plinkarr, that he might purify your soul."

Like Li'ila's husband, Jig feared her and hoped to do away with her before she grew too powerful. That didn't explain why they had killed Slash, too. Then again, Slash was a hobgoblin. How much reason did they need?

Veka turned around. Maybe she should go back. Jig might try to hide and flee from battle, but she was Veka. She had the power to defeat ogres and goblins both. She grinned, remembering the giddiness of riding the giant bat through the pit, her cloak billowing, her hair blowing in the wind. All she lacked was her staff.

She scowled, trying to recall where she had lost it. She had been trying to release the spell on Slash. For some reason, she hadn't been able to undo the magic, and then . . .

"He kicked me!" Remembering that indignity was the final insult. She rubbed her scalp, feeling the blood clotted to her hair. Of all the ungrateful, cowardly, hobgoblinish things to do! It made her feel a little better about his ugly demise.

She wouldn't have been so upset if it were Slash who had been planning to kill her. She was a little surprised he hadn't tried already. But to hear Jig and Grell talking about who should be the one to stab her . . . "They wanted to kill me." The words sounded distant and unreal.

Her throat hurt, as though she had tried to swallow a rock, one with lots of corners. "I went to Jig for help!" How many times had she imagined the day he would see her potential and share the secrets of his magic, teaching her the things he had never shared with any other goblin.

He had seen her potential all right, and it had terrified him. Jig was no Hero. Nor was he a Mentor. What kind of Mentor plotted the murder of his own apprentice? Even if she had never officially been his apprentice.

But Jig had failed. He had made a mistake, killing the hobgoblin first. Veka was no longer the helpless fool everyone thought she was. She would go back there and show Jig Dragonslayer what real magic could do. She would—

She glanced at her legs, which refused to budge. She pinched her thigh and winced. Why couldn't she move?

She tried an experimental step backward, toward the bottomless pit. Her legs obeyed, but when she tried to go forward again, her muscles went rigid.

"What's wrong with me?" Maybe it was a curse of some sort. She wouldn't put it past Jig. She turned around and tried walking backward toward him, and again her body rebelled. She could flee, but she couldn't go back to confront him.

"Trying to fight Jig Dragonslayer will get you killed, either by Jig himself, or by the pixies searching for him," she whispered.

One hand reached up to touch her lips. That was her voice, but it certainly didn't sound like anything she would say. Though it was a reasonable point. Assuming the pixies were searching the pit, they would eventually find this tunnel.

"Jig means well, but he's going to get every last goblin killed."

It was her mouth. Her voice. Her teeth that nearly pierced her fingers when she grabbed them and tried to stop herself from talking. She waited to make sure the voice had finished before asking, "What's going on?"

"Currently, you're standing in a tunnel with your fingers in your mouth." The inflection was slightly off, emphasizing different syllables and blurring the sentence together so it sounded like one long word. The fact that her fingers were still probing her lips didn't help her enunciation much either.

"Who are you?" She folded her arms and braced herself. Her legs twitched, but she tightened the muscles. She might not be able to walk back to the others, but she could stop herself from leaving. "I'm not budging until I get some answers."

"Fine. My name is Snixle," Veka's own voice said,

sounding exasperated. "I'm the guy who helped you cast that illumination charm on your hobgoblin friend. The one who guided you through the levitation spell. The one who helped you take control of that bat before he could eat you. I'm the guy trying to save your life, who can teach you far more powerful magic than anything you've done so far, but only if you get out of there. It's much more difficult to teach the dead."

Veka started to argue, but her lips refused to open. Her neck and jaw muscles began to cramp as she struggled against herself.

From the direction of the pit, a faint purple light began to fill the tunnels. "Pixies." She couldn't tell if she or Snixle had been the one to speak.

Veka frowned. "The pixie following us was pink, not purple."

"Which means there's probably a second pixie. Lights combine into new colors. Don't you goblins know anything? If they're sending another pixie out into your world, they must really want your friend Jig."

The rock in her throat grew sharper at the mention of Jig's name. "Why him?"

"Look, if I promise to answer your questions, will you please get out of the tunnel? We passed a crevasse near the floor a little way back. You can hide down there."

"Heroes don't hide," Veka said. "If these pixies are coming for Jig, they won't expect me. I'll have the element of surprise."

"I'm sure that will be a tremendous comfort when your bones begin to grow through your skin. Look, no matter how surprised they are, they'll either kill you on the spot, or they'll wrest control from me and make you fling yourself into the pit or slam your own head against the wall until your skull cracks. You can fight me, but you won't be able to resist them. Is that really how you want to meet your end?"

"I can—"

"No, you can't," Snixle said, cutting her off. He sounded absolutely certain. "Not yet, at least. You can't save your people if you're dead. Do you really think the pixies would send anyone but their strongest warriors to hunt in your world?"

Reluctantly, Veka allowed Snixle to take control of her legs, hurrying back a short distance. A smell like damp seaweed marked the place. She lay flat on the ground, feeling the outline of the opening, an irregular crack on the edge of the floor. She hadn't even noticed it before. Snixle must have been attuned to her senses for some time.

She should fit, though it would be tight. The ground beyond angled sharply downward. She heard water trickling from overhead. The crevasse extended up as well.

"Goblins have a rule about surviving strange tunnels," she muttered. She pulled her cloak tight around her body and slipped her feet into the hole. "A rule for figuring out which ones are dangerous."

"What rule is that?"

"They're all dangerous." She scooted deeper, grimacing as her hips and stomach scraped the rock. By now the approaching pixies were bright enough for her to distinguish the individual colors. The left side of the tunnel was more pink, while the right was bluer. If they found her here, wedged halfway into a hole, they wouldn't even need to attack. She would die of humiliation.

The soles of her boots touched the far side of the

crevasse. She squeezed her fingers in next to her stomach and pulled. Her feet searched for traction, anything she could use to help drag herself through. This was worse than the time a group of older goblins had threatened to plug a privy with her.

No, on second thought, it wasn't quite that bad.

Her hand slipped, scraping skin from her knuckles. Gritting her teeth, she reached down and tried again, straining and tugging.

The edge of the crevasse scraped her stomach as she finally slid inside. She clung to the rock as her feet searched for traction. The crack fell away at an angle, passing underneath the tunnel. Water trickled along the bottom. Already it had begun to soak into her cloak.

"They're almost here," Snixle whispered. Without warning, her hands relaxed. Only Snixle's control of her jaw kept her from screaming as she slid into the darkness.

She stopped moving almost at once as her legs jammed into the rock. Cramped as it was, it would be nearly impossible to really fall. The hole dropped more sharply here. She lay on her stomach, staring up at a crack of light with one leg dangling into the dropoff. The other pressed against the rock, bracing her in place.

As the pixies passed, their lights briefly illuminated the crevasse. Water and brown sludge covered the rock. A quick glance showed that same sludge now covered her cloak and boots. She waited until the light disappeared, then pushed herself up.

"What are you doing?" Snixle whispered.

"The pixies are gone. I'm getting out of here."

"There will be others. Pixies and worse. They'll be

even more vigilant now that the queen has awakened. All they care about is eliminating every possible threat to the queen's safety."

"The queen?"

"She came over before, asleep in a shell of magic to protect her from the shock. This place is so warm and dry. Even with all of the changes below, the transition will be quite a shock. But soon she should be ready to leave the dragon's cave. She might already be on her way. That's why they must capture Jig Dragonslayer."

Veka decided right then that the next one to mention Jig Dragonslayer's name would get a knife in his gut. "Why does everyone—?"

Her jaw clamped shut. Through pressed lips, she heard Snixle say, "This place isn't safe. We have to go deeper. Then we'll talk."

The water was cold enough to chill her hands and arms, and her sodden cloak was beginning to weigh her down. Gritting her teeth, she pressed her hands against the rough stone and lowered herself farther, searching for footholds in the algae-slick stone.

Her stomach rumbled as she climbed. How long had it been since her last meal? Heroes' stomachs weren't supposed to rumble. Of course, Heroes weren't supposed to have to squirm down dark, tight, wet holes, talking to themselves and hoping their friends didn't come along to stab them in the back either.

Her fingers slipped. She dropped hard, landing in a shallow puddle on a ledge. The rock fell away by her ankles. As the water soaked into her undergarments, she closed her eyes and fought for control. When she thought she could speak without screaming, she said, "We're deeper."

Snixle didn't argue. Maybe he heard something in her tone. "The tunnel slants back down toward the pixie cavern. If we're lucky, we can just follow the water all the way home."

Veka rested her head on the rock. "We're running away from two pixies so we can drop in on a whole army of pixies?"

"Most will be busy preparing to escort the young queen to her new home. This place still isn't safe for her. There are a few ogres roaming free, not to mention you goblins and hobgoblins. But no pixie queen likes to wait. Everyone will be concentrating on her, so depending on where this drainage crack leads, we should be able to get you out unnoticed."

"Why do they want Jig?" Veka asked.

She felt Snixle taking control of her hand, running through the familiar motions of the binding spell. She recognized the enchantment; he was trying to create light. "It's no good," she told him. "Without a source of light, the spell won't—"

Her fingers began to glow from the inside with a soft green light. The bones and veins in her hand appeared as dark shadows.

"*That* is why they wish to capture Jig Dragonslayer," Snixle said. Veka suspected it was supposed to sound dramatic, but mostly it just irritated her. "That is why they would want you as well, if they knew what you could do."

"They would?" Knowing the pixies would want to capture her made her feel a little better. She stared at her hand. "They want us to make light? I wouldn't think that was a problem for pixies."

"The magic of your world follows different rules. Your magic is richer, full of power, but also rigid.

Learning to manipulate magic here is like learning to breathe stone. We can learn faster if we have a practitioner of your magic."

"You're one of them, aren't you?" she asked, turning her hand. Even her claws glowed.

"I used myself as the light source," Snixle said.

The dragon's cave. When she and Slash had gone to spy on the pixies. The pixie who found them in the tunnel had been this exact shade of green. But she remembered defeating him. She had told the others how she bested him. "You changed my memories from Straum's cave."

"No, you did that all by yourself," said Snixle. "You swung at me with your staff. That's when I cast my spell. By the time you got back to the others, you must have convinced yourself you'd killed me. We control the body, not the mind. We can't touch your thoughts or emotions. Well, the queen can, but not the rest of us."

Veka shook her head. "I remember hitting you, and then—"

"Your staff only brushed the tip of my wing. Then you turned around and dragged your friend out of the tunnel."

"He's not my friend." So why had she bothered to drag him out, unless that had been Snixle's doing? He must have enchanted them both. "That's why Grell stabbed Slash. They knew you were controlling us."

"They must have," Snixle agreed. "Jig's smarter than I realized."

Jig hadn't been threatened by her after all. He wasn't afraid of her. He was afraid of Snixle and the pixies. To him Veka was nothing. Just like she was to every other goblin.

"Why did you let us go?" she asked, her voice dull

and flat. "Why not turn us over to your queen when you had the chance?"

"I . . ." Snixle's voice trailed off. Her shoulder blades flexed, and she stared at the ground. After a moment, she realized these were Snixle's movements. He must be flexing his wings. A nervous gesture? "I'm not strong enough," Snixle said. "If I tried to force you both, I was afraid you'd break free. I thought I'd let you and the hobgoblin go back so I could try to learn more about you, maybe find something that would help me earn the queen's respect. She was so depressed at the thought of leaving our home. I never imagined you held the key to this world's magic."

Her spellbook. "That's why you wanted me to hide from the other pixies," she said. "So you could keep me for yourself."

"If I bring you to the queen, she'll reward us both," Snixle said. "Veka, right now they mean to cleanse the mountain, to kill every last hobgoblin and goblin. Come with me, and maybe we can show her she doesn't have to kill you. She may let your people leave peacefully."

Veka shook her head. She didn't like the sound of that *may*.

"Look at what I've already shared with you," Snixle said. "Imagine what else we could accomplish. You can tap into the magic of your world. I can teach you to use that power to save your people. Jig Dragonslayer wants to fight us. The queen won't like that. She'll order you all killed. She'll send more pixies up into the tunnels to—"

"I thought you couldn't use magic here," Veka interrupted. "Our tunnels should be safe." She frowned. If that was true, the two pixies who had flown through above should have been powerless.

"*I* couldn't," Snixle said. "But the strongest warriors can wrap a bit of that magic around themselves when they leave the safety of our home. It's like a magical blanket. They have enough power to fight you goblins at least. Eventually our magic will fill this entire mountain. Then all your people will be destroyed, unless you help me."

"I know what you're doing," Veka said, shaking her head. "This is the Temptation of the Hero."

"The what?"

"Josca wrote all about it. This is part of The Descent, where the Hero is tempted away from the Path, drawn by promises of power and glory. You're trying to trick me into betraying my companions."

"The same companions who wanted to stab you in the back?"

That was a good point.

"We need you, Veka," Snixle said softly. "There's a limit to the power we can bring from our own world. We're exiles, every one, and we would be killed if we tried to go back. We must learn to live in your world. Help us, and you could be the savior of our people. Our people and yours as well."

Before Veka could answer, a loud snarl rose from the darkness below.

"What's that?" asked Snixle.

Veka's stomach tightened. "Tunnel cat." Naming the beast made her mouth go dry. She nearly lost control of her bladder. Which, given that the tunnel cat was creeping around beneath her, would have only made the situation worse.

This chimney of rock would be the perfect hunting ground for a tunnel cat. They had little fear of water, and their paws could find purchase on the smoothest stone. Prey would be hard-pressed to escape in such close, treacherous confines.

"Can you take control of the tunnel cat?" Veka asked. "Like you did with the bat?" Her heart pounded as she imagined herself returning to the goblin lair astride her own pet tunnel cat. She could almost hear the terrified screams of the goblins as they fled. Hobgoblins might be able to train the tunnel cats, but Veka would master them. She—

"No," said Snixle, shattering her fantasy with a single syllable. "The bat was stupid and frightened, both of which made it vulnerable to my magic. I doubt this beast shares those weaknesses."

"No." As far as Veka knew, tunnel cats didn't have any weaknesses.

"I might be able to help another way," Snixle said. "But you have to choose. Save us. Save our queen. In return, I can save you, and I can help you save your people. If not, you and the rest of the goblins will die."

Veka hesitated. Josca was quite clear on the fate of so-called Heroes who yielded to temptation. In the end, most broke away from their evil ways, but a high percentage died in the process. No, defying the temptation was almost always the right choice. Though in this case, defiance seemed to have a high chance of death too, and that couldn't be right.

"Wait, you said you were exiled?" Veka asked. She fumbled for her books.

"This is hardly the time to catch up on your reading," Snixle said.

Veka ignored him, flipping through *The Path of the Hero* until she came to the appendices. "Appendix A," she said, reading by the light of her hand. "One Hundred Heroic Deeds and Triumphs." She skimmed through the list. " 'Number forty-two: saving a village from invasion.' The goblin lair isn't exactly a village, but I think fighting off a pixie invasion would count."

"What are you doing?" Snixle asked. "I told you, if you try to fight us, you—"

"Shut up and listen to this," she said excitedly. " 'Aiding a banished prince or princess to regain his or her throne' is number thirty-seven!"

"Thirty-seven?"

"Do you know what this means?" Veka said, slamming the book closed. "Helping your exiled queen is even more Heroic than trying to save the goblins. Josca says so himself!"

"Does that mean you'll help us?"

She could save the pixies and the goblins both. Better still, she would save the goblins from the very doom Jig Dragonslayer would bring down on them. Jig still wanted to fight, but Veka would be the one who led them to safety.

"Can we fight the tunnel cat now?" Snixle asked.

She blinked. "Sure."

"Put your hand into the water."

Veka obeyed. Snixle gave her an extra push, thrusting her hand forward until her fingers smooshed into the wet, fibrous mass of algae. The slime and water shone green with the light emanating from her hand.

She twisted her head, trying to see into the darkness below. She couldn't see the tunnel cat, but she could hear it making its way toward her. The rough barbed skin of those paws let them climb almost as quickly as they walked. Those barbs would also strip the skin from their prey in a single swipe.

"Okay, I *think* we need to cast another binding. That's the key, you realize. Back home, we're constantly tied in to the magic, but here—"

Veka yanked her hand back. "You think? You don't know?"

"Do you have a better plan?"

Scowling, Veka relaxed and allowed Snixle to trace a quick binding. Lines of magic wove from her fingertips into the algae, knitting them together.

"Excellent. Now push, like so, joining your power to the very life of the algae."

Her hand flexed, and a bubble of magic pulsed outward from her palm. Veka grimaced. "It feels like I'm farting through my hand."

"You should have been a poet."

The tunnel cat's nose poked up through the darkness, surrounded by a halo of long white whiskers. A pale face stared up at her, the pink eyes never blinking.

A new sensation flowed through her hand and arm: a cool, calm feeling, as if the water were trickling over her own body, refreshing and reenergizing her flesh. She was feeling what the algae felt.

"You're bound to the plant," said Snixle. "Forget the clumsy second-rate sympathetic magic you were doing with that levitation spell. This is pure power. The magic is an extension of your body, and the algae is an extension of your magic. Now reach out and grab that tunnel cat before he rips your legs off."

The cat climbed closer. Muscles twitched along its back as it shifted its weight, searching for the next hold. Tunnel cats rarely rushed. They climbed easily and surely, waiting for prey to panic and fall.

"Grab it how?" Veka asked.

"Less thinking, more doing." Before Veka could react, Snixle took control of her feet and yanked them from the wall. She began to slip.

Veka grabbed the algae, and the algae grabbed her.

Slime coated her fingers and wrists. Even as her legs kicked the air, drawing a hungry growl from the cat, the sludge tightened its grip. Hair-thin tendrils coiled around her fingers, stronger than any rope.

"Excellent! Now do the same thing to that beast below."

"Shut . . . up," Veka said. She could feel the cat now as it crept through the slime. Each time a paw pressed into the algae, she felt it on her own skin. The tail tickled as it lashed through the water.

The next time that tail splashed into the water, Veka grabbed it. A great mass of brown plant matter clumped onto the tail and held fast.

The tunnel cat yowled, a furious squeal that echoed through the tight crevasse.

"Don't let go!" Snixle yelled.

Stupid pixie. As if she couldn't figure that much out on her own. Veka fought to hold on. Slime crept farther up the cat's tail, tendrils weaving through fur and clamping around the bones and joints beneath. By now the tunnel cat was clinging to the rock with all four paws, pulling and twisting to escape. It twisted its head, bending its spine nearly double to bite at its own tail. Veka reached out, using another bit of algae to pluck several whiskers from its face.

That was too much for the poor tunnel cat. Fur ripped free as it dropped away, hissing and spitting. She could hear claws scraping against stone as it fled down into the darkness.

"Not bad. We'll have you commanding the elements and smiting your enemies in no time."

Veka laughed, no longer caring whether anyone heard. Forget Jig and his temple tricks. Had Jig ever ridden a giant bat or turned plants against a tunnel cat? Josca wrote that the Hero descended into darkness, where she would face her greatest trials and come into true power. Well, this crevasse was not only dark, it was smelly too. And if facing a hungry tunnel cat wasn't a trial, she didn't know what was.

"Do you think I should have a new name?" she asked. "Josca says a lot of powerful wizards have more than one name." Plus it might stop the other goblins from ever calling her Vast Veka again. "According to Josca, a truly heroic wizard name should be several syllables, often with some kind of animal worked in. Birds are best, but any powerful animal will do. What about Kestrel Shadowflame? Or maybe Olora Nightcrow?"

"Veka Bluefeather of the Flatulent Hand?" asked Snixle.

She rolled her eyes. Not even the pixie's mockery could pierce her excitement. She was going to be a wizard!

Veka rested with one leg propped against the top of the tunnel. By twisting the upper part of her body, she could press one cheek into the dripping water. After climbing for so long without food or drink, the sharp, silty water tasted like the finest wine. Wine mixed with plant slime and the occasional slug, but that simply added flavor.

She massaged her hand, trying to work out the worst of the cramps. Her magically glowing hand was fine. Somehow the enchantment kept the muscles loose and strong. If she could, she would have spread the spell over her entire body, but Snixle said that would only dilute the magic.

"Hurry up," said Snixle. Veka found herself glancing around, searching the darkness overhead as his nervousness translated into her body.

"Why are you in such a rush?"

"I have to get you to the queen. If she finds out I concealed your presence—" Veka's body shivered. "Queens are especially temperamental after drastic changes. That's one of the reasons for transforming your caves, to give her a familiar space. I remember how long it took my former queen to adjust after the death of her favorite mate. She ordered her guards to rip the wings from a worker's body simply because she didn't like the color of the shimmers he had brought to her quarters."

"Shimmers?"

"Wingless insects," said Snixle. "They weave intricate patterns of light wherever they crawl, which lures smaller bugs toward them. My former queen hung them for decoration. The bugs are nasty to feed, though. A bite will ooze blood for days."

"Why did this queen come here at all?" Veka asked. "Weren't there better places to invade? Places that would have been less of a change from your world?"

Snixle shook her head. "Opening a gateway is easy enough. The trick is to stabilize the other side. Magic calls to magic, even between worlds. The more magic you have on the other side, the stronger the link. Otherwise your gateway might flash off to some other world, and suddenly you're flying into a flaming mountain or the middle of an icy sea. This mountain was full of magic, especially the dragon's cave. That makes it safe."

Veka nodded. "Legend says the whole mountain was carved out by magic." She flicked a snail away from her hand and pushed herself away from the water, wincing at the tightness in her back and shoulders. She kept the algae twined around her hand and wrist as she lowered herself off the ledge. The crevasse was nearly vertical here.

"Best of all," Snixle added, "this place was unguarded. Aside from a few ogres and you goblins and such, of course."

"Jig will still try to fight you," she said. "He's like that."

Snixle was shaking Veka's head. "If he fights, he condemns you all to death."

"What if—"

"Less talking, more climbing," Snixle snapped. "The pixies have probably already captured him." Her shoulders twitched with his anxiety. "If they bring him to the queen before we get there—"

"I don't think so," Veka said. "Not Jig." Her mind leaped ahead. Jig would escape somehow. He always did.

Snixle didn't appear to be paying attention. "Do you see that? Down below?" Golden sparks floated upward, some nearly reaching her feet before disappearing.

This tunnel couldn't have been much longer than the one they had walked through before, on their way to the bottomless pit. But she felt as though she had been crawling and climbing through the tight confines for an eternity.

"We're almost home. I'm not sure where this comes out, so be careful."

Veka's heart started to pound. She knew what she had to do. She had to stop Jig Dragonslayer before he doomed them all.

She relaxed her legs, using the algae to slow her descent as she slipped toward the hole at the bottom of the rock. A thick haze filled the air below. Her feet emerged into open air, and only now did she stop to wonder how she would reach the ground. There was no ladder, and she—

Her shoulders spasmed, and her hand released the algae. With a loud squawk, Veka fell. Her arms and legs wheeled madly, and then the ground hit her like an angry ogre.

"Sorry," said Snixle. "I was excited. I forgot you don't have wings."

Veka spat snow and blood. One of her lips was split, and her face would be one enormous bruise. She rolled onto her side.

Slabs of ice covered the ground, high enough to completely hide the dead grass and bushes. Snow swirled through the air, reducing visibility to nearly nothing. That was good, she decided. Hopefully nobody had seen her graceless fall.

"So flat," Snixle muttered. "So overrun with plants and dirt. I miss the ice spires of the palace back home, watching the young pixies light up the mists from the nests as they flew their mating dances. . . ." He turned her in a slow circle and began to mumble. "Magic is flowing from your right. That should be the direction of the gateway. From the feel of it, you're on the far side of the cavern, well beyond the Necromancer's pit."

"Can you lead me to the Necromancer's lair?" Veka interrupted.

"What? No, we have to get you to the queen."

Veka shook her head. "What if there's a way for me to bring Jig Dragonslayer to your queen?"

She shivered. A drenched cloak didn't provide much warmth in the best of times, but down here it was little better than going naked.

"You can do that?" Snixle asked.

"Can you teach me to command creatures like that bat?" she countered.

"I think so. Like I said, I'm not the greatest warrior, but—"

"Teach me that spell, and I'll bring you Jig Dragonslayer." She cocked her head to one side. "If you're no warrior, exactly what *do* you do?"

She found herself walking as Snixle talked. Hopefully he was guiding her to the Necromancer's lair.

"Mostly I use magic to . . . well, to clean things."

Veka frowned. "What do you mean?"

"I'm a worker. I may not be a trusted bodyguard for the queen, but I'm wicked fast when it comes to getting stains out of clothing. Spills, infestations, anything like that. I was coming to dispose of that dead ogre when I found you and your friend."

That couldn't be right. Her Mentor simply could not be the pixie equivalent of a carrion-worm.

"There," said Snixle. He pointed.

Veka squinted, barely able to make out the dark rock overhead. The illusory sky Straum had maintained for as long as anyone could remember was gone. She searched the rock, trying to make out the spot he was pointing to. "That's the Necromancer's lair?"

Snixle was already casting a levitation spell. Moments later, the snow was gone, and Veka stood in the dusty emptiness of the Necromancer's throne room. She untied her belt and tossed her cloak on the floor, grimacing at the sloshing sound it made when it landed.

"Jig says the Necromancer was a pixie," she whispered. Something about being in this place alone made her uncomfortable, as if the dead still lurked beyond the doors, waiting for the slightest sound to resurrect them once again.

"Probably exiled here," said Snixle. "I wonder how long it took him to learn the laws of magic."

"Can all pixies command the dead?"

"Technically, yes," said Snixle. "The magic is the same kind of spell I'm using on you. We don't do it, though."

"Why not?" Forget commanding a giant bat. If he taught her this magic, Veka could lead an army of the dead!

"It's . . . icky. Necromancy is like wearing a corpse. You need a lot more power to keep the bodies from rotting, or else your host starts to drop bits and pieces everywhere they go. And you always have to be careful not to let your body get too connected to the host. That's bad enough when the host is alive, but you can imagine what happens if you get too attuned to a corpse."

Right. Forget Necromancy then.

"Are you serious about being able to beat Jig Dragonslayer?"

Veka retrieved her copy of *The Path of the Hero* and wiped water from the cover. The edges were damp. She opened the book and fanned the pages to dry them. "I can beat him," she said. "I have to. It's the only way to save my people and yours, right?"

"Assuming he hasn't already been captured," Snixle said nervously.

Veka didn't bother to respond. Clearly these pixies didn't know Jig Dragonslayer. But they would . . . just as Jig Dragonslayer would soon learn to know and respect the real Veka.

CHAPTER 9

"Sure he killed the Necromancer, but can you imagine a bunch of goblins trying to sing 'Hail Jig Necromancerslayer'? And then you've got to come up with a rhyme for it."

—Goblin Songwriter

The ogres didn't leave Jig completely empty-handed. No, they did something worse: they gave him a torch.

Regular torches were annoying enough. Unless you dipped it in muck, the flames would flicker and start to die every time you moved. Nor was muck the answer, not unless you wanted the stuff dripping onto your hand and burning your fingers off.

This was worse. The ogres had no muck, so they had fallen back on what they did have.

"Flaming goblin dung on a stick," Slash muttered, waving one hand in front of his nose. He kept his eyes averted from Jig, whose shirt had begun to stiffen with drying blood.

"Would you rather leave it behind?" Grell asked.

"You can go first. Let us know if you find any rock serpents."

"What does it matter?" Slash asked. "The pixies are going to kill us all anyway."

"They're not—" An unfortunate puff of wind sent smoke directly into Jig's face. He held the torch at arm's length, coughing and gagging. To make matters worse, the smell was drawing flies that constantly buzzed about Jig's head and landed on his ears. Smudge kept climbing onto Jig's head, trying to catch them.

"Here," said Grell, fishing a knotted bit of cloth from her shirt pocket.

"What is it?" Jig asked, his voice hoarse.

"Sugar-knot. Hardened honey candy." She grabbed his fang and pulled him down. With an easy, well-practiced motion, she tied it around his fang and tucked the knot inside his lower lip. "It calms the kids down. Ought to block the smell a bit."

Jig gave the sugar-knot a tentative suck. The cloth was rough and gritty, but the candy inside had a too sweet, fruity taste. Better than dung smoke, at any rate, though it left a bitter aftertaste. He frowned as he recognized it. "Is that klak beer?"

Grell shrugged. "Like I said, it calms the kids down."

His tongue and mouth tingled as he sucked the candy. He could still smell the smoke, but he no longer felt as if he were about to vomit.

"So what do we do?" asked Braf. He was swinging his hook-tooth through the air, probably attacking imaginary pixies.

"How should I know?" Jig had the overpowering urge to smash the flaming end of the torch right into

Braf's face. Why did they keep asking him? "The only reason Kralk sent me on this little quest is so I'd get myself killed. I don't know how to fight pixies. I don't know how we're going to get back home. Stop asking me! I don't know."

Braf had stopped in midswing. Slash stood leaning against a wall, his arms folded.

"No more sugar-knots for you," Grell muttered.

His outburst finished, Jig's weariness returned. He stifled a yawn, knowing how foolish it would appear to the others.

"You told the ogres you'd take care of the pixies," Braf said.

"They were going to kill us!" Jig said. "This way—"

"This way the pixies do it instead." Slash snorted. "Nice of you to save the ogres the work."

They were right, and Jig knew it. But it was their own fault. They were the ones who kept calling him Jig Dragonslayer, expecting him to find a way out of any situation. Didn't they understand how many times he had nearly died on that stupid quest? He could barely keep himself alive, let alone two other goblins and a hobgoblin.

Smudge tickled the back of Jig's neck as he scooted to the other shoulder, trying to get away from the torch smoke.

Okay, so he had managed to protect Smudge so far, too. He stroked Smudge's head, wishing he could scurry away and hide in a crack somewhere until the pixies gave up. Really, wasn't that what the ogres had done? Hiding deeper in the tunnels and hoping the pixies wouldn't follow? Of course, if Jig tried to lead the others after the ogres, one of two things would happen. Either the pixies would find them and kill them, or the ogres would find them and kill them. The only thing left was to decide which would be the quicker death.

Even Tymalous Shadowstar didn't know how to fight an army of pixies. What was Jig supposed to do?

One step at a time, Jig. First you need to beat the pixies who are hunting you. Then you worry about the rest.

If Tymalous Shadowstar had been a physical being, Jig would have punched him in the face. *This is your fault! You're the one who told me to go with Walland. You—*

The pixies were here whether you went or not, Jig. Sure, you could have hidden in your temple like you always do, but in the long run you're better off facing them now.

How does that help me if I die in the very short run? Jig asked.

The god didn't answer. Jig sat down, sucking hard on his sugar-knot. Fine. So he was supposed to fight the pixies. No, wait. Shadowstar said he had to beat them. That didn't mean he had to fight them himself. He could order Slash or Braf to do it.

One look at them did away with that idea. Slash had no weapon, and as for Braf, the pixies would fly circles around him until he killed himself with his own hook-tooth.

Smudge twitched, growing a bit warmer. The pixies were coming. What Jig needed was a giant fire-spider. With smaller prey, Smudge could be as vicious as any goblin, catching and cooking his food in a single jump.

Slowly, Jig climbed to his feet. On the way in, they had passed an opening that smelled of soot and ash. He hadn't recognized it then, being a bit distracted by his ogre captors, but the air had smelled a lot like one of Smudge's abandoned webs. Only stronger.

"What is it?" asked Braf.

"The pixies are coming," Jig said. He stepped away from the others, who made no move to follow. Good.

Grell coughed and spat. "You've got a plan, then?"

"I'm a goblin, remember?" Jig said, fighting a completely inappropriate giggle. Was giggling in death's face a sign of hysteria? "We don't make plans."

Jig hadn't gone far when he spotted the pixies approaching in the distance. Purple light slowly resolved into sparkling pink and blue orbs. The pink one flew ahead of the blue, wings humming. She folded her arms as she drew to a halt, hovering in front of Jig. He could feel the wind from her wings.

"You're Jig Dragonslayer." It wasn't a question.

Jig nodded. "Who are you?" To his surprise, he got the words out with barely a tremor.

"Pynne." She landed on her toes. Her wings continued to buzz, supporting most of her weight as she stared up at him. Her small face was overly round, almost swollen, with puffy cheeks and a wide forehead. White hair surrounded her head like a cloud. Yellow beads decorated her white wrap. Her nose wrinkled as she studied his torch, but she didn't say anything.

Jig had grown up a runt, always looking up at the other goblins. Dodging the larger goblins' fists, to be precise. Now he found himself staring down at his enemy. Pynne was so small. She looked like one good kick would break her against a wall.

"Try it," Pynne said softly.

Jig didn't move. Despite their difference in size,

those two whispered words were enough to make him feel as though Pynne were the one looking down at him.

"*You're* the one who killed the dragon?" Pynne asked.

Annoyance momentarily overpowered his fear. Hadn't he been through this once before with Walland? "Yes, that was me."

"There were others with you when you escaped the bottomless pit," she said. "What happened to them?"

Jig hesitated. Where was Veka, and how much did the pixies already know? "The ogres killed them."

Pynne frowned. "What ogres?"

Whoops. Trockle wouldn't be happy. But how could they not know about the ogres? *Are you sure Veka was being controlled?*

I'm sure, said Shadowstar.

Pynne sighed, a whistling, chittering sound. "I told the others some ogres had escaped, but did they believe me?"

Behind her the blue pixie rolled his eyes. "Yeah, yeah. You're always right and everyone else is wrong. You want me to fly along to deal with them?"

"No, Farnax" said Pynne. Her light had brightened as Farnax spoke, and even Jig could hear the annoyance in her voice. "We've found Jig Dragonslayer. Our duty is to bring him to the queen."

Farnax drifted higher, and sparks exploded from his wings as he brushed the ceiling. He dropped to the ground, cursing and flexing his wings. "How do you creatures survive in these horrible, hot, filthy tombs? You've barely room to breathe without hitting stone."

"Enough," snapped Pynne. Farnax shrank back, then nodded. No question who was in charge here.

"Why does the queen want me?" asked Jig.

Pynne's wings stilled. "You are Jig Dragonslayer.

When you killed the dragon, you opened the way for us. You served the queen once, and you will serve her again by helping us master the magic of your world."

"What about—?" Jig clamped his jaw before Veka's name slipped out. Somehow Pynne didn't know about Veka. If she did, would she still see any reason to keep Jig alive?

Jig stared at her as the rest of her comment sank in. *He* had opened the way? The pixies had to be mistaken. Jig was certain he would have remembered opening a portal to another world.

"What about what?" asked the Farnax.

"The other goblins," Jig said. "The ones up above in the lair. What are you going to do to them?"

Pynne shrugged and hopped into the air. "The same as we would do to any pest who infested our home."

She turned, gesturing at a smaller rock serpent who had been creeping up the tunnel toward them. At first nothing appeared to happen. Then the snake hissed and began to bite at its own scales. The snake's struggles grew more frantic, dissolving into spasms and convulsions that flung it right off the ground. The snake made one last, frantic attack, sinking its fangs deep into its body, and then it was still.

Only when the rock serpent was dead did Jig see clearly enough to understand. Blood seeped from the edges of the scales. Pynne's magic had caused the scales to grow inward, digging through the skin until they killed the snake.

"Do we understand one another, goblin?" Pynne asked, smiling.

Jig thought he might throw up. It wasn't fair. Goblins worked so hard to be loud and ferocious and intimidating. Pynne had them all beat with a smile and a wave of her hand.

Jig stared at the snake. They intended to kill or enslave every last goblin in the mountain, and they thought Jig would help them do it, just to save his own life.

They knew goblins pretty well. Jig took a step back. "You said you wanted to control the magic of our world?"

"That's right," said Pynne, moving so close Jig could feel the warmth emanating from her wings. Smudge was still hotter, and growing more so the closer Pynne came, but the pixie generated a respectable warmth.

"When I ran away from the ogres, I was coming to get the power to fight them," Jig said. He was a horrible liar, but hopefully Pynne would have as much trouble reading his expressions as he did with the pixies. "After I fought Straum, I found a wand, one with more magic than I could ever hope to keep for myself. Enough to reshape this entire mountain."

The pixies glanced at one another. "Where is this wand, goblin?" asked the blue one.

Jig stared at the snake. He had never imagined he could feel sorry for a rock serpent. "I'll take you to it."

There were advantages to traveling with pixies. For one thing Jig could do away with that awful torch. Almost as good, the insects that had been harassing Jig now turned their attention to the pixies, drawn to their bright lights. Jig smothered a grin as he watched Pynne swing her hand at a particularly amorous moth.

Another advantage was that Jig no longer needed to worry about the rock serpents. Twice more the snakes slithered toward them. Pynne didn't bother with such dramatic magic this time. She simply used her power to make the snakes bite themselves to death.

"I thought you didn't know how to use our magic," Jig said as he watched the second snake die, fangs still sunk into its own back.

"We don't," said Pynne. "The strongest among us learn to store magic within ourselves, but if we're away from our world for too long, our power will fade. Even the enchantment we use to speak your language would dissipate."

Farnax scowled. "Don't misunderstand her, goblin. We're still strong enough to destroy you if you betray us."

"Oh, Jig wouldn't dream of such a thing," Pynne said, smiling. It was the same smile she had worn after murdering the first rock serpent. Her light turned a brighter pink as she circled Jig's head. "Tell us more of this wand."

Jig tugged his ear as he tried to remember the stories. "A wizard used it to create these tunnels and caves. It has the power to transform people, things, just about anything."

"A perfect tool," said Pynne.

"If you know about this wand," said Farnax, "why haven't you used it against us?"

"I didn't have it with me." Even if he had, he wasn't sure the Rod of Creation would work inside the pixies' world-bubble. "I have a hard time just keeping the other goblins from taking my boots."

Jig held up one foot. All his climbing and running away had scuffed the blue leather, and the white-furred fringe at the top was tangled and matted. "Goblins have a different view of property and ownership than most races."

"A communal relationship?" asked Farnax. "Things are shared and passed along to those who need them?"

Jig shook his head. "No, things are taken by those who are bigger and stronger than the ones who had them."

"With the power you describe, you could destroy anyone who tried to take the wand from you," Pynne said.

"I'd have to kill the whole lair," Jig muttered. Not to mention he would never again be able to sleep. How many times had he woken up to find goblins tugging at his boots?

The wind had begun to increase as they moved toward the pit, and the air was drier. Both pixies were having a bit of trouble flying. Farnax in particular kept bumping into the rock and swearing.

Jig coughed, trying to clear his parched throat. His nose wrinkled. The pixies certainly smelled better than the ogres' torch, but in some ways, their scent was equally disturbing. They smelled of burning metal mixed with something sweet, like the flowers that used to grow by Straum's cave.

"Why did you leave your world?" Jig asked.

"We had no choice, once the queen was born," Pynne said.

"She ordered you to leave?" Jig didn't know much about kings and queens, but that made no sense.

"Her birth was an accident," Pynne explained. "The current queen almost never gives birth to a successor until she nears the end of her life, but occasionally it happens. Once the new queen was born, exile was the only option. Otherwise war would have devastated our people."

So it was a power struggle, and the pixies in this

world had been the losers. Given what Jig had already seen them do, that wasn't as reassuring as it might have been. "Why didn't the other queen just kill the new one when she was born?"

Both pixies froze. Was it his imagination, or had their lights grown brighter?

"Nobody can kill a queen," whispered Pynne.

Alien though the pixies might be, Jig could still read them enough to know this was a good time to stop asking questions. All his instincts screamed at him to change the subject. Of course, if he had listened to his instincts, he never would have left the goblin lair to begin with.

"Even if she's too powerful, wouldn't another queen be equally powerful?" he asked, cringing in anticipation. "She has to sleep sometimes, doesn't she?"

Pynne actually shivered, a strange sight, since she was still hovering in the air. Her whole body vibrated, and it hurt Jig's eyes to look at her. "You couldn't understand. None can look upon a pixie queen without loving her. That's her power. That love is even stronger when the queen is young. When she is asleep or vulnerable. A newborn queen will even steal the loyalty of her mother's followers. She was raised in isolation until she was old enough to travel to your world. The most black-hearted villain would die to protect her, once he laid eyes upon her."

"As will you, goblin," added Farnax.

Jig struggled to comprehend that kind of loyalty. Goblin politics were swift, decisive, and deadly. Goblins followed their chief because they would be killed if they didn't. The trouble was, the chief couldn't be everywhere at once. In the midst of battle, the immediate threat of an enemy with a big sword took precedence over a chief who might or might not survive long enough to punish you. If Farnax and Pynne were telling the truth, the pixies would never flee from battle. They would never stop fighting, and they would use every bit of their strength to destroy their enemies. Enemies like Jig and the other goblins.

He was so absorbed in the ramifications, he nearly missed his destination. Only Smudge's sudden excitement made him stop and look around.

"There," he said. A flat opening near the top of the tunnel, to his right. That was the origin of the ashen odor he had smelled before. If he was wrong, the pixies would probably kill him. But if he was right . . .

Who was he fooling? The pixies would probably kill him either way.

"The wand is in there?" asked Farnax, flying closer to the entrance.

Jig jumped and grabbed the lower edge of the hole, then struggled to pull himself up. His boots scraped uselessly against the moss-slick rock. Finally, muttering under her breath, Pynne grabbed the bottom of one pantleg and flew up. Farnax did the same with the other leg. With the pixies' help, Jig managed to pull himself into the cramped tunnel.

There was barely room to crawl, and Jig tried not to imagine what would happen if the tunnel grew any narrower.

"This had better be worth it," Farnax said from behind Jig. "I can't stand much more of these tunnels. I feel like I've been buried alive." He had landed on the ground, and he glared distastefully at the rock with each step. There was no room for them to fly. They probably couldn't even see anything but Jig's backside. No wonder they were so grouchy.

Jig's sword hilt jabbed his side as he started to crawl. Smudge crouched on his shoulder. The fire-spider was warm, but this wasn't the intense heat of fear. Heat wafted from Smudge's body in waves, in time with the spider's rapid heartbeat. Smudge was making no attempt to hide. Rather he seemed eager to continue, racing down Jig's arm, then turning as if to ask what was taking so long.

Jig hoped that was a positive sign. He had heard other goblins talk of fire-spider nests, but he had never seen one. Usually fire-spider eggs were abandoned in pools or puddles of water, and the young spiders that survived scattered throughout the tunnels to find their own hunting grounds. But down here, with all the insects attracted to the filth and garbage, there would be no need to leave. At least, he hoped so.

Jig stopped to remove his spectacles, doing his best to wipe the lenses on his shirt. Sweat and steam still streaked his vision. Tiny insects kept landing on his neck and ears.

"This seems a strange place to hide your treasure," said Farnax. "A dismal cave you can't even reach? How would you have retrieved it if we hadn't been here to help lift you into the tunnel?"

Jig bit his lip. Most goblins wouldn't have caught that discrepancy. "I can reach it," he protested. "My arms were just tired from fighting ogres, that's all."

He wished there was enough room to look behind so he could try to guess whether the pixies believed him.

"More likely your legs were too tired from running away from the ogres," Farnax muttered. The pixie didn't seem to like him much.

Jig twisted sideways to pull himself up and through a narrower bit of tunnel. As he did, his body blocked the light of the pixies, and he noticed a faint red light coming from farther on. The air was warmer, and the smell of ash was even stronger. "Almost there," he whispered.

Smudge hopped off Jig's shoulder and skittered ahead. Jig grabbed for him, but he was too slow. The fire-spider disappeared. "Smudge, wait!"

No, this was probably for the best. If things went wrong, Smudge would be safer away from Jig. Still, as Jig pulled himself along, a hard lump filled his throat. Smudge had been his companion for so many years, and now the stupid fire-spider had abandoned him.

Jig crawled past a drop in the tunnel and looked up. His breath caught.

The cave was larger than he had imagined, and it was full of fire-spiders. Hundreds of webs stretched across the walls and ceiling, dotted with dried bugs of every size, from tiny gnats to a green moon moth as big as Jig's hand. There were so many spiders that their combined heat and magic actually generated the red light he had seen: just enough to attract more insects.

"How far must we travel?" asked Pynne. "I feel like these tunnels are shrinking around me."

Fire-spiders twitched and crawled in response to her voice, some crawling deeper into their webs, others moving toward the source of the sound. Jig searched for Smudge, wondering if he would even know his own spider from the rest.

"We're here," whispered Jig, trying to block the cave from their sight. He spotted a patch of mirrored ebony on the ground near the back of the cave. That would be the pool where the fire-spiders laid their eggs.

The pixies would kill him the moment they suspected betrayal. No, that wasn't true. Farnax already suspected him. Regardless, Jig would have to move swiftly.

He studied the webs. The majority hung near the entrance, which made sense. Few insects would survive to make it deeper into the cave. The only real gap was directly in front of the tunnel, which helped the air flow freely through the cave. That opening gave Jig his only chance. He tensed his legs, drawing them up as much as he could in the confines of the tunnel. His hands gripped the rock to either side.

"What is it?" asked Pynne.

Jig kicked her as hard as he could. He heard Farnax swear as Pynne crashed into him, and then Jig was launching himself into the cave. He stayed low to the ground, but his ear tore through one web, then he caught another with his arm.

The fire-spiders reacted instinctively, the way fire-spiders always reacted to threats. They retreated, igniting their webs as they fled. Jig crawled as fast as he could, flinging himself into the shallow pool even as his sleeve and hair went up in flames. Water hissed and steamed. Jig rolled over and squinted through streaked lenses as the pixies burst into the cave at full speed.

Farnax was first through, flying too fast to avoid the webs. His blue light nearly disappeared as he tore through the flames. His body crashed into the far side of the cave and dropped, completely engulfed.

Pynne fared slightly better. Farnax had torn enough of an opening that only her wings caught fire. She spun and flew back into the tunnel, tumbling to the ground.

Jig crawled back out, doing his best to avoid the furious fire-spiders and the remains of their webs. Up ahead Pynne was frantically trying to rip the flaming bits of web from her wings. Jig slid his sword free, holding it ahead of him.

Pynne's light brightened when she saw him. Ignoring her smoldering wings, she raised her hands to cast a spell. Jig didn't have room for a proper attack, but he managed to smack her arms with the flat of the blade.

Pynne screamed, clutching her arms. Jig crawled closer and pressed the tip of his blade to her chest.

"Stop!" Pynne shouted. She twisted back, breaking part of her burned wing in her desperation to avoid the sword. "Please, keep it away." Dark burn marks covered her arm and hand where Jig had struck her.

Her right wing was mostly intact, but the left was barely half its previous size. The ragged edge glowed orange, like an ember.

Jig risked a quick glance back, to make sure Farnax was dead. He needn't have bothered. Fire-spiders swarmed over the body, leaving only the faintest cracks of blue light visible.

He heard Pynne moving and lunged, but she twisted aside. She pointed at Jig, and his sword twisted in his hand. No, not the sword itself, but the leather wrapped around the hilt.

Pynne stumbled back. "Your blade might be deathmetal, but the leather is nothing but dead flesh." Already the tightly wound cord slithered between Jig's fingers, loosening from the hilt and wrapping around his hand and wrist. He tried to drop the sword, but the leather dug cruelly into his skin, binding his hand in place.

"You betrayed us," Pynne said.

"I'm a goblin." Jig tried to grab the cord with his other hand, and nearly managed to get both hands bound to his sword. He yanked his free hand away so hard his elbow smashed into the tunnel wall.

"The queen would have honored you for your help," said Pynne. "Instead, the last thing you feel will be your own weapon choking the life from your body. You thought this ruse would defeat us? I promise you, goblin, we will destroy every last one of your ilk." Her face glowed with pink light as she lay back, gasping.

The cord was already coiling around his elbow. Jig shook his hand, trying to fling the sword away. The blade clanged against the rock, jarring his bones. "Wait. I thought you needed me to learn how to use magic in our world."

Pynne smiled and shook her head. "You would have simplified the process immensely. But we have adapted to other worlds before. And there are always others willing to share their knowledge in exchange for the rewards you've thrown away."

The end of the cord tickled Jig's chin. He twisted his head away, but how was he supposed to avoid his own arm? The leather brushed his neck, waving like one of Smudge's forelegs, reaching . . . reaching. . . .

Jig looked down. Only a single loop of leather remained knotted around the bare wood of his sword hilt. The leather wasn't quite long enough to reach his throat.

Pynne realized it at the same time. She raised her hands, and Jig lunged. This time Jig was faster. His sword was nearly as long as Pynne herself. She died quickly and messily.

Jig pulled his hand back, hoping the spell would dissipate with Pynne's death, but the only change was that the end of the cord grew still, stiff as rock. It jabbed his chin when he turned his head.

The sword rang against the rock as Jig turned to

search for Smudge. So many fire-spiders, all feasting on crispy pixie. He tried to smile. Crispy Pixie would make an excellent title for a song.

"Good-bye, Smudge." Jig backed away from the cave. Smudge was probably safer here anyway. There was plenty of food, and he was surrounded by other fire-spiders. Most importantly, he wouldn't be anywhere near Jig when the pixies came to wipe out the goblins.

A small, dark shape broke away from the mound of spiders, scurrying toward Jig. He could see it dragging something with its rear legs, something that glowed faintly blue.

Jig grinned so hard his cheeks hurt as he set his free hand down for Smudge. The fire-spider crawled up to his shoulder pad and began to feast.

"I'm sorry about that," said Jig. "It's been a while since I fed you, hasn't it?"

Come to think of it, he hadn't eaten in quite some time either. Jig turned back around to where Pynne had collapsed. . . .

Braf, Grell, and Slash were still waiting where Jig had left them. Jig heard their voices long before he got close enough to see the light of their small fire. They were arguing loudly enough Jig was surprised a tunnel cat hadn't eaten them all.

"I say we go after the ogres," Slash was shouting. "They're so busy running away with their tails between their legs they won't notice us tagging along."

"Ogres don't have tails," countered Braf. A moment later he grunted sharply, as if he had been struck with a cane.

"All it takes is for one of them to glance back, and

they'll squash us like bugs," said Grell. "The way you smell, I'd notice you at a hundred paces."

"What choice do we have?" asked Slash. "Head back and ask the pixies to let us through? Beg them not to hurt us, the way you goblins do when you want to pass through hobgoblin territory?"

"Jig should have let you stay dead," Braf said. "When he gets back—"

"You think Jig's coming back?" Slash asked, laughing. "If he's smart, he ran like a frightened ogre. If he really tried to fight those pixies, he's probably—"

Jig's sword banged against the ground. He had been trying to hold it out in front of him, but the blade seemed to grow heavier with every step. "It's me," he called out. He could hear them shifting positions.

"What are you doing still alive?" Slash asked.

Jig could see them now, standing behind a small, foul-smelling fire. Braf had his hook-tooth out. Grell held one of her canes like a club. Slash had a rock. Jig couldn't tell whether they had been preparing for a pixie attack, or if he had arrived just in time for them to start killing one another.

"The pixies are dead," Jig said.

"All of them?" Braf asked.

With his sword pretty much permanently attached to his arm, it would have been so easy to run Braf through. "No," Jig snapped. "The two who were following us."

"Looks like you had a little trouble with your sword," Slash said. "Lost a bit of hair, too."

Jig reached up to touch the short, singed patch of hair. Hair wasn't supposed to feel so crunchy.

"How do we know they're really dead?" asked Grell. "You told us the pixies were controlling Veka and the scarred simpleton here. They—"

"Hey," said Slash. He stepped toward Grell, only to catch the butt of her cane in his throat. He turned away, gagging.

Jig pulled a bundle from inside his shirt and tossed it onto the ground between them. "Here's your proof."

"What's that?" Braf asked, poking it with his hook-tooth.

"Leftovers." Jig's sword dragged against the ground as he walked toward Grell. His whole arm tingled with every movement, and his fingers were swollen and cold.

Consider yourself lucky. If I hadn't strengthened the vessels and forced your blood to keep flowing through your arm, your fingers would have fallen off by now.

Jig grimaced. Given that the pixies were going to wipe them all out anyway, and the only way he could think of to get back home was more than a little unpleasant, he was having a hard time feeling lucky. "I need to borrow your knife," he said to Grell.

Braf had already opened the bundle and stuffed a bit of glowing meat into his mouth. As Grell slapped the handle into Jig's free hand, she said, "Going to carve up what's left for the rest of us?"

"No," said Jig, sitting down beside the fire. He tried to work the tip of the curved blade beneath the cords on his arm, but the leather wouldn't budge. All he managed to do was slice his skin. He changed tactics, trying to cut the leather where it looped around the hilt. The blade didn't even scratch it.

He knew the knife was good. The blood dripping down his arm proved that. Pynne's magic must have hardened the leather. "Stupid pixies." Jig was going to spend the rest of his short life with a sword stuck to his arm.

"So how do you propose we get out of here?" Slash asked.

Jig handed the knife back to Grell. "The ogres said that stench came from goblin garbage."

Grell was the first to figure it out. "I've dealt with some vile messes in my time, but I'm not climbing through that."

"Fine," said Jig. "Stay here and wait for the pixies." He stared at his sword, wondering if he would be able to climb the crack one-handed. Grell would certainly need help as well, assuming she changed her mind. "Braf? Slash?"

"You want us to climb through goblin filth?" asked Slash.

"I really don't care." Jig was too tired to argue. His sword dragged along the ground as he trudged toward the ogres' abandoned cavern. He heard the others fall in behind him, not without a bit of muttering on Slash's part.

A short time later, Jig realized he had given all three of them a clear shot at his back. As the smell of rotting garbage grew strong enough he could taste it in the back of his mouth, he was almost disappointed they hadn't taken advantage of his vulnerability.

CHAPTER 10

"The astute reader may notice gaps in the old tales, unexplained spans when the Hero disappears from the narrative. The Hero emerges later, more powerful and prepared for the final conflict. Some argue these omissions are due to the highly secretive nature of the Hero's transformation. Others say the storyteller simply wanted to skip to the good parts."

—From the introduction to Chapter 7 of *The Path of the Hero (Wizard's ed.)*

Despite the awkwardness of the blade affixed to his right arm, Jig still managed to climb a goodly distance. From his own informal calculations, he had now climbed approximately twelve times the height of the entire mountain. That was what it felt like, at any rate. In reality, it couldn't be more than thirty or forty feet from the ogres' cavern to the goblin lair.

Jig's sword arm hung leaden at his side. His thigh throbbed with every movement where he had sliced himself before thinking to tie the scabbard over the naked blade. He stank of rotten food, mold, and far worse things. And tiny burning stings covered his scalp and shoulders from brushing against . . . he still wasn't sure what the nasty things were.

At least they give off light, Shadowstar offered.

True, and Jig would take a few stings over the stench of the ogres' torches any day. He peered upward, where more strands of what appeared to be blue-white hair dangled from the filthy stone. The ends of the strands slowly changed from blue to green and back again. Jig braced himself, watching as a huge black fly approached one of the strands, drawn by the shifting light.

The instant the fly touched the end, the strand flashed, shocking the unfortunate insect. The rest of the strands shot out, coiling around its body and dragging it toward the oversize sluglike body stuck to the underside of the rock.

Shadowstar thought it must have come from the pixies' world. Jig didn't care where it had come from, as long as it was too busy with the fly to go after him. He had moved Smudge down into his belt pouch after the first attack. Smudge was a tough little fire-spider, but these creatures had a lot more filaments than Smudge had legs.

He reached up with his left hand and pressed his feet to either side of the rock, dragging himself a bit higher. The creature ignored him. A tiny carrion-worm scurried over Jig's fingers, clutching a broken bit of bone in its claws as it fled. The light of the tendrils turned the worm's white skin pale blue.

"Ouch," shouted Slash. "I'm going to rip that hairy glowing slug apart with my bare—Ouch!"

"Keep your hands to yourself before you kill us

all," snapped Grell. They had rigged a crude rope harness to help her climb, using scraps of rope scavenged from the abandoned ogre camp. Braf and Slash both supported some of Grell's weight, leading to numerous complaints from all involved.

"Are you sure this will take us home?" asked Braf.

"Smells like goblin filth to me," muttered Slash.

"Quiet," said Jig, twisting his head so his good ear was aimed upward. Footsteps, and the creak of a door. His sword clinked against the rock as he drew himself higher. He could see light from above: not the pale, sickly light of the slugs, but the cheerful green of a goblin muck lantern. They were here. They had made it to the goblin lair. He opened his mouth to tell the others.

Broken, dripping shards of pottery showered down on them. Jig yelped as one piece jabbed the top of his head. The shards smelled of spoiled beer.

Jig pushed himself up. He dug his toes into the rock and summoned one last burst of energy to drag himself out of the pit.

He found himself staring at a young goblin girl. Before Jig could say anything, she screamed, threw her lantern at Jig's head, and ran screaming.

Jig dropped back into the pit, barely dodging the lantern. One foot landed on Slash's shoulder. The hobgoblin grunted and strained to keep from falling, which was probably the only thing that stopped him from flinging Jig down with the rest of the garbage.

"Sorry," Jig muttered as he climbed back out. The muck lantern had shattered on the back wall, casting green light over the small, stuffy cave.

"At least that oversize, rat-eating wizard never made me swim through goblin trash," Slash muttered as he followed Jig out. He turned and hauled on his rope, pulling Grell and Braf out after him.

"Where is Veka, anyway?" asked Braf.

"I wish I knew," said Jig. He had been wondering the same thing. Pynne and Farnax hadn't said anything about her. Maybe she was dead. She could have run afoul of a tunnel cat or rock serpent, or maybe she had tried to jump onto another giant bat and missed. Given that she was still pixie-charmed when she escaped, Jig's life would be much simpler if she were dead. That, more than anything else, convinced him she was still alive.

A heavy door blocked the only way out of the cave. Jig gave it a quick shove, but the door was barred on the outside. The goblin lair had few real doors, since the rock was too hard to work, but there were a few areas deserving of special attention. In this case a full frame had been constructed around the cave opening, secured with a batch of Golaka's raknok paste. The sticky-sweet paste was great on fish, but more importantly, raknok was the favorite food of a kind of black mold that clung tightly to both wood and stone. After a week the frame would be secure enough to support a door. After a month an ogre could probably still rip down the door, but it would take at least four or five goblins working together to do so. Given how often goblins worked together, the door would likely stand for years.

Jig jabbed his sword tip into the crack at the edge of the frame, trying to reach the bar on the other side, but the blade was too thick.

He stared at the sword, remembering the fear on Pynne's face as he shoved his sword at her. She had called it death-metal. The blade had left burns on her skin. If all pixies shared her vulnerability, the goblins might have a chance.

No, the only reason he had gotten close enough to kill Pynne was because they wanted him alive. The pixies wouldn't make that mistake when they came to wipe out the goblins.

They might not attack right away, Shadowstar said. *The first two pixies to venture out from the protection of their world were killed by a single goblin. They'll be more cautious next time. You might have bought your people a little more time to prepare.*

A strong hand shoved Jig aside. Slash pounded on the door. "If you don't let us out of here now, I'll feed your private parts to the tunnel cats!" He stepped away, searching the debris-strewn cave. "There has to be something we can use to bash this thing down. If I have to spend another moment immersed in this stench—"

"You call this a stench?" asked Grell. "Try changing diapers when the whole nursery comes down with the green squirts." She shook her head. "Babies never get sick alone. Once one of 'em starts dripping and crying, you can bet the rest of them will come down with it in a day or so."

Jig grimaced and stepped toward the edge of the waste crack, away from the others. He had managed the entire climb without relieving himself, but if he didn't go now, his bladder was going to burst. He stared at the sword tied to his hand. This was going to be tricky.

He fumbled a bit, giving himself a nasty pinch involving the sheath and crossguard, but he managed. Then he got another shock. Apparently the pixies' glow followed them through death and beyond.

Jig's sword dragged along the ground as he returned

to the door. He could hear several sets of footsteps outside, along with low voices. Slash and Grell were still arguing.

The door creaked open. Slash started to push past Jig, then noticed the armed goblins gathered around the cave. He moved aside. "Why don't you go first?"

As Jig stepped outside, he breathed deeply for the first time in what seemed like forever. The air smelled of muck smoke and the sweat of too many goblins, but compared to the waste pit, this was paradise . . . if paradise included one very angry goblin chief.

Kralk stepped forward, her morningstar hanging from one hand. To either side goblin guards stood with drawn swords. The rest of the lair had gathered at a safe distance, no doubt eager to see who would get a taste of that morningstar.

"You've returned," Kralk said. "Alive." That last was added with a long stare at Grell and Braf, who still waited in the shadows. "And you've swapped your ogre for a hobgoblin. Not a wise trade, I think."

A few goblins laughed at that. Slash growled.

Kralk hesitated, taking in Jig's bedraggled appearance. No doubt she had already gotten past her disappointment at seeing him alive and was now trying to figure out how best to turn this to her advantage. She began with mockery.

"So tell us, Jig Dragonslayer. What menace so terrified the ogres that they turned to you for help?" She smirked. "Perhaps we can make a new song for you. 'The Triumph of the Filth-Strewn Hero.' "

To Jig's great annoyance, his mind seized on the title and spliced a tune to it.

In comes the filth-strewn hero,
his sword nicked and rusted,

his bones bruised and busted,
his body still sticky with blood so blue.

Beware the filth-strewn hero.
His temper is strained,
a stink fills his brain,
and he'll triumph by running you through.

Jig allowed himself a quick, wistful sigh. "Pixies," he said.

Kralk cocked her head, momentarily taken aback. "Did you say pixies?"

"They've enslaved or killed most of the ogres," Jig said. "The rest have fled the lower cavern. The pixies are going to destroy us and the hobgoblins if we don't stop them. We—"

A harsh laugh cut him off. "Pixies conquering the lower cavern?" Kralk said, her face twisting into a sneer. "That's the best story you can invent? How could they have gotten to the ogres without first passing through our tunnels?"

She turned to glare at the other goblins, who started to jeer and laugh. The sound of their mockery triggered flashbacks from Jig's childhood. Most of his adulthood too, for that matter.

Jig hunched his shoulders, remembering what Pynne had said about him being the one to open the way for the pixies. He still didn't know what she meant by that, but why would she make up such a lie? "They opened a magical gateway into Straum's lair. A portal from their world."

To Jig's surprise, the laughter began to die. They actually believed him?

"Have you seen this portal?" Kralk snapped.

Jig hesitated. "Not exactly." He had thought his

problem would be in convincing the goblins to fight the pixies, not in proving the pixies existed in the first place. Perhaps he should pee for her.

He pointed to the waste room, where Slash and the goblins still waited. "They were there. They've seen—"

"You expect us to take the word of a hobgoblin?" Kralk said quickly. "Or two goblins who failed to carry out their orders?"

"What orders?" Braf asked. Grell grabbed his ear, yanked his head to her mouth, and whispered. Braf's eyes widened. "Oh, that's right. I forgot." He drew his hook-tooth. "Should I do it now?"

Grell dragged his head back down and smacked his forehead with her other hand.

The head of Kralk's morningstar swung back and forth as she twitched the handle. As Jig watched, it slowly dawned on him that she wasn't nervous about the pixies. She was worried about *him.*

She had sent him on this mission hoping to be rid of him. Instead he had returned alive, if a bit smelly, and bringing word of an invasion into the mountain. Kralk couldn't afford to believe him. If she did, she would make Jig a hero all over again. He would be the one who had discovered the threat and returned to tell of it. He would be the logical choice to lead the goblins against their new enemy. No matter what happened, Jig, not Kralk, would be the one the goblins remembered.

"You're lying," said Kralk. "And even if these pixies did exist, why should we worry? They'll have to fight through the hobgoblins first."

"You rat-eaters think we're going to do your dirty work?" Slash shouted, stepping forward. One of the goblin guards advanced to stop him. Slash shoved him, knocking him into the crowd. Several more goblins rushed forward with swords and spears.

"Wait!" Jig said. He grabbed Slash by the arm and tugged him back.

Kralk and the others were all watching him. Jig had always thought hobgoblins were the experts on traps, but the one Kralk had created when she sent Jig out with Walland Wallandson had ensnared them both. Kralk had to kill him. If he was lying to the chief, death was the only punishment. If he was telling the truth, she had to kill him to keep control of the other goblins.

On second thought, it seemed like Jig was the only one who had been snared in this little trap.

"You should probably talk to the warriors," Jig stammered, searching for a way to back down. "You can prepare the lair against the pixies. I wouldn't be much use. I barely escaped. They nearly killed me. Look what they did to my arm."

He stepped forward, flourishing his arm so everyone would see the way the leather bindings bit into his skin. As he did, the sheath slipped free, flying from the blade and striking Kralk's shoulder.

Jig's throat tightened so quickly his breath squeaked. He now stood with a bare blade pointed directly at the goblin chief.

Kralk's smile threatened to split her face. She flexed her arms, then switched to a two-handed grip on her weapon. The other goblins fell back like ants fleeing a muck spill. Kralk kicked the sheath away, out of Jig's reach, so he had no way to cover his weapon. "I wondered when you'd finally summon the courage to challenge me, runt," said Kralk.

Jig backed away. It appeared as though Pynne was going to succeed in getting him killed after all.

Kralk was stronger, larger, and faster than Jig. He didn't need the warmth coming from Smudge's pouch to tell him he was in trouble. *Help?*

Jig, she might be stronger, but you're smarter. You can defeat her.

Right. What was the smart thing to do? That would have been not going on this stupid mission in the first place!

Kralk stepped forward, swinging her morningstar in a wide arc. The spiked ball smashed Jig's sword, spinning him in a full circle. Shock and pain tore through his arm, shaking his very bones. He staggered back, barely dodging a second blow.

Like most goblins, Kralk attacked with brute force but very little technique. Unfortunately, she had a great deal of brute force.

Her morningstar whooshed through the air, driving Jig toward the garbage cave. Her attacks were predictable enough for Jig to avoid getting hit, but he couldn't attack without opening himself up at the same time.

If he timed it right, he might be able to dive through the door of the cave and crawl back down the waste crack before Kralk smashed his skull. He doubted that was what Shadowstar meant by "smarter," though.

Kralk switched her grip, swinging at an angle that knocked Jig's sword downward. Jig dropped to one knee. Kralk's morningstar blurred in a circle, smashing Jig's sword against the floor. A handsbreath of steel snapped off the end.

Jig stumbled into the doorway, staring at the broken end of his weapon. At least the blade was a little lighter now.

Kralk was still smiling. She was sweating a bit, but Jig was so tired he could barely keep his sword up.

She didn't even have to hit him with her morningstar. Much more of this, and he would drop from exhaustion.

"Your precious god isn't going to save you this time, Jig," said Kralk.

Jig snorted. His precious god was the one who had gotten him into this mess to begin with. He pushed sideways, trying to get to the doorway. The morningstar gouged the door frame near his head.

"See how he scampers," Kralk shouted. "Jig Dragonslayer, cowering like a cornered rat."

Jig tried to stab her while she gloated. He barely avoided having his elbow shattered as a reward for his clumsy lunge.

Kralk's foot shot out, catching him in the shin. He rolled away as the morningstar rang against the floor next to his head. The next strike was even closer. He flattened his ears, trying to shut out the worst of the noise as he scrambled to his feet.

"They'll sing a new song before this day is done," Kralk yelled. "How Kralk the Chief triumphed over Jig the Coward." She glanced around as she was speaking, but it wasn't long enough for Jig to attack.

She was playing with him, stretching out the fight for the other goblins. She wanted to make a show of it, to prove beyond any doubt who was the strongest. To Kralk Jig was already dead. She fought now to defeat anyone else who might have considered trying to overthrow the chief.

If there was one thing Jig knew, it was fear. Kralk was afraid. Afraid of Jig, and afraid of the other goblins. She had seized control through treachery and deceit, which meant she had to live every day in fear that someone would do the same to her.

Fine. Treachery and deceit it would be. Jig raised his sword and shouted, "Now, Braf! Attack her now!"

Kralk never took her eyes from Jig. She smirked as she twirled her morningstar. "A poor choice for a bluff, Jig. Braf lacks the imagination for treachery."

She raised her morningstar, and a wooden hook caught her wrist. She staggered sideways. A powerful jerk of her arm yanked her attacker to the ground.

Jig thrust as hard as he could. His shoulder nearly wrenched out of its socket as the broken tip of his sword skidded off her breastplate. Jig fell forward. He twisted to keep from squishing Smudge. As a result he landed off-balance, hitting his chin on the floor hard enough to rattle his teeth.

Kralk's eyes were wide, her teeth bared. Jig didn't know why she was so upset. His attack hadn't even scratched her armor. She raised her morningstar to crush Jig's skull . . .

. . . and a yellow hand snaked out to catch her right fang. The other hand seized her by the hair. With a sharp twist, Slash broke Kralk's neck.

Jig stared at Kralk, who lay twitching on the ground. Then he stared at Grell, who was climbing back to her feet, Braf's hook-tooth in one hand. Then he stared at Slash. The hobgoblin was looking around at the stunned goblins with a wary expression that suggested he wasn't sure whether to gloat or run away.

"Why did you do that?" asked Jig.

Slash wiped his hands on his vest. "No blood this way."

That wasn't what Jig meant, but before he could clarify, one of the goblins whispered, "Does this mean the hobgoblin is our new chief?"

"What's that?" Slash looked like he had swallowed a rock serpent. "Me?"

"You did kill Kralk," Jig said. From the muttering of the crowd, they didn't like the idea any better than Slash did.

By now Braf had retrieved his hook-tooth, and was walking toward Jig. He nudged Kralk's body with his foot. "That was great. Everything worked exactly the way you planned it, Jig."

"The way I what?" Jig bit his lip. Throughout the cave goblins were whispering and pointing and generally wondering what was going on. Jig knew exactly how they felt.

"Yeah," said Braf. "Jig knew Kralk would try to kill him, so he made a plan to kill Kralk instead." He clapped Jig on the back, hard enough to stagger him. "Grell told me all about it when she borrowed my hook-tooth."

Jig turned to stare at Grell, who shrugged and said, "Good plan. I guess that means you're chief."

"Me?" His voice squeaked.

Kralk's body lay face-up, a grimace of rage frozen on her dead face. *I suppose it's too late to heal her so she can be chief again?*

Even if she wasn't already dead, how long do you think you'd keep breathing if she could get her hands on you?

How long do you think I'll keep breathing now? Everyone was watching him. No matter which way he turned, half the goblins would have a clear shot at his unprotected back. What was a new chief supposed to do in a situation like this anyway? Usually they bellowed something loud and triumphant and scary, but Jig's throat had constricted too tight for him to say anything at all.

Grell nudged Kralk's body with her cane. "Hey Jig,

if you don't want to claim that malachite necklace, I'll take it."

She didn't wait for an answer. With a bit of groaning and creaking, Grell hunched down and began untying the necklace. Braf picked up the morningstar and handed it to Jig.

The weapon was heavier than he had guessed, especially one-handed. The handle was still warm. He dug his claws in to keep it from slipping out of his sweat-slick grip. Should he tuck it through his belt, the way Kralk had always worn it? The weight would probably drag his trousers down to his knees.

"Feast!" shouted one of the goblins, a cry that swiftly echoed through the crowd.

Feast? What . . . oh. The chief was dead. Goblins usually marked the occasion with a feast. The choosing of a new chief always provided plenty of fresh meat.

They hadn't feasted when Kralk became chief, but that was because the former chief's body had already been eaten by hobgoblins, and nobody had been certain whether her other opponents' bodies had been poisoned or not. "What about the pixies?" Jig asked weakly.

"You really want to deny this crowd their feast?" Grell asked, glancing up. The necklace hung nearly to her waist. Malachite clinked as she held the rough spikes to the light.

"What's going on out here?" The voice thundered through the cavern, cutting a path through the goblins as Golaka the chef stormed from her kitchen. Even larger than Braf, and strong enough to give Slash a good fight, Golaka waved her huge stirring spoon like a sword as she approached. She stopped when she saw Kralk. "Who did this?"

Every set of eyes turned toward Jig.

Golaka shook her spoon. "I've been marinating a pan full of moles all day, and now you're telling me I have to throw them out and cook her?" She tilted her head to one side, and her voice grew thoughtful. "Though the hobgoblin opens up some interesting possibilities. I could make skewers, alternate goblin meat with hobgoblin, add sliced mushrooms and rat livers, and garnish the whole thing with fried cockroaches for texture. Hobgoblin, do you drink a lot of alcohol?"

Slash stared. "Why do you want to know?"

"It affects the taste of the liver," said Golaka. "Doesn't matter, I can always baste you with—"

"No," Jig said. Blast it, he was squeaking again. "No," he repeated.

The lair fell silent, and Jig tried to remember if anyone had dared say no to Golaka before.

Golaka tilted her head. She was older than any goblin had a right to be, and her hearing was as poor as a human's. "What did you say?"

"Slash—the hobgoblin, I mean, we—"

"Slash the hobgoblin!" yelled one of the younger goblins, raising a sword.

"No!" They didn't understand. They hadn't seen the entire lower cavern transformed. They hadn't talked to the handful of ogres who had survived the invasion. They didn't care about pixies.

This was a hobgoblin, a threat they knew. How many of them had endured the taunts of hobgoblin guards? How many bore scars from the hobgoblins' "playful" jabs? And now Jig's first act as chief would be to deny them their revenge?

Jig turned around, wondering if it was too late to retreat back into the garbage pit. Anywhere he could put a heavy door between himself and the rest of the goblins would do. But the only places that merited doors were the nursery, the distillery, the kitchen, the garbage pit, and Kralk's quarters.

No, *his* quarters now. "The hobgoblin comes with me," Jig said. He forced a smile, trying to appear as nasty as possible while he reached up to stroke Smudge's head. "I've got something special planned for him, and my pet hasn't eaten in far too long."

Jig started to walk toward the brass-hinged door on the far side of the cave, only to draw up short when Golaka refused to budge. Jig held his breath as he stared into those greasy, dark-veined eyes.

Eventually Golaka shrugged. "Bring me the left-overs, chief. We haven't had hobgoblin jerky in a long time."

The goblins cheered, shaking their weapons and causing several injuries in the process. Golaka stepped aside.

Glancing back at Slash, Jig whispered, "You can either follow me, or you can stay with them."

"Do you want us to help carve?" one of the goblins asked before Slash could respond.

Jig shook his head. "I think I can handle one hob-goblin by myself." Slash cocked his head at that, but the only sign of annoyance was a convulsive twitch in his hands, his fingers curling much the way they had when he broke Kralk's neck. Silently he followed Jig across the lair, glaring at any goblin who dared ap-proach too closely.

The bottom of the door scraped the rock as Jig hauled it open. Inside, two muck pits sat to either side of the doorway. One was empty, the other nearly so. The lone flame flickered weakly, but it was enough. Gleaming metal lined the walls, like a miniature version of Straum's old hoard. Swords, spears, knives, as well as more exotic weapons, were all stacked against the walls, some piled atop one another. To one side, a longbow with a broken string sat half buried in a rickety stack of yellow-fletched arrows. A spear so long it barely fit within the cave was propped against the opposite wall.

The door slammed shut behind him. Jig spun, nearly cutting Slash's ankle with his sword. Slash stepped to one side, and his hand clapped Jig's shoulder. The nails dug through Jig's shirt. "I've killed one goblin chief today," he said. "Do I need to kill a second?"

Jig shook his head. Slash was too close for him to stab with the sword, even if his arm hadn't been useless after the fight with Kralk. "They would have killed you," Jig said.

Slash stared at him for a long time. "Pah. You rat-eaters are too cowardly to take on a hobgoblin warrior." But he made no further move against Jig. He picked up a peculiar-looking knife with two thin spikes angling out from the main blade. "They're going to eat you alive, you know. You're no chief."

"I know." Jig stepped away, rubbing his shoulder. Out in the lair, Jig could still hear the chant of "Feast, feast!" from the goblins, and then Golaka shouting, "If you don't shut up, there'll be more than one goblin on the cookfires!" The lair was much quieter after that.

Jig's new quarters were relatively small, and the abundance of weapons made the place feel even more cramped. A mattress made from the skin of a giant bat sat against the far wall. Jig could smell the dried moss stuffed within the skin. His eyelids drooped at the mere thought of such luxury. He stepped toward the mattress, but Slash grabbed his ear and yanked him back. Jig yelped, then covered his mouth and hoped nobody outside had heard.

Slash pointed to the floor, where a thin string stretched through a metal loop, up to a tripod of battle axes beside the door. The base of the nearest ax was secured to a wooden rod. From the look of it, the ax would swing down to split the skull of anyone who snuck in uninvited.

"A three-year-old hobgoblin could do better," Slash muttered, kneeling by the string. "The line's too high. Not only does it catch the light of the muck fires, but it leaves a clear shadow. If nothing else, you ought to blacken the line." He studied the ax briefly. Holding the handle in place, he broke the string with his other hand.

Jig examined the room with new respect, not to mention fear. What other surprises had Kralk left behind? Several vials and clay jars sat in a rack by the far wall, padded with dried leaves. Her collection of poisons? A wooden box with rusting hinges sat open on the other side of the room, revealing rumpled clothes in bright blues and reds and oranges. Near the head of the bed sat a jar of candied toadstools. Jig's mouth watered, but he stopped himself after a single step. Knowing Kralk they were probably poisoned.

Slash squeezed past him to examine the mattress. Strange that Jig felt safer in here, alone with a hobgoblin, than he would have with another goblin.

Slash poked the leather in a few spots, then grabbed the edge and lifted the mattress to reveal a thin metal spike affixed to a broad wooden base. Moss flaked out of the hole in the bottom of the mattress where the spike had been. Jig tried not to think what would happen to anyone who snuck in to catch a quick nap.

"Some of these are hobgoblin tricks," Slash said.

"Poorly done, but I'm guessing your chief had help setting this place up. Another benefit of your precious truce." He sat by the door and dipped his fingers in the empty muck pit. Humming to himself, he began to smear the ashen film along the string. "The first thing we need to do is run the line from the top of the door, where nobody will see it," he muttered. "Those axes are too obvious. Though if I could mount one to the ceiling, it might work. That's the first rule of traps: nobody ever looks up."

Jig sat gingerly on the corner of the mattress, half expecting it to stab him in the backside or trigger an avalanche of sharp rocks. Smudge started to crawl down to explore, but Jig snatched him and shoved him into his pouch. Until he knew everything Kralk had done to this place, he wasn't about to let Smudge wander about. The fire-spider probably wasn't heavy enough to trigger most traps, but paranoia had kept Jig alive so far.

Now that he was chief, paranoia might not be enough. *Why did you do this to me?* he asked.

What are you talking about? I didn't do anything. Despite his vast powers, Tymalous Shadowstar was a piss-poor liar.

When my sword came unsheathed. You did that. I could feel the magic. Jig was too exhausted to be angry.

She was going to kill you one way or another.

Jig shook his head. *You've been pushing me ever since Walland showed up. Why?*

You would have preferred to go back to your little temple? To hide all alone while the world goes on without you?

That was unfair. *Better than another adventure. I hate this.*

I know. But I also know your people would never survive against the pixies. I'm trying to keep you all alive.

No, said Jig. *You didn't know about the pixies. You didn't know anything except that Walland 'felt wrong.' Oh, you also knew Kralk wanted me killed, and that she would probably use this as a way to get rid of me.*

But you're still alive, and Kralk is getting basted as we speak.

I'm chief, Jig said. *Do you know how long most goblin chiefs survive?*

Jig, it doesn't—

Less than one day. Usually we go through at least seven or eight goblins before one survives long enough to really seize control. Kralk had been an anomaly, killing her foes with a ruthless efficiency that had gone a long way toward cowing the other goblins into submission. Jig, on the other hand, had nearly died. He would have died, if not for the help of an old woman and a hobgoblin. No doubt half the lair was already plotting his death.

Jig stiffened as he realized what Shadowstar had done. "You set me up," he whispered.

"What?" asked Slash, glancing up from a half-assembled crossbow.

You didn't want me to save Walland. You wanted to pit me against Kralk. You wanted me to be chief.

I wanted both. I wanted to know what was happening, and I wanted to help you change things for the goblins. You can lead them, Jig. You can help them be something more. You've already begun to change the goblins who are closest to you. Grell saved your life when Kralk was about to kill you. Doesn't that seem like an odd thing for a goblin to do? Why do you think she did that?

Jig hesitated.

Grell saw you go off to fight those pixies. She saw something few have ever seen: goblin courage.

Lots of goblins run into battles against more powerful enemies.

Goblin stupidity is as common as lice, but you're not stupid. Grell saw that. So did your hobgoblin friend. You saved his life. Look at him, sitting there and not killing you. When you defeated those pixies, you inspired them. You showed them they could be something more, something greater.

Jig's stomach was starting to hurt again. Hunger and anxiety worked together to twist his guts into a knot. He wondered if he would be able to keep anything down at his own chief's feast. He grabbed his numb arm by the wrist, setting the sword across his legs to examine the broken steel.

It's rude to ignore your deity, snapped Shadowstar. No goblin could sound half as petulant as a cranky god. *Forget the pixies, think about your people, living and dying in the dark, trapped in a cramped, smelly cave as they kill one another off. Would you rather live like you did before you faced Straum, scurrying about on muck duty and hoping the bigger goblins didn't try to unclog the privy with your head?*

Jig didn't answer. To tell the truth, he rarely thought ahead. Most of the time he was content simply to make it through the day without getting killed.

Horrible as that adventure a year ago had been, his life was better now. It had been free of privy-related incidents, at least. *We happen to like caves*, he said. As protests went, it was weak and he knew it.

What do you want, Jig? You're chief now. You're responsible for what happens to the goblins.

That was even more frightening than an imminent pixie invasion.

What do you want? Shadowstar's voice was louder, more insistent, prompting Jig to blurt the first thing that came to mind.

"Stuffed snakeskins and klak beer."

"What?" asked Slash. He held several crossbow quarrels between the fingers of his right hand, and a length of copper wire in his left. A steel tool like a tiny flat-tipped dagger protruded from his mouth.

"That's what I want," Jig said, ignoring a sigh of divine exasperation. He wanted one brief respite where he didn't have to worry about pixies or ogres or goblins trying to kill him. Or hobgoblin traps misfiring, he added as a crossbow quarrel shot into the ceiling and ricocheted into the mattress beside him. "And now that I'm chief, I should be able to get it."

He headed for the door. Golaka's stuffed snakeskins were legendary. She stuffed shredded meat, sautéed mushrooms, and boiled tubers into snakeskin, fried the whole thing, then sliced them into bite-size chunks. Best of all, snakeskins and klak beer would help wash away the sour aftertaste of pixie meat.

You can't run away from this, Jig. You have a responsibility to your people.

Can't you see I'm busy? Jig asked. *Besides, if I order them to do anything before they've had their feast, they'll throw me onto the fire alongside Kralk.*

As he thought about the pixies, wondering how he could possibly lead the goblins against them, he couldn't help wondering if maybe Kralk had been the lucky one.

CHAPTER 11

"You have to understand, this truce doesn't mean we can't kill goblins. It only means we can't get caught."

—One-eyed Tosk, Hobgoblin Weaponsmith

Jig stood in the main cavern, burping up snake and watching the satiated goblins. As a rule, goblins with full stomachs were slightly less dangerous than hungry goblins. He had no doubt they would still kill him if he dropped his guard, probably even if he didn't, but maybe now they wouldn't be quite so brutal about it.

He remembered how foolish Veka had looked with her cloak and staff, trying to be a wizard. Jig's pretense at being chief was even more absurd. One look and anyone would know Jig was no chief.

His sheath once again covered his sword, but with the blade broken, the end of the sheath flopped limply along the ground. He had already stepped on the end twice, nearly tripping himself as he walked.

His clothes had been so saturated with blood and filth there was nothing to do but burn them. Even his favorite boots were scuffed and scratched. The pixies would pay for that.

Unfortunately, most of Kralk's clothes were ridiculously large on Jig's scrawny frame. Given the choice of raiding Kralk's wardrobe or facing the lair naked, Jig had chosen the ridiculous.

His belt cinched garish yellow trousers that ballooned over his thighs. He had also picked out a red vest with silver tassels. On Kralk those tassels would have hung just below her waist. On Jig they tickled the tops of his knees when he walked.

"Well?"

Jig jumped. He hadn't noticed Grell sidling up to his right. Braf followed close behind her, groaning and rubbing his stomach.

Why now, when he was in more danger of being killed, was Jig having such a hard time staying focused?

"They're waiting for you to tell them what to do," Grell said. "They know things aren't right. They may not have seen the pixies, but they know the air is colder, and they see how restless the snakes and bugs have been. One of the guards says a rock serpent attacked his muck lantern, and Topam swears he saw a giant bat flapping around over the lake a few days ago. There have been more carrion-worms crawling around the tunnels, too."

Which you would have known, if you didn't spend all of your time in your temple, Shadowstar whispered.

"The tunnel cats have been pretty restless lately, come to think of it," said Slash as he stepped out of Kralk's—out of *Jig's* quarters. "By the way, don't push your door open more than forty-five degrees, and you should probably let someone else light that muck pit from now on."

Jig wondered if he would ever have the courage to set foot in that room again. This was probably for the best, really. If not for Slash's traps, Jig would be too tempted to retreat back to his quarters and lock the door behind him.

Shadowstar was right. They had to do something about the pixies. The longer they waited, the more time the pixies would have to adapt to this world. The next time Jig faced pixies, they would be far more dangerous than Pynne and Farnax.

He stepped away from the wall to address the goblins, and his throat went dry. It looked as though every single goblin in the whole mountain was here, joking and smirking and waiting for him to speak. So many goblins, all staring at him.

Wait . . . all the goblins? "Who's on guard duty?" Jig asked.

A pair of well-fed, belching goblins near the back raised their hands, and Jig groaned. "I told you the pixies were going to try to kill us. Don't you think someone should guard the lair?"

The guards nodded, but made no movement to return to their posts. "Someone should, yeah," said one. The other laughed.

"Don't ask them," Grell whispered. "Tell them. You're the chief!"

Jig cleared his throat. Both guards waited, silently daring him to utter an order. How was he supposed to make them obey? His sword arm was so numb he could barely move it, even if the sword hadn't been broken. Jig looked at those guards, and all he could see was himself as a child, fleeing the older, bigger goblins who wanted to put a carrion-worm down his pants.

"Fine," Jig said, anger helping his voice carry throughout the cavern. "Leave the lair unguarded." He glanced at Grell, hoping she had been right about the goblins' mood. "I'm sure the pixies will appreciate it, when they send their ogre slaves to slaughter us." He raised his voice and pointed at the guards. "When the ogres start tearing you apart, and the pixies are disemboweling you with their magic, remember it was those two goblins who let them stroll right into the lair."

Finally the attention of the goblins shifted away from Jig. Angry muttering spread through the crowd.

"We're going, we're going," said one of the guards, shooting a hateful look in Jig's direction.

They didn't make it out of the lair. A loud snarl announced the arrival of a group of armed hobgoblins. Two tunnel cats strained to break free of braided leather harnesses, nearly pulling their hobgoblin keeper off his feet. "Where is Jig Dragonslayer?" shouted the largest of the hobgoblins.

And that brought the attention right back to Jig. He didn't get the chance to speak before the hobgoblins were making their way toward him, tunnel cats snapping at anyone who failed to get out of the way. "Our chief wants a word with you, goblin."

Another of the hobgoblins stared. "Hey, Charak. What are you doing with these rat-eaters?"

Charak? They were looking at Slash. From the look of things, he had been trying to disappear into the shadows.

"Chief's going to want to see you, too," said the hobgoblin holding the tunnel cats. "He's going to be real happy when he finds out you're still alive. Now where's Kralk? He told us to bring back the goblin chief, too."

Maybe I should have just stayed in the garbage pit. Jig raised his hand. "I'm the chief." The words sounded strange, like someone else had spoken.

A tunnel cat swatted a goblin who had gotten too close, sending her to the ground with four gouges bleeding down her arm. "Makes our job easier, I guess," said a hobgoblin. "Come with us, rat-eater."

"You can't come in here and give Jig orders," Braf shouted. "He's the chief. You're lucky he doesn't slay every last one of you hobgoblins."

"Braf?" Jig asked.

"What?"

"I'm chief now, right?"

Braf nodded.

"So you have to do what I say?"

Braf nodded again.

"Good. Shut up." Jig studied the hobgoblins. Two tunnel cats and five warriors to escort a few goblins. The hobgoblin chief was serious. Still, if the whole lair attacked together, they would overwhelm the hobgoblins. Judging from the nasty smiles beginning to spread through the crowd, the goblins had figured that out too.

What they hadn't figured out was what the rest of the hobgoblins would do in reprisal. The last thing Jig needed was to have hobgoblins screaming through the layer on a vengeance raid when he was trying to worry about pixies. He could only manage one war at a time.

Actually, he doubted he could manage even one.

"Braf and Grell, I want you to come with us to the hobgoblin lair," Jig said loudly. "The rest of you, keep the muck pits filled and burning, and could somebody please make sure we get a guard at the entrance?"

"Why us?" asked Grell.

Because Grell and Braf had both been under orders to kill him, and neither one had done so. Jig hoped that trend of not killing him would continue. "Because I'm chief and I said so."

Jig tried to look on the bright side as he followed his escort out of the lair. If the hobgoblins killed him, at least he wouldn't have to worry about the pixies.

The lead hobgoblin took one of the tunnel cats, who sniffed the air and the ground as they walked. Another cat followed behind, straining at its leash. That one actually drooled as it watched Jig, barely even blinking.

Hobgoblin lanterns painted the tunnel the color of goblin blood. Jig glanced at Slash, trying to guess whether he was a captor or a prisoner. The other hobgoblins hadn't given him a weapon, but they weren't jabbing him in the back of the legs with their spears either. Lucky hobgoblin.

Jig jumped and walked faster, trying to avoid another poke as he studied his escort. A large, ugly bruise covered one side of the lead hobgoblin's face. Recent, from the looks of it. They didn't say much, but they didn't have to. Three lanterns were overkill for such a small group. They kept peering into the shadows and letting the tunnel cat peek around bends and turns. They were afraid.

"Have the pixies attacked already?" Jig asked.

That earned him another jab, this one in the thigh. From then on, Jig kept his guesses to himself.

When they reached the hobgoblin lair, Jig saw that the number of guards had doubled. Four hobgoblins stood in a rough square at the junction of the tunnels. Lanterns hung from both ears of the glass statue. Several of the guards growled softly as they saw the goblins approaching.

Braf puffed his chest and opened his mouth. Jig smacked him with his sheathed sword. Whatever Braf had intended to say came out a startled, "Hey!"

"No weapons," said one of the hobgoblins, catching Jig's wrist. Jig's arm was so numb he could barely feel the fingers digging into his skin. The hobgoblin grabbed the crossguard and gave a quick yank that nearly dislocated Jig's shoulder.

"Try cutting it off," suggested the hobgoblin who had yanked Braf's hook-tooth away.

"I already did," said Jig. "The leather is enchanted. Cursed, really. It's too strong to cut."

The hobgoblin grinned. "I didn't mean the cord." He drew a short, flat-tipped sword from his belt. The blade was only sharp on one side, an obvious chopping weapon.

"Go on, cut it off," Grell said, leaning against the wall. "Course, then you'll have to explain why your guest bled to death before he could talk to your chief."

The hobgoblin's smile melted away. The thought crossed Jig's mind that nobody had actually specified whether they wanted Jig alive or dead. Though if they wanted him dead, they probably would have killed him by now.

The hobgoblin shoved Jig's arm away. "Draw steel, and you'll wish I'd killed you, goblin." He pushed Jig for good measure, knocking him to the ground next to the glass statue. Blue light reflected from the chipped glass. The hobgoblin warrior stood so tall his head nearly touched the top of the tunnel. Aside from a helmet, he wore only a loincloth, no doubt to emphasize the muscles covering his body.

Lying on the floor, Jig wondered if anyone else had

ever bothered to examine the statue from this angle. He also wondered why the sculptor had made the hobgoblin anatomically correct.

"Get up." Strong hands hauled Jig to his feet, then dragged him through the open archway. They pushed Slash after him, saying, "Make sure he doesn't step in anything." Grell and Braf followed, probably assuming they were safer with Jig than out here with cranky hobgoblin guards.

One of the tunnel cats stayed behind. A guard tied the leash around the legs of the statue. The statue would keep the cat from running off, but all the guard had to do to loose the cat on an enemy was cut the leash. Whatever had happened, the hobgoblins were taking no chances.

A few paces into the tunnel, the hobgoblins pressed themselves to the walls as they walked.

"Pit trap," said Slash, shoving Jig against a wall hard enough to bang his head. Grell did the same to Braf who, despite Slash's warning, had almost walked right into the trap. "Fall in there, and the goblins will have to find someone else to play chief."

"What's down there?" Jig asked, keeping his body as close to the wall as he could.

"Used to be a pair of giant carrion-worms." Slash shook his head glumly. "A group of adventurers fell into the pit and slaughtered them. Do you have any idea how long it takes to breed and raise giant worms? The chief decided rusty spikes at the bottom would be faster and easier. Not as much fun though."

"Oh. I see." Jig fought to keep his face neutral, though he couldn't quite stop a shiver at the memory of those worms.

A few paces later, Slash pushed him again. "See that stain on the ground?"

Jig stared. The ground was dusty rock, the same as the rest of the tunnels. Squinting, he could just make out a faint discoloration in the dirt where Slash was pointing.

"We spread a mix of blood, rock serpent venom, and diluted honey there. The venom keeps the blood from clotting, and the honey makes it stick to whoever steps in it." Slash licked his lips. "Tunnel cats love the stuff. Step inside the lair wearing that scent, and they'll be on you before you can draw your sword." Indeed, even as Slash explained, the tunnel cat tugged its leash, trying to reach the dried stain. The hobgoblin kicked the cat in the side, earning a loud hiss, but the cat didn't attack. That was a well-trained animal. Jig wondered if the hobgoblins would be willing to train the goblin guards.

Before Jig could say anything, Slash hauled him to one side. This time it was a scattering of tiny metal spikes resting on the ground.

"They're so small," Braf said.

"And they're coated in lizard-fish toxin," Slash said.

Oh. Jig stared at the hobgoblins with newfound respect. If he tried to set such traps to protect the goblin lair, half the goblins would be dead within a week.

"Watch your step," said Slash.

Jig stopped, fully expecting to be shot, poisoned, crushed, or maybe all three at the same time. "What is it now?"

Slash pointed to a pile of brown, slimy goo in the center of the tunnel. "Hairball."

Eventually the tunnel opened into a broad cavern, similar in size to the goblins' lair. But the hobgoblins had carved out a very different home for themselves. For one thing, instead of using muck pits in the floor, the hobgoblins hung wide metal muck bowls from large tripods, so the light came from overhead. Every time Jig took a step, three shadows followed him along the floor. As if he wasn't jumpy enough already!

Even stranger, there were hobgoblin *children* running about. Jig stared at a girl whose head barely came past his waist. She had a knife tucked through her belt, and was swinging a club at a larger, similarly armed hobgoblin boy. As Jig watched, the boy knocked her club away, then kicked her in the stomach. The girl crawled away to retrieve the club. To Jig's amazement, the boy stood there, waiting as she attacked again.

"What's she doing?" Jig asked.

Slash glanced over. "Practicing."

Jig could see other children working throughout the cavern. A few near the entrance scraped lichen from the walls by one of the lanterns, while a boy farther in helped butcher a pile of lizard-fish. Jig even saw a baby hobgoblin slung to the back of a female. He grimaced. The baby had wrinkly yellow skin, green toothless gums, and a misshapen skull.

"Hobgoblin babies are ugly," said Braf.

Grell snorted. "You weren't exactly pleasant to look at yourself."

The female with the baby noticed them staring and bared her teeth in a scowl before ducking behind a large, painted screen mounted on a wooden frame.

Similar screens were set throughout the cavern, partitioning the space into smaller chambers. Crude paintings decorated most of the screens. They seemed to tell stories of hobgoblin triumphs, whether it was a single hobgoblin leading a troll into an ambush, or a group tossing goblins into a pit full of tunnel cats.

The guards led Jig and the others toward the rear of the cave. Several hobgoblins spat as Jig passed. He heard two others making a wager over how Jig would be killed. He held his sword close to his leg, trying to appear unthreatening. So many hobgoblins. Men and women, young and old, armed and . . . well, they were all armed. And they all looked angry.

"What happened?" Jig asked.

One of the guards shoved him forward. "That's for the chief to explain."

"No," said another. "That's for him to explain to the chief."

The chief was an older hobgoblin, sitting on a much-abused cushion near the back of the cavern. A half-eaten skewer of lizard-fish meat sat on the ground beside him. Screens to either side created a smaller artificial cave. Another frame stood in front, but the screen had been rolled up and tied overhead, opening the small chamber to the rest of the cavern.

The hobgoblin chief rose, ducking past the wooden frame to stand in front of Jig and the others. He slipped a bit of greasy lizard-fish to the tunnel cat, then wiped his hands on his quilted, brass-studded jacket. A long wavy sword hung on his hip. The cast bronze head of a hobgoblin warrior capped the hilt, and the crosspiece was a pair of long barbed spikes. Jig had seen the sword once before, when he and the chief had negotiated the truce between goblins and hobgoblins. According to hobgoblin law, whoever held that sword commanded all hobgoblins.

"Hello, Jig," said the chief. His thinning hair was bound into a dirty white braid. He glared at the other hobgoblins. "I said I wanted to speak to the goblin chief too."

"That's me," Jig said.

"I see." He studied Jig, his expression never changing. His cool appraisal was far more worrisome than the gruff threats of the other hobgoblins. At least with them, Jig knew what to expect. Not so with this hobgoblin. He might offer Jig a bit of lizard-fish or cut the head from his body with that huge sword, and he would do both with the same stone expression. Finally he grunted and said, "About time someone killed that overbearing coward Kralk."

He turned to Slash. "Ah, Charak. The others tell me you let a goblin outwit you. A fat female, one who claimed to be a wizard of some sort. They say she humiliated you and led you away, slinking like a cat who's been beaten once too often."

Jig took a small step away from Slash. Charak. Whoever.

"Doesn't matter anymore," Slash said. "The stupid rat-eater went and got herself enchanted by pixies."

"Pixies?" the chief asked. "What are you talking about?"

As fast as he could, Jig stepped forward to explain about the pixies and their conquest of the ogres. He told the chief how they had fled to the Necromancer's pit and how the steel of his blade seemed to have broken the spell on Slash. "Ask them," he added, pointing to Braf and Grell. "They've all seen the pixies and what they can do."

The chief was shaking his head. "So, Charak. Not only does a mere goblin get the best of you, but then you let yourself fall prey to a fairy spell? I should probably kill you now and save us all the trouble."

The threat was uttered in an easy, casual tone, but Jig saw several hobgoblins reach for their weapons.

"Falling in battle against an invading army I could forgive," the chief continued. "But letting a goblin get the better of you?"

Slash mumbled something incomprehensible.

"And now she returns," said the chief.

Jig's ears perked up. "You have Veka?"

"Not exactly." The chief took another bite of lizard-fish as he studied Jig. Pale strings of meat protruded from between his teeth. "Your goblin wizard killed nine of my men. She refuses to let anyone get to the lake. If we can't get down to hunt in the caverns below, we'll be reduced to scavenging for bugs and rats. Living like goblins, in other words."

He stepped closer, until Jig could smell the meat on his breath. "She tells me she'll let us through if we present her with Jig Dragonslayer."

For once, Jig wasn't afraid. He raised his chin and said, "You can't. She'll turn me over to the pixies, and they'll kill me."

The chief shrugged and spat a few bones onto the floor. Jig could hear the guards moving closer, and Smudge crouched down at the junction of Jig's neck and shoulder to hide.

"If I die," Jig went on, "the truce between goblins and hobgoblins ends today. The truce, and everything that came with it. The same goes if you kill my companions. Even him," he added, nodding toward Slash. He tried to fold his arms defiantly, but he had forgotten about the sword. The sheath whacked him in the leg, to the amusement of the hobgoblins.

The chief stared at Jig for a long time. His wrinkled face gave no clue what was running through his mind. He was a crafty one, even for a hobgoblin, and Jig began to wonder if he had miscalculated.

"Veka told us she wanted Jig Dragonslayer," the chief finally said. "She never specified how she wanted him delivered . . ."

The hobgoblins guarding the entrance to the lair appeared quite surprised to see Jig and the others alive.

"Give me that," Braf said, reclaiming his weapon.

One of the guards stared at Slash. "What happened?"

"We're going to kill Veka," Slash said, grinning.

"I don't suppose any of you mighty warriors know how we're going to accomplish that?" Grell asked.

Nobody answered. Personally, Jig had been giving serious thought to running away and hiding back in the goblin lair. If Veka had slaughtered nine hobgoblin warriors, Jig and his companions weren't going to last very long.

But retreating would only lead to other problems. Problems like angry hobgoblins butchering their way through the goblin lair, demanding Jig's head.

Slash grabbed one of the muck lanterns, but Jig shook his head. "No light. We don't want her to see us coming."

Jig studied his companions as they left the hobgoblin lair. Grell's canes made too much noise. They might be better off leaving her behind altogether, but she seemed to do a good job of keeping Braf in line. As for Braf, he was barely bright enough to know which end of a sword to grab, but Jig needed all the help he could get. Without the two goblins, his only backup would be a hobgoblin who fainted at the sight of blood.

"Wait," Jig said, struggling to draw his sword. After the incident with Kralk, he had used a bit of cord to knot the sheath in place. Those knots had tightened, and he had to bite through them to free the blade. His shoulder burned with newly awakened pain as he used the sword to cut off the tails of his vest. "Grell, give me one of your canes."

He wrapped the material around the end, then used a broken piece of twine to tie it into place. He did the same with the other cane. Hopefully that would muffle the noise a bit.

He shoved the sword back into the sheath and rested the whole thing over his shoulder. Smudge scurried to the top of Jig's head for safety.

As the light dimmed toward blackness, Slash stepped closer. "Why didn't he kill you?"

"Who?" Jig asked.

"The chief. You defied him, and he let you live."

"A good thing, too," said Braf. "You hobgoblins need to treat us with a bit more respect, or else—"

The thump of Grell smacking Braf was quieter than usual. The cloth Jig had tied around the ends of her canes appeared to be working.

"Because of the truce," Jig said. That earned a disbelieving snort. "No, it's true. He's afraid that if I die, he'll lose what he got out of the deal."

"I've always wondered about that," said Slash. "A lot of us have. What possible reason could you give us to leave you rat-eaters alone?"

Jig brushed the fingers of his free hand along the wall for guidance as blackness swallowed the last of the lantern light. "He was sitting on his cushion when we arrived, right?" Jig asked. "Before the truce, when was the last time you saw him sit?"

"He didn't," Slash said. "He was always up and moving. Training the warriors, inspecting traps, overseeing the cats' handlers. He's chief. He doesn't have time to—"

"No, he *couldn't* sit. He had . . . an injury. I healed it." He grimaced at the memory. "Not an experience I'd choose to repeat."

"What?" From the sound of things, Braf was barely holding back his laughter. "You mean this whole truce was nothing but a reward for you healing a hobgoblin's ugly behind?"

Jig stopped. "What did you think, Braf? That I threatened them? That I stomped through the hobgoblin lair and told their chief I'd bring the full wrath of the goblins to bear if they didn't stop killing us?"

"Well . . . yeah."

Jig shook his head. How in the world had Braf survived to adulthood?

The smell of water told Jig they were close, as did the sudden flare of warmth from Smudge. Faint light shone from the beach ahead. Pixies? Jig hoped not. The hobgoblin chief hadn't known about the pixies, which suggested Veka was alone.

"Hello, Jig." Veka's voice was as cheerful and grating as ever. "I know you're there. You and your three companions. Why don't you come out and meet my new friends?"

So much for Veka being alone. How could she know they were coming? Jig wrapped his free hand around his sword handle. With the muscles of his sword arm bound and numb, this was the only way he'd be able to use it.

Veka *couldn't* know, not unless one of his group was possessed.

No, none of you have the taint of pixie magic.

Then how? They had been as quiet as tunnel cats stalking their prey. Veka couldn't have heard them. Jig backed away.

He had only gone a few steps when Smudge grew warmer. Had Smudge only now recognized the danger? Jig was moving away from Veka. That should be safer!

Jig ripped a handful of frayed threads from the bottom of his vest. Putting the threads in his mouth, he reached up to move Smudge to his shoulder. Much hotter, and Smudge would burn the rest of Jig's hair . . . which would give him the light he wanted, but Jig preferred to keep what little hair remained. Once the fire-spider was crouched on his leather pad, Jig twisted the ends of the threads together and reached up to poke Smudge from behind.

The threads burst into flame. "Eight eyes, and I can still scare you," Jig whispered. In the faint, dimming light, he could see Grell, Braf, and Slash standing behind him, weapons drawn.

"No light," Slash said, mimicking Jig's voice. "We don't want her to see us coming."

"Here," said Grell, holding out a rag. She touched one corner to the dying flame, and the tunnel brightened.

"What is that?" Braf asked.

"Another diaper. Useful things, really." She knotted the burning diaper around the end of Jig's sword. "Don't worry, it should be clean."

Normally the odor would have bothered Jig, but the ogres' torches seemed to have overloaded his sense of smell. And the diaper burned quite well, he had to admit.

Mold covered the tunnel walls, thriving in the damp lake air. Jig saw nothing out of the ordinary, aside from himself and his companions. Maybe Smudge was getting jumpy in his old age. Considering everything they had been through together, Jig could certainly understand that. He took another step back.

"What's wrong, Jig?" Veka shouted. "Running away won't save you."

"It's always worked before," Jig muttered. She

could see every move they made. "That's not fair," he whispered, turning toward the others.

As he did, a shadow overhead caught his attention. No, three shadows.

"Good fire-spider," Jig whispered. Clinging to minuscule irregularities in the obsidian, three lizard-fish watched Jig from the ceiling. They were so still they could have been a part of the rock, save for a slight quiver in the closest lizard-fish's tail. "First rule of traps," Jig muttered, remembering what Slash had said before. "Nobody ever looks up."

He tried to watch them without moving his head or giving Veka any indication that he had discovered her spies. He stepped toward Slash, a move that brought him almost directly underneath the lizard-fish. The tails of the other two began to twitch now. Jig recognized that motion. They tensed their muscles like that right before they lashed out with those poisonous spines.

Why hadn't they struck when Jig and the others passed underneath the first time? Something must have held them back. The same power that had driven them from the comfort of their lake, pushing them beyond the damp sand and onto hated rock. Veka.

Jig locked eyes with Slash, hoping the hobgoblin would understand. Slowly and deliberately, Jig turned his eyes upward.

"Look out!" Braf shouted. "Lizard-fish!"

Even as Jig thrust his sword at the closest lizard-fish, a part of his mind hoped he would live long enough to hide a few lizard-fish in Braf's undergarments.

His sword clanged into the ceiling, still sheathed, but the flaming diaper drove the lizard-fish back. They circled around, their tiny legs scrambling in unison. How could they cling upside down like that? Then he remembered Veka's levitation spell, back at the bottomless pit. She must have been practicing.

A rock cracked off the ceiling, and one of the lizard-fish fell. It wasn't dead, but its body bent sharply in the middle, and the tail was still.

Jig leaped back as the other two lizard-fish dropped to the ground to attack. One landed on its back, while the other scurried after Slash. Jig saw Grell crushing the inverted lizard-fish with her cane.

Slash was still unarmed, and he leaped out of the way as the lizard-fish charged. He grabbed Braf by one arm. As Braf squawked in protest, Slash kicked the back of the goblin's knees and flung him to the ground. Braf landed on his back, directly on top of the attacking lizard-fish.

As Braf scrambled to his feet, cursing and spitting, Jig could see the squished lizard-fish still stuck to the wooden shield strapped to Braf's back.

A crunching sound told him Grell had finished off the first lizard-fish, the one with the broken back. "Who threw that rock?" Jig asked, as much to distract Braf from going after Slash as anything else.

"Oh, that was me," said Braf. "I've always been good with rocks."

"You've always . . ." Jig's voice trailed off. He stepped away, shaking his head in disbelief. He waved his light around the floor until he found the stone Braf had thrown. Tucking it into his shirt, he wandered farther down the tunnel, collecting a few more. He came back and dumped the rocks into Braf's hands. Without a word, he snatched the hook-tooth away and handed it to Slash.

This time, there were no taunts from Veka as Jig approached the lake. He could hear the others following behind.

Jig peeked around the edge of the tunnel and nearly wet himself.

Hundreds of lizard-fish waited on the beach. Veka must have emptied the entire lake to amass so many. They stood facing the tunnel, each one about arm's length from the next. Aside from the occasional flicking of a tongue, they were absolutely motionless.

Then they spotted Jig. Each and every head turned in unison.

Braf tugged Jig's arm. "I think I'm going to need more rocks."

Veka herself sat atop the tunnel that led into the lake. The edges of her cloak trailed along the surface of the water. Her eyes were closed, but she was smiling at Jig. "I knew those pixies wouldn't capture you." She patted a pocket in her cloak, doubtless one of those stupid books. "The end of the Path brings the Hero to her final, fateful trial. I should have known destiny's decree would bring us together for this climactic confrontation. You've thwarted me at every pass, Jig Dragonslayer, mocking my efforts to master the mysteries of magic."

Jig rolled his eyes. Veka's "Heroic" dialog had grown even worse. Had she always used such clumsy alliteration?

He turned his attention back to the beach, particularly to the hobgoblin corpses scattered among the lizard-fish. He counted eight or nine, most of which had died within a few steps of leaving the tunnel. A few dead lizard-fish lay beside them.

"What we need is about a hundred more hobgoblins," Grell said.

"Don't worry, I can get her," said Braf. Before Jig could react, Braf stepped into the open and flung one of his rocks. It arced through the air, directly toward

Veka's head. The rock slowed as it neared, coming to a halt just before it hit Veka's forehead. Without opening her eyes, Veka reached out to tap the rock with her finger. It reversed direction, picking up every bit of speed it had lost and more.

Jig ducked, and the rock slammed into Braf's stomach, knocking him onto his back.

"Nice try," Veka called out.

"We should run," said Jig, keeping his voice low. "Her magic is too strong."

"Don't you have magic of your own?" asked Slash.

Jig shook his head. "She's using wizard magic. I only have priest magic."

What are you talking about?

Jig jumped. *I can't do wizardly things like Veka. I can only—*

Magic is magic. The universe doesn't divide its mysteries into priest magic and wizard magic any more than you divide the air down there into goblin air and hobgoblin air.

Wait, does that mean I'm a wizard? Jig's eyes widened. *But I have a sword! And I don't have a staff or a beard or long robes or—*

You're as bad as Veka, you know that?

Jig stiffened. *So why can't I use magic to make those lizard-fish turn on Veka?*

That kind of magic takes years of study and discipline.

A gritty wind began to blow. Veka held her fingers fanned toward the tunnel, her magic shooting sand into their faces.

Years of study and discipline, or getting possessed by pixies, Shadowstar amended.

Can you help me fight her magic or not? Jig demanded.

You'll need time to learn and practice that style of magic. Ask Veka to meet you back here in about a year or so.

Jig grimaced and spat sand from his mouth. "I can't fight her magically." He stared at the beach, using his fingers to block the worst of the sand from his eyes. Why hadn't Veka simply sent the lizard-fish into the tunnel to kill them?

He studied the lizard-fish more closely. Even the twitching of their tails was synchronized, just like the three that had been spying in the tunnel. The only time that had changed was when the lizard-fish dropped from the ceiling and their instincts had taken over. If Jig and the others hadn't been in the way, would the lizard-fish have left them alone? Free of Veka's control, they might have fled for the comfort of the beach.

How much power did Veka need to control all those lizard-fish? "We have to go out there," he whispered.

"If you don't want to be chief, there are easier ways to quit," said Grell.

Jig shook his head. Already the sandstorm was beginning to die down. She couldn't have much power left. Enough to deflect a few rocks maybe. "All the hobgoblins charged straight through the middle," he said, pointing to the line of bodies. "We need to split her focus. I don't think she can send them against us all at the same time."

"So you're saying only some of us will get killed?" Braf asked.

Jig's shoulders slumped. That was precisely what he was saying. And they reacted precisely the way he would have expected goblins and hobgoblins to react. Grell chuckled. Braf shook his head and backed away. Slash rapped the end of his hook-tooth against the wall, testing its weight.

"Surrender to me, Jig," Veka said. "Come with me, and your companions will survive. The pixies will spare you all, but only if Jig gives himself up."

"Sounds good to me," said Slash, stepping toward Jig.

"Wait!" Jig waved his sword at them. The flaming diaper dropped to the ground. He licked his sand-chapped lips, searching for sympathy and finding none.

If he tried to run, Slash and Braf would both be able to tackle him. Or Slash could loop the hook of his weapon around Jig's feet. Jig would never get past them both. "She's lying," said Jig. "Remember what Trockle said? The pixies want us all dead!"

"Trockle said they wanted all of the ogres dead," said Braf. "Who can blame them?"

"Braf, think about it," said Jig. "If she gives me to the pixies, who's going to help you the next time you get a fang rammed up your nose?"

He turned to Slash. "And you, hobgoblin. I guess this means you'll be heading back to your chief to tell him how one goblin female was too much for you to handle? Veka's been getting the better of you since she first laid eyes on you!"

He had saved Grell for last, mostly because he wasn't sure what he could say to convince her. She was too old to threaten, and too smart to fall for any bluff. He stared at the dwindling diaper fire on the ground, and then it came to him.

"Help me, and when we get back, I'll take you off nursery duty forever. You'll never wipe another goblin butt as long as you live."

Nobody spoke. Braf and Grell glanced at one another. Slash had a scowl on his face, but he always had a scowl on his face.

"You really think Veka and the pixies will just go

away and leave you all in peace if you give me to her?" Jig asked.

"I've been patient with you until now," shouted Veka. "It's time to make your choice."

The others looked at one another. Slash was the one who broke the silence. "I'd never hear the end of it," he said.

"Do you really think this will work?" asked Grell.

"Of course," Jig said.

Grell poked him with a cane. "Liar." Groaning, she limped toward the beach. When nobody else moved, she turned around again. "Well, what are you all waiting for?"

CHAPTER 12

"Great power carries a great cost. But there's no rule that says you *have to be the one to pay it."*
—Grensley Shadowmaster
From *The Path of the Hero (Wizard's ed.)*

Nowhere in either the ragged remnants of Veka's spellbook or in her copy of *The Path of the Hero* did there exist a single warning that the overuse of magic could leave the wizard with such a raging headache. She had never seen Jig suffer this kind of pain after one of his little healing spells. On the other hand, Jig had never tried to control well over a hundred individual minds.

She kept her eyes closed, seeing through the eyes of the lizard-fish and struggling to merge it all into a single coherent image. So long as she remained still, the feeling that a team of ogres were digging a hole through her skull wasn't quite as bad. Only a single ogre, and he wasn't using quite so heavy a pickax.

"How much longer?" Snixle whispered. By now, she

had gotten used to the pixie speaking with her mouth. He had a tendency to curl her tongue into a tube, though, and that was annoying. She could do without the twitching of her phantom wings, too. No wonder Snixle had a hard time controlling other creatures: he insisted on treating them like pixies.

Veka knew better. Her lizard-fish weren't miniature goblins to command. The more she tried to control their every movement, the clumsier they became. One of the hobgoblins had crossed half of the beach before she realized she could let the lizard-fish's own instincts take over, keeping only enough control to aim them at the appropriate prey.

"Throw more sand at them," Snixle said, trying to raise her hands. The pounding in her head grew worse. Three ogres worth, at least.

"I'm not sure I can." She probably could, but if Braf threw another rock at her, she might not have the strength to stop it. "Be patient. Jig will be out soon, one way or another. The others have a choice between their lives and his. I have no doubt what they will choose."

She concentrated on the lizard-fish closest to the tunnel. Lizard-fish didn't see very well. Their vision was blurred, and she had a harder time distinguishing colors. Not to mention how odd it was to have to look *up* at everything. On the other hand, lizard-fish had excellent hearing. Not as sharp as the giant bat she had ridden, but good enough to hear the goblins whispering. She couldn't quite hear Jig's words, but she could make out the rising fear in his voice. If they hadn't killed her three lizard-fish in the tunnels, she could have listened in on the conversation easily.

"Once Jig realizes he's out of options, he'll be ours," she said. Excitement made her shiver, which sent new pangs through her skull. This was worth the pain. Her former days of sitting alone in the back of the distillery, painstakingly struggling through the faded instructions of an old spellbook, were behind her now. Veka had become a wizard. Or sorceress. Sorceress sounded more impressive. *Veka the Sorceress.*

"At least send a few more lizard-fish into the tunnel," Snixle whined.

"Jig will come to me," Veka said. Whether he came willingly or was thrown out by his companions was another question.

As if he had heard her thoughts, Jig stepped out of the tunnel. Even through the blurry vision of the lizard-fish, Veka could see that he was breathing fast, like a rat about to be dropped into the stew pot. He had his sword drawn, but he didn't seem to be attacking the lizard-fish. The broken tip of his blade hung by his ankle. What was wrong with his arm? A sour taste hinted at pixie magic. The pixies had cursed his sword, from the look of things. Apparently Jig hadn't come through his last battle unscathed.

Behind him, Slash poked a weapon toward Jig's back, urging him onward. Veka's throat tightened. The hobgoblin was supposed to be dead! She had seen Grell shove a sword into his chest. Jig must have healed him, though she couldn't understand why he would waste that much magic on a hobgoblin.

Grell held a makeshift lantern of some sort that burned with a foul black smoke. Braf stood on Jig's other side, seemingly empty-handed.

"Go back," Veka shouted to them. "Tell your people not to resist, and the pixies may let you live."

"Right," Jig said, turning around to leave. "I'll pass that along."

"Not you," Veka snapped.

Jig stopped at the edge of the sand. His eyes fixed on the closest lizard-fish.

"Fear not, Jig Dragonslayer," she said. "They obey my will, and mine alone." To demonstrate, she commanded those lizard-fish nearest Jig to move aside, opening a path for him.

"Veka, do you really believe the pixies will let us live?" Jig shouted.

"They want this mountain," Veka called. "Whether we're dead or departed doesn't matter. The strongest will rule this place. Isn't that the way it's always been? Before it was Straum and the Necromancer who commanded the bulk of the mountain. The pixies are even more powerful, and they've chosen this place as their own."

She could see Jig shaking as he stepped forward, past the hungry lizard-fish. Veka gritted her teeth as she continued to clear his way. Would it kill him to walk a little faster?

"Drop your weapon," Snixle shouted, using her voice.

Jig struggled to raise his sword arm. Now Veka could see how leather ties secured the sword to his hand and arm. The skin had turned purple where it bulged between the cords. "I wish I could."

When he was halfway across the beach, Veka raised her hand. "That's far enough, Jig Dragonslayer. From this point onward, you shall submit to my will." Let him try to fight. His healing magic was no match for her power. She stilled the lizard-fish and opened her eyes, focusing on Jig alone. Controlling lizard-fish was one thing. This would be her first attempt at controlling another intelligent being. She grinned. Not just any being, but Jig Dragonslayer.

"Look out!" Snixle yanked her to one side, nearly

dumping her in the lake. A stone grazed her head, clattering off the top of the tunnel before splashing into the water. Veka recovered to see Jig running as fast as he could, his sword dragging through the sand. He wanted to test himself against her power? So be it. She drew herself to her feet.

Before she could do anything more, her vision erupted into rippling, blinding light. No, not her vision, but that of her lizard-fish. One segment of her sight now burned with orange fire, rippling through her composite view of the beach as the burning lizard-fish frantically tried to escape the flames. She severed the spell binding her to that lizard-fish, then turned to see what had happened.

Grell! She had flung a rag of some sort onto the lizard-fish. Even now another burning rag flew from her hand. Trapped by Veka's spell, the lizard-fish were unable to dodge, and another segment of her vision exploded into flame.

Veka cut that lizard-fish free, then commanded the others to surge forward. They had barely begun to move when yet another layer of her sight began to spin and whirl. Slash had crept out of the tunnel, and was using the hook end of his weapon to fling lizard-fish into the air.

Another lizard-fish died as a rock smashed its skull. Braf was throwing rocks again, aiming for the lizard-fish nearest Jig. She tried to intercept the next stone with magic, but Grell lit a third lizard-fish on fire, and Slash was still flinging them to and fro. Much more and Veka would lose the contents of her stomach.

Enough of this. She relaxed her control over those lizard-fish closest to their attackers. Some immediately scurried for the water, but others were too close to Slash and the goblins. Braf shouted a warning as the lizard-fish broke formation, and he began throwing at the lizard-fish racing toward Grell.

"Now we help them," Snixle said, bouncing with eagerness. Seizing control of her arms, he moved her through a quick binding, then cast a levitation spell. The spell ripped the hook-tooth from Slash's hands and sent it flying point-first toward Braf.

"Nice move," Veka said.

Slash kicked a lizard-fish and shouted, "Watch out!"

Braf yelped and ducked, and the point of the hook-tooth splintered against the wall.

"Drat," said Snixle.

"It doesn't matter," Veka assured him. Braf was almost out of rocks, and Slash was unarmed. She turned to Grell, casting another levitation spell to try to rip the rags from her hands.

Grell had a surprisingly strong grip for such an old goblin.

"Concentrate on Jig," Snixle said. Jig was the only one not fighting lizard-fish. He seemed solely intent on reaching Veka. He ran at top speed, several times practically stepping on lizard-fish in his haste.

Veka grinned in anticipation. Here was the battle she had dreamed about. Veka the Sorceress against Jig Dragonslayer. The new Hero stepping forth to vanquish the old. He had suppressed her for so long, but finally she was ready. She would have to make sure at least one of his companions survived to take the story back to the goblins and the hobgoblins. Grell would probably be the best choice. Slash was a hobgoblin, and Braf would mess everything up in the telling.

Veka strode toward the front edge of the tunnel, where it rose out of the lake. Here atop the arching stone, she had the advantage of height. Jig would have to scramble up to face her. Would it be better to wait for him, or should she strike him down as he climbed? The former would make a better story, but she might be wiser to kill Jig when he was most vulnerable. Strictly speaking, that might not be the most heroic decision, but it was certainly a goblin decision. She cast another levitation spell, lifting one of the lizard-fish and floating it spine-first toward Jig's back. She would plunge those spines into Jig's neck as he climbed, and—

The lizard-fish squealed in pain as a rock smashed it aside. Braf! She clenched her teeth, wishing she had tossed Braf into the middle of the lake, but there was no time. Jig was almost upon her. She braced herself, releasing the rest of the lizard-fish as she prepared to strike.

Jig disappeared.

Veka's mouth opened in disbelief. Jig had run straight into the tunnel. He hadn't even stopped to fight her. He was fleeing to the Necromancer's domain. What kind of Hero ran right past his enemy without even a token exchange of insults?

She stepped to the edge.

"What are you doing?" asked Snixle.

"The Necromancer's home was a maze of tunnels," she said. "Jig could disappear in there for days, and we'd never find him."

"You promised me Jig Dragonslayer," complained Snixle.

"Relax. We'll get him." Snixle was such a whiner. A wave of her hand cleared the lizard-fish from the tunnel mouth. Another spell gathered the flaming rags from the sand, summoning them to Veka. Jig might be fast, but he couldn't have reached the end of the tunnel yet.

Her magic compressed the rags into a single ball as she prepared to fire the flames into the tunnel. He would be badly burned, but he should survive. With the fire hovering over her hand, she jumped to the sand below.

Snixle screamed as Jig's broken sword took Veka in the chest.

Veka could hear lizard-fish splashing back into the lake. There was sand in her hair, and Jig's knees dug into her belly. Every time she inhaled, someone punched her in the chest. No, that was the sword. There was tremendous pressure, but less pain than she would have imagined.

Her body began to spasm as her lungs fought harder and harder for breath. "Snixle?" Her lips formed the word, but no sound came out.

Someone was shouting. Jig? He appeared to be in pain. With an effort, Veka managed to focus her eyes. Only one set of eyes . . . how odd.

Jig's arm was twisted at a painful angle, still lashed to the sword which had sunk into Veka's body. He must have wrenched his shoulder when Veka fell.

She would have laughed, had she been able to catch her breath. The only injury Jig had taken in his fight with Veka, and he had done it to himself.

Through watering eyes, she saw Grell come up beside Jig, carefully carrying a burning lizard-fish for light.

"Help me get her on her side," Jig said.

Grell was no use, but Veka felt a large boot slide beneath her shoulder, kicking her to one side. Jig flopped into the sand.

"Thanks, Slash," Jig said, spitting sand. He braced his feet on Veka's chest and yanked.

A true Hero would have made one final, defiant declaration as her blood spilled onto the sand, but all Veka could manage was a whimpered "Ouch." Then she passed out.

When she awoke, she found her face pressed against Slash's back. There was no light, but the smell of hobgoblin hair grease was unmistakable. Her arms were around his neck, and her feet dragged along the rock as he hauled her through the tunnel.

"Jig, she's drooling again," the hobgoblin complained. "It's gross."

"Could be worse," Braf said. "At least she's not bleeding on you."

Slash groaned, and Veka felt him swallow.

"You're alive?" Veka asked. It came out a dry croak. "All of you?"

Slash dropped her. Her fangs cut into her cheeks as her jaw hit the ground.

"The lizard-fish all fled back into the water when you dropped your spell," Jig said. "You kept them out of the lake for too long. Their skin was dry and cracked, and they were climbing over one another to get back."

So once again Jig had escaped unscathed. An entire army of lizard-fish, and he had won. All her power, and she was the one who had taken a sword through the stomach.

Hesitantly, afraid of what she might feel, she reached down to where she had felt the horrible pinching sensation of Jig's sword. There was a ragged hole in her cloak. Both the cloak and the shirt beneath were still sticky with blood. But her skin was soft and whole. Jig had healed her.

"You were under a pixie spell," Jig said. "They've been controlling you since you left Straum's cave."

Veka kept silent. Let him believe the pixies were responsible.

"What happened after you ran away?" Jig continued. She could hear him sitting down beside her, his sword dragging on the rock.

"I descended," she whispered. Her hands automatically moved to check her pockets. Both books were still there. She pulled out *The Path of the Hero*, holding it with both hands. "I descended through darkness and sludge and tunnel cats, and emerged into the silver light of Straum's cavern."

Her eyes watered as she quoted chapter five. " 'The Hero's Path shall descend into darkness, but upon the Hero's return, her symbolic rebirth, she shall have the power to triumph.' That's what Josca said. And I descended!" Her hands shook so hard she could barely hold the book. "I descended and returned, and you stabbed me!"

"You were trying to kill us," Braf said.

"You don't understand," Veka said, tears tickling her face. "I was supposed to be strong. Jig wasn't supposed to beat me. All that magic, and he still beat me."

She flung the book away. Pages flapped, and the book thumped against the tunnel wall.

"Watch it," snapped Slash. "Stupid goblin. Jig should have left you for the lizard-fish. Gods know there's enough of you to go around."

Veka sniffed. She couldn't summon up the slightest bit of anger at Slash's jab. It was no different from the taunts goblins had flung at her all her life. Slash was right. Jig should have left her to die. Now there would be new songs of Jig Dragonslayer and his victory over Vast Veka at the lake.

"I did everything Josca said," she mumbled. She had followed the Path, descended into darkness, acquired an admittedly unusual mentor, and returned to face her greatest challenge. But Josca said the Hero was supposed to win.

"The pixies said the queen had come into our world," Jig was saying. "Do you know where she went? How many pixies are we up against? Where are all their ogres?"

"I don't know," Veka whispered. *The Hero was supposed to win.*

"She's useless," Slash said.

"Like a hobgoblin guard who's afraid of blood?" asked Braf.

"Shut up, both of you," snapped Jig. "The pixies will know Veka's no longer enchanted. Next they'll probably send their ogres up to wipe us out."

Jig had beaten her.

"So what?" asked Braf. "They'll have to go through the hobgoblins before they can get to us."

"You rat-eating coward!" shouted Slash.

"We've taken the brunt of every group of adventurers, explorers, and heroes who ever came to this mountain," Braf shouted back. "It's about time you hobgoblins took a turn."

"Or else the pixies could wait and let us kill each other," Grell said.

Veka coughed and spat. Evidently she had gotten a bit of blood in her throat after Jig stabbed her. It tasted awful. "Snixle said something about bringing the queen to her new home."

"Snixle?" asked Braf.

"The pixie who . . . who controlled me." She

flushed, ashamed. Let them think it was Snixle who had lost the fight against Jig Dragonslayer, not Veka.

"Where was this home?" Jig asked. "In Straum's cavern, or somewhere else?"

She shook her head. "He didn't say."

"Why leave Straum's cave at all?" Slash asked. "That's the safest place in the whole mountain. In all those years, how many adventurers ever reached the dragon?"

"The cave is too cramped for pixies," Jig muttered. He was sitting so close. She could reach into her cloak and pull out her knife. In the darkness he would never know it was coming.

No, his pet fire-spider would know. Smudge would warn Jig, and Jig would stab her again. No matter what she tried, Jig would beat her. Just as he had beaten the dragon and the Necromancer. Just as he had beaten the pixies who tried to capture him. Just as he had beaten her at the lake, destroying Snixle's spell.

"How did you overcome the pixie's control over me?" she asked.

"Steel," Jig said. He sounded distracted. "The pixies called it death-metal. Something about it disrupts their magic. That's how we freed Slash. When he got stabbed . . ." His voice grew faint, barely even a whisper. "Oh, no."

"What?" asked Grell.

"The pixies told me I opened the way for them when I killed Straum," he said softly. "They said it was my fault. Do you remember what Straum's lair was like, right after he died?"

"Full of clutter and junk," said Braf. "Books, pots, paintings, coins, armor, every bit of garbage that old lizard had collected in his lifetime."

"Including weapons and armor," said Jig. "Every sword, every knife, every shield and breastplate, all of it was mounted on the cave walls. He lined the whole cave with steel, and after he died—"

"We picked the place clean," said Braf. "Oh. Whoops."

Veka felt herself nodding. "Snixle said it took powerful magic to open a gateway. The greatest concentration of magic over here would have been Straum's cave, where the dragon's own power had seeped into the rock over thousands of years."

"We should get back to the lair," Jig said. "We'll send some of the goblins to help the hobgoblins, in case the ogres come up through the lake."

"Kralk will never agree to that," Veka said.

Slash began to chuckle. "I don't think Kralk's going to object too much, seeing how she's dead."

"Dead?" Veka asked. "Then who . . . ?" She didn't finish the question. She knew. Who else could it be? While Veka had been descending and returning and wasting her time trying to master pixie magic, Jig had not only fought off ogres and pixies, he had taken control of the goblins as well.

"Come on," said Jig.

Veka trudged along behind them. Her foot brushed her copy of *The Path of the Hero* where it had fallen. She hesitated, then continued after the others.

Veka remained silent as Slash tried to convince the hobgoblin guards she was their prisoner and that Jig was taking her back to the goblin lair to make her pay for what she had done. The hobgoblins were reluctant at first. One kept twitching the leash to his tunnel cat and talking about how hungry the beast was.

Then Jig stepped forward. He looked filthy and exhausted. In that pitifully small, squeaky voice of his, he said, "We fought through an army of enchanted lizard-fish to get this goblin." He grabbed his sword in both hands and pointed the bloody tip at the closest guard. "Move aside."

The hobgoblins backed down. Jig was small, his weapon was laughable, and any one of the guards could have killed him bare-handed, but they backed down. How did he do it? He didn't boast, he didn't raise his voice, he didn't even try to threaten them. He simply . . . told them the truth.

Jig had defeated the lizard-fish, and Veka as well, and the hobgoblins knew it. They knew what Jig Dragonslayer could do. Jig didn't have to boast. He simply had to remind them who he was. Jig was a Hero.

Two goblins stood outside the goblin lair, and they actually appeared to be standing guard.

"Come with us," said Jig. The guards grinned. Why wouldn't they? Jig had just ordered them to stop working.

Veka could feel the tension the moment she stepped into the lair. The muck pits were all full and burning. Goblins cast wary looks at the entrance until they saw who it was. A pair of young goblins outside the kitchen were strangely quiet as they played Stake the Rat. From the look of it, the female had a three-rat lead.

"Now what?" asked Slash.

Jig raised his battered sword over his head and slammed it three times against the ground. Sparks flew from the steel, and a shard of metal broke away, but it got the goblins' attention.

Jig took a deep breath. "The pixies and the ogres have taken over the lower caverns. Soon they'll be coming after us. I'm betting they'll come through the lake to attack the hobgoblins."

Immediately the goblins began to whisper to one another, setting odds and making wagers. A few goblins gave a tentative cheer. Veka kept her attention on Jig. His face shone with sweat, and his clothes were torn and bloody. His sword arm hung limp at his side, and he kept playing with his right fang. Hardly the picture of a Hero.

Jig swallowed and said, "So we're going to help them."

Silence blanketed the lair, broken only by the occasional cough.

"Help the hobgoblins or the pixies?" someone asked.

"The hobgoblins," Jig said.

"Why?"

Veka could see Jig searching the crowd, trying to pick out the speaker. Not that it mattered. Every goblin was silently asking the same thing.

"Why not let the hobgoblins wear them down, then we can finish off whoever survives?" yelled another goblin. Veka thought it was one of the guards from outside, but she wasn't sure.

Nobody had ever questioned Kralk's orders. Then again, Kralk had never given such bizarre orders.

Veka waited to see what Jig would do. How would he prove himself, bringing the goblins into agreement and obedience?

But Jig simply stood there, looking more and more nervous. If he rubbed that fang anymore, he was going to twist it right out of his jaw. The goblins were starting to whisper among themselves again.

Veka couldn't believe it. Jig didn't know what to do.

Grell's canes rapped the floor as she stepped forward. Her dry fingers dug into Jig's shoulder, pushing him aside. "You idiots couldn't stop one lone ogre from marching through this place before, and he wasn't even trying to kill you. What are you going to do against an army of 'em? Hobgoblins too, most likely. Every hobgoblin who falls could be enchanted, sent out to fight the goblins. If we help the hobgoblins fight, we might be able to do some damage, but only if you stop asking stupid questions and start listening to what the chief has to say!"

"There's an even better reason," said Braf, coming around on Jig's other side. "If we help the hobgoblins, then every time you see one of those yellow-skinned freaks, you can gloat about how we had to save their worthless hides from the ogres!"

That earned a rousing cheer. Several goblins pointed at Slash, snickering. Others were grinning and nodding to one another.

Slash, on the other hand, was staring at Braf and clenching his fists.

"You should do it because it's Jig's idea." The words slipped out before Veka even realized she had spoken. She almost thought Snixle had taken control of her again, but no . . . the words had come from her. She saw Jig's mouth open in disbelief.

She couldn't even look at him as she stepped forward to address the goblins. "Jig fought an ogre and won, down in Straum's cavern. He killed two pixies. He killed the Necromancer. He killed Straum himself. Not only did he win every one of those battles, he kept his companions alive as well." She sniffed and wiped her nose on the sleeve of her robe. "If Jig says we have to help the hobgoblins, you can bet it's the only way we're going to survive."

"Actually we're probably going to die," Jig whispered. He was still staring at Veka.

"I'm thinking you shouldn't mention that," Grell answered just as softly.

Many of the goblins were already swinging their weapons in anticipation. Veka saw one warrior nearly slice the ear from his neighbor with a crude hand ax. Others had begun to sing "The Song of Jig."

"The strongest warriors will go to the hobgoblins to help fight," Jig shouted. "The rest stay here. Some of you will barricade the lair, and a handful will come with me."

Only Veka was close enough to hear him mutter, "And you're not going to like where we're going."

CHAPTER 13

"No plan survives the first encounter with your enemy, so why bother to make one?"
—Farnok Daggerhand, Goblin Warleader

Twenty-three goblins waited outside the doorway as Jig and Slash searched through Kralk's armory, collecting every knife, sword, mace, morningstar, and ax they could find. Anything would do, so long as it was steel.

"Any reason you didn't share these toys with the goblins heading out to the hobgoblin lair?" Slash asked.

"I'm betting they won't be fighting pixies," Jig said. "Not many, at any rate. The pixies will stay in their own world as much as possible. That's where they're strongest. And if I'm right, we're going to need all the help we can get."

He picked up a quiver of steel-tipped arrows. He had also spotted an enormous bow, but he hadn't been able to find a bowstring. Not that he or any other goblin knew how to shoot a bow. And the only crossbow had been disassembled so Slash could use the string in one of his traps. But the arrows were long and heavy enough he might be able to use them as spears, which could be useful against an airborne enemy.

He had to make several attempts to get the leather strap over his pixie-cursed arm, but once he managed, the quiver fit fairly well. Jig turned his head to search for more weapons, and the end of an arrow poked him in the ear.

Slash laughed as he stooped to pick up a nasty-looking barbed trident.

"Leave that," said Jig. "Leave everything longer than your arm."

"Why?" Slash asked. "You goblins not strong enough for real weapons?" He hefted a thick quarterstaff with iron bands around either end. "This could do some serious damage without drawing much blood, don't you think?"

Jig ignored him. Carrying weapons under his arm, he stepped through the doorway, being careful not to trigger Slash's traps. Several knives clanged onto the ground. Jig dumped the rest in a pile.

"Take whatever you can carry, but don't overload yourself," Jig said. He studied the goblins closely as they scrambled to arm themselves. He hadn't tried to pick and choose who would accompany him. Instead he had let the goblins choose for him when he ordered the strongest warriors to help the hobgoblins.

As a result, Jig had been left with the weakest goblins in the lair: the scrawny, thin-limbed goblins who slunk into the shadows and hid from danger. The ones who survived through thievery and betrayal rather than facing their enemies head-on. The ones who had to be twice as cunning as the rest of the lair just to survive. These were the goblins Jig wanted.

Braf and Slash towered over the others. Even Jig didn't feel like such a runt among this crowd. Most of the weapons had disappeared, and the goblins eyed one another warily as they waited for Jig to speak. However, the bulk of their suspicion was reserved for Jig himself.

Jig kept his back to the wall. They weren't going to like this. He thought about Farnax and Pynne, remembering their reactions to the cramped tunnels of the mountain. If the other pixies felt the same way, they wouldn't stay in Straum's cave. No, if Jig was right, there was only one place they would go.

"The pixie queen sent a handful of pixies into our world to prepare the way," he said. "They killed or enslaved most of the ogres, but instead of moving up into the Necromancer's tunnels, they burrowed through the rock until they reached the bottomless pit, where they've been hunting and destroying the giant bats."

To a goblin, a cave was the safest place to hide, with solid stone protecting you on all sides. For pixies, safety lay in the open. They would choose a place where they could fly, where they could ride the wind, and where any attacker would face an enormous disadvantage.

"They're building their lair in the bottomless pit," Jig said. "That's where they'll bring the queen. If we can get there before they do, we might be able to ambush them."

As he had expected, his own companions were first to understand the implications. Unless they wanted to make their way through the Necromancer's maze and a possible ogre attack, there was only one way to get back to the bottomless pit.

"I still smell like goblin filth," Slash shouted. "Now you expect me to climb back down through—"

"No, I don't," Jig said. He had counted on Slash being the first one to complain. "This is a goblin mission. I'll understand if you prefer to stay behind, where it's safer."

"I'll go!" Braf yelled. "The hobgoblin might be a coward, but I'm—"

"Who are you calling coward, rat-eater?" Slash demanded, shoving goblins aside as he advanced on Braf.

Jig's plan had worked. Now all he had to do was keep them from killing one another.

"I'll go too." Veka's flat voice momentarily drew the attention away from Slash and Braf.

"Why, so you can get yourself pixie-charmed again?" Slash asked.

"You were enchanted too," Braf pointed out.

Grell hit them both, one with each cane. Braf took it on the shoulder, and Slash received a sharp smack on the knee. Grell staggered forward a few steps before recovering her balance. Then, to Jig's surprise, she whacked him on the arm as well. It was his sword arm, and the flesh was so numb he barely felt it.

"Stop standing there with your mouth hanging open," Grell snapped. "You're chief, remember? Try to act like it."

Jig nodded. "We're going to climb down through the garbage, to a tunnel that will take us to the bottomless pit." He glanced at Braf and Slash. "You two stay in the back. Make sure nobody tries to sneak away. You too," he added, nodding at Grell.

Grell raised both eyebrows but said nothing as Jig

turned to lead the goblins toward the waste pit. More than pixies or the bottomless pit, this was the part of his plan he had been dreading. But it had to be done.

He stroked Smudge, perched comfortably on his left shoulder. Climbing down the pit was too dangerous . . . too vulnerable. It wasn't a question of whether one of the goblins would try to kill him. It was simply a matter of when.

He strained to keep his sword from dragging along the ground. His good ear twisted back as he listened for every whisper, every footstep. What was taking them so long? They didn't actually believe everything Veka had said about Jig being so dangerous and heroic, did they?

There it was. A slight change in footfalls. One set drawing nearer, while the others pulled back, giving the chosen goblin room to make his or her move. Smudge crept closer to Jig's neck, warmer, but not yet hot enough to burn.

Jig kept walking. His timing would have to be perfect. What were they waiting for? Working up the nerve to attack? His back was turned. How hard could it be?

There, a quick indrawn breath. At the same time, Smudge's feet seared Jig's skin. Jig lunged forward, hunching his head and shoulders as he grabbed his sword arm with his free hand and spun, hoisting the blade into the path of his would-be killer.

His attacker slammed onto the broken sword, knocking them both down. Jig found himself staring into the face of Relka, one of Golaka's kitchen assistants. The knife in her hand clattered to the ground.

Jig kicked her off of his sword. His shoulder felt as though someone had ground metal shavings into the socket.

Relka wasn't dead. She clutched her bleeding stomach and scooted back, her huge eyes never leaving Jig's sword.

"Stay here," Jig said. "Have Golaka bandage you up. If you're still alive when we get back, I'll heal you then. Assuming we get back."

He turned his back on Relka, trying not to feel too bad as she crawled away. He hoped she would survive. She made the best snake egg omelettes. But her attack had done what Jig hoped. The other goblins looked terrified.

Jig shook his head. *It wasn't hard to guess one of them would try to kill me.*

Maybe, said Shadowstar. *But think about what they saw. You just took out a potential assassin without even looking. They won't try to stab you in the back again any time soon.*

No, Jig agreed glumly. He had never imagined he would feel sympathy for Kralk. *Next time, they'll try something sneakier.*

Climbing up through the waste pit had been bad enough. Climbing down, leading a group of twenty-plus goblins and one grumbling hobgoblin was far worse. Only the cramped confines of the pit, which kept them all moving one at a time, prevented bloodshed. Even so, goblins were constantly stepping on one another's hands, or dislodging dirt and worse onto the ones below.

Jig had ordered several goblins to carry muck lanterns. As an unexpected bonus, the light and heat seemed to frighten off the tendriled slugs that had stung Jig before. Unfortunately, the goblins kept accidentally igniting the waste that clung to the sides of the pit.

Even with several ropes anchored in the goblin lair, it was a miracle nobody had fallen.

Jig relaxed his grip and let himself drop a bit, away from the bulk of the group. His sword tip caught a rock, jamming his arm and nearly breaking his elbow before he managed to stop. To make things worse, his spectacles kept sliding down his nose. He tried to use his shoulder to scoot them into position, but they immediately slid back down his sweaty face.

"How many ogres and pixies do you think we'll get to kill?" Braf asked, nearly falling as he shoved past another goblin to catch up with Jig.

"None if you keep talking so loudly," Jig said. The noise shouldn't give them away, not this far from the pit, but better to silence Braf now. They should be about halfway down by now, roughly level with the Necromancer's maze.

Braf bit his lip and nodded.

Jig frowned as he studied the other goblin. "You didn't get a weapon?"

Braf tried to shrug, and ended up hoisting his body higher on the rope. "I stocked up on rocks instead. If we're going to fight pixies at the pit, I thought we'd want some kind of ranged weapon."

Jig hesitated. "You thought of that yourself?"

"No," Braf said quickly. A strange, frightened expression flashed across his face, then disappeared again. "Grell did. She told me I'd better stick to rocks, or else I'd hurt myself." He scrunched up his forehead. "Or did she say *she'd* hurt me?"

Jig climbed a bit lower, thinking hard. "Braf, back when I was trying to get the goblins to help the hobgoblins, you told them they should do it because we'd be able to gloat. What made you say that?"

"Because it's true!"

Maybe, but it had also been the perfect thing to say, the pebble that had started a rock slide, bringing the lair around to Jig's plan. Just as Braf had done later, outside Kralk's quarters, when he mocked Slash. Once again Braf had helped to persuade the goblins to do exactly what Jig wanted them to do.

Jig squinted up through sweat-smeared lenses, and in that instant, he saw it. Braf was studying Jig . . . trying to figure out whether Jig had guessed his secret? The expression vanished as soon as Jig noticed, but it was too late.

"You're not as dumb as you pretend to be, are you?" Jig whispered.

Braf's eyes narrowed. Suddenly Jig was very aware of exactly how big and strong Braf was. And Jig's sword was pointed down toward his feet, with no easy way to lift it here in the cramped confines of the pit.

"Maybe," Braf said, his voice as quiet as Jig's.

They were still at least a body's length ahead of the next closest goblin. Higher up Jig could hear Grell cursing and trying to rearrange her canes. Slash was swearing right back, threatening to cut the rope that held her harness. Others still stood around up top, waiting to follow.

Jig turned his attention back to Braf. "Then why—"

"You'd do the same thing if you were me."

Jig stared, not understanding.

"How does a goblin captain take command of his group?" Braf asked.

"The same way a goblin becomes chief. Kill the former captain, along with anyone else who opposes you."

"Look at me, Jig. Big, strong, and threatening. If you're . . . well, someone like you, you'll see me as a bully, and you'll try to kill me in my sleep. If you're a warrior, you'll see me as competition. If you're a captain, you see me as a threat. If you don't kill me outright, you'll send me out to fight tunnel cats or ogres or order me to march into a hobgoblin trap. You think it's coincidence there are no old goblin warriors?"

Slowly, Jig shook his head.

"So I play dumb. I drop my weapon. I let others play their stupid tricks." He grimaced and rubbed his nose. "I didn't expect to get a fang punched up my nose, but the point is, if I'm dumb, I'm not a threat. The teasing and the jokes are annoying but better than the alternative. Oh, and a carrion-worm is about to crawl onto your hand."

Jig yanked his hand away from the wall, which knocked his back and shoulder into the rough stone. The pale, segmented worm was almost as big as his arm. Jig waited until the worm squirmed away, dropping into the darkness with a bit of charred meat and bone clutched in its black pincers.

"So why do you let Grell hit you all the time?" Jig asked.

Braf laughed. "Grell knows what I'm doing. She helps me. I can pretend to be stupid, and she stops me before I do anything too dangerous." He gave Jig a sheepish smile. "It's kind of fun."

"Fun?"

"Sure. You're always so uptight, so afraid of messing everything up. With me, people expect it." His smile faded. "Naturally, if you tell anyone, I'll strip the skin from your body and feed it to the worms."

"Naturally," said Jig.

Braf grinned. "Hey, when did it get so cold down here?"

Sweating and warm from climbing, Jig hadn't really

noticed, but Braf was right. The stone was cool to the touch, and the air below . . . "Can someone lower one of those lanterns?"

A flare of heat from Smudge warned him just in time. Jig twisted, pressing himself to one side as a burning muck lantern tumbled past, splattering green flames as it went. Braf swore and flicked a bit of muck from his arm. Overhead, goblins yelled and cried out in pain as they tried to pat themselves out. Then the goblin who had dropped the lantern squealed as his fellows pummeled him for his mistake.

Still, it did what Jig needed. The droplets of burning muck illuminated a silver fog creeping slowly up the pit below.

"Where are we?" The words echoed through the abandoned cavern.

Jig wasn't sure who had asked the question. He could feel the heat of the goblins gathered behind him. He took a few steps to the side, trying to get his back to the wall. He probably didn't need to worry. These goblins hadn't seen the pixies' world yet, and they were too shaken to think about killing him . . . at least for the moment.

The rippling texture of the obsidian combined with the lead-colored frost created the illusion of being surrounded by molten metal. The light of their lanterns had taken on the same bronze tinge he remembered from his excursion into Straum's cavern.

Shadowstar? Can you hear me?

Silence. The pixies' world was expanding much faster than he had expected. That couldn't be good.

Jig looked around, and for one panicked moment he wasn't sure which tunnel led out to the pit. Everything was so different with the fog and the snow. They had come from the right, hadn't they? Rubbing his fang, he began following the cavern wall. His sword dragged lines through the frost beside him.

"This looks a bit like our lair," Braf commented.

Jig glanced around. Braf was right. The cavern was larger, but he could easily imagine goblins or hobgoblins making a home of this place. He hadn't seen much the last time he was here, being too eager to escape, but now he looked more closely. Bits of rotted rope still circled one of the obsidian pillars, far too old to have been left by the ogres. When they reached the tunnel, Jig spotted a rusted hinge hanging from a scrap of wood beside the opening. He tried to pry it free, and the wood crumbled in his hand.

Jig had never heard of goblins living this far down, but clearly someone used to inhabit this cavern. Their own lair might look like this one day, if they failed to stop the pixies.

"Keep your weapons ready," Jig said as he stepped into the tunnel. "The last time we were here, we faced ogres and pixies both."

"And rock serpents," Braf piped up. "Don't forget about them!"

The response from the other goblins was less than enthusiastic. Jig saw several glance longingly into the cavern, no doubt wondering if they would be better off climbing back through the garbage. Veka remained at the rear of the group. She hadn't spoken at all since they left the goblin lair. He still wasn't sure bringing her along was such a great idea, but so far she seemed safe enough, if a bit subdued.

"Come on," Jig said, hurrying into the tunnel.

They passed a mass of carrion-worms, a knee-high mound of the squirming creatures huddled together to one side of the tunnel. They seemed to be climbing over one another, all trying to get to the top of the pile.

"They're freezing to death," Grell said. "They pile together for warmth. We do something similar with the babies, tossing them all into a single crib when the air gets too chilly." She kept her arms close to her chest, and she kept stamping her feet. She was wearing an old pair of sandals, and her toes had already begun to turn a paler shade of blue.

The cold appeared to be even harder on the rock serpents. Jig saw several snakes coiled into tight spirals for warmth. They weren't dead—one snake still struck out when a goblin poked it with his sword—but the snake's reflexes were so slow the goblin actually survived the attack. For all practical purposes, the tunnel was unguarded.

"Smother the lanterns," Jig whispered. As the flames died, he began to make out the open space at the end of the tunnel. A long stiff shape lay on the ground near the edge: Veka's staff, right where it had fallen when Slash kicked her in the head. Jig glanced back. Veka had seen it too. She stepped past him, her eyes never leaving the staff. Several of the beads and cords broke free as she pried the staff up, leaving a perfect impression of the wood in the frost and ice. Jig wrapped his good hand around the handle of his sword, wondering if Veka was about to try something heroic again. But she seemed content to stand there staring at the staff.

Jig edged around her, wondering if the pixies had damaged her brain. Some of the other goblins were pointing and whispering. Jig heard muffled laughter. They hadn't seen what Veka could do, back at the lake. He held his breath, but Veka appeared deaf to their jokes.

Praying it stayed that way, Jig crept to the edge of the tunnel. Wind blew snow and dirt into his face. The buzzing of wings warned him, but even so, when he looked out into the pit and saw the swarm of pixies darting through the darkness, he found himself wondering if he should just throw himself over the edge. At least that way he might hit one on the way down.

They had changed the pit itself. Shimmering silver bubbles, each one larger than Jig himself, covered the walls. In most places, the bubbles pressed against each other, their sides flattening where they touched. In one spot the bubbles were two or three layers thick.

As Jig watched, a pair of green pixies flew out to hover near a bare patch of rock. These were smaller than the pixies Jig had seen before, and they had only two wings, not four. Their lights faded somewhat as they touched the stone. When they drew back their hands, a thin transparent bubble followed. Ripples of color spread across the bubble's surface as it grew. The pixies floated, motionless except for the blur of their wings, as the bubble grew. When it was as large as the others, they dropped away. The color continued to spread across the bubble's surface, rings bouncing back and forth before gradually fading to a more uniform silver.

One of the green pixies pressed her hand against the bubble. Her hand disappeared, and the pixie squeezed through the surface and disappeared inside the silver shell. Her companion floated back, allowing the wind to carry him up until he reached another patch of bare rock.

"What is it?" Braf asked.

Jig took a deep breath. "They're building a hive."

The other goblins had crept up behind Jig, straining to see into the pit. A younger goblin, Grop, was leaning so far out that his shadow was visible on the roof of the tunnel. Jig grabbed him by the hair and yanked him back.

"How are we supposed to fight that?" Grop asked, rubbing his head.

"Quiet," Jig snapped. He didn't think anyone could hear them over the wind, but he wasn't about to take any chances. He lay down in the frost and peered up, toward the old bridge connecting the Necromancer's tunnels. A handful of pixies buzzed around the bridge. Darker shapes resolved into ogre warriors as a pixie flew past. Wonderful.

"It gets worse," Veka said.

Jig didn't even blink. "Of course it does."

She pointed down to the thickest cluster of bubbles, down where the pixie tunnel emerged from Straum's cavern. "The queen is down there."

"Are you sure?"

Veka nodded. "It's hard to describe. I can feel their magic, like a wind."

"Do you think maybe, just maybe, that could be the wind?" Slash said.

Veka ignored him. "It's like she's sucking the magic into herself and drawing the rest of the pixies to her. Not physically, but their magic, their minds, everything about them revolves around the queen."

Jig adjusted his spectacles. He thought he saw a spot of pure white light below, but it was hard to be sure. What had Pynne said? *None can look upon a pixie queen without loving her.*

Either that light wasn't the queen, or Jig was too far away to be affected. The only thing he felt was sheer, gut-churning fear.

"We should go back," said Grop. "We can help the others barricade the lair and—"

"And what?" asked Jig. The pixies were moving too quickly. Look what they had accomplished in a single day. "Why didn't they leave guards in this tunnel?"

"This crack isn't easy to see from out there," said Veka. "The overhang makes it look like part of the rock. The pixies aren't telepathic. If you killed the only two who found the tunnel, they might not know about it yet. And Snixle . . . he didn't tell anyone about me and Slash."

"Lucky us," Slash muttered.

Jig peeked into the pit again, trying to see how high the pixie's world reached. Only the occasional spark marked the expanding border between their world and his own, but that border appeared to be well past the Necromancer's old bridge. "They needed weeks to take over Straum's cavern," Jig whispered. At this rate their world would overtake the goblin lair within a day at most.

"We need to cut off the source of their magic," said Veka.

"I know that," Jig snapped. "I thought we could destroy their gateway after we killed the queen and eradicated her army of pixies. And then I figured I'd resurrect Straum the dragon and use his breath to toast my breakfast rats."

He closed his eyes, trying to calm himself. Why worry about future battles when he probably wouldn't survive this one?

"Are you sure we shouldn't go back?" asked another of the goblins, Var.

Jig shook his head. They were spreading too quickly. If he and the others left, that hive would fill the pit by the time they returned. "The pixies are like insects," he said. Magical bugs with ogre slaves and enough magic to conquer the whole mountain, but bugs nonetheless. "What do you do when you find wasps building a nest in the lair?"

"Burn it," said Var.

"Knock it down and use a stick to hide it in Captain Kollock's chamber pot," muttered Grop.

Jig grinned despite his fear, wishing he had thought to try that. "Everything the pixies do, they do for their queen. We attack the nest, kill the queen, and their whole purpose for coming here is gone."

Grell scratched her ear. "You know, I've seen wasps get pretty riled up when someone pokes their nest. Even if we manage to kill the queen, we're still going to have an army of angry pixies after our hides."

"We'll have that anyway," Jig said. He was trying very hard not to count the number of bubbles. How long would it take them to produce a pixie for every chamber in that nest? If pixies reproduced as quickly as they did everything else . . .

"Jig's right." Veka stepped away from the others, her staff clutched tightly in both hands. "As long as the queen lives, every pixie you see will fight to the death. With her gone, they might be willing to negotiate." Her eyes widened, as if she were surprised at the words coming from her own mouth. "Like Jig did with the hobgoblins."

"Or they might kill us all for revenge," said Slash.

Veka shook her head. She closed her eyes, and said, "The climax of the Hero's journey is the battle through death. No reasonable person could hope to survive this final conflict, but the true Hero shall discover a way." Her smile was wistful, almost sad. "This is that battle, and Jig will get you through it."

Grell shrugged. "Only one way to find out."

Before Jig could think up something inspirational to say, Veka moved closer. Jig started to back away, but she reached out and tapped his sword arm with her staff.

"What are you—" Jig stopped in midprotest as the leather cords on his arm began to loosen. The ends slipped from his shoulder. "You mean you could have done that the whole time?"

"I'm sorry," Veka whispered. "I didn't . . . I couldn't bring myself to try any magic until now. I should have, but—" She swallowed. "The spell is straightforward, even easier than controlling the lizard-fish. Just a simple command to the residual life in the leather."

The sword dropped to the ground. Jig winced and glanced out at the pit, but the pixies didn't appear to have noticed the sound. His fingers were still molded to the shape of the hilt, and deep wrinkles marked his arm. The flesh was so pale it was almost white, with dark lines and bruises where the skin had pinched and folded over itself. "So why didn't you—"

That was as far as he got, and then the blood began to flow through his veins again. Jig clamped his jaw, biting back a high-pitched squeal as he fell back. With every heartbeat, a thousand hammers smashed the bones of his arm and hand. Tunnel cats chewed the joints from the inside out, and the skin was molten lead.

Jig stared at the frosted rock overhead until tears blurred the patterns into a field of gray. If he could have reached his sword, he would have cut off his own arm at the shoulder to stop the pain. *Shadowstar?*

The god couldn't hear him, not down here. He felt fingers prying at his jaw, shoving something between his teeth: one of Grell's sugar-knots, laced with klak beer. He bit down on the sugar-knot so hard his teeth crushed the candy inside.

"Give him a little time." Grell's voice sounded as if it were coming from the far end of a tunnel.

Easy for her to say. His arm felt as if it had swollen to triple its normal size, but when he opened his eyes, he found he was mistaken. It was only double.

Gradually the pain began to ebb a bit, becoming a deep prickly feeling that began at the skin and penetrated all the way to the marrow. Jig grabbed his sword with his left hand and used it like one of Grell's canes to push himself to his feet.

"See, I told you he'd be fine," said Grell. "So tell us how you plan to get through this battle, oh heroic one?"

Jig scowled and sucked on the crushed remains of his sugar-knot. He had been wondering the exact same thing. He could tell the other goblins weren't happy about the situation. Goblins weren't subtle when it came to expressing displeasure. Weapons drawn, they were moving into a rough circle, trapping Jig between the edge of the pit and a lot of sharp steel.

Jig raised his sword. His right arm was still useless, but so was the sword, really. The blade had lost another chip from the end. Old blood stained part of the hilt blue. The hilt itself was bare wood, held in place only by the dinged, worn pommel. A long string of leather dangled down to the floor. The nicked, dented edges of the blade would have a hard time cutting even the skin of a child. Unfortunately, it was all he had.

The goblins stopped. "Well?" asked one.

"Well what?"

"When do we attack?"

They weren't preparing to kill him. They were preparing to kill pixies. They . . . they were getting ready to follow him into battle. To follow *him*!

He turned back to the pit, trying to flex his arm.

His hand and wrist twitched a bit. He spotted Braf watching him. Now that Jig knew what to look for, he saw past the slack-jawed expression to the way Braf's eyes shifted from Jig to the other goblins to the pit and back, watching for threats from either side.

"Braf, what's the best way to stir up a big wasp hive?" he asked.

Braf grinned and fished a rock out of his trousers.

"How many rocks are you carrying down there?" Jig asked with a grimace.

"Don't ask. I'm fine as long as I don't sit down." He slipped past Jig and hefted the rock. "Who do you want me to hit first?"

Jig pointed to a bubble on the far side of the pit. "No, wait." Why bother throwing rocks when Veka could use her magic to shoot them across—

He glanced around, searching the shadows. Veka was gone. So was Slash.

"What is it?" asked Grell.

"Nothing." If he pointed out that two of their number had already slipped away, who knew how many would follow? "Wait for my signal to throw. The rest of you, back into the darkness. We don't want to reveal our numbers yet. Braf might be able to hit two or three pixies before they figure out where the rocks are coming from. They'll send a few up to investigate, and we'll draw them into the tunnel. They hate it in here, and they can't maneuver as well."

He turned back to Braf, wishing he could talk to Tymalous Shadowstar about this plan. Annoying and condescending the god might be, but he had helped Jig through a few messes in the past. Not to mention that Shadowstar would have been able to help him heal any injuries the goblins might sustain . . . starting with Jig's arm, which felt like one enormous blister.

On the other hand, at least this way Shadowstar wouldn't be around to make snide comments if they failed. Jig raised his sword and backed into the shadows. "Do it."

CHAPTER 14

"The gods mark their favorites. I was born with a birthmark in the shape of a flying dragon, and I became the mightiest beastlord in history. My sister wasn't so lucky. Her birthmark looked like a lopsided bowl of raisin pudding."

—Theodora of June, Beastmaster of the Elkonian Isles
From *The Path of the Hero (Wizard's ed.)*

Veka hurried through the darkness, pulling her cloak tight with one hand for warmth. She had ripped the remaining beads and bones from her staff to stop them from rattling, but she couldn't quite bring herself to leave the staff itself. The thick wood was her best weapon, and who knew what creatures she might encounter on the way to Straum's lair? She needed the staff for defense, that was all. It had nothing to do with her shattered dreams of wizardry. Nothing at all.

She slowed, searching for the crack where she had descended to the pixies' cavern. She poked her staff at the rock as she went. Several times she nearly slipped on the frost and ice. Stupid pixies. No wonder they flew everywhere. Who could walk on all this ice?

Her cloak helped against the cold, but it did nothing to block the sensation of alien magic that permeated the air like the stench of a dead hobgoblin. The pixies' magic was like a living wind, cutting right through her clothes to chill her skin. The pixies flew upon that magic just as much as they did the air, riding its currents and drawing power through themselves, replenishing their strength with every breath. Magic was as much a part of their diet as food and drink.

Veka could barely grasp that power long enough to channel it into a spell.

But she had done it before. Snixle had shown her the way. How many times had he taken control of her body, dictating her gestures as he struggled to master the magic of her world? Those gestures had made little sense in the beginning, but she had learned. Pixie magic was less a matter of control and more about suggestion. The slightest whisper was enough to shape that magic. Grasp too hard, and it crumbled in your fingers. But she could do it

If she could figure out how to use their magic, the pixies could do the same. That was the only explanation, the only way their world could have begun to grow so quickly. The pixies had found a way to tap into this world's magic to feed the expansion of their own.

The only one who could have helped them do that was Snixle, and the only one he could have learned from was Veka.

This was her fault.

Muttered curses interrupted her thoughts. The sound came from behind her. She raised her staff and sniffed the air. "Slash?"

She heard him hurrying toward her. "I hate that name, you know."

"What are you doing here?"

"I saw you slipping away from the others."

Her shoulders slumped. "So you came to stop me from running away like a coward?"

Slash snorted. "I came to join you. If you really thought Jig had any chance at all, you would have stayed. No, the only thing that crazy runt is going to do is get himself and the rest of his little band slaughtered."

Veka shook her head, forgetting he couldn't see her. Jig would survive. He might even keep a few of the others alive too. Her lip trembled. How did he do it? He had magic, but hers had been stronger when they fought. She was bigger, stronger, and younger, but Jig had beaten her.

Jig had been the Hero all along, not Veka. She was simply another of Jig's trials, an obstacle to be overcome and forgotten. She wondered if she would even rate a line in Jig's next song.

"I'm going to destroy the gateway from the pixies' world," Veka whispered.

"My mistake. For a moment there I forgot that *all* goblins were crazy."

"Most of the pixies will be with the queen. She's more important than anything." Though Veka doubted they would be foolish enough to leave the portal completely unguarded. She didn't know if she would find pixies at Straum's cave, but she would not enter unchallenged. Perhaps she would have to face something like the multiheaded snake creature the pink pixie created in the tunnels, only without that construct's intestinal design flaw.

She shivered as she thought about it. Before, she

would have been eager to face such a challenge, but that was when she had believed herself the Hero. Now she was afraid, and she hated it.

She turned her attention back to the rock, searching for the opening. How far had she run when she fled from Jig and the ogres? She hadn't bothered to count her steps or memorize every twist and turn, and her struggle to control her own body had further confused her sense of distance. She stopped, fighting despair. Was she even on the right side of the tunnel?

With one hand, she tried to conjure up a light, but without a source she could do nothing. Pixie magic swirled around her fingers, taunting her with her own impotence.

"So you have a way to sneak down into Straum's lair?" Slash asked.

"There's a crevasse, where water runs down through the rock. Snixle brought me down, before I—" She bit her lip.

"Before you came back to murder some hobgoblins?"

Veka backed away.

"That's right, I was under the pixie's spell too, remember?" Slash asked. "But I didn't march into the goblin lair and start slaughtering rat-eaters. Nobody forced me to do anything. You *wanted* to kill those hobgoblins."

Veka tried to remember if Slash had taken any weapons from Kralk's old chambers. He had Braf's broken hook-tooth, if nothing else. And in the darkness blood wouldn't bother him one bit.

"I didn't care about the hobgoblins," she whispered. Let him kill her, if that was what he wanted. "I wanted to fight Jig."

"Why?"

She started to repeat the reasons she had given to Snixle, the reasons she had repeated to herself. Because Jig had treated her like a child when she came asking for help. Because Jig would get the goblins killed, and Veka could save them. Because it was the only way.

No. Part of being a Hero was making your own way, like Jig was doing.

"I wanted to prove I was better than he was." She tried again to create a light, but as before, nothing happened. "Better than all of them."

"Oh." Slash stepped past her. "Well come on, where is it?"

Veka wiped her nose on her sleeve. "Where is what?"

"This secret runoff of yours."

"I don't understand. You're not going to kill me?"

He snorted. "With enslaved ogres going after the hobgoblins up above, and Jig fighting the bulk of the pixies down here, I'm starting to think you've got the best idea. Straum's cavern might be the safest place in this whole cursed mountain." His voice changed, becoming quieter. "It's not like I'd be much use in battle anyway."

The very first casualty would leave him passed out on the ground. For the first time Veka wondered what it had been like for him, a hobgoblin warrior who couldn't bear the sight of blood.

"This way, I think," she said. She raised her ears, listening for the sound of water, but either they weren't close enough to hear it, or else the water had frozen in the cold. "Tap your weapon along the other side of the tunnel, near the bottom. Let me know if you find it."

Slash sighed as he began rapping his hook-tooth

against the rock. "Just promise me we won't have to climb through any more garbage."

Veka found the crack eventually. The water had indeed frozen, turning the rocks even more treacherous. The algae and slime were dying, but enough life remained for her to use them to help control her descent. She moved faster than before, thinking about Jig and the other goblins.

Her staff she simply dropped. It clattered down a short distance before getting stuck. She kicked it again, knocking the end loose so it fell a bit more. Above her head Slash yelped as his feet slipped. Like Veka's staff, he fell only a short way before catching himself on the rock. She couldn't hear everything he said under his breath, but she caught her name, along with the phrase ". . . grind her into tunnel cat kibble."

Though she never would have admitted it, especially to Slash, she felt better with the hobgoblin along.

"There," she whispered. Below her feet, silver light outlined a jagged opening. Her staff had dropped through and now lay in the snow and ice below.

She squinted, waiting for her eyes to adjust. She could probably use pixie magic to levitate herself down. Her backside was still bruised from the last time.

Slash made the point moot, losing his grip and falling hard enough to knock her free. With frozen, dying algae still twined around her hand, she slipped into the open air and landed, once again, on her behind. This time Slash came with her. His legs slammed into her stomach, knocking the wind from her lungs.

"Graceful, as always," he said, resting his head in the snow.

The top of the cavern appeared to be much lower

than before. If she held one end of her staff, she would be able to tap the rock overhead. She rolled onto her side, wincing as the movement revealed new bruises on her elbow and shoulder. "We're here."

Here was an enormous slab of silver ice. The top of the cavern wasn't low at all. Instead the ice lifted them to the height of the trees. Veka could see withered treetops poking through various spots. The slab itself had cracked and broken in places, leaving the surface slightly tilted. Pushing herself to her knees, Veka could feel her body starting to slide to the right, away from the crack. She grabbed her staff and jabbed the end against the ice for balance.

The ice directly beneath the opening overhead was smooth, almost like a puddle. Water must have continued to drip down after the cavern froze. She wiped her hand on her robe, leaving a dark, damp algae stain.

"Which way?" asked Slash.

Fog and snow swirled through the air, and the ice made every direction the same. She closed her eyes, concentrating on the flow of the magic. Down here it was strong enough to make her feel like she was standing in the center of a river. A fast river, deep enough to cover her head and strong enough so she nearly fell.

Veka pointed toward the source of the flow. That should be the gateway, clear on the far side of the cavern. Tightening her cloak, she took one step, lost her footing, and began to slide down the ice. She tried to grab a tuft of pine tree in passing, but the brown branch snapped off in her hand, and then she was falling. Again.

This time snow cushioned her landing. She found herself in a canyon of ice, three times as tall as any ogre. The gap was barely wide enough for her to fit.

The fog was thickest here, curling up from the snow and the icy walls.

She could hear Slash laughing as he made his way after her. She closed her eyes again, tapping into the magic to cast a quick levitation spell, just enough to nudge the hobgoblin behind the knees. Moments later Slash plunged into the snow beside her, cursing.

The ice had a copper, cloudy hue when viewed from down here. Veka imagined a huge slab covering the entire cavern, then fragmenting into uneven blocks like these. Was this what the pixie world was like, a world of ice and fog and cold? That would explain their glow at least. It would be the only way for them to find one another.

"This way," she said. The canyon didn't go in precisely the right direction, but she could always levitate them out and over the ice. For now though, staying down here kept them out of sight of any pixies who might have stayed behind.

Then again, trying to cross the ice above offered the possibility of sending Slash for another spill.

Reluctantly, she decided to stick with the canyon. The ice walls closed in on them before they had walked very far, but the slab on the right tilted upward enough for them to crawl beneath the edge. Veka sighed and tightened her robe, then dropped to her knees. A short distance away, she could see a triangle of light from the far side of the slab. It should be a simple matter to scoot beneath it and continue along the other side. Keeping her staff in one hand, she began to crawl past a thick tree trunk that rose right through the ice.

She had only gone a short distance when Slash seized her ankle. Veka yelped and twisted, and Slash slammed into the ice above them.

"Sorry," Veka said. A part of her was delighted at how easily she had used magic to defend herself, but her heart was still pounding too hard to truly enjoy it.

Slash's hands and knees dug long gouges through the flattened, muddy earth as he tried to break free, but his body remained pinned to the ice overhead. After a few more undignified attempts to pull himself down, he asked, "Would you mind?"

She dropped him.

"Stupid goblin witch," Slash muttered. Silver clouds floated from his mouth as he spoke. "I ought to let you keep going for that."

Veka hesitated. "What do you mean?"

"Look at the ground," Slash said. "Dead and dying grass, broken splinters that used to be saplings, a few stray vines, and muddy ice overhead. Except for that spot right in front of you."

Veka stared, trying to understand. "So there's a puddle. Do you think it might have something to do with all the ice?"

"Do you see any other puddles? It's a trap. Look at the ice."

Most of the ice was rough and muddy, full of stones and twigs and at least one buck-toothed squirrel still clutching a nut in his claws. He had probably frozen to death and been trapped in the swift-forming ice. If she hadn't been in such a hurry, she would have chipped him free to see if the meat was still good.

Directly in front of her, however, the ice was clear and clean. A few bronze-colored vines crept around the edges, defining a roughly circular patch. Clusters of swollen globules dangled from the vines by knife-like leaves. Within the clear patch, long needles of ice hung like the malachite formations back at the lizard-fish lake. She could see water dripping from the ends.

They looked a bit like the ice spikes she had seen in front of Straum's lair, but these were thinner, and she saw no sign of the wormlike creatures she remembered. As she watched, a drop of water fell from one of the spikes. "What is it?"

Slash reached into one of the pouches on his belt and pulled out several metal objects no wider than his thumb. Each one had four barbed spikes protruding from the center.

"Goblin prickers," he explained, grinning. "You scatter them on the ground and wait for some dumb goblin to run past. If you're feeling really nasty, you do it near a tunnel cat lair. The goblin steps on the pricker. His scream wakes up the cats. The cats smell the blood, and we sit back and make wagers on how far the goblin will be able to limp before the cats get him."

He crawled past her and tossed one of the goblin prickers into the puddle. The instant it hit the water, the ice above exploded. A coiled snake of gold fire streaked to the ground and seized the goblin pricker in its mouth.

The snake was fairly small, about the size of the average carrion-worm. Veka could see several sets of rudimentary wings pressed flat against its burning scales. The snake wasn't truly on fire, she saw. Like the pixies, it gave off a great deal of heat, light, and sparks. Those sparks brightened, turning almost white as the snake realized what it had caught. Water splashed as the snake flailed its head, trying to rid itself of the goblin pricker. One of the barbs had stuck in its lower jaw. Smoke trailed from the snake's mouth.

"I guess they aren't too fond of steel either," Slash said.

Eventually the snake dislocated its own jaw, then used its fangs to rip the goblin pricker free. With its wings folded back like armor, it shot up into the ice and disappeared.

Slash scooted ahead to reclaim his goblin pricker. "I doubt the pixies did this. The labor-to-victim ratio is all wrong: too much work for too few victims. This is a natural trap, probably how that thing hunts for food. Lizard-fish do something similar. They'll hide in the sand beneath the water, waving their spines until some stupid cave fish swims over to take a nibble."

Veka rolled onto her back, trying to see where the snake had gone. How many more might there be? Snakes could be the least of the predators. She squinted, imagining she could see faint lines of light wiggling through the hazy silver ice.

Her back scraped the damp ice overhead as she turned around. "We need to get out of here. We'll go over the ice and hope they don't spot us. That will be faster anyway."

Slash was still muttering about goblin indecisiveness as he followed her out from beneath the ice. When they reached the canyon, Veka wiped damp, muddy hair from her face and stared at the sky.

"How many of those goblin pricks do you have?" she asked.

"Goblin *prickers*," Slash said. "Eight, though one is still a little slimy from that snake. Poor fellow."

Veka stared, but he appeared serious. He really felt sorry for the snake that would have killed them. Hobgoblins were weird. "Give them to me."

He handed her a small jingling pouch. She pulled out one of the goblin prickers and tried to levitate it. Almost immediately the metal grew so hot she had to fling it away. The pricker bounced off the ice and dropped to the ground, completely unaffected by her spell.

"Interesting strategy," said Slash. "How exactly is this going to get us to Straum's cave?"

"Shut up." While she waited for the first goblin pricker to cool, she pulled out another and examined it more closely. The whole thing was steel, rusted a bit toward the center, but gleaming brightly at the points. She drove one of the goblin pricker's barbs deep into the wood of her staff, then concentrated.

The staff began to float. She could feel heat coming from the metal, but as long as she focused her spell on the wood, she could control it. "Help me find more wood. Small pieces, but solid enough to hold a goblin pricker without splitting."

After a bit of scrounging, they gathered enough broken branches for all eight prickers. She embedded each one into a chunk of wood. The last goblin pricker ripped a long splinter from her staff when she pulled it free. She grimaced and rubbed the wood. She would have to sand that out with a rock later, assuming she survived. She tucked most of the goblin prickers back into her pouch, but kept a few in her hand just in case. "Ready?"

"Ready for what?" Slash asked.

Veka grinned and waved her staff. Ideally her robe should have fluttered around her feet as she floated into the air, but after her aborted crawl through the mud, all it did was drip a bit. A casual glance at Slash was all she needed to summon the hobgoblin up after her.

"You'd better know what you're doing this time," Slash snapped. "Otherwise I'll give you a lot worse than a kick in the head."

They flew over the cracked plain of ice, the wind ruffling her cloak. She spun Slash over and raised him higher, until his nose nearly scraped the top of the cavern, then brought him back down. "Keep an eye out for pixies. Most of them will probably be with the queen, but there may still be a few down here with us."

She flew between the protruding treetops, trying to stay as low as possible. Avoiding the brown, dying branches was easy enough. Keeping Slash from crashing through them was trickier. More than once she heard him plotting her death and spitting dead leaves from his mouth.

Veka grinned and increased their speed.

At most Veka had expected to face only a handful of pixie guards. She had been correct. Only five pixies perched on the rock around the entrance to Straum's lair, clinging to the icy stone like glowing flies. A sixth stood on the back of what might have been a cousin to the winged burning snake that had tried to ambush them beneath the ice. The only real difference was that this snake was as wide as Slash's thick head, and long enough to wrap its body around them both from head to toe without a bit of space between the coils.

"So much for sneaking in," said Slash.

Veka guided herself and Slash down behind the top of a nearby tree. Dry papery leaves offered some cover, assuming the pixies hadn't already spotted them. The snake reared up, wings fluttering as it looked around. It actually left the ground, flying low over the ice as it hunted. A tongue of green fire flicked from its mouth. She could feel tremors passing through the magic around her, like waves in a pool.

The snake was *tasting* the magic, searching for them. For her. The instant she tried to cast a spell, the huge snake would find her.

"Amateurs," she muttered.

"What are you talking about?"

She pointed to the snake. "Making giant versions of normal creatures. It's a fairly basic bit of magic. Most apprentices learn to do it in their first year of studies. There were notes in my spellbook. Giant bats, giant rats, giant snakes, giant earwigs . . . most of the time they all die within a few days. The larger body isn't proportioned right. But occasionally someone gets lucky. That's why you get giant weasels rampaging through a village, or giant toads hopping around and crushing people, or giant dung beetles rampaging across the country in search of giant privies."

"Can you do it?" Slash asked. "Better yet, can you undo it?"

Veka flushed. "The notes in my book . . . they weren't complete."

Slash didn't say anything. She almost wished he would.

She opened her hands, staring at the goblin prickers she had carried. Her palms were dotted with blood from clutching them too hard. She hadn't even felt the spikes pierce her skin.

They were outnumbered. Any magic she used would give them away. Not to mention that six pixies could bring a lot more magic to bear than a single goblin. And then there was the giant flaming snake.

"What next?" Slash asked.

Veka had no idea. She stared at him, then back at the pixies. *Jig would have found a way.*

The thought made her stomach hurt. Jig would have slain not only the pixies, but the giant snake as well.

No, he wouldn't. That was the sort of thing a Hero from her book would do, but Jig wasn't like that, whatever "The Song of Jig" said. He would have done something different. Something unexpected. Something goblinish . . .

"I think I have an idea," she whispered.

CHAPTER 15

"Hero or coward, they all taste the same with a bit of harkol sauce."

—Golaka, Goblin Chef

Jig's hands shook as he watched Braf throw his rock. It arced through the air toward the silver bubbles on the far wall. Would the pixies attack en masse, or would they see Braf standing alone and decide he wasn't worth a full assault? If they sent only a few pixies, the goblins might have a chance.

The rock hit one of the silver bubbles and stuck.

Nothing happened. Jig glanced at Braf, who shrugged. Eventually another of the two-winged pixies flew up to investigate the rock. This one was orange in color. He glanced up, then back at the bubble. With both hands he pried the rock free and dropped it into the pit. He whistled loudly, presumably to warn the pixies below to watch out for falling rock.

"Tough nest," Braf muttered.

"Yes, it is," said Jig.

The pixie was already descending toward a lower cluster of bubbles.

Movement up above drew Jig's attention. Apparently one of the pixies up on the bridge had noticed something. He started to fly lower, in the general direction of Braf and the others.

"Can you hit him?" Jig asked.

Braf produced another rock and let fly. The pixie tried to spin out of the way, but he was too slow. Purple sparks exploded as the pixie spiraled downward, his light fading.

Two more pixies hopped off the bridge, searching for their attacker. These were the four-winged pixies, who seemed to be the warriors and guards. Jig could see the ogres peering down as well. "Them too?"

Another rock flew. This time the pixies managed to dodge, though the rock did hit an ogre on the shoulder. The ogre didn't appear to notice. One of the pixies pointed toward Braf. "Get him!"

The enslaved ogres leaped from the bridge and began to plummet into the pit.

Jig stared. Grell shrugged and said, "Nobody ever said ogres were bright."

That was when the first of the ogres spread her wings. On Jig's shoulder, Smudge grew so hot he began to glow. Jig could smell his hair burning as it curled away from the terrified spider. Jig patted out the hair with one hand, never looking away from the flying ogres.

"Unfair," he whispered. He counted four ogres, circling lower on enormous black wings. Bat wings. The pixies had been hunting giant bats, trying to capture them alive. Somehow they had grafted the wings onto the ogres, creating flying ogres. Similar to what Pynne had done to create the snake guardian with too many heads and no tail. Jig doubted he could defeat these ogres by feeding them though. "Weren't ogres scary enough already?"

He wondered briefly what had happened to the bats. Without their wings, they were essentially giant blind rats. Then the first ogre reached the tunnel, and Jig and Braf were leaping away to avoid a spear thrust.

Braf threw another rock, which bounced off the ogre's wing with no apparent effect. The ogre stabbed again. Braf fell, yelping with pain.

"Are you hurt?" Jig asked.

Braf shook his head. "She missed me. I landed on my rocks, that's all."

Beyond the tunnel, the ogre dropped out of sight. Another appeared from above, armed with a large club. He hovered for a moment, then flung his club at Jig.

Jig's sword dropped as he rolled out of the way. Arrows spilled from his quiver, and he nearly squashed Smudge. "Sorry," he whispered. He tried to scoop Smudge off his shoulder, but the little fire-spider was too terrified, not to mention too *hot*, for Jig to move. Sucking his blistered finger, Jig turned his attention back to the ogre. He peeled away from the cave, to be replaced by yet another.

"They can't get into the tunnel with those wings," Jig said, gathering his fallen arrows. Their wingspan was too great, and if they stopped flapping, they would fall. "Braf, get back. They can't come in after us."

The new ogre scowled. He couldn't reach Braf or Jig, but he did manage to use his spear to drag his companion's club back out of the tunnel. Jig cursed himself for not throwing it out of range. They could have disarmed at least one of the ogres.

"Well this is an amusing little standoff," Grell said from the darkness. "What next?"

The ogre with the club returned. This time a bright green pixie warrior rode her shoulder.

"Rock!" Jig shouted.

Braf fumbled for a stone, but the pixie was faster. He flew into the tunnel and pointed. Braf fell, fumbling at his boots and howling in pain.

The pixie turned to Jig. Jig grabbed his sword and prepared to charge, already knowing he couldn't get there fast enough. But before Jig had taken a single step, the pixie yelped and clawed at his shoulder. Smoke spiraled as the pixie fell to the ground, where he yanked a tiny dart from his shoulder and flung it away.

Jig ran up and kicked the pixie. He slammed into the wall and slid to the ground.

"That's mine," Grop said, hurrying to retrieve the dart. He lowered his voice. "I use it back at the lair. The others blame it on wasps. If you tie a thin line to the dart, you can yank it away before they swat it, and nobody knows—"

Jig stepped away. Ogres hovered outside, and Jig could see other pixies streaking toward them from above and below. He turned to face the other goblins.

Braf was using Grell's knife to pry his boot from his foot. The pixie had tried the same trick Pynne had used on Jig, constricting the leather. Braf had managed to get one foot free before it tightened too badly. The other appeared immovable. His face was tight from pain.

"I heard bones snap," Grell said. "Can you fix him?"

Jig shook his head. "Even if I could, I can't break

the pixie's spell on the boot." Veka could, but she had disappeared. "You and Braf stay here. Our attack should draw them away from the tunnel. If you see an opening, try to hit a few more pixies with rocks."

One of the goblins coughed. "Our attack?"

"I'm guessing their nest is strong enough to hold us," Jig said. "We can jump down and—"

"You're guessing?" repeated the goblin, Ekstal. He was another distillery worker, like Veka. Ekstal waved his sword at Jig. It was in far better shape than Jig's weapon. The slender, double-sided blade looked as though it had been forged solely to slide through goblin throats. "You're going to get us killed!"

"Probably," admitted Jig. He didn't have time to argue. He glanced at Braf, who nodded and pushed himself into a sitting position.

"I'm not going out there," shouted Ekstal. "If you try to—"

There was a sharp thud, and Ekstal's sword dropped to the ground, followed by Ekstal himself. A bit of blood trickled down his neck where Braf's rock had hit him.

Jig scooped up the sword and gave it an experimental swing. Much better than his own weapon. He pointed to two of the goblins. "Toss him onto the nest. Then we'll know whether it can hold a goblin."

The two goblins looked at one another, then at Ekstal. "Right!"

"What about the ogres?" one asked.

Jig scooped up the dead pixie. Hopefully the ogres wouldn't realize he was dead. He flung the body out of the tunnel.

All four ogres dove, trying to catch him.

"Go," said Jig.

Ekstal groaned. His eyes opened wide as the goblins pushed him over the edge. A high-pitched squeal echoed through the tunnel.

Jig peered down. Ekstal had nearly missed the nest. He lay at an angle, his feet pointed upward, looking as though the slightest movement would send him slipping into the abyss. Already the pixies were zooming toward the panicked goblin.

"Here!" Jig called. He started to throw Ekstal's sword down to him, reconsidered, and tossed his own old broken sword down instead.

Ekstal caught it by the blade, which would have been a problem if the weapon hadn't been so dull. He clawed his way back to the rock, where he stood and waved the sword with both hands.

That answered the last of Jig's questions. Sticky as the nest was, they could still move about. "Everyone get your weapons ready. Spread out. Try to cut your way into the nest. Make them come up close to fight so you have a chance to stab them before they use their magic."

A rock flew by his head, momentarily driving the pixies back. Below, Ekstal was frantically cutting a hole in the nest.

None of the goblins had moved. The two who had tossed Ekstal down were still standing at the edge, watching and cheering him on. Jig sighed, tucked his sword under his arm, and pushed them both down to join their frantic companion.

It took a bit of threatening, with both his sword and Braf's rocks, but eventually the other goblins followed. Jig caught the last three before they jumped.

"You're the smartest goblins I've got," Jig said.

"Why do you say that?" asked Grop.

"You haven't jumped yet." Already Jig could hear shouting and screaming from below. "So you're the ones I need with me."

"Doing what?"

Jig swallowed and tried to sound like he knew what he was doing. "We're going to kill the queen."

He unstrapped his quiver and handed a few arrows to each goblin. "The tips are steel. Throw them like spears to keep the pixies back, but save one or two for when we reach the queen. We'll have to fight our way through any guards."

Jig put two arrows back into the quiver, keeping a third ready in his hand. Ekstal's sword was too long and slender for his old sheath, but he forced it. A handspan of steel protruded from the bottom, but if he was careful, he should be able to avoid slicing off his own foot.

He stepped to the edge and froze. The others stood close behind, waiting for Jig's order. Wind buffeted his face. He tried to tell himself he was waiting for the right moment, giving the other goblins time to spread around the nest. Several had already fallen into the pit, and the rest were scrambling away and cutting into the silver bubbles as fast as they could.

He could imagine Tymalous Shadowstar's derisive laughter as he said, *Waiting for the right time? You're cowering while the others get themselves slaughtered.*

Jig shrugged. Cowering while others died was a perfectly acceptable goblin tactic. Unfortunately, once the pixies finished with the others, they would return to thc tunnel.

The hive was right below, only a short jump. The others had landed safely. Well, aside from Jallark, who had leaped a bit too enthusiastically. Even Braf's rock had stuck. Jig wasn't going to fall. The nest would hold him.

"This is crazy," whispered one of the remaining goblins, Noroka.

Jig agreed completely, but he forced himself to shake his head, then gave them his best conspiratorial grin. "We're going to let the others fight pixies while we sneak down through the hive. Do you think I'd be doing this if it wasn't the safest part of the whole plan? If you want, you can stay behind, but look what happened to poor Braf."

With that, Jig sat down on the edge, put his arrow in his mouth, and before he could stop to think about what he was doing, pushed off. Fear locked his jaw as he fell, and he bit clean through the arrow. The short drop felt like an eternity, and he was certain he had somehow missed the nest. He would fall forever into the bottomless pit, unless one of the pixies was kind enough to kill him in passing.

His feet hit the nest. Jig spat splinters of wood from his mouth and tried to make himself start breathing again.

The silver bubble felt like warm clay, sinking beneath his weight and sticking to his boots. The smell reminded him of burned mushrooms. Some of the fog rose from the nest itself, the warm surface interacting with the cold, damp air. With one hand pressed to the icy wall of the pit, Jig made his way to the next bubble. He looked up. "Hurry!"

Nothing happened at first. Then he heard the distinctive sound of a cane smacking a goblin skull. Grop dropped down a moment later, rubbing his head.

Several pixies were already streaking toward them. Jig hurried to the next bubble. He could see where some of the goblins had cut their way into the hive. The punctured cells sagged and wiggled as the goblins moved about. Farther on the pixies had added a second layer of bubbles, thickening the hive. If Jig could reach that point, the extra layer might help to conceal him.

On the far side of the pit, a goblin poked his head out of a damaged bubble and threw his knife at an unsuspecting worker pixie. The pixie fell. The goblin's gleeful expression vanished as pixies and ogres swarmed toward him.

Jig drew one of his two remaining arrows and threw it at the closest pixie. The pixie veered away, and Jig hopped to the next bubble, landing beside the smashed body of one of his goblins. Peeling the goblin from the bubble, Jig flung him onto the head of an unsuspecting pixie below.

The goblins who had gone first all appeared to have followed Jig's instructions, spreading out and taking cover in the hive. They were doing quite well for goblins, which meant they weren't all dead yet. From what Jig could see, almost half were still alive and fighting.

One of the goblins crouched within a broken bubble, fighting a pixie. As Jig watched, the pixie flew away, and an ogre soared in to take its place. Instead of trying to escape, the goblin actually tried something heroic. He raised his sword and swung for the ogre's head.

The ogre took the blow on the shoulder without slowing. His body smashed the goblin against the rock. That was what happened to goblins who tried to be heroes.

So what am I doing here? The ogre dove away from the gruesome remains of thc goblin, then swooped up again, apparently unaffected by the collision. He was coming directly at Jig. Jig drew his remaining arrow and waited. The ogre drew closer . . . closer. . . .

Jig feinted with the arrow, then leaped to the next

bubble. The ogre hit the rock headfirst and fell back, clutching his scalp. The impact didn't seem to have stopped him, reinforcing Jig's private theory that ogre skulls were stone all the way through.

It did make the ogre an easy target, though. Grop threw one of his arrows. The point lodged in the ogre's wing, and he screamed and moved away, flapping his other wing harder to keep from falling.

Jig jumped one more time, and he was there. This part of the hive was firmer, supported by the second layer of bubbles. Praying this would work, he reversed his grip on the arrow and shoved the head into the silver surface.

Sour air rushed from the puncture. The walls were thicker than they looked. He could probably push his thumb into the hole, and his claw would just reach the other side. The wall sizzled and smoked where the arrowhead touched. Moving as fast and as carefully as he could, Jig carved an opening wide enough for him to squeeze inside.

This was too much for Smudge. The fire-spider raced down over Jig's chest, smoke rising with each step, and stopped near his pouch. He turned, all eight eyes pleading for Jig to open his hiding place. Jig loosened the laces with one finger to let Smudge scurry inside.

Sweat dripped down his face as Jig crouched within the bubble. These chambers might be quite cozy for a pixie, but Jig barely fit. He jabbed his arrow into the floor, punching through to the next one. The air was warm and damp, like the breath of a dragon with an infected tooth.

Purging that image from his mind, Jig prepared to cut through to the next cell. He bent down, and the end of his sword pierced the side of the bubble.

Jig grabbed his sheath, pulling the blade back, but the damage was done. A long, smoking gash opened into the next bubble, where a bleary-eyed yellow pixie was stirring. Apparently when pixies slept, they slept hard. The pixie blinked, horror replacing weariness as he spotted Jig. Jig drew back the arrow to throw, just as the pixie's light flared. The wooden shaft crumbled, and the feathers of the fletching twined together and tried to fly away.

Jig squeezed through the opening and punched the pixie in the face. The pixie bounced off of the far side of the chamber. Jig grabbed him by the wings and threw him against the flattened part of the bubble, the side that clung to the rock. As the pixie collapsed, Jig realized he was grinning. He liked being bigger than the enemy for once.

The nest muffled sound well enough he could barely hear the battle outside. No wonder this one hadn't woken up. He wondered how many more sleeping pixies they would encounter.

The bubble shook slightly as Grop dropped into the one behind him.

"Are the others still coming?" Jig asked.

"Var got pixie charmed and tried to stab me in the back, but Noroka tossed her into the pit." He scowled. "Or maybe she wasn't pixie charmed. Var never did like me that much."

Jig shook his head. If he was remembering right, they had a long way to go before they reached the thickest part of the nest, where he hoped to find the queen. He looked at his lone remaining arrow, then at his sword. The arrowhead was small enough to control, but the sword was faster.

He was a goblin. Caution was for those who actually expected to survive a battle. Jig returned the arrow to his quiver and climbed back into Grop's chamber.

Squeezing past the other goblin, he drew his sword and slashed a hole in the far side. He lost his balance and fell. His sword opened a huge hole in the floor. The chamber below held another two-winged pixie, but Jig impaled him as he plunged downward.

Jig grinned. Sure he was down to three goblins against the pixie queen and all her guards, but in the meantime, this was how goblins should fight. Sneaking around, pouncing by surprise, and stopping only for a very quick snack.

One problem with cutting through the inside of a pixie nest was that you had no way to know when you reached the bottom.

No, that wasn't true. There was one way.

Jig rolled away from the gash in the floor, pressing his body against the rock and gasping so hard he nearly passed out. He rested his sword across his chest, making sure the steel came nowhere near the walls of the bubble. His shook so hard he could barely hold on. From below, the wind of thc bottomless pit fluttered the edges of the gash.

He tried to tell himself he wouldn't have fallen through. The hole might be big enough for his leg, but not his whole body. "Don't come down!" he whispered to Grop and Noroka.

Grop poked his head down from the chamber overhead. Jig could see Noroka settling in above him. "Now what?"

Now he had to figure out where they were. He pulled out his remaining arrow and poked a tiny hole in the wall of the bubble, widening it just enough to see. He pressed his eye to the wall.

Only a handful of goblins still fought. Jig saw an orange pixie swoop in to cast a spell, then tumble to the side. Jig hadn't seen the rock that hit him, but he was relieved to know Braf had survived so far.

The queen was easy enough to find: a point of brilliant white light, orbited by pixies of every color. The white light perched in the center of a cluster of bubbles, a rounded area of smaller bubbles that bulged from the rest of the hive. Jig closed his eyes, hoping that one brief glimpse wouldn't be enough to enchant him. He didn't *feel* particularly loving.

"The pixies say all who look upon their queen will love her, so don't wait," Jig said, turning back to Grop and Noroka. "We're going to cut our way through the hive until we're close enough to attack. If we're lucky, we'll have one chance before she enchants us."

"And if we're not lucky?" asked Noroka.

One of the surviving goblins from the fighting above chose that moment to go tumbling past, screaming.

"Any other questions?" Jig stood up and began cutting a path to the next bubble. He used his arrow, unwilling to risk a mistake.

Noroka and Grop both had several arrows left. Grop had already proven his aim with that dart. A thrown arrow didn't have the force to penetrate deeply, but as they had seen with the flying ogre, even a weak hit was enough. As long as the steel lodged in the queen's flesh, they might actually succeed.

A few bubbles over, Jig poked another hole to gauge their progress. He tried not to look directly at the queen, judging her location from the shadows and the other pixies. It looked like the pixies had taken over a small cave to use as the queen's chamber. An ogre stood at the edge, two warrior pixies perched on her shoulders. Other pixies sat on the bubbles above the cave, like tiny, glowing gargoyles.

"How much closer do we need to get?" Grop asked.

"A few more chambers," Jig guessed without looking back. "We should try to attack from the side. Noroka, you distract the guards long enough for Grop and me to cut through."

This could work! What would Tymalous Shadowstar say if he could see Jig now?

That was when something punched him hard in the back. Jig twisted his head to see Grop's arrow sticking out from beneath his rib cage. There was no pain, just blue blood dripping down the shaft.

No, wait. *There* was the pain.

Jig dropped to his knees. Grop pulled out another arrow. "That was a good plan," he said to Noroka, who was staring from the next chamber. "The two of us will attack together. Help me toss Jig's body out for a distraction."

Goblins really are as stupid as they say. Less than a day as chief, and I already turned my back on another goblin. Are you happy now, Tymalous Shadowstar? You're the one who wanted me to lead my people. Is this what you meant when you talked about inspiring the other goblins? I inspired Grop so much he thought he'd try his hand at being chief!

He tried to reach around, but the effort made the arrowhead move inside him, and he squealed in pain. Maybe he would just hold still.

Shadowstar? Of course. The god couldn't hear him down here. Jig had no way to heal himself. He was alone.

At least Grop and Noroka might still reach the queen. Not that it would do Jig much good.

Then he saw Noroka contemplating her own arrow, looking from the tip to Grop's exposed back. Jig wanted to weep. They were so close! "Noroka, don't—"

Grop spun as Noroka leaped. She landed on top of Grop and stabbed her arrow into his hip. The arrow broke, leaving a splintered shaft in her hand. With a shrug she stabbed the broken end into Grop's side.

Grop screamed and elbowed her in the head. There was no room to fight, and both goblins kept stepping on Jig. Claws and fangs ripped flesh. Jig moaned and tried to curl his body into a ball, keeping his wounded back away from the fight.

The bottom of the bubble began to glow with golden flames. A hole opened in the floor beneath Noroka. Jig would have warned them, but he was too busy bleeding and cowering.

An ogre grabbed Noroka by the ankles and yanked her out. Grop followed, his fangs still locked in Noroka's arm. Another ogre caught Grop by the neck and squeezed until he let go. Jig grimaced. Goblin jaws were stronger than any other muscle in their bodies, and the ogre had plucked Grop off Noroka like he was a rat.

Jig yelled as another ogre pulled him down, bumping the end of the arrow against the nest. Hanging upside down by one leg, Jig closed his eyes and concentrated on not blacking out.

The beating of the ogres' wings was almost as loud as the pounding in Jig's head. As they flew toward the queen's chamber, he found himself feeling jealous of Veka. Wherever she had gone, at least she hadn't been stupid enough to rely on goblins to help her.

The ogres dumped them on rough stone. Jig raised his arms and tucked his head as he landed, trying to protect Smudge and keep from bumping the arrow in his back at the same time. He managed to avoid squishing Smudge at least.

Unlike the pit and the tunnel above, the air was

warmer here, and there was no frost. Now that he was here, Jig realized this was the same tunnel that the ogres had dug from Straum's cavern. The back had been narrowed, with two-winged pixies constantly squeezing in and out, carrying small fruits or clearing bits of stone from the cave. Hardly a single speck of rubble littered the ground. Sparkling blue and green crystals covered the rock. They felt like sand, scraping Jig's skin when he moved.

He rolled onto his side, grimacing. The entire right side of his body hurt with every breath. His sword and arrow were both missing. The ogre must have taken them, or else they had fallen into the pit. Jig hadn't even noticed.

He touched Smudge's pouch and felt the fire-spider moving about inside. He loosened the ties. Hopefully Smudge would have a chance to escape.

Grop and Noroka lay bleeding beside him. Jig pushed himself up just enough to give Grop a quick kick in the stomach, a move that probably caused Jig more pain than it did Grop. Jig kicked him again anyway.

"I hate this place."

Jig still hadn't looked up, nor did he intend to. Faint shadows spun around his body as the pixies circled behind and overhead, but the white light shining from the queen overpowered them all.

"Everyone promised me we'd be safe. That you'd build me a nest even bigger than my mother's. You never said we'd be underground, in this hot, dark, horrible place. What if these goblins had gotten through? They could have killed me!"

Her voice jumped and dipped like music. Other pixies swarmed and buzzed overhead, drowning each other out with their hasty apologies.

Jig saw bare feet moving toward him and the other goblins. They were larger than he had expected. The queen must be almost as large as a goblin. Either that, or she was simply a normal pixie with grotesquely oversize feet.

Sweat dripped onto one of his lenses. Jig flinched and closed his eyes. How much of the queen did he have to look upon to be enchanted? Were feet enough? He didn't feel overcome with love or worship yet. He raised his hand to block her from view as he glanced at the others.

Grop was doing the same thing, shielding one eye. The other was bruised and swollen shut. Noroka had gotten in some good blows.

Noroka looked equally battered, but she didn't seem to care about her wounds. She didn't seem to care about anything. The queen's light turned Noroka's skin to white gold. She lay on her back, her mouth open and her eyes wide as she stared up at the queen. Until now Jig had clung to the faint hope that goblins might somehow be immune to the queen's charms. So much for that.

Could they still attack? Jig twisted his head, quickly losing count of the pixies buzzing around their heads. He could hear several ogres hovering outside as well. Attacking now would be suicidally stupid.

Grop attacked. He had managed to palm his little dart, and he flung it at the queen. Four pixies swooped down to intercept the missile. Grop swore as one of the pixies squeaked and fell. He drew a knife from inside his shirt.

Noroka kicked him in the knees, knocking him to the ground. Moving faster than any goblin had a right to move, she pounced and sank her fangs into his neck. Grop stabbed his knife into her arm, but she didn't even notice.

The queen giggled. "Stupid goblins."

Noroka rose and backed away. Grop whimpered on the floor, blood dripping from his throat. He would be dead soon, from the look of it.

The queen stepped closer. Through squinted lids, Jig saw a slender, pale hand grab Grop's hair, wrenching his head back. Grop's eyes widened, and his face relaxed into a slack, peaceful smile.

"What's your name?"

"Grop." His wound bubbled.

"What an ugly name." She struggled to lift him up. Instantly four pixies flew down to help, hoisting Grop up until only his toes still brushed the ground. "Go away and leave me alone, Grop."

Still smiling, Grop turned and began to jog away. He ran right out of the chamber, dropping into the pit without a sound.

Jig began to tremble. Given the arrow still sticking out of his back, he wasn't terribly upset about Grop's death. But Grop had acted so cheerful about it. Jig hadn't seen the slightest trace of hesitation on that blissful face as he trotted to his death.

"Oh, yuck. This one's bleeding all over my cave."

Jig glanced down. His blood formed a small puddle on the floor. The pain had begun to recede a bit, but he was light-headed, and every movement made him dizzy. Was he dying?

"That's Jig Dragonslayer," said Noroka. She moved in front of Jig, positioning herself between him and the queen. "He's the one who forced us to try to kill you."

Jig groaned. He scooted back, toward the edge of

the pit. If he was going to die, wouldn't it be better to do so himself, while he was still his own goblin?

He stopped. Blood loss was starting to affect his mind. Death was death. Veka might opt to die heroically, but Jig planned to go out cowering and pleading for his life.

Smudge darted down Jig's leg and scampered up the wall. Nobody appeared to notice. Their attention was on Jig. He hoped Smudge would be able to climb back out of the pit. Did he still remember how to find the fire-spider nest?

"Make him look at me!"

Two pixies seized him by the ears, yanking his head up.

"Want me to cut off his eyelids?" Noroka asked.

Jig's eyes snapped open.

The queen stood before him. Her gown sparkled like platinum, though it was clearly too small for her. Several stitches had popped along the side, and the hem barely reached past her knees. Rows of black pearls highlighted the contours of her skinny body. A golden circlet was twined into her long black hair. Had she been a goblin, Jig would have guessed her to be no more than seven years of age.

Her ears were narrow and pointed, rising well past the top of her head. Her eyes were pure blackness, reminding him of the bottomless pit, save for the spot of white light at the center of each eye.

Her wings were small and shriveled. Jig wondered if that was a result of injury, or if queens simply didn't get real wings. He saw no scars, nor did the wings appear deformed. They were simply too small, too flimsy. She had four wings, like the warrior pixies, but hers gave off no light. The queen's light came from her skin, her eyes, even her nails.

"Stand up."

Sweat poured down Jig's face as he obeyed, despite the pain the movement caused. He stood hunched, one hand reaching around his back to hold the arrow still.

The queen was . . . beautiful. It was an alien beauty, but Jig couldn't look away. The angular features of her face, the curves of her body, the gracefulness of her movements that made her every step look like she was flying. . . . Every being Jig had ever encountered seemed crude and ugly in comparison. Admittedly, Jig had spent most of his life with other goblins.

"Jig Dragonslayer," the queen whispered. "I remember your name. They told me about you. You're the one who opened the way so we could come here. Everyone was so excited when they found this place. I would be safe. We could start our own kingdom, away from my mother. I could raise my own army of warriors as soon as I was old enough to breed. All thanks to you."

Jig shivered. What was he supposed to say? "You're welcome."

"I hate you!" the queen said. She stomped around Jig, her withered wings rustling with her despair. "Why couldn't *I* stay behind, and my mother come through?"

"You know your mother's followers were too great in number for—" one pixie said.

"Shut up! How many more of these horrible goblins are going to come crawling into my cave?" She wiped her nose on the sleeve of her gown. "I hate them," she said again.

She wrapped both hands around the arrow in Jig's side and prodded him toward the edge. Tears streamed down his face, and he was gasping so hard he nearly passed out. Pixies and ogres flew back, clearing space for him to fall.

Jig turned around. Everyone was watching, waiting for that last order that would send him to his death. The queen wrenched the arrow from his back. Jig gasped, and tears filled his eyes.

"I wish you'd never opened that stupid cave for us," she whispered, too low for the others to hear. Even her tears glowed. "I wish you'd just left me there to die."

The poor queen was scared and miserable. Jig sympathized. He had felt the same way ever since that ogre first came to the goblin lair.

A small, dark shape dropped down to land on the queen's withered wing. She didn't appear to notice. Nor did she notice when smoke began to rise from that same wing. "Go on," she said. "Follow your friend into the pit."

Noroka acted first, leaping toward the queen and screaming, "Jig's fire-spider!"

That was too much for the young queen. She whirled around and flailed her arms in panic, knocking Smudge to the ground. "Somebody kill it!" she screamed.

Jig leaped. Agony tore his wound as he grabbed the arrow in the queen's hand and ripped it from her grasp. Before the queen could react, he plunged the arrow into the her back, directly between the wings.

She screamed. Jig flattened his ears against the terrible, high-pitched shriek. Pixies swarmed around the cave. Others fought their way through the opening at the back, bloodying one another in their desperation.

Before anyone could reach the queen, Jig yanked hard, pulling her toward the edge, then let go. The queen staggered, her arms waving madly. Jig saw her wings shiver once as she teetered on the edge, and then she was falling.

Every single pixie and ogre dove to follow, trying to save her. Jig scrambled out of the way and pressed himself to the floor.

When Noroka tried to follow the queen, Jig reached out with one hand and snagged her ankle. She flopped face first onto the rock and didn't move. Only then, with Noroka unconscious and the rest of the pixies and ogres gone, did Jig drag himself back to peer into the pit. A tiny spark of white was quickly fading into darkness, pursued by swirls of color.

Everything felt fuzzy. He thought something in his back had torn when the queen yanked the arrow free, and his blood was flowing faster than before. His head slumped to the ground, just past the edge. He watched a bit of his own drool fall into the pit. Why wasn't he dead? He had looked upon the queen, just like Grop and Noroka. Not that it mattered. He would be dead soon enough.

His ears and nose hurt. He pushed himself back and reached up to adjust his spectacles. The frames were so hot they burned his fingers.

The *steel* frames.

Jig started to giggle. Every time he had looked at the queen, he had seen her through circles of steel.

Shadowstar? There was no answer. He was alone.

Hot footprints made their way up his arm. Not alone after all. Jig smiled and rested his head on the stone. At least he would die with the one creature in this world he had always been able to trust.

CHAPTER 16

"You think Heroes have it rough? Try cleaning up after them."

—Chandra Widowmaker, Proprietress of
The Dancing Zombie Tavern
From *The Path of the Hero (Wizard's ed.)*

"So what's this plan of yours?" Slash asked. He lay on his stomach, burning designs in the ice with one of his goblin prickers. Veka frowned and looked more closely. He had drawn a fat goblin cowering behind a tree. Now he sketched a pixie circling the tree, with bolts of lightning shooting from his hands. Slash appeared to be a fairly skilled artist. He held the pricker by the wood, pressing two points into the ice as he drew the parallel lines of the giant serpent's body.

By the cave, the flaming serpent undulated through the air, almost as if it were swimming.

Veka's fists clenched. "Can I borrow that?"

Slash sat up and handed her the goblin pricker. Veka jabbed one of the points into her forearm, then pinched the skin around the wound. Blood dripped down her forearm.

"What are you doing?" Slash asked.

She squeezed harder, and a tiny spray of blood misted Slash's drawing.

"Stop that." He turned away, his face pale.

Veka grabbed his shoulder. Blood dripped down her arm. The pain was annoying, but the discomfort on his face more than made up for it. "I need a distraction," she said. "The only way one of us is getting through is if the other gets the guards out of the way."

"I'm not going out there."

"If you say so." She squeezed again, spraying a bit of blood onto his chest.

That was too much for the poor hobgoblin. Slash groaned and fell face first onto the ice. Veka pressed the goblin pricker into his hand and closed his fingers.

Almost instantly Slash was up again, suspended by Veka's magic. She could see the giant serpent stiffen and turn, tasting her spell. She maneuvered the unconscious hobgoblin like a puppet, marching him toward the pixies. One of the pixies flew out to meet him, shouting a challenge. The pixie didn't appear worried. A lone hobgoblin shouldn't be much of a threat.

That was what he thought. Splitting her concentration, she cast a second spell that tore the goblin pricker from Slash's hand and propelled it upward. The point drove through the pixie's wing.

The pixie fell, screaming with pain and fury. Veka turned her full attention to Slash, levitating him over the pixie and dropping him several times. She didn't know if it would be enough to kill the pixie, but it should keep him from getting up any time soon. One pixie down. Five more to go, along with the flying fire snake.

"Sorry, Slash," she whispered. To her surprise, she realized she meant it.

Already the other guards were rushing to attack, the serpent in the lead. Veka sent Slash running as fast as she could, guiding him away from herself and the pixies. No hobgoblin could move so quickly, but the pixies probably didn't know that. Sure his movements were stiff and awkward, but so were most hobgoblins. And if his feet didn't quite touch the ground with each step . . . well, hopefully the pixies would be too intent on catching him to notice such details.

Veka edged out from behind the tree and began to run toward the cave. Slash's movements grew even clumsier. She couldn't watch where she was going and control him at the same time. Maybe she would have been better off trying to take over his mind, but that was a more complicated spell. Dominating lizard-fish was one thing, but Snixle had told her that intelligent creatures fought much harder. Grudgingly, she admitted that Slash would probably qualify as intelligent.

She glanced back in time to see Slash run right through the tip of a pine tree. He stumbled and slid along the ice. Veka tried to yank him back to his feet, but before she could, he simply dropped out of sight. He must have fallen into another crevasse.

Good enough. She was almost to the cave. The ice near the entrance was melted smooth and slick, probably from that oversize snake. She saw no sign of the tiny worms and their ice spike traps. In a way, the flaming serpent had done her a favor, driving off the smaller predators.

A few more splashing steps brought her to the darkness of the tunnel and relative safety. Thankfully the ice was high enough she didn't have to climb up to the entrance.

She was past the guards. Using her helpless companion as bait wasn't the most heroic tactic, but it had worked.

The tunnel had changed since her last visit. Orange insects filled the air, zipping this way and that, riding the currents of the magic. One tried to bite her arm, and she slapped it. She wiped glowing bug guts off her arm and hurried down the tunnel.

Glittering gray frost coated the rock. The dead ogre from before was gone. She looked back, wondering what the pixies would do to Slash. She hoped they wouldn't kill him.

The tunnel never became truly dark. The orange bugs continued to circle her. Their light reflected from the frost, illuminating the walls as she ran. As she neared Straum's lair, the light grew stronger. The warmth of the magic increased as well, making her sweat beneath her cloak. She pressed to one side of the tunnel and peered into the cave the dragon had once called home.

Crystalline ice lined the walls, the facets reflecting colored light in every direction. The ice itself seemed to glow, as if some of that light had been frozen within.

A bone-white mound sat in a depression on the far side of the cave. Golden sunlight spilled from a round, jagged hole in one side of the mound. She could feel the magic from here, enough to make the hair on her arms and neck stand at attention. If that wasn't the portal, she would eat her spellbook.

As far as she could tell, there were only two pixies in the cave. Two-winged worker pixies, not the warriors from outside. It would have been her luck to show up right as an army of pixie warrior-wizards were coming through, but for once, fate's dice had fallen in her favor.

A bright yellow pixie hovered on the far side of the cave. Her green companion crouched on the ground, struggling to maneuver a long pole-arm. Swarms of orange gnats circled angrily as he tugged. The point of the weapon slowly scraped along the rock, toward what appeared to be some kind of hive.

"You're mad," the yellow pixie said. Veka's heart pounded as the pixie flitted in Veka's direction, but then she turned back. "The queen ordered all death-metal buried beneath the ice."

"She also—" The green pixie grunted and strained as the pole-arm started to slip away. There was something wrong with his wings, but from this angle, Veka couldn't tell what. "She also ordered us to take care of the sparks. I for one don't intend to stand around swatting bugs all day."

The hive was a frosted, warty bulge in the ice about the size of a goblin's skull. The tip of the pole-arm brushed the hive, sending up a tiny geyser of steam. More gnats exploded from the hive, swarming toward the pixies.

"Don't drop it!" the yellow pixie shrieked.

The one on the ground grunted as he jabbed the tip deeper into the hive. He stepped back and fished a small bronze fruit from his vest. It looked like the globules she had seen growing beneath the ice. He popped it in his mouth, sucked for a moment, then spat out the wrinkled skin. "There's not enough metal in this stick to damage the portal."

"But if the queen comes back—"

"She won't." He pointed at the hive, and Veka felt

the tremors of magic. It reminded her of the spell she had used on the lizard-fish, back at the lake.

Orange bugs streaked toward the head of the polearm. The pixie's magic drove them into the steel, where they died in tiny flashes of light. Bodies sprinkled down on the green pixie like rain. "Ha! What do you say now, Wholoo?" He laughed and danced a victory jig as the bugs continued to dive to their deaths.

Veka's jaw clenched as she realized who it was. She had never actually seen Snixle before, but she recognized the inflection of his voice, the way he moved. It was easier to recognize someone when they had inhabited your body for a time.

Why wouldn't Snixle be here? He was the muckworker of the pixie world, cleaning up their messes and doing the jobs nobody else wanted. While the others went off to defend the queen, he was stuck here fighting bugs.

With the worst of the bugs littering the ground, Snixle bent down to adjust the butt of the weapon. Where his wings should have been, two tattered fragments protruded from his shoulders. He gave off less light than the yellow pixie, Wholoo. A deep green fluid had oozed over the torn ends of his wings. This was a recent injury then.

That meant he wouldn't have adjusted to his loss yet. Veka had seen it before, watching the younger goblins torture rats. The maimed rats needed to learn how to move all over again. Snixle's reflexes would be wrong.

Veka grabbed the rest of her goblin prickers and launched them at the yellow pixie. The pixie saw them coming and tried to dodge, but it was too late. Two caught her in the back and leg. Wholoo fell like the bugs she had been working to kill. Snixle let go of the pole-arm, which tipped over backward.

Already Veka was up and running. She saw Snixle leap back, then fall, unable to complete his instinctive retreat to the air.

Veka smacked Wholoo with her staff, then pounced on Snixle, wrapping her fingers around his slender body.

Snixle squirmed briefly, then his head slumped. "Go ahead and eat me," he mumbled. "That's what you goblins do, isn't it?"

Veka hesitated. The maimed pixie was, in a word, pathetic. Skinny, too. There was hardly enough meat on those tiny bones to make him worth the effort. "What happened to you, Snixle?"

His head jerked back up, and his glow brightened slightly. "Veka?" A tentative smile spread across his bruised face. "Is that you? I thought Jig Dragonslayer killed you!"

Veka shook her head. "When he stabbed me, it broke your spell. Then he healed me."

"The disruptive effect of death-metal, yes," Snixle said, nodding. "That makes sense. But why did he save you?"

"Because he's Jig. That's what he does." She turned him around to examine his wings.

"The queen," Snixle whispered. "When she learned how I failed to capture Jig Dragonslayer, and that I had kept you a secret . . ." Tears filled his eyes. "I didn't mean to disappoint her. She should have killed me. You can't know the agony of disappointing her, Veka. I wish she had killed me, but she ordered me to remain, to clean the sparks out of our cave."

Glowing snot dripped from his nose. He was a pitiful sight. The queen's magic was strong indeed, to command this kind of loyalty. She wondered how Jig would overcome it. "Sparks?"

He tilted his head toward the insect hive. "Nasty things. They feed on the blood and magic of pixies and other magical creatures." He sniffled and bent his neck, wiping his face on Veka's thumb. "How did you get in? There were guards—"

"I snuck past," she said.

"You're going to try to close the gateway, aren't you?" He shook his head. "Twenty of the strongest pixies worked together to open that portal. You'll never be able to destroy it."

She stepped toward the white hill, feeling the magic wash over her body. Snixle was right. Even this close, the sheer power pouring from the gateway made her want to shield her face. Enough power to transform the entire mountain. She knelt, trying to peer through, to get a glimpse of the pixies' world, but the sunlight was too bright.

"It's not too late," Snixle said. "We could still go to the queen—"

Veka shook her head. "Jig's leading an attack against the queen."

"No!" He couldn't have looked more distraught if she had eaten his legs. He twisted and squirmed, pounding Veka's fingers with his tiny fists. "I have to help her. I have to fight—"

Veka gave him a shake. "You have to show me how this gateway works."

"I can't! I have to save the queen." He closed his eyes, and Veka felt a swelling of magic within her hand as Snixle fought to take control, to reestablish the spell he had used on her before.

Veka strode to the edge of the cave and rapped him against the ice on the wall. "Stop that."

Snixle's spell dissipated at once. He groaned and closed his eyes. Another rush of magic swept past her.

The buzzing of insects warned her what Snixle had done. Veka leaped aside as a swarm of sparks rushed after her. Her staff clattered to the ground. She spun and flung Snixle into the middle of the swarm.

He yelped and curled into a ball. Bugs flew in every direction. Snixle's torn wings fluttered uselessly, and then he hit the ground and skidded into the wall. Veka hurried to scoop him up, but she needn't have bothered. Snixle swayed as he tried to stand. Even with one hand on the wall, he could barely keep himself upright.

Veka picked him back up and flicked a spark off of his neck. "Next time, I'll just squeeze."

Snixle nodded. "But the queen. I can't abandon—"

"Hush." Her ears twitched. She could hear shouting from the tunnel. She bit her lip, recognizing Slash's voice. At least he was still alive.

Snixle used her distraction to try one more time to enchant her. Her skin tingled, and her muscles grew heavy. Veka couldn't help but admire the little pixie. Bruised and battered, he still tried to fight.

She bounced him against the wall again, then stuffed his unconscious body into her pocket as she searched for a place to hide. The only shelter was the hill itself, the white mound that housed the pixies' portal. She crouched behind it, pulling her cloak around her body. The dark material wouldn't do much to conceal her, not when everything from the ice to the bugs generated its own light, but it was the best she could do.

Flickering flames marked the arrival of the giant serpent. Several pixies flew into the cave ahead of the snake. "Hey, Snixle, Wholoo, we caught a hobgoblin prancing around outside. He says his friend was coming this way."

Veka's fangs pressed her cheeks. The stupid hobgoblin had probably started babbling the moment he woke up. Cowards, all of them.

Then again, she had sent him bouncing over the landscape as a distraction. She might not feel terribly loyal either, if he had done something like that to her.

"Down here," said another pixie. "Wholoo's dead."

"Where's Snixle?"

Their lights danced along the ice as they flew down to investigate the body of the pixie Veka had slain. She didn't have much time before they found her. She had to figure out how to destroy the gate.

"Stay back. Let Moltiki deal with her."

Veka peeked around the hill, trying to figure out which one was Moltiki. The other pixies retreated to the entrance. Surrounded by pixies, Slash pressed himself to the wall as the giant snake slid into the cave, sniffing the air. As Snixle had taught her, she tried to reach out, to touch the snake's body with her magic. She had commanded hundreds of lizard-fish. How hard could a single giant snake be?

She wove magic like a shell, a second skin she could use to surround Moltiki, to control the snake's movements. Slowly that shell shrank into place.

The instant the magic touched the snake's skin, her spell shattered. She bit back a scream of pain. Moltiki reared, tongue flickering madly. One of the pixies shouted, "She's by the hill!"

She wasn't strong enough to break their control over the snake. All she had done was reveal her position, giving herself a skull-splitting headache in the process.

She edged around the hill, toward the back of the cave. She thought about simply running through the gate, but what would she accomplish? Even if she survived, she would be alone and lost in another world. Better to end things quickly, but how?

She could sense the magic pouring through the portal, but she didn't have the slightest idea what to do with it. If she tried to block the flow, that magic would rip her apart.

Moltiki crept closer. Veka pressed her hands and face against the hill. The mound's rough surface scratched her skin. What was this thing made of? Unlike the ice and stone of the cave, this was dry and warm. Too hard and uniform for wood, and too rough for stone. More than anything else, it reminded her of bone.

Veka backed away, staring at the mound and imagining . . . That bulge around the base could be a tail coiled against the body. The other side of the hill narrowed like a neck, with the great skull resting between his feet.

The pixies needed a powerful concentration of magic to serve as an anchor for their portal, and what greater magic than the body of Straum himself? They had fused the bones into a single invulnerable shell. The skull housed the actual gate. To physically destroy the hill, she would need to shatter the skeleton of a dragon. Easier to rip apart the mountain itself. No wonder they hadn't left more guards. What could a single goblin do against this?

"I see her!" One of the pixies waved his hands, and Moltiki lunged for her. How could something so big be so fast? Veka's size had only ever slowed her down.

She dove away, stumbling into the icy wall. Strange that she didn't feel cold. Oh yes, that would be because Moltiki had set her cloak on fire. She stripped the cloak from her body and flung it at Moltiki's face. Wearing nothing but her old muckworking clothes, she backed away.

The giant snake slid around behind her, positioning his huge body between Veka and the exit.

"What did you think you were doing, goblin?" asked the lead pixie.

Moltiki's tail smashed her side. It was like being hit with a tree. A burning tree. With rough scales that shredded her apron and the skin beneath. Old muck stains on her clothes smoked in response to the flames. Veka cowered against the hill, her hands up in a futile gesture to ward off the next blow.

"This is what you want," Slash shouted from the entrance. He held up a small rectangular box that appeared to be made of wood. "This is what she planned to use to close the gate."

The pixies hesitated. Moltiki's burning eyes stared into Veka's. His mouth was open, and he could have swallowed Veka whole before she could draw breath to scream. For now, though, everyone's attention was on Slash.

Veka rubbed her head. What was that stupid hobgoblin talking about? Where had that box come from?

"I stole it from her," Slash said. His face was bruised and bloody, either from being dropped into the ice crevasse, or from the pixies' rough handling. "No hobgoblin would trust a rat-eating goblin with something this important."

One of the pixies flew toward Slash and plucked the box from his hand. "What is it?"

"There's no magic in that," said another. "If they think their little toys are powerful enough to scratch our gate, they're delusional."

Veka glanced at the pole-arm Snixle and Wholoo had been using against the sparks. Was that enough iron to scratch the gate? Probably not or they never would have used it here. She needed something bigger. A spell powerful enough to kill this stupid serpent and destroy the portal at the same time.

While she was at it, why not wish for the pixie queen's unconditional surrender to Veka the Sorceress?

"How do you open it?" asked the pixie, studying the box. "I see no hinges—No, I see it now. Clever workmanship." He pressed one end of the box. "The lid pops open like so, and—"

Even Veka's goblin ears could barely make out the sharp *twang* from the box. The pixie screamed and flung the box away. A slender pin protruded from the center of his palm. Smoke rose from the wound.

"Kill him!" the pixie screamed. Moltiki rushed away, closing the distance to Slash before the poor hobgoblin had taken a single step. Moltiki's body blocked her view as he lunged, and then the giant snake drew back. Slash dangled from the snake's jaw. Moltiki's fangs had pierced the hobgoblin's leg. Slash flailed about, shouting in pain.

"No!" Before Veka even realized what she was doing, she had wrapped a spell around the pole-arm and launched it at the snake. The steel blade cut through the scales and lodged deep within the neck. Moltiki roared in pain. Slash dropped to the ground and didn't move.

"Get the goblin, get the goblin!" screamed another pixie.

The pole-arm was embedded too deeply in the snake for Veka's magic to remove it. She cast a second spell, grabbing her staff from where it had fallen and sending it spinning through the air. The whirling ends batted one pixie aside, then smashed a second. She shot the staff at a third pixie, but this one waved a hand, and the staff disintegrated. So she flung Wholoo's body at the pixie instead. She missed, but it bought her time to scramble around behind the hill.

Two pixies down, a third with a metal pin through his hand. That left two uninjured, along with one bleeding, very angry snake. She could try again to control it, but—

No. She stared at the hill, remembering Snixle's words. *Necromancy is like wearing a corpse.* But the magic was the same as she had used on the lizard-fish.

Straum had been dead for an entire year. His bones were warped and fused by pixie magic. She had never tried to control anything so big, or so dead.

And if she didn't try now, she would be snake food.

Blood dripped into her eye. When had she cut her head? Not that it mattered. As the pixies regrouped, she pressed her body against the hill and cast her spell.

Snixle had taught her that pixie magic was practically a living thing. So were Straum's remains. The dragon might be dead, but those bones were still warm with power. They welcomed Veka's magic, drawing her spell into themselves like a starving goblin stuffing himself in Golaka's storerooms.

Her vision blurred and darkened. Her joints felt like ice, stiff and cold. She slipped to her knees as the magic threatened to crush her. No, it wasn't the magic. It was Straum's remains. The weight of those massive bones pressed her to the ground, grinding her into the ice and stone. She couldn't hear. She couldn't see. Where were the pixies, the giant serpent? Moltiki could be rearing back to strike, and she wouldn't even know.

She fought to stand, but her body wouldn't obey. Straum's body. Magic and ice and decay had turned the skeleton into a solid mass of bone. She would have to break the bones to move them. This had been a mistake. How could she have been so foolish? She tried to release the spell, but even in death, Straum was too powerful. His body sucked Veka's power and refused to let her go. She was inside Straum's bones, but she couldn't move them. She would have laughed at the absurdity, but even that was beyond her.

Veka felt nothing. No cold, no pain, nothing but magic. The river of magic pouring from the portal in her mouth, the currents flowing through the room, the tiny spot of warmth on her side . . . no, that was Veka herself, felt through Straum's body. Her jaw throbbed, as if she had tried to swallow one of Slash's goblin prickers. Was that the portal causing her such pain?

There was Moltiki, crawling around the front of the hill toward Veka.

Would she even feel the strike, or would her existence simply end? Worse yet, would her mind remain trapped inside Straum's skeleton, blind and deaf and forever unable to move? Despair began to weigh her down as much as the bones themselves.

Time seemed slower, trapped inside the dragon. She could feel each ripple of Moltiki's muscular body as the great snake drew back to strike. The pixies darted about, sending currents through the magic like bugs on the lake.

As she waited for the serpent to finish her, a single thought wormed through her mind. *Jig would have found a way.*

Anger burned through despair. Jig *always* found a way. He always won. Veka was the one who got captured by a pixie peon or eaten by a flaming serpent or stabbed through the gut by *Jig Dragonslayer*! Jig had slain Straum, and Veka wasn't even strong enough to overcome the power in the dragon's dead bones. It wasn't fair!

The portal pulsed in her jaw as waves of magic poured from the pixies' world. Veka tried to shut out everything except that portal. Forget the pixies. Forget Moltiki. Forget Slash. She didn't even know if the hobgoblin was still alive.

Jig would have succeeded. So would she.

Straining every bone in her neck and jaw until they felt ready to shatter, Veka wrenched Straum's head to one side and snapped the great jaws down on the serpent.

There was a moment of tremendous pressure. She thought about the younger goblins who, when harassed by mosquitoes and other bloodsuckers, would pull their skin taut to trap the bugs in place. Blood would continue to bloat the mosquitoes until they exploded. At that moment, Veka felt a great sympathy for those poor bugs.

The skull shattered, and Veka lost consciousness.

Rough hands shook Veka's arm. She opened her eyes and wished she hadn't. The light felt like knives going straight to her brain. "No goblin should have to wake up to that ugly face," she mumbled, shoving Slash away.

"About time you woke up." Slash sat against the wall of the cave. He had wrapped torn singed strips of her cloak around his leg. Water dripped down from the melting ice.

Veka looked around. Moltiki's body had been cut completely in half, either by Straum's jaws or by the explosion that followed. Huge shards of bone littered the cave floor. If the pent-up magic had done that to a dragon's bones, she wondered how bad the damage had been on the pixies' side of the portal.

She reached up to touch her face. Her fangs had driven right through her cheeks when she clamped Straum's jaws down around the serpent.

Blue blood. She stared at her hands. The metallic glow of the pixies' world was gone.

Slash was holding up one hand to block the sight of her blood. "Do you mind?"

She wiped her hands on her apron. "That box. What was it?"

"Needle trap. I pried it out of one of the Necromancer's doors a few months back. Dipped the needle in lizard-fish poison for good measure." He pointed to the pixie who lay dead near the tunnel entrance. "I had been planning to install it in a little chest and leave it in front of the goblin lair."

He gave a sheepish shrug. "The chief only told us not to kill goblins. Is it my fault if you hurt yourselves on one of my toys?"

Veka was too exhausted to do anything but shake her head. Even that was a mistake. The bones in her neck popped and cracked, shooting pain down her spine. All she wanted was to lie down and sleep for the next few days.

"How do you think Jig did?" Slash asked.

Veka snorted. "He's probably back at the goblin lair, sipping klak beer while the other goblins make up new verses for 'The Song of Jig.' "

Slash chuckled. "Forget 'The Song of Jig.' I want to know what they're going to sing about this." He waved an arm to encompass the snake, the bone debris, the dead pixies, and the multicolored slush dripping from the walls and ceiling. "I'll tell you this much, though. The first goblin to call me 'Slash' in a song gets a lizard-fish spine in her boot."

Veka stared at the scar running down his face. For the first time she thought to wonder how it had happened. "Who did that to you?"

He flushed. "I did it myself. An ax trap I was working on misfired." He shrugged. "Could be worse. You should see what my friend Marxa looked like after her fire trap went off prematurely."

Veka nodded absently. Reality was gradually beginning to seep through her shock. She was still alive. The portal was destroyed. The pixies had all died or fled.

She glanced at the tattered remains of her cloak, wondering what had happened to Snixle. She had forgotten all about him when she tossed away the burning cloak. If he had remained inside her pocket, she would have been able to smell his burned remains. She crawled over and poked the cloak. A bit of ash floated free, all that remained of her spellbook.

"Hey, Veka." Slash still wouldn't look at her. "That snake was going to kill me. One more bite. . . ." He grimaced and touched the bloody bandages on his leg. "I mean, if you hadn't stabbed him like that. He . . . you . . ." He shook his head. "Sorry, I can't say it. Not to a goblin. If the other hobgoblins found out a stupid, fat, ugly rat-eater like you had saved my life, they—"

"Shut up, Slash." Veka rolled her eyes. After everything else she had been through, the hobgoblin's insults were no more bothersome than gnats. The normal kind, not the orange pixie gnats. Besides, if he got too uppity, she could still bounce him off a few walls. "You're welcome."

She tried to stand up, and her head began to pound. "Forget that," she muttered. With the portal closed, she had to try several times to cast her levitation spell. The pixies' magic was still here, but it was dissipating fast, like smoke in the wind. Eventually she managed to tap into that fading power. Ever so gently, she lifted herself from the ground. A second spell scooped Slash after her. Together they floated out of Straum's lair and into the wider cavern, toward home.

CHAPTER 17

"Well, *that* didn't go quite the way we had planned."

—Poppink the Pixie

Jig had experienced plenty of unpleasant awakenings in his life, from the time he woke up to find a group of goblins preparing to drop a baby rock serpent in his mouth to the time he discovered Smudge building a web in his loincloth. This one topped them all. Not only was Tymalous Shadowstar's voice booming loudly enough to crack his skull, but when he finally opened his eyes, Braf's face filled his vision.

Braf grinned so widely a bit of drool slipped from his lower lip. "It worked! You're alive!"

You weren't joking, were you? asked Shadowstar. *Less than a day, and already you've got goblins trying to kill you.*

Jig groaned and sat up. "Yes, I'm alive." He stopped. The pain in his back was gone. Drying blood covered his vest, but the wound itself had disappeared. *Why am I alive?*

Because Braf fixed that nasty hole in your back.

Jig stared, trying to absorb that piece of information. Braf had healed him. Braf, who was now standing next to Jig. Standing on two bare, perfectly healthy feet. Grell sat on the ground behind him, tending a small fire. She had taken the remains of Jig's muck pouch and set the whole thing aflame.

You . . . he healed me? But I thought you couldn't do anything down here. The pixies—

Look around, Jig.

The tunnels were the same red and black obsidian he was used to. The flames rising from his muck pouch were a healthy green. This was the chamber where he had fought the pixie queen. Without the sparkle of magic and the flurry of pixie lights, Jig barely recognized the place. The blood on the ground gave it away though. A sticky blue puddle showed where Jig had passed out.

Noroka still lay face first on the ground, snoring loudly. "You healed her too?"

Braf nodded. "Those pixies broke her nose pretty good, but she wasn't dead."

"Pixies. Right." Jig looked out at the bottomless pit. "How many others survived?"

"Counting us?" Grell asked. "Maybe five or six. I'm not counting you, because you should have been dead. Would have been, if Braf hadn't stuck his finger in your back and—"

"Thanks," Jig said, cringing.

"The others already started climbing back up to the lair," Grell went on. "I wanted to follow, but this clod kept insisting you were alive, talking about how he had to save you. When I asked how he planned to do that with the bones of his foot all crushed to gravel, he sat down and started fixing his own foot. After that I figured maybe he knew what he was talking about for once."

"How did you get here?" Jig asked.

Braf pointed to a rope hanging down the side of the pit. "One of the ogres tried to fly straight into the tunnel. Snapped his wings, but he nearly got me. Grell snuck up and jabbed a knife in his ear. We tied the rope around his body and climbed on down."

Jig stood up, testing his balance. He was filthy, hungry, and exhausted, but everything appeared to be working. He crouched by Noroka and shook her until she stirred. "Watch her," Jig warned. "Stop her if she tries to go over the edge."

Braf and Grell looked confused, but they didn't argue. Braf stepped toward the pit, arms spread.

"My head hurts," Noroka said. "I think the mountain punched me in the face." She gasped. "Grop. He—"

"Took a dive into the pit," Jig said. "Do you want to do the same?"

Noroka scowled. "Is that a threat?"

"No." Jig realized he was grinning. He didn't know how long he had lain there, but it was long enough for the pixie queen's magic to disperse. If the steel arrowhead hadn't killed her, the wind would eventually do the job, smashing her against the walls of the pit. Most of the pixies had probably suffered the same fate as they flew so recklessly after their queen, trying in vain to save her.

He stepped to the end of the tunnel and looked into the darkness. The muck fire gave enough light for Jig to see the nearest bubbles of the pixie nest. They sagged gray and broken from the walls. He saw pieces flaking away, spinning as they disappeared into the dark.

Of all the goblins who had come with him, only a handful still survived. He wondered how the goblins back at the lair had done against the ogres. If things had gone as poorly there, Jig might have single-handedly overseen the extermination of half the goblins in the mountain.

Is that why you spoke to Braf? he asked. *To replace me with a follower who doesn't get everyone around him killed?*

Don't be daft, snapped Shadowstar. *I spoke to him because it was the only way to keep you from bleeding to death. I actually asked Grell first, but she told me to go to hell. I wiped it from her mind, so she doesn't remember. But that left the idiot.*

Braf isn't—

I know he's not as dumb as he pretends to be, but he's still a goblin.

Thanks.

"What now, Jig?" Braf asked.

Jig stared for a long time before realizing what Braf meant. Jig was still chief. Braf and the others still expected him to tell them what to do. Jig groaned and rubbed his head. "We should go home," he said. "We have to find out if anyone survived up there."

"Braf and I will go first," Grell said. "He can haul me back up, and then you two follow. We shouldn't put too much weight on the rope. That ogre was a big fellow, but we don't want to push our luck."

Jig nodded.

"Watch out for that nest too," Grell added. "Those chunks are hard as wood when they fall, and they'll scratch you good. The big ones could knock you clean off the rope."

"I will," Jig said.

"Of course some of the pieces are pretty sharp. We'll be lucky if one doesn't cut the rope clean through as we're trying to—"

"Will you just go?" Jig snapped.

"Hmph." Grell grabbed a bit of rope and began tying herself to Braf. "See if I ever share my sugar-knots with you again."

Jig climbed slowly, despite his fears. He had hesitated at first, not sure whether he should go first and give Noroka a clear shot at his back. But if he followed, it would be just as easy for her to cut the rope, sending him into the pit. In the end he decided he was too tired to worry about it. If she killed him, at least he wouldn't have to be chief anymore.

His mind hurt as he tried to absorb it all. What had happened to the pixies' world? No matter how he thought about it, he kept coming to the same answer: Veka. She and Slash must have found a way to close the gateway. Jig spent a fair amount of time wondering how in the name of the Fifteen Forgotten Gods she had managed to pull that off.

Then there was Braf and Shadowstar. By all logic, Jig should have been happy. Let the goblins come to someone else for a while with their broken bones and their bloody wounds. Let Braf be the one the ogres sought out when pixies invaded. Braf could have Tymalous Shadowstar, and Jig could have some peace and quiet.

Yet every time he thought about it, the idea of Braf taking his place made his teeth clench tighter.

Why, Jig, I think you're jealous.

Jig rolled his eyes. *Can't you snoop around in his mind for a while?*

I did. It's boring. Besides, who says I can't snoop in two places at once? Now tell me, what's really bothering you?

You, said Jig. *You pushed me to go to the lower caverns with Walland. You pushed me to fight the pixies. You pushed me into that fight with Kralk. You've been trying to control me all along, just like the pixies controlled their ogres.*

Haven't we already been over this? Shadowstar asked, sounding a bit testy. *Jig, what do you think would have happened if you hadn't gone? The pixies would have swept through this mountain, and every last goblin would be dead or a slave.*

Jig wrapped his arms and legs around the rope and rested briefly. *Kralk could have led that fight.*

Jig, the goblins are dying.

Jig snorted. *That's what happens when goblins fight ogres.*

That's not what I mean. Think about that cavern where the ogre refugees were hiding. Who do you think used to live there, and what happened to them?

Jig didn't answer.

You goblins have always lived in the dark, dank holes of the mountain. Even before you sealed the way out a year ago, you isolated yourselves from the world. You hid, and you fought, and you died.

I sealed the entrance to protect us, Jig snapped. *And if this is your solution, I'm not impressed. All you did was speed up the process.*

No, the pixies did that. Jig, you can't go back to hiding in your temple, and the goblins can't keep hiding in their mountain. Straum's cavern is wiped out. The Necromancer's tunnels were already dead, if you'll forgive the pun. And there are other empty lairs, places where goblins and hobgoblins and other creatures used to live before they died out. If things don't change, empty lairs will be all that's left.

You want us to leave? Jig asked.

I want you to stop isolating yourselves. Jig, your race was brought here to help protect the treasures of the mountain. Those treasures are long gone. The goblins have no purpose. All you do is fight the hobgoblins and the other monsters, when you're not fighting yourselves.

Jig shook his head. *I can't—*

You have to lead, Jig. Kralk couldn't have done it. The hobgoblins won't. If the goblins are going to survive, you have to be the one to guide them.

It all sounded so reasonable. Jig rested his face against the rock. *Why didn't you tell me? Why not trust us to make our own decisions?*

Shadowstar didn't respond, and Jig didn't bother to repeat himself.

The goblin lair was empty. Braf and Grell had opened the door from the waste pit, and the cavern was as quiet as the Necromancer's throne room.

"Do you think the ogres won?" Braf asked.

Jig shook his head. The pixies' control over the ogres should have been broken, but that probably didn't matter. The ogres would have found themselves free, in the midst of a battle with goblins and hobgoblins. Being ogres, they probably reacted the same way the goblins would have: by finishing the battle. But if that was the case, why hadn't they overrun the lair? Where were the goblins who had remained behind? There were no bodies, no signs of battle, aside from day-to-day goblin messiness.

He hurried past the others, running toward the kitchen. Dying muck fires flickered to either side as he peered through the doorway.

The kitchen was empty. The cookfire was little more than embers.

"Golaka left her kitchen?" Braf whispered, sounding shaken.

Jig wanted to weep. He didn't have the strength for another battle. He reached up to pet Smudge. The fire-spider didn't seem worried. Maybe the events of the past few days had burned out his ability to feel fear.

By now Noroka had emerged from the waste pit. She cocked her head to one side and said, "Jig, listen."

He tilted his head and twitched his good ear. Screams coming from the hobgoblin lair. He started to reach for his sword, forgetting the pixies had thrown it away. Grimacing, he snatched a large kitchen knife and headed for the tunnels.

The closer they came to hobgoblin territory, the stranger the sounds became. He didn't hear the ring of steel or the high-pitched squeals of wounded goblins. The taunts and shouts weren't as loud or hateful as he would have expected either. Some of the voices actually sounded like they were singing.

A group of hobgoblins stood near their statue, guarding the entrance. One raised a copper mug. "Who goes there?"

"Filthy beasts, aren't they?" asked another of the guards.

Jig glanced down at himself. Perhaps he should have changed clothes after coming through the waste pit.

"Looks like a bunch of carrion-worms masquerading as goblins." That earned a laugh from the other hobgoblins.

"This is Jig Dragonslayer," snapped Grell. "The goblin who singlehandedly killed the pixie queen."

Jig flushed as the hobgoblins peered closer. A horrible thought entered his mind. Would they start calling him Jig Pixieslayer now?

"Jig Dragonslayer, eh?" The guard was clearly skeptical that the goblin chief would be wandering about in such a state. He glanced at his companions and shrugged.

"Put that thing away," said the largest of the guards, pointing at Jig's knife. Two others ducked into the hobgoblin lair. "They already carved the meat."

Already carved the meat? Jig stared at the knife in his hand. It wouldn't do much good against the hobgoblins anyway. The blade fit loosely into the empty sheath on his belt. "I don't understand. What—"

The other hobgoblins returned carrying large, wooden buckets. Before Jig could react, they tossed the contents over him and the other goblins. Jig barely had time to shield Smudge before the frigid water knocked him back.

"That's better," said the closest guard, swishing the half-empty bucket. "Folks are trying to eat and drink back there. If we don't rinse you down, you're going to ruin their appetites."

Jig was too confused to do anything but nod and turn around. They had a point, he supposed. He did smell pretty rank. Smudge was even worse, since fire-spiders cleansed themselves by burning whatever dirt clung to their bodies.

Still, there was no reason the water had to be so cold.

Eventually they were deemed suitable for hobgoblin society, whatever that meant, and led into the larger cavern. The dead goblin they passed along the way did nothing to calm Jig's fear. The hobgoblins stepped around the body. One of them muttered, "Makkar was supposed to clean up the traps. Looks like she missed one."

"This is weird," whispered Noroka.

Jig only nodded. Most of the partitions that had divided the hobgoblin lair were gone, torn down and piled to the sides. Hobgoblins and goblins crowded around an enormous bonfire, and as far as Jig could see, nobody was killing anyone else. He spotted a few fights, but they were weaponless spats. A hobgoblin bludgeoning a goblin here, a gang of four goblins piling on a hobgoblin there, nothing out of the ordinary. And those few fights were the exception to the overall sense of . . . of celebration.

Jig made his way toward the fire, where two hobgoblins were turning an enormous spit. Both hobgoblins cast nervous looks at Golaka, who rapped her ever-present wooden spoon against her palm as she supervised.

She supervised one hobgoblin on the back of the head, hard enough to knock him away from the spit. "Don't turn it so fast," she shouted. "Give the ogre time to cook. Give the sauce time to work through the meat. Otherwise you might as well eat him raw!"

Braf tapped Jig on the shoulder and pointed to the bonfire. "Isn't that Arnor?"

Jig squinted. Golaka's garnishes hid some of the features, but he thought Braf was right. Apparently some of the ogre refugees hadn't managed to escape from the pixies.

Grell sniffed the air. "Smells like Golaka broke out the elven wine sauce."

A loud, harsh voice cut through the noise. "Jig Dragonslayer!" From the far side of the cavern, the hobgoblin chief waved his sword. "Someone drag that scrawny excuse for a leader to me."

Jig waded through the crowd, doing his best to avoid the larger goblins. Cheerful as things appeared, he was still the goblin chief, and there were a lot of ambitious goblins crammed in here. Nowhere near as many as there had been before, thanks to the fighting, but more than enough for Jig's comfort. Not to mention the hobgoblins, one of whom left claw marks in Jig's arm as he tried to hurry Jig along.

The chief sat on one of the rolled-up partitions, basically a log of heavy red cloth. One of his tunnel cats sat with its paws tucked beneath its chin as it worked the marrow from an ogre bone. Veka and Slash stood to one side, drinking klak beer. Veka had lost her robe and staff. Both she and the hobgoblin looked bruised and battered, and it was strange to see Veka in her ragged muckworking clothes. They made her look smaller somehow. Younger.

The hobgoblin chief pointed his sword at Jig. "A beer for the goblin chief!"

Veka rolled her eyes, then gestured. Across the room a cup jumped from a hobgoblin's hand and floated toward Jig. Veka bit her lip. From the looks of it, she was concentrating much harder than she had before. That thought cheered Jig immensely.

"You're using your magic to serve drinks now?" Jig asked. Veka scowled, and the cup wobbled just enough to spill beer onto Jig's arm. He grinned and snatched the cup. The smell of klak beer would help mask the odors still coming from poor Smudge.

"What a battle," the chief said. "They'll be singing songs about this one long after you and I are gone. Those blasted ogres drove us all the way through the tunnels to the entrance of our lair." He pointed. "That's where we hit them with our first ambush. I had your goblins come at them from the tunnel. Pathetic as you rat-eaters are in a real fight, it was enough to confuse the ogres. They're tough to kill, I'll tell you that much. No matter how many times we drove them back, they kept coming. Eventually they broke into the lair. We led them into the tunnel cat kennels near the back. Your little wizard here showed up around then, using her magic to fling weapons left and right. Not enough to kill an ogre, but she certainly kept them on their toes while our cats tore into them."

Veka's mouth wrinkled, as if she couldn't decide whether or not to take offense at the "little wizard" remark.

"A number of the ogres fled in the end. Your wizard thinks some pixies survived as well. I don't know where they'll get to, but I plan to be ready." He waved at Slash. "Charak here has been sharing some ideas for pixie traps, and I want them set up in your lair as well as ours."

Slash pulled a folded packet of parchment from his vest. Charcoal arrows and drawings covered the page. "I'm designing a pixie net using steel wire," he said, sounding more excited and animated than Jig had ever seen him. "I haven't figured out how to set a trigger for an airborne target yet, but I will. We can also stretch netting across any opening we don't want pixies coming through, like your waste pit or the privies. Can you imagine sitting down right when a pixie—"

"We'll need to do something about Straum's lair too," said Jig. "The dragon lined his cave with steel and iron to keep the pixies from coming through. Most of those weapons will have to be returned. Otherwise what's to stop the next group from recreating the portal?"

"The fact that I blew Straum's remains to pieces,"

Veka mumbled. She sounded dejected, which confused Jig. From the sound of things, she had done everything she ever dreamed of: fought pixies, destroyed the gate, and helped to save the goblins. Her magic was clearly stronger than before, and somehow she had survived the whole mess. What was wrong with her?

"You want us to give up our weapons?" The hobgoblin chief scowled, and Jig took a step back.

"Not all of them," Jig said. "But enough to line the walls of Straum's cave. Goblin and hobgoblin weapons both."

The chief's scowl faded. "Why not? If we need more swords, we can always come pound a few more goblin warriors and take yours, right?" He clapped Jig on the arm and stood up. "If we're going to do it, best to start now, before these fools sober up."

Despite his age, his shouts cut through the noise of the celebration like . . . well, like his sword. "Listen up! We're going to lock those pixies out of this mountain forever. To do that, I need you hobgoblins to gather every sword, knife, shield, and any other bit of steel or iron you can find. Once we see what we have to work with, we'll decide how much we need."

He glanced at Jig, clearly expecting him to make a similar announcement. Already hobgoblins were crowding around the chief, dropping weapons and armor at his feet. The sight of it confirmed something Jig had been thinking about ever since leaving the pixies' pit:

No matter how loudly he shouted, no matter how many songs the goblins sang about him, no matter how many pixie queens and dragons and Necromancers he killed, the goblins would never leap to obey him the way these hobgoblins did with their chief . . . the way the pixies obeyed their queen. Even the old ogre Trockle had been able to control her family.

Jig wasn't cut out to be a leader. Sure, they followed him into battle after a bit of prodding and bullying. Then he turned his back on Grop and nearly got himself killed.

His attempts to rally the goblins into battle with the hobgoblins had been humiliating, and his first official act as chief had been to flee to Kralk's quarters and hide.

Everyone stumbles in the beginning, Shadowstar said.

When a goblin stumbles, there's usually another goblin to make sure he doesn't get back up.

By now many of the hobgoblins were watching Jig, as were a number of goblins. He could see their suspicion building. Was this a trick to disarm the hobgoblins? The hobgoblins looked angry, and the goblins looked eager.

"Bring your weapons to the goblin chief," Jig said, wincing at how hoarse his voice sounded. Drawing a deep breath and hoping it wouldn't be his last, he pointed to Grell. "Bring them to her."

Grell's cane jabbed him in the side before he could say anything more. "Did my withered ears deceive me, runt? If you think you can foist this job off on me, you—"

"Isn't it better than working in the nursery?"

"I'm looking after children either way. At least the babies don't poison you in your sleep. Not until they're two or three years old at least. If you want me dead, cut my throat and be done with it."

She was right, of course. Grell was one of the few goblins who would be even more vulnerable than Jig himself. He could already see the hunger in the eyes of the goblins, the calculating expressions. Jig had lasted several hours before his first assassination attempt. Grell would be lucky to last five minutes.

"Grell's smart enough to have survived this long," he said. "That's something we need from a chief."

Grell reached beneath her blankets and drew her knife, which she jabbed at Jig's throat. New odors wafted from Smudge as he grew hot from fright. "That's right. I survived by avoiding suicidal situations like this one. I'm not about to—"

"I'm not done!" Jig squeaked, backing away from that blade. He raised his voice. "I know you're already plotting to kill her, so I should warn you. Whoever kills Grell will die a slow, horrible death. I've cast a spell of protection on her. Every hurt I've healed over the past year, every broken bone, every gash, every split lip and chipped tooth, every gouged eye, hernia, and wart, all of them will be inflicted upon whoever dares lay a hand on her."

Oh, really? Shadowstar asked.

Shut up. As long as they *believe it, who cares?* The goblins looked nervous. They kept glancing from Jig to Grell and back again. He held his breath, hoping it would be enough. If not . . . if they didn't believe him . . .

"Yeah," Braf piped up. "And then I'll kill you." He was unarmed, but he pounded his fist into his palm for emphasis. Whatever else he might be, Braf was a big goblin. The crowd began to mutter.

One of the hobgoblin swords floated from the pile of weapons and began to spin. Veka stepped forward to stand beside Braf. She didn't try to shout, but every other voice in the cavern went silent to listen. "But before he kills you, I'll seize control of your body. I'll make you smile as you eat your own limbs." The sword cut an arc through the air, driving the goblins back. "Cooked or raw, it's your choice."

The goblins backed down. A new pile of steel began to grow next to Grell. Jig knew most of the goblins were keeping knives or other weapons hidden, just as the hobgoblins were doing, but hopefully it would be enough. Given how sensitive the pixies had been to the touch of steel, they shouldn't need to line every bit of the cave. Just enough to disrupt their magic.

He turned to Grell. "Now will you be chief?"

Grell muttered and spat.

"I watched you," Jig said, lowering his voice. "You helped Braf. You helped me. You were the one who convinced the goblins to follow my orders. You know how to get them to do what you want. I don't."

He looked around. "You *care*. You won't let them die. You'll keep them safe and make them stronger." He swallowed, remembering what Shadowstar had told him. Angry as he was, he couldn't ignore the truth in Shadowstar's words. "We can't keep going on the way we have."

He held his breath. If he were in Grell's position, he would ram that knife right into Jig's belly. Sure, Jig and Braf and Veka had all sworn to avenge her death, but that didn't do anything to change the fact of her death, did it? Most goblins would be too afraid of Jig's bluff and the others' threats to do anything, but there were always a few clever enough to trick another goblin into doing their dirty work. Jig would have to keep an eye on those.

Grell poked him with her cane again. "If I'm going to be chief, I'm going to enjoy it. Grab me a pitcher of klak beer and a plate of Arnor."

Beside her the hobgoblin chief chuckled and turned

his attention back to the growing pile of weapons and armor. Mostly weapons . . . neither hobgoblins nor goblins worried too much about armor. Jig reached around to rub the spot where Grop had stabbed him. Maybe he ought to snatch a scrap of armor for himself before all that steel went back to Straum's cave . . .

Two beers and a bit of heavily spiced ogre meat later, Jig was sneaking out of the hobgoblin lair toward home. Smudge sat on his shoulder, happily charring the scrap of meat Jig had saved for him.

"Jig, wait." Veka hurried after him, carrying a borrowed muck lantern. Blue light illuminated the tunnel, nearly washing out the few specks of orange that swirled around her head. "Pixie bugs," she muttered. "They were all over Straum's cave."

Jig didn't answer. She couldn't be planning to ask him about magic again. Whatever tricks Jig could do, Veka had clearly surpassed him. So what could she possibly want?

"Jig . . ." She grabbed his arm and dragged him to one side of the tunnel.

Jig tensed, suddenly very aware that he still hadn't replaced his sword.

But Veka only sighed and looked away. Her huge body seemed to deflate a bit.

"Jig, Braf told me what you did. How you led the goblins through the nest and killed the pixie queen."

Jig nodded, still unsure where this was going. For a moment, he nearly panicked, thinking Veka might somehow still be under pixie control, here to avenge his attack on the queen.

She swallowed, and her eyes shone. "How did you do it?" she asked softly. "I needed all of my magic just to survive, and even then . . . even then, Slash had to help me. I needed a hobgoblin's help to keep me alive long enough to kill the giant snake and destroy their gateway. I had all that power at my fingertips, and you had nothing. I know you couldn't talk to your god. You had no magic, nothing but a few goblins and some old weapons to fight an entire army of pixies and ogres, not to mention the queen herself, and you *won*. You killed her."

Jig touched his spectacles. "I was lucky."

Veka shook her head so vehemently her hair whipped Jig's face. "Nobody is that lucky." She patted her apron as though she was searching for something, and then her shoulders slumped even more. "In *The Path of the Hero* Josca wrote a list of one hundred heroic deeds. I read it so many times I could list the top ten in my sleep."

She closed her eyes. "For deed number one, Josca wrote, 'The mark of the true Hero, the one feat that scores above all others on the dimensions of courage, strength, cunning, and sheer nobility, is the slaying of an evil dragon.' "

With a weary sigh, she looked at him and said, "You're a Hero, Jig. A scrawny, half blind, weak runt with no real magic to speak of, but still a Hero."

"Thanks," said Jig.

She shook her head again. "You don't understand."

Should he tell her the only reason he had survived his encounter with the pixie queen was because of his spectacles? Or that if she examined every one of his so-called victories, what had kept him alive wasn't strength or nobility, but pure, unadulterated cowardice?

Veka swatted another bug. "I always thought you were weak. Hiding in your temple, letting Kralk bully you, flinching away from the larger goblins. I never wanted to be like you. But ever since you came back from your adventure, I wanted . . ." Her voice trailed off. Jig wasn't sure, but he thought she had said, "I wanted to *be* you."

"Veka, what—"

"I lost my spellbook. I lost Josca's book. I even lost that ridiculous cloak." She cocked her head to one side. "Which is probably for the best. That thing was too heavy for these caves. The material doesn't breathe at all, and I was always drenched in sweat. But, Jig, what am I supposed to do now?"

"I'm sure Grell wouldn't mind if you took one of Kralk's old outfits."

Veka rolled her eyes. "I thought . . . I wanted to go on adventures and save our people and discover ancient treasures and all that. But you're the Hero, not me. I'm not the one who killed the queen or slew the dragon. I—"

"Veka, I didn't kill the stupid dragon," Jig blurted.

She froze with her mouth half open. "What?"

Jig grimaced as he sang a bit of that blasted song, " 'While others fled, Jig grabbed a spear, and he threw.' The song doesn't say I actually killed Straum."

Veka blinked so rapidly Jig thought one of those orange bugs had flown into her eye. "I don't understand. Straum's dead."

"He's dead, but I didn't kill him."

"I *know* he's dead, Jig." She pointed to a long cut on her arm. "I got that when his bones exploded!"

Jig rubbed his head. Were goblins really this dense? "I threw the spear, just like the song says. I threw it right at Straum's eye, but the stupid dragon blinked. The spear lodged in his eyelid. Straum was going to have me for a snack when someone else grabbed the spear and finished the job."

"But you're Jig Dragonslayer."

He shook his head impatiently. "Not really."

Veka looked so stunned Jig thought she was going to fall down. Instead, she leaned against the wall and whispered, "You didn't kill the dragon."

"That's right."

Her quivering lips began to smile. "What about the Necromancer?"

Jig shrugged. "Well, yeah, I killed him."

"But . . . killing a Necromancer isn't even *in* the top hundred heroic deeds and triumphs. The closest thing would be defeating a dark lord who had returned as a spirit or body part. That was number eighty-three, I think. Though Josca wrote a footnote that you could score it a little higher if nobody else believed the dark lord had come back, and everybody teased you about your so-called obsession."

"Body part? Like a disembodied nose?" Jig cringed, trying not to think about a flock of glowing pixie noses chasing him through the tunnels.

"There was something about the black foot of Septor," Veka said. "Legend has it the foot appeared in the boot of the weather mage Desiron, and when he tried to pull on his boot, the black foot grew teeth and—"

"Veka, stop." It was too late. As if he needed more fodder for his nightmares. "If you want to go on adventures, go."

"But I'm not—"

"Not what? Not a Hero? Just because you didn't find 'Destroy a pixie portal in an abandoned dragon's lair' on Josca's list?" Jig couldn't believe he was saying this. "Would a real Hero let some dusty old book tell her what she could and couldn't do?"

"I guess not."

"And that giant snake you fought. Slash told me a

bit about it. Flames and scales and wings and teeth . . . That sounds pretty dragonish to me."

Her face brightened. "That's true."

"Veka, we need goblins like you. Goblins who will delve into the abandoned tunnels and caverns of the mountain, or go out to explore the rest of the world."

"But you closed the entrance to the mountain," she said. Her eyes widened. "You're going to reopen the way?"

Jig gritted his teeth. Shadowstar hadn't spoken in some time, but he knew the god was listening. "I was wrong. We can't cut ourselves off from the rest of the world, Veka."

Veka stared at him for a long time, until Jig began to wonder if all this arguing had somehow broken her mind. When she finally spoke, her voice was quiet and tentative. "But what about you? Shouldn't you be the one to explore? To continue your adventures and add new verses to your song?"

Jig stepped back. "Nothing you, Grell, or even Tymalous Shadowstar say could make me set off on another adventure."

Ah, whispered Shadowstar. *That sounds like a challenge.*

No!

Veka had begun to smile. She looked like a nervous child, ready to bolt at the first sign of danger. "You really think I should be the one to go out there?"

"Better you than me." Jig pointed toward the goblin lair. "You'll want to gather some supplies. Clothes, food, weapons, that sort of thing."

"Thank you!" Veka grabbed his arms and squeezed. Then she was racing down the tunnel.

Jig watched the blue light of her lantern disappear into darkness. He was about to follow when he heard footsteps coming up behind him. Whoever it was, they were running. Only one person, from the sound of it. Jig backed against the wall, hiding in the darkness. Smudge remained cool, but Jig wasn't taking any chances.

His pursuer stopped almost within arm's reach and shouted, "Jig!"

Jig grabbed his ears and winced. "I'm right here, Braf!" He heard Braf jump away.

Hey, Jig said. *Couldn't you have warned him I was here before he deafened me?*

I could have, sure.

"What is it?" Jig asked. He sounded more brusque than he intended, but he didn't have time for another long conversation. Hobgoblins used big cups, and those two beers had gone straight to his bladder.

"It's about *him,*" Braf whispered. "Tymalous Shadowstar. He never really told me what I was supposed to do. Except to heal you when you were dying, I mean."

Jig groaned. He wasn't even chief anymore. Why did everyone still expect him to tell them what to do? "Heal the other goblins. Hobgoblins too, if they need it. And he's not too keen on stabbing people in the back or killing them in their sleep."

"Weird," said Braf. "What else?"

Jig started walking. "Well, he might make you do stupid things like helping ogres or challenging the chief or battling pixies who can kill you with a wave of their hand." He glared skyward. "Not that he'd ever tell you what he's doing at the time."

"He's a god," said Braf. "They're supposed to be manipulative and incomprehensible to mere mortals, right?"

Jig scowled. "I guess."

"So that's it? Heal a few goblins, wake people up before you kill them, and fight a few creatures we would have had to fight anyway? That doesn't sound too bad."

"Wait until tomorrow, when you've got a mob of cranky goblins threatening to rip you apart unless you cure their hangovers."

Braf had stopped walking. "So what does he get out of it?"

"He gets to laugh at us as we're running around, trying to save our hides," Jig muttered. He waited for Shadowstar to chastise him, but his head remained mercifully silent.

"He did save your life," Braf pointed out.

Much as he hated to admit it, Braf was right. For all Shadowstar's meddling, he had saved Jig on several occasions.

"Um . . . Jig?"

"What?"

"You said Shadowstar's magic could cure hangovers?"

"I guess so," said Jig. "Why not?"

"Thanks!" Braf's footsteps retreated swiftly toward the hobgoblin lair.

There was a time when any priest of mine who drank himself into a stupor would have been stripped of his robes and driven out of town.

You want Braf to strip for you? Jig asked.

Gods forbid. No, these days one makes do with what one can. Goblins are a grubby, selfish, violent race, but they have their moments.

We're not children, Jig said.

What's that?

You're like Grell in the nursery, tricking and kicking the children to get them to do what she wants. Don't do it again.

Shadowstar's voice grew louder, and Jig imagined he heard thunder in the distance. *Are you trying to command a god, goblin?*

Jig didn't answer. He knew how far he could push Tymalous Shadowstar, and he had done nothing to truly enrage the god yet. He didn't think so, at least. There was one other thing he had learned about Shadowstar, something he hadn't shared with Braf: Tymalous Shadowstar was lonely. He had been one of the forgotten gods, alone for centuries until chance brought him and Jig together.

You're right, said Shadowstar. *I'm sorry.*

Jig was so surprised he nearly fell. He wondered how many people could claim to have gotten an apology from a god.

You know, back in the old days, worshipers wouldn't dare set terms to their gods.

Back in the old days, gods would rather disappear forever than take goblins as worshipers, Jig countered.

True enough.

Jig perked his ears. He could hear singing from the tunnels ahead, and faint green light flickered at the edge of goblin territory. He was almost home.

Go on. Eat, rest, and enjoy the peace while you can. You deserve it.

Jig stopped. *While I can? What do you know that I don't?*

Do you really want to spend the rest of your short life listening to that list?

The pixie queen is gone. The portal is closed. Veka and Grell and Braf can worry about helping the goblins to grow and explore. What's left?

Nothing. Nothing at all.

Jig grunted. "Good."

It's just that . . .

Jig closed his eyes. He hated gods. Almost as much as he hated himself for asking what he was about to ask. He knew he should let it go. Let Shadowstar taunt Braf with his foreboding hints and dire warnings. *What?*

Nothing really. You're right, you know. You beat the pixies, and you survived your little adventure, just as you survived that messiness with Straum.

So what aren't you telling me?

A faint tingling of bells filled the air: the sound of Tymalous Shadowstar's laughter. *Haven't you ever noticed? In all the songs and all the stories, adventures so often come in threes?*

Jig gritted his teeth. *I hate you.*

More bells, then silence. Shadowstar was gone.

Jig reached up to pet Smudge. He had no doubt Shadowstar was right. Shadowstar was always right about things like that.

With a shrug, Jig continued toward the goblin lair. Golaka should have plenty of leftovers, and with most of the other goblins still celebrating, Jig might actually be able to relax and rest for a little while.

Really, what more could any goblin ask for?